LIKE HEAVEN

NIALA MAHARAJ

LIKE HEAVEN

HUTCHINSON
LONDON

Published by Hutchinson in 2006

1 3 5 7 9 10 8 6 4 2

Copyright © Niala Maharaj 2006

First published in 2006 in the United Kingdom by Hutchinson

Hutchinson
The Random House Group Limited
20 Vauxhall Bridge Road, London SW1V 2SA

Random House Australia (Pty) Limited
20 Alfred Street, Milsons Point, Sydney
New South Wales 2061, Australia

Random House New Zealand Limited
18 Poland Road, Glenfield
Auckland 10, New Zealand

Random House South Africa (Pty) Limited
Isle of Houghton
Corner of Boundary Road & Carse O'Gowrie
Houghton 2198, South Africa

The Random House Group Limited Reg. No. 954009

www.randomhouse.co.uk

A CIP catalogue record for this book
is available from the British Library

Papers used by Random House are
natural, recyclable products made from wood grown in
sustainable forests. The manufacturing processes conform to
the environmental regulations of the country of origin

Typeset by Palimpsest Book Production Limited
Polmont, Stirlingshire
Printed and bound in Great Britain by
Mackays of Chatham plc, Chatham, Kent

ISBN 0 09 179656 3 (Hardback Edition)
ISBN-13 987 0 09 179656 3 (From Jan 2007)

ISBN 0 09 179712 8 (Airport/Export Edition)
ISBN-13 987 0 09 179712 6 (From Jan 2007)

for my sister
Chandra
in memory of our father,
Harry Persad Maharaj

Acknowledgements

Like Heaven is the result of years of prodding by people who believed I could write fiction despite my own self-doubt. Camini Narayansingh-Chang telephoned me every day from Trinidad to nag me, while Lin and Martha McDevitt-Pugh found jobs to keep me alive in Amsterdam so I could write. My editor, Paul Sidey, offered encouragement at an early stage; Rhonda Cobham-Sander arranged a Copelard Fellowship with Amherst College in the US and Leslie Epstein of Boston University gave advice on style. Sally Sontheimer provided a frescoed dining-room as a studio in Rome. My unbelievably generous brother Ashram and his wife, Lorenza, offered emotional sustenance all the way from Canada, while Patricia Collette, Jochen Hippler, Rob van Gemeren and Gaston Dorren did so in Europe. Rhonda Tracey, Jeremy Taylor and the late Fitzroy Nation commented on the first draft, while Anand Narayansingh checked my depiction of male sexual feelings.

I am immensely grateful to all of these friends, as well as to that great story-teller, my mother Balmaty Maharaj, who taught me the power and delight of narrative.

'And here they are, all in a single Caribbean city, Port of Spain, the sum of history, Trollope's "non-people". A downtown babel of shop signs and streets, mongrelized, polyglot, a ferment without a history, like heaven.'

'The Antilles: Fragments of Epic Memory', The Nobel Lecture,
Derek Walcott, 1992

Prologue

I read in a magazine recently that good-looking people have greater chances of success in their careers.

Maybe that's what I should say at business seminars, I thought. It might be more useful than the inane tips I usually dole out. 'Get plastic surgery!' I could exhort all those mid-rank executives in ill-fitting suits looking eagerly to me to hear how I made money.

But I'm never going to do it, am I? I'm such a fraud. A failure. One big, beautiful failure.

I'm six feet one, which is tall for a guy from Trinidad. A little taller than my father, who claimed to be descended from the Rajputs, a race of legendary warriors in India. But I don't look like my father at all. Pa had ashy-grey skin and a long sad face with dangling jowls like a labrador. In my memory, he's just a shadow in a corner, bent in two over some dingy account book, muttering dark imprecations about the cost of things. I didn't inherit that darkness. I have light-brown skin, like my mother's. For the rest, my features are just regular as far as I can see. Straight nose, straight teeth, clear brown eyes, thick, curly hair that is greying now. But people used to say I was good-looking. And women used to claim I had a sexy voice.

I think I also got that from my parents. My father's speech was a disagreeable growl, my mother's an irritated whine, so, from early, I adopted a firm, low tone to make it clear I was not going to be swayed by them. In our home, speech just seemed to be a means of expressing your dissatisfaction with the world around you. I had no reason to be dissatisfied with that world. Growing up in the Croissee, about a mile east of the capital of Trinidad, where people of all races met and mingled in a glorious cacophony, I loved the world around me. 'Croissee' means 'crossroads'. It is here that all Trinidad passes to get to and from the city centre, from the four corners of the island. There were always things to see, to hear, to marvel at. With two older sisters and an older brother to absorb the

I

brunt of my parents' bad tempers, I was free. I would stop off at Aranguez Savannah on my way home from school to find a game of cricket or football, a kite-fight involving razor blades, or a communal effort to stone down tamarinds from the big trees that surrounded the savannah. To set myself apart from my family's reputation for bad-tempered isolationism, I adopted a quiet affability, an ease when somebody failed to return my comic books or lost my cricket ball. I would have read the comics before I lent them anyway, and other cricket balls were available in my father's dry-goods shop on the Eastern Main Road. When adults cooed over me, saying I was cute, I thought this was the kind of stupid thing grown-ups said because they couldn't think of anything better to say.

I took it all for granted. Success in school, success with women and success in business. I was always just trying out things, just following my nose, indulging my curiosity, and everything succeeded and succeeded . . . till it all crashed in on my head.

I think too much. I know it. But being aware of failure while the world proclaims you successful forces you into a syndrome of loneliness. You keep asking yourself where you went wrong. What was the point when you should have stopped and reflected on what you were doing? Was it when you first met Anji? Should you have left that butterfly of a girl alone, to find her way to another ending? Was it later, when you began to recognise the trap you were in, but told yourself it would all come out right just as everything else had come out all right in your life? The fates had always rescued you when you were in a jam before, why wouldn't they rescue you now? Then you realise that they did rescue you, but they forgot to rescue Anji. She was sacrificed to your success – she, the slim girl in the blue dress with splotches of red flowers that swung around her thighs, who still dances in your mind's eye even now, when you should have forgotten her.

Before now, I never thought my looks had anything to do with my business success. I thought they just gave me an unfair edge with women. That was clear from early. I remember noticing it when I was only eight years old.

I had just arrived at the seaside district of Dorado to spend my summer vacation on my grandfather's coconut estate. My cousin Ashok and I were walking to the village along the palm-fringed road. The heavy sea breeze was making the palms dance, and I had that wide-open feeling of wonder that Dorado always brought. It was another world, a world dictated by the power of sea and wind, where nature had its way, and man just adapted.

I had been given pocket money for my holiday. Ashok suggested I buy some Wrigley's Juicy Fruit chewing gum. Juicy Fruit? I wrinkled my nose. I had been thinking of other things: materials for making a box-cart, for example.

'Juicy Fruit!' Ashok insisted.

Ashok was also eight, but he had a more worldly air. Growing up in the countryside, he possessed an in-depth knowledge of the dark side of life. Poisonous snakes and scorpions that could kill you in two hours flat. Foul-mouthed fishermen who beat their wives and sent them flying out of the house naked in the middle of the night. Jellyfish invasions. Tides that could come up and snare you even if you were only ankle-deep in the sea. Beautiful women who lived in the forest, one of their feet a cow's hoof, and lured men to their destruction. Children with their feet turned backwards who were to be feared for some reason never explained.

I tried to figure out where Juicy Fruit figured in this constellation, but didn't want to ask. I was already feeling at a disadvantage. Ashok was wearing his dingy everyday clothes, while I was still in my neatly pressed travelling outfit. My mother had made me use rose and cucumber soap when I had showered before the trip, so I suspected that I smelled girly-girly.

Ashok grabbed my arm. His skin was nearly black against my pale-ness. Naturally dark like the rest of my father's family, he spent his days under the baking sun of the beach.

'You know Donna?' he asked.

I vaguely remembered that one of the girls in the village was called Donna, but I couldn't place her.

'Donna will let you lie down on top of her if you give her a Juicy Fruit.'

I kept walking. I knew grown-ups lay down on each other, men on women. Ashok had informed me of this a year before. But I couldn't imagine my big, tall father lying on my little wasp of a mother, and, more to the point, couldn't imagine her permitting it. I had just accepted the hypothesis and stored it away till evidence turned up to verify it.

'I will show you,' Ashok said.

He led the way into a lane full of broken-down old concrete houses.

Before I knew what we were up to, we had stopped in front of the most broken down of all.

'Donna!' he called, then turned to me. 'Her mother working on our estate right now.'

A girl of about our age came round from the back of the house. She had golden-brown skin, and looked like she was mixed with Chinese. Then I remembered who Donna was. She was the village retard, a mongoloid with bandy legs. Ashok crossed a crumbling bridge over a filthy drain and approached her. I followed.

'You want a Juicy Fruit?' Ashok asked.

Donna nodded absently, tilting her face to one side and gazing at me out of her oval eyes. Then, abruptly, she began shaking her head. Ashok's face dropped.

'You don't want a Juicy Fruit?'

She shook her head harder. 'I have a hole in my teeth and Juicy Fruit does make it hurt.'

She opened her mouth wide to point at a back molar. I was relieved. I wanted to keep my pocket money intact till I had decided what to spend it on.

I began to turn to leave, but Donna came up to me and touched the starched blue and white sleeve of my dress-up shirt. She began caressing the fabric.

'What about a Spearmint,' Ashok asked, his big eyes lighting up in his dark face. 'Spearmint doesn't hurt your teeth.'

Donna shifted her eyes to his. 'You sure?'

'Sure, sure, sure.' Ashok held up two fingers in a cross. 'Kiss the cross. He will buy a pack of Spearmint if you let him lie down on you.'

Donna looked around at me again, tilting her face to study me. 'OK,' she said. She turned and went up the four stairs to the house.

'Go on!' Ashok gave me a shove.

I stumbled up the stairs, while Donna turned and waited at the top for me. She reached out and stroked my face. 'You pretty,' she said. 'You prettier than him.' She gestured in Ashok's direction.

'Hurry up,' Ashok hissed. 'We have to go and buy the chewing gum.'

I had had enough. 'I don't want no chewing gum,' I said, and turned to go back down the steps.

Donna caught my hand. Her palm was hard, rough. 'You not going to buy Spearmint?'

I shook my head more emphatically. She continued holding my hand, gazing into my face admiringly. 'Well, all right,' she said slowly. 'You could still lie down on me.'

She turned and moved towards the inside of the house, then looked back at me expectantly. I followed her into a bedroom. She lay down on a dingy bed and raised up her dingy dress. Then she pulled her dingy panties down. Gingerly, I made to lie down on top of her.

'You have to take off your pants,' she informed me.

I hesitated. This was going too far. But Ashok was waiting outside. I eased myself out of my shorts and lay on top of her. She began humming a song. I wondered what to do next. This was rather boring, lying here on her, while the beach and the forest and river waited in the bright sunlight outside. She just hummed contentedly away. I got up and pulled up my shorts. 'I gone,' I said, and dashed down the steps to where Ashok was waiting.

This set the pattern for my later relations with girls. Not that I ever lay on top of a mongoloid again. But by the time I was fourteen and knew more about sex, some girl had snatched my virginity away from me when I wasn't looking.

She was a fifteen-year-old girl named Carlene, who hung around the steel-band yard in the street behind our house in the Croissee. Our store faced the Eastern Main Road, but the lot of land on which it stood was long and narrow. The wooden house we lived in at the back faced a street running parallel to the Main Road. As soon as January began, the thrill of steel drums began emanating from the pan-yard every night. By the time Carnival arrived in February, our house seemed to vibrate slightly around midnight. Nigger-noise, my mother called it, but I loved the sound. On the evenings when there wasn't a cricket game in the savannah, I wandered over to the pan-yard to watch the band practise. Many people in the area did this, and there was a joyous atmosphere around that empty lot. Next door was a dilapidated wooden house where Carnival costumes were made. Women and girls hung around its verandah sewing sequins on satin fabric and gluing feathers on headdresses. The atmosphere was chaotic, with constant jokes and flirtation, and occasional bursts of dancing when the steel band got going. Little boys like myself would be given simple tasks to perform on the four stairs that led to the verandah, like painting broomsticks to make flags for the masqueraders to carry on Carnival day. I was the only Indian on the scene, so I kept quiet and tried to be as useful as possible. But the women wouldn't let me keep a low profile.

'Indian boy!' one exclaimed as I painted a broomstick one evening. 'But how you could paint neat-neat, so!'

Another woman came down the stairs to watch what I was doing. She slung a heavy arm around my shoulders. 'You taking the boy slight, because he small and skinny,' she said to the first, 'but the boy know how to handle his wood.'

There was uproarious laughter at the sexual innuendo. My ears started burning.

'That is Mr Saran good-good boy-child, you know,' a woman who sat at a sewing machine warned. 'If he father know what kind of talk allyou talking with him, he will come with he big-gun to shoot allyou.'

'Leave the boy alone!' the band-leader growled as he passed by. 'He does paint better than all them other hooligan who does hang round here. I don't want him to get shy and stay away.'

I went pinker from the compliment. I hadn't thought the band-leader ever noticed me; he always looked busy and preoccupied. The people in the pan-yard called him Charlo, and he commanded automatic respect, even though he must have only been in his early twenties. His face was a smooth, shiny black, with no discernible nose-bridge, just a flare of nostrils. His body, on the other hand, bulged with muscle. He had thick biceps with prominent veins running down their length that you couldn't help noticing since he always wore just a sleeveless undershirt.

Soon, people began to take me for granted as one of the regulars at the mas' camp. Charlo would ask me to hold wire taut for him when he was making wings for the costumes. He grew to like me so much, he shortened my moniker to 'Indian'. 'Indian!' he would call from the yard. 'Leave that broomstick and bring the pliers for me.'

I loved working with Charlo, observing how mysterious concepts in his imagination got transformed into glimmering reality. I had patience for even the smallest tasks, and would stick with him when he made mistakes and had to re-do things that had been badly conceived.

'Hear, nuh,' he growled one day, 'you don't have a name? How come everybody does call you "Indian"?'

I didn't like to remind him that it was he who had given me that nickname. 'My name is Ved,' I said, pronouncing it the usual way, 'Vade'.

Charlo stopped what he was doing and trained his eyes on me. 'Ved?' he asked. 'What kind of name is that?' His eyes, when he looked at you, were big and very clear.

I smiled at him. 'Indian,' I said, imitating his own grunt.

Charlo wouldn't let it go at that. In the long hours of hand-fabrication at the mas' camp, repartee had to be strung out as long as possible. 'But they couldn't have named you Krishna, or Vishnu, or Ramkhelwansingh, or something normal?' He shook his head as he went back to what he was doing. 'Saran is a true, true miser, you know,' he said. 'He wouldn't even spend a few more letters on his son name.' He unrolled a length of wire. 'Ved? Ved?' He stopped to look at me again. 'What the hell kind of name is that to give a smart little boy like you.'

I felt a warmth in my chest from the praise. 'Ved kind of mean smart, you know,' I explained diffidently. 'It's the name of the Hindu books of knowledge.'

He passed me the end of the wire and measured off a piece. 'Hindu books of knowledge, eh?' he grunted. He wrapped one end of the wire around the top of a broomstick.

'The oldest books in the world,' I boasted.

Charlo took the other end of the wire from me and curved it into an arc. I gripped the broomstick tight while he bound the wire onto it. The frame was complete. Now I would just have to fill in the arc with kite paper. Charlo straightened up.

'So,' he asked, training his eyes on me again, 'if you name Knowledge, how you does let all these ignorant nigger-people call you stupidness like Indian-Boy?'

I was hugely embarrassed and just looked down at my feet. From then on, Charlo called me by my name, and upbraided anyone who addressed me as 'Indian'. 'The man have a name!' he would growl at the others. 'How you would like it if he call you "nigger"?' And with that, my status changed. 'Ved!' Charlo would call when I arrived from school. 'I have a job for you. Bring some glue and crêpe paper.'

This brought me to the attention of the young girls who hung around the mas' camp. They wore tight shorts and were always moving to the music of the steel band, occasionally stopping to 'put down a wine', as they called it – and no one can wind a pelvis like a Trinidadian. It's a slow, sensual movement with legs spread and knees bent. Those girls at the mas' camp, with their thick, fleshy bottoms straining against their shorts, could put down a wine that was a first lesson in sex education.

Over that summer, as I grew taller and my voice began to change, I became a target for their wining antics. They would shuffle up to me while my back was turned, put their arms around me and gyrate their pelvises against my bottom. They would approach me from the front, spread their arms wide, and wine a millimetre away from my crotch. They would turn away from me and begin wining backwards till their pert bottoms were swivelling chock-a-block against my penis. 'Wine back!' Charlo urged me. 'If you give them a good solid wine in their backside, they will run! The way you does just blush, you will always have them terrorising you.'

I tried it, but I was too timid. My efforts only encouraged the girls. Eventually I got used to the physical contact. It was delicious and I began to want more.

One evening, the girl, Carlene, had a lot of heavy bags to take back home with her. She asked me to help. When we got to her house, no one else was there. She offered me a soft drink and I perched on a broken-down old sofa. She sat next to me and began teasing me. One thing led to another. By the time I left that house my sexual education was well on its way.

Thinking about it now, those early experiences must really have helped to form my character, for I lost my self-consciousness very early. I never thought about the way I looked. If it weren't for my mother, I would go around in rumpled clothes, my T-shirt on inside out as I hurried from my room to get to whatever I was doing at the time. At secondary school, the other boys talked endlessly about girls and sex, scheming to get a glimpse of parts of their sisters' bodies, but I was accustomed to girls' body parts. Those girls at the mas' camp would try on half-finished costumes with only the most perfunctory gestures towards modesty. They would play with my hair if I was sitting down, sometimes leaning over the back of my chair and letting their breasts rest on my head. They would tickle me if I was too quiet and I'd have to slap their hands to get some peace.

I never revealed this at school, though. I acted as though I was just as needy as the rest. There were enough things to prevent me fitting in. Being Indian, for example, at Queens Royal College, which was populated mainly by black boys from middle-class families. Being Hindu. Having all these Hindu antics going on at home. Having a family like my own, a mother and two older sisters whose behaviour didn't correspond with female norms I had ever heard of in fact or fiction. I never seemed to have much in common with anyone. I avoided talking about myself, even to myself. That became a lifelong habit, which I'm only now breaking. It was a habit, I think, that led to my immense success and my terrible failure.

This book is about Anji. She is like a bass drum in my head whose deep, resounding echoes stay with me no matter what I'm doing. They say acknowledging your mistakes helps you move on. But I don't want you to misunderstand me as she did. So I'm going to have to start before I met her, long before, at where everything began. I think everything began with Ma.

Book One

GRAND OPENINGS

Chapter One

My mother is the rudest person I ever met in all my forty-nine years. Ma would tell God to go to hell if He got in her way. And He often got in her way. Ants, for example, were an indication of His incompetent approach to creation. Listening to my mother on the subject of ants, you would think they constituted a biblical plague, not just a nuisance around the sugar jar. I once tried to explain to her about biological diversity, and everything having a role in nature. 'They must be have a role in nature, but they ain't have no role in my kitchen,' she snapped. 'You does only talk shit.'

I retreated, thinking that she did have a point.

Dust was another failure on God's part. The world would never have included dust if my mother had had her proper place as designer of the universe. It would never have included black people, who didn't fulfil her concept of propriety. It wouldn't have included any of our relatives, who were just fools, or my father, who was the worst fool of all, or any servant she ever had, or the colour green, which she despised for no reason I have ever heard. As far as my mother was concerned, she was born to be the sole arbiter of taste and propriety in the entire universe. The fact that no one except she recognised this was only a reflection of the stupidity of the human race. It wasn't going to stop her from carrying out her duties as judge and jury of everything around her.

'Pundit!' She would call out, as an eminent Hindu priest performed a sacred ritual in front of a considerable gathering.

The priest would pause.

'You making a mistake with that puja!'

Used to being revered, the pundit would look from left to right, not knowing what action was prescribed in the event of being insulted.

'You supposed to light the camphor before you pour the milk!'

The pundit would begin stammering and stuttering.

'They too lazy!' Ma would expound to nobody in particular. 'They does want to give people short-cut work and finish the puja fast, so they could go and make more money somewhere else.'

To say that my mother wasn't a very popular person is to understate the matter. But Ma didn't care for the good opinion of people she despised. Since she had never met anyone she didn't despise, she gave a piece of her mind to everyone she came across. She told off government census officials that came to our house, informing them that it was none of their business how many people lived there. She told off customers who came to the shop asking for something we didn't have in stock at that moment. She told off doctors who didn't agree with her self-diagnosis. She told off policemen as a matter of principle. Ma only had to glimpse a police uniform to get into a bad mood.

How she got to be this way can only be a matter for speculation. Her sisters claimed she was born a hot-mouth. She was the last of four of them, and tiny in size. Perhaps she developed this personality to avoid being bossed around by a lot of older siblings. But whatever the excuse, Ma was, by all accounts, a pain in the ass from early o'clock. Her father was a well-to-do landowner who lived on the other side of the Croissee, at the back of the Caroni Savannah. When it came time to marry his daughters off, he found husbands within a few miles of his home – in Tunapuna, Champs Fleurs – or around the pleasant southern borough of San Fernando. For my mother, he identified a bridegroom at the farthest reaches of the known world, Dorado. To find one any further away he would have had to cross the sea.

Needless to say, my mother didn't take this lying down. Being banished to a coconut estate, where the only creatures available to her correctional bent were jelly fish and scorpions, was not what she had intended herself for. She took one look at Dorado and despised it. She took one look at my father and despised him. He was only interested in picking up his shotgun and going off to hunt in the nearby forests. She took one look at her mother-in-law, a plump, jovial woman, and decided she was too stupid even to despise. She took one look at her father-in-law and decided he didn't bathe often enough. She decided to get the hell out.

'Sand!' she snaps whenever Dorado is mentioned. 'That is all Dorado is. Sand!' Other people see a spectacular landscape of waving coconut trees and magnificent sunsets, a wide vista of beach that goes on for ever. 'Sand up in your nose-hole; sand in your crotch,' is all my mother has to say about her early married life. 'Sand in every blasted thing. You expect me to stay there?'

To be fair to Ma, at the time she got married there were no electric lights in Dorado, or running water. An outside latrine must have been a horror for her. And Pa was no company. But Ma was never one to appeal to anyone's sympathy. She preferred to give as good as she got. If Dorado had the effrontery to offer her kerosene lamps and wood fires, she would reduce it to sand. The only other aspect of nature that could compete with ants for my mother's contempt is sand.

The minute she got pregnant, Ma's escape route was assured. It was conventional to return to your own family's home to give birth. Once she had returned to the Croissee, she forgot her marriage and took up permanent residence at her parents' house. 'Sand will get in the child's bottle,' she informed anybody who dared question her decision. 'It will get in her diapers. You think I mad to go back there?'

In the end, her father made a compromise. He gave her a piece of land on the Eastern Main Road as a sort of belated dowry. My father was designated shopkeeper. The problem was, Pa didn't want to be a shopkeeper. He was used to the wide-open spaces of Dorado, to the sound of wind and surf, to the easy, irregular life of the coconut estate. But it was an offer he couldn't refuse. Everybody said it was the chance of a lifetime. The Eastern Main Road was prime commercial property. He would become rich there.

My father defied them. He managed to stay poor on the Eastern Main Road. He stocked his shop with the most unattractive items available at the wholesalers – brooms and enamel basins and such-like – jumbling them together to create a dark hole in the wall that people entered only out of utmost necessity. Ma's contempt for him grew. Her relatives were making money out of the land her father had accumulated in the urban centres of Trinidad. They were starting gas stations and Chinese restaurants. Her husband chose to sell chamber pots. She refused to participate in this embarrassing pursuit, barricading herself in the wooden house at the back of the shop to produce another generation of women to carry on her work of condemning the rest of creation.

My oldest sister turned out looking like Pa. She was tall and husky and dark, with a long face and heavy jowls. The expression on her face did nothing to lighten these looks. She seemed to have absorbed Ma's attitudes with mother's milk, but, lacking Ma's wasp-like swiftness, they just made her dour and haughty. She was named Raywatee, but somehow everybody took to calling her Queen. My second sister, Indrawattee, upped the ante. She was pretty. Slim and of a nice height, she reacted to

Queen's grumpiness by being bitchy. When I learnt about Marie Antoinette in high-school history classes, I immediately started visualising her as Indra.

You can see why I took to the pan-yard and savannah from early in life. With three people at home who thought they had a share in mothering me, I would put up with anything outside. My brother, Rabindranath, who was born three years before me, tried to assert his independence, but he was outnumbered. Robin was the spitting image of Pa, and the female members of the family were determined to ensure he didn't develop the same personality – or kill him trying.

Children have a native intelligence, they say. I knew from early that discretion was the better part of valour. When the going got tough, I got going. And the going was always tough in our house. The mahogany chairs in our living-room weren't meant for sitting in. They were there to be polished. The curtains weren't to budge an inch from the way they were hung. Doormats should remain as clean as towels and towels were to be as straight as curtains. I retreated to the dust of the savannah, the ripe mangoes you could stone down and then eat without washing them, the jaunty bawdiness of the mas' camp.

School only gave me other escape routes. My mas' camp experience made me valuable in the drama club, which was a focus of college life. One of the English teachers, a portly Chinese man with a reputation for fornication, fancied himself as a literary type and fuelled his ambitions via college theatre. I was happy to create props and help build sets for *Julius Caesar*, *The Tempest*, *Oedipus Rex*. When he went one step further and mounted a play without a set, I was so chagrined I sat through several rehearsals of *Waiting for Godot* trying to figure out what the goddamned thing was all about. Another English teacher, meanwhile, aspired to being a jazz performer. That was a hopeless ambition. Trinidad was wrapped up in steel-band and calypso and Indian music. So he created his own ensemble from some of the older boys at school. While trying to recreate Ancient Rome on the stage in the assembly hall, I would hum along to the strains of modern jazz coming from the back.

I was perfectly content. These folks at home were just the backdrop to my life, like God, who sent rain to wash away a long-awaited cricket match. Like Latin, with its declensions and conjugations that you had to learn for no good reason that you could see. I honestly never thought my family would ever have any influence on my life at all. Like all teenagers, I guess.

But when I turned fifteen everything started turning on its head. My grandfather in Dorado died, leaving the coconut estate to my father and his brother, Ashok's father. Pa proposed to pack us all up and resume life among the coconut palms.

I was torn – I loved Dorado, but I had a full life in town. Ma was not. 'You could go if you want,' she informed my father. 'I staying right here.'

Pa blustered a bit, but he was outnumbered. My sisters were married by this time, but Ma alone was enough to outnumber Pa. When he argued that the shop wasn't making money, Ma snapped that that was his fault. 'Anybody with any sense would have bought the lot next door a long time ago, and extend the shop to the corner.'

Our shop was long, narrow and dark. Next door was a large plot of land that did indeed extend to the corner. If we had both, our shop could extend along the Main Road and be more visible.

'What I going to buy land with?' Pa asked.

'Sell Dorado,' Ma snapped.

My father blanched. Sell Paradise Lost?

'What Dorado good for?' Ma said. 'Coconut don't make money.'

Coconut plantations were afflicted with a disease called witchbroom. Income was much reduced.

They eventually came to a compromise. Pa didn't sell Dorado. Instead, he let his brother manage his share of the coconut estate and used the income to send my brother Robin to study law in England. Ma mortgaged her property in the Croissee to buy the land next door, then mortgaged that land to raise a loan to extend our shop. She wanted a large concrete building with our living quarters upstairs. 'Ants can't climb stairs,' she informed us.

I didn't at all approve of this idea. I liked our wooden house. It was built in the Spanish style with white fretwork wreathing its doors and windows and verandah. Only the three of us were left to inhabit it now, and it was quite sufficient. But arguing with Ma was a waste of breath. Her sisters and brothers all had gigantic concrete houses and lived upstairs.

'Dust can't climb stairs,' was all the explanation she would give.

Plans were drawn for the massive new building. Pa developed a look of full-time worry. Ma's querulous voice was permanently raised. She railed at the government for making laws and regulations that limited her building ambitions; she railed at the bank for its high rates of interest. 'You don't see bank don't have no conscience?' she asked. 'Fourteen per cent for twenty years?'

I tried not to listen. I was sixteen and studying for my A-level exams. Apart from all my other activities, I now had gigantic books of mathematics, additional mathematics, physics and chemistry to cover. But not listening to Ma was a contradiction in terms.

'You know how much fourteen per cent will add up to over twenty years?' she demanded as I sat at the dining-table with my calculus books.

'Ma,' I said patiently, 'the bank has to make money too. You think they will lend you money for nothing?'

She leaned over and stared fixedly at me. 'I asked you a question,' she said. 'You know how much fourteen per cent will add up to over twenty years?'

'No I don't know,' I said shortly, and turned back to my books.

'Well I know!' She named a figure. An astronomical figure. I forget what it was now.

'Ma,' I looked up, 'what stupidness you talking?'

'I talking stupidness? I talking stupidness? Look, boy, I must be never went to college, but we do compound interest in elementary school.'

She went to the shop and came back with an adding machine. 'Here!' she said. 'Work it out! Since you think you so smart.'

Ma's arithmetic was correct.

I sat back and looked at her as she ranted on. Perhaps, I thought, Ma was such a pain in the ass because she was too bright for her boots. I had wondered where my own facility with numbers came from. Mathematical reasoning was an instinct with me. I now realised that it came from Ma. Maybe that's why she was so frustrated with Pa. He took a year and a day to figure out the profit margin on a two-dollar basin.

I went back to my books. Nothing I could do about it, I thought. I couldn't have been more wrong.

A few months later, when the building plans were nearly ready, Hurricane Vera struck Trinidad. It was a once-in-a-lifetime event. Trinidad was never usually hit by hurricanes. By some accident of geography, it lay just off the traditional hurricane path. But Vera had wandered off the beaten track and managed to brush the eastern coast of the island with her tail.

The eastern coast was Dorado. Pa's face was ashen as he studied the newspaper photos. We got into the car and drove up to the estate. It was like a landscape on some strange, undiscovered planet. The coconut palms were flattened, twisted, contorted by the swirling winds into gravity-defying shapes. Some were bent over and curved like prehistoric serpents. There wasn't a palm frond left on a tree, and there was debris everywhere: houses collapsed, bridges broken and water all over the road. And, beyond the tree-line, the sea went on, pounding the sand of the beach as if nothing had happened.

There would be no coconut crop that year. My brother's expenses in England would have to be paid out of the bank loans. Repairs on the estate would have to come out of the loans as well. Fences had been destroyed; my grandmother's house was damaged; the storage sheds were drenched and all the copra was sodden and useless. Ma shrugged. 'Didn't I tell you to sell that land? But no, you want to hold on to your navel-string!'

Pa's face grew longer in the ensuing months. He struggled to try and speed up the building preparations, but only ended up making mistakes. He spent weeks searching for a contractor who would undertake the project cheaply. Eventually, he had to give in and go back to the first one he had approached. By that time, it was Christmas and the contractor was busy. 'And when January come, I can't guarantee I could get a builder,' the contractor added. 'Once Carnival time start, builders does forget about building. You will have to pay a lot for labour.'

Pa decided to put off the building work till after Carnival. 'It's better to wait a couple of months than pay double price,' he said, and spent the next two months worrying over his account books.

Once Carnival was over, the contractor turned up with a crew ready to begin work on the building. I was overjoyed to discover that the leader of the crew was none other than my good friend Charlo.

'Just keep that lady away from me,' Charlo warned, gesturing with his head in my mother's direction. 'If she get me too vexed one of these days, I will pick up one of these big stones and lick her down.'

We began work on the foundations of the building. My A-level exams were approaching, so I didn't need to be in school full-time, just when I had classes. I was expected to be studying on my own, so I had time to help Charlo and his crew.

'You don't have to study, boy?' he asked.

'I could study in the night.'

We measured and dug and poured concrete. I had applied to study engineering at the University of the West Indies, which was about five miles down the Eastern Main Road. I felt I was getting good practical experience of building principles, and could observe some of the physics I was studying at school in practice.

But after the first two loads of bricks were delivered, disaster struck. Trinidad's only brick factory burnt down. 'Flat, boy,' Charlo said. 'Flat to the ground.'

The building work had to be stopped. The contractor disappeared. 'He take so much money for people building in advance, he up shit-creek now,' Charlo informed us. 'He gone underground.'

'You see!' Ma told Pa. 'It's a good thing I never let you give him no money in advance.'

It was the only good news. Pa went back to his account books, calculating how much of the bank loans he was spending on interest payments. I went back to my studies.

May came and I began working till late at night to be ready for my exams in June. In the wee hours, I would hear Pa rise from his bed and go into the kitchen to take Eno's Fruit Salts for his dyspepsia. He would then proceed to the verandah to pace up and down there. I would join him sometimes for a few minutes.

'Why you don't go and see the doctor?' I suggested.

'Doctor can't do anything for indigestion. They will just take my money and give me Milk of Magnesia. I could buy Milk of Magnesia on my own.'

'I feel it's an ulcer you have.'

One night, he stopped pacing. I didn't notice as I was preparing for an exam the next day. It took a while before I realised he was quiet. I went out to the living-room. He was sitting on one of our low mahogany chairs, rubbing his chest.

'What you doing?' I asked.

'Nothing. Just sitting down here.'

He contorted his face in pain. I went and got him some Milk of Magnesia.

'You want to go to a doctor?' I asked. I had got my driving licence a couple of months before.

'What doctor?' he replied. 'It's two o'clock in the morning.'

We repeated this a couple of times. I would leave my books, go outside, and find him rubbing his chest.

At three, Pa was moaning softly in the living-room. 'Let's go to the hospital,' I said, beginning to wonder if it might be his heart, not his stomach, that was the trouble.

He shook his head. 'Hospital does only kill people.'

I went out to the verandah. His groans grew louder. 'Pa, come on! I taking you to the hospital.'

'When they carry my father to the hospital, he come back dead.'

At three-thirty I woke up my mother. For once she was quiet. 'Go to the hospital,' she urged.

He only groaned and shook his head.

'Put your clothes on,' I told Ma, and went to do the same.

'Come on, Pa,' I said when I got back, putting one arm round his back and levering him out of the chair. 'I taking you to the hospital whether you like it or not.'

He let me lead him out to the car. He was sweating profusely. By the time we got to the casualty department, he was retching. The staff took one look at him and rushed him to intensive care. By 7 a.m. he was in the operating theatre. Ma and I sat on a bench outside and waited. She complained a bit about the doctors and the dirty hospital, but it was only habit; she didn't have her usual verve. I felt that there was something choking my own chest now.

Pa came out of the operating theatre at about 11 a.m. By then I had missed my physics exam.

The next day, the employees of the shop turned up at our house. There were two of them, young girls called Nerissa and Suzanne. They had hung around the locked doors of the shop the day before and then gone back home. I explained that my father had had a massive heart attack and would take months to recover. Once he was released from intensive care, he would have to spend some weeks in a nursing home.

'And the shop?' Nerissa asked.

I shrugged. The shop was the last thing I was thinking of. In fact, thinking was a hard thing to do at that point. The inside of my head was like a mass of loose wires.

'You will have to open it,' Nerissa said.

I stared at her. She was a very thin, dark girl of about seventeen with big, scared eyes.

'Don't worry.' She shook her head. 'We will do everything. You only have to stay by the cash register.'

I shrugged again. I had already missed my physics exam and would have to wait a year to do it again. I could miss the rest as well. Until the loose wires in my head came up with something better to do, I might as well preside over the shop. I went and found the keys and opened the doors.

Man, that shop was the most boring place in all creation. Occasionally some fat woman would come in to buy a bucket and argue with me over whether it should cost $1.30 or $1.36. Nerissa and Suzanne dusted the shelves all day, but it couldn't dispel the gloom. They bought salt-prunes and munched them in tiny bites to while away the time. By the end of the week, I was munching on salt-prunes as well, and pepper mango, and plums with salt and pepper. 'What you think this is?' Ma asked. 'A shop or a nursery school?'

I pulled down an old Scrabble set from the top shelf where it had lain unbought for about a decade and taught the two girls to play. They were fairly hopeless, but I persisted. Charlo dropped by occasionally to chat.

'How this place so dead, boy?' he asked.

'How much doormat people could buy?' I retorted.

'They does only buy them thing for Christmas . . .' he agreed. 'But you have some nice, nice glass over there. People does need glass when they have fete and break up all the old one.'

'Who going to see them in this jumble sale?' I asked. 'If we had the new building, we could lay things out better and attract some customers.'

One morning, he went and gazed at the concrete floor of the new building thoughtfully. I followed him. 'You know,' he said, 'we could finish this building . . .'

'You have a couple hundred bricks in your back pocket?' I asked.

'We don't have to use brick,' he replied. 'When we run out of crêpe paper in the mas' camp, what we does use?'

'You want me build a store with kite paper?' I asked. 'What happen? You think we is the three little pig in the story-book? Waiting for wolf to huff and puff and blow the house down?'

Charlo shook his head from side to side. 'You ain't studying your brains,' he said. 'Worries have you stupid! When we don't have something, ain't we does improvise? Well that is the same thing we could do here. We going to build with glass.'

22

'Glass?'

Charlo held up a finger. 'You never hear the saying, boy? Those who live in glass houses could show off their wares? What all them big, big store in town does build out of? Not glass? So people could see the things they selling?'

It was a very good idea. The extended shop would front onto both sides of the corner. We could construct giant plate-glass windows between the concrete pillars and minimise the need for bricks.

I consulted Ma. 'And have all them ignorant people in the Croissee pelt big stone and break the window?' she asked. 'We will be fed up paying for more glass.'

I shrugged. 'We could use the money we paying as interest on the loan right now,' I said.

That caused her to pause. Then she put on her most bad-tempered voice. 'Do what the hell you want, you hear! But don't come crying by me when it don't work.'

That gave me something to do apart from worry about the exams I hadn't finished and watch boring old household wares. Charlo and I threw ourselves into the building project with enthusiasm, joking about everything, trying to defy Ma by succeeding. And we eventually did. Once we had had the plate-glass windows installed, the new shop was magnificent, total showroom. Light flooded in from two sides, making the goods sparkle. Suzanne and Nerissa acted like they were in heaven. They started dusting things and putting them out on the glass shelves Charlo had built.

'Ved!' Suzanne called. 'Come over here a minute.'

Suzanne was a gorgeous honey-coloured girl with pert tits, the smoothest of skins, and hair neatly pressed and combed back from her face. I went over to where she was standing holding a chamber pot in one fist, the other fist clenched on her waist.

'You really, really expect me,' she asked, 'to put this posy on this glass shelf?'

I was amused at her worried tone. 'No,' I said, taking the chamber pot from her, 'I expect you to put it on your head.'

'Ved, man!' Nerissa pleaded, her eyes big and round in her face. 'Get serious, nuh! How this place will look with all this old junk your father gathering since Noah was in short pants? You ever see anybody use something like this?' She held up an enamel teapot with pink and blue flowers on it.

Nerissa looked like a breeze could blow her away. She had very dark skin, but, unlike my father, it gave her a mysterious, insubstantial air, like a drift of smoke.

'Send it to the museum,' I said, patting her shoulder. 'I will buy some new stock.'

That would be a very good use for some of the loan-money that was waiting till we could construct the upstairs portion of the building. I went to wholesalers and ordered gleaming glassware, china dishes, stainless-steel implements.

'You expect these Croissee people to buy those things?' Ma whined. 'You never hear corbeaux don't eat sponge cake?'

'When they see our window display,' Charlo told her, 'all the corbeaux round here will be lining up for sponge cake.'

He had marked off big areas around the windows and was constructing wooden platforms to fit in them.

'Here we having we eleegant-living display. Next window is we back-to-school section. The other one . . .'

'Hear, nuh!' Ma put her hands on her hips. 'You feel you move your mas' camp over here?' Indeed, the shop was like a mix of mas' camp and stage set.

Nerissa and Suzanne were perfectly capable of running the business without me. I had taught Suzanne to use the cash register and to make sure her cash balanced at closing time. Nerissa and I devised inventory systems and drew up record books, and she managed the stock. I could devote myself to creating décor in the windows that would encourage Croissee customers to eat sponge cake.

We needed a dining-table to lay out our table settings. Charlo insisted that it had to be an 'eleegant' table. He and I went to the nearby Santa Cruz valley to meet a guy named Antoine he had heard about. Antoine turned out to be a short, stocky man of Corsican derivation who made teak and mahogany furniture. He had a crop of curly grey hair that stood up away from his head, and a golden-brown wife, twice his height, who upholstered the chairs he made.

'I been making furniture for generations,' he said, when I admired his handiwork. 'My family came here in the eighteenth century to make furniture for the French plantation owners who moved to Trinidad to escape the revolution in Haiti.'

His talk made dull history lessons of my past seem suddenly to have meaning. I looked around at the lush valley I had taken for granted in the past. Mr Antoine's house was humble, but there was a vast crenellated estate house next door that was falling to bits. With its curved verandahs and little turrets, its crumbling, weather-beaten wood, it made me think of Miss Havisham's place in *Great Expectations*. It was like one giant gingerbread house that hadn't been eaten and had been left to decay on its own. Most of the houses in Santa Cruz were like this. If you pushed at an exterior wall, you felt, the whole thing would crumble into dust like a forgotten cigarette left burning in an ashtray. The cocoa plantations of the valley had been abandoned by the French Creole families, who had moved to the city. They were returning to jungle under a canopy of giant immortelle trees, whose blossoms studded the sky with vivid flecks of red.

'I don't get many orders nowadays,' Mr Antoine said. 'But it's enough to keep going.'

I felt the pity of it. His pieces had beautiful clean lines. The reddish Guyanese teak gleamed warm and eleegant. We bought a dining suite, a couple of coffee tables and a small desk. Mr Antoine's prices were cheap. We stacked them carefully in the back of Charlo's pick-up, padding them with scraps of cloth Mrs Antoine gave us, and headed back to the Croissee.

Within a week of opening the new store, a burly man came in and asked whether he could buy one of our window displays. 'I haven't seen a table like that since I left home,' he said in a thick Guyanese accent. 'That will last till I die, and my children die. I was thinking of shipping in some furniture from Guyana, but it's very expensive.'

As I chatted with him, I discovered that he was a lecturer in the human-ities department of the university. His research area was the calypso songs sung at Carnival in Trinidad. I enjoyed our chat so much, I got willing to disturb my window display for him. I charged him double what I had paid Mr Antoine for the dining-room furniture, then went back to Santa Cruz to collect a replacement.

A week later, a big, light-skinned woman turned up. She was a librarian from the university. She spoke with a Jamaican accent. 'My neighbour bought a dining set from you,' she said in a haughty fashion. 'I would like one like it, but to seat eight.'

I shook my head. 'I don't have any more in stock.'

'When will you get more?'

'You want to check back in two weeks?'

She butted around the store and bought some dishes. 'I didn't know these were available in the Croissee. I thought only Ross carried this Italian pottery.' Ross was the most exclusive store in the city, a place I'd never been into. Then she caught sight of the teak coffee table in the window display. 'Can I get one of those as well?'

'I think there's one in stock. I can probably get it for you tomorrow. I can also get some nice matching side-tables.'

I went to Mr Antoine's and bought every scrap of furniture in his workshop. Mrs Antoine showed me some cushions she was making for a family in the poshest residential area of the city. I ordered as many as she could churn out.

Soon, the little Antoine homestead was a hive of activity. 'Boy, I can't keep up with you,' Mr Antoine told me happily. His two sons, both of whom worked at businesses in the city, had the family touch for making furniture. They helped in the evenings and on weekends. A couple of young boys worked on the polishing and sanding, and Mrs Antoine farmed out some of the sewing to other women living in Santa Cruz.

'You know Christmas coming,' she said one day. 'Then is when people does buy new furniture. My niece will come to spend the holidays here and we going to make hundreds of cushions.'

'I will take leave from my job,' said her younger son, Bernard. 'I have plenty leave I didn't take this year. From November to December I will work full-time.'

We were in the shed at the back where the furniture was made. I usually lingered there as long as I could, passing my hands along the pieces in various stages of construction, playing with fragrant wood shavings, inhaling the odours of new wood and polish. Mrs Antoine brought me slices of warm bread she made in the oven, chunks of coconut pone, cups of tea flavoured with cinammon. Bernard liked showing me how they made joints in the furniture, discussing new designs he had thought up to modernise some pieces.

'The problem is the wood, you know,' Mr Antoine remarked. 'If we run out of wood, we dead as a duck. Bernard could take his leave, but production will still grind to a standstill.'

'Why you don't stockpile wood?' I asked.

'Where? On my head?'

I looked around. There was no space in his lot for anything more. But in the plantation yard next door there were a number of unused out-buildings.

'You think your neighbour will let you use some space to store the wood?'

Mr Antoine straightened up from what he was doing, his face a mask of shock. Mrs Antoine let out a splutter of laughter. Her husband tried to explain. 'You don't know my neighbour, boy! That man mad as a hatter. Some of them French Creole so inbred, they doesn't know if they mother is their cousin or their cousin wife. That one so crazy, all his children run away to Port of Spain to get on mad there theyself, and leave him here to make noise every full moon.'

I stared at the madman's lot. It was very attractive for someone who needed storage space.

'We could offer to pay rent for one of those old cocoa-houses,' I said. 'He's not doing anything with it.'

'Boy!' Mr Antoine struck a pleading note, 'you thinking like a sane man. This is a madman you talking about! Who know how the moon striking him these days?'

I meandered across to the estate house. What did I have to lose by asking? I shouted a bit while a pack of wild-looking dogs barked at me. Eventually, a gnarled old man emerged on the verandah. He had dingy cream-coloured skin and was bent over at the waist, with dirty grey hair and a few days' worth of stubble around his face. He looked like somebody who hadn't brushed his teeth for months.

'Good afternoon,' I said.

He stared at me from under bushy grey eyebrows.

'My name is Saran.'

No response.

'From the shop in the Croissee.'

Still no response.

'I was wondering if I could rent that building from you.'

He glared at me. I remained silent. 'Rent?' he croaked.

I nodded warily. There was a long silence. Then he opened his mouth again. 'You think I want any coolie living here?' he demanded in a hoarse rasp.

I was taken aback.

'What the arse I will want a coolie living here for?' the old French Creole croaked. 'For you to nasty up my place?'

I glanced around. The place was filthy, piles of dog shit everywhere. He took a breath.

'Who the arse tell you I looking to rent my place?' he bawled. 'You see my place stand up here good good good, and, just so, you decide that you could come and live in it?'

'Actually,' I said, in a conversational tone, 'I don't want to live here.'

'So what you come here to waste my focking time for?' he snarled. 'Get the arse out of my yard!'

He turned as if to go back into the house.

'I want to rent the building for storage,' I said quickly.

He turned back again and glared some more.

After about an hour and a half of bizarre exchanges, I got the cocoahouse for rent at a very cheap price. Mr de la Guillame, as the madman was called, must have last done business at least a decade before. He had no idea about property values.

By the time we had reorganised our production system to accommodate the new workshop and incorporate more workers, Christmas was upon us. Charlo and I thought long and hard about our Christmas window displays. Every other shop sprayed their windows with tins of fake snow. We decided to go one better. We put together a North Pole scene with Santa Claus and his dwarfs loading up the sledge with toys. We doused everything in flour to create snowdrifts. Charlo stared at our creation critically.

'I wonder if we could make this snow actually fall, boy?'

I got a strainer from the household department and we studied how flour sifted through it. Then we got wire mesh and constructed a large strainer of a ceiling so it was snowing inside our window. What was particularly satisfying was when the snow piled up and made avalanches. Children stopped at the window to wait for a big clump to fall off Santa Claus's roof and bury a couple of dwarfs. Nerissa took to shovelling snow with a toy shovel every morning.

We moved on to the next window. There, we wanted to construct a skating rink out of a mirror, and magnetise some dolls to get them to skate around it.

'The two of allyou worse than any child I ever see,' Ma snarled. 'All allyou really want to do is play with the toys in this shop. And allyou does only mash up the toys!'

'What you expect, Ma?' Charlo looked up at her from where he was crouched on the floor unscrewing a toy aeroplane. He had taken to calling her 'Ma' just to annoy her. 'You take a little boy out of school and put him to run store. You don't expect him to play with the toys when he get a chance?'

'He is a little boy?' Ma asked. 'When I was his age, I had two children already.'

Charlo put down the aeroplane and stared up at her, his big eyes opened wide. 'Ma,' he asked, 'how you know Ved don't have two children heself? The way them girls does be chooking up under him, I wouldn't put my head on a block that you don't have a couple grandchildren running round Trinidad, nuh.'

Ma put her fists on her hips. 'And who fault it will be?' she shrilled. 'It's you who does encourage him in slackness! Before he know you, he was a good boy, only playing cricket and football.'

'Me?' Charlo pointed at his chest and opened his eyes wider. 'Me? I encouraging Ved in slackness? Ma, wake up and take a good look at your son. Ved don't need me to encourage him in slackness.'

I was seventeen, but I looked a couple of years older. When hair had started growing on my face a few years before, I had simply ignored it, and now I had a bushy beard. I still played football and cricket in the savannah, but now I went to drink beer at a bar afterwards. My cousin, Ashok, had come down from Dorado to go to university in nearby St Augustine, and had rented a little apartment he called his 'bachie'. I only had to drop by there to find myself involved in a girl-chasing expedition of one kind or the other.

'A sister in Trinity Hall having a birthday party,' Ashok would say. 'Let we go.'

'You get invited?'

'Well, I didn't get uninvited. Let us put it that way.'

We'd go and hang around outside the party till we were invited in. The girls liked Ashok for his jovial manner and cute face. He had a strong, stocky build from fighting waves and helping fishermen pull in nets, and his skin was jet black, with a healthy sheen from years of beach-life. He plied the girls with obvious invitations to seduction that made them laugh. 'I not sneaky like you,' he said. 'With me, what you see is what you get. You does just stand up by the door and stroke your beard and play man of mystery. That too long-winded for me. I like quick action. Live fast, die young and make a pretty corpse.'

I wasn't being sneaky. I was just being my normal self. I liked being among people, but didn't care to be the centre of attention. I had confidence from my evenings in the mas' camp. I knew that if you didn't pursue girls, their own hunting instincts became aroused. Beards were in fashion on the campus then; those were the revolutionary days. As soon as a girl began remarking that I looked like Fidel Castro, I knew my way was clear.

But Ashok hadn't grown up in the mas' camp. Before this, he had only had coconut trees and jellyfish to practise his seduction techniques on. The few girls at his country high school had been church-going and parent-bound. The middle-class girls at the University of the West Indies, ready to doff their virginity at the drop of a pair of male trousers, blew his mind. He was like a fly in a cake shop, flitting from glass case to glass case, trying to sample every colour of icing on display.

It was Ashok who started the tradition of crazy discounts at Saran's. 'I come to buy a bed!' he announced to Nerissa one day when he showed up in our furniture department. 'A very strong bed. You understand what I mean, girl? A bed that could take a good roughing up.' He jiggled his eyebrows up and down at her in a mock-lascivious gesture. Nerissa sucked her teeth.

'Look, we have a good bed here.'

He stared at her, his eyebrows suspended in shock. 'A single bed? How you could show me a single bed, girl? I look to you like a man who does sleep alone?'

'You look to me like a man who does dream a lot,' Nerissa replied.

'You see allyou Croissee girls!' Ashok pointed his finger at her face. 'Allyou don't know nothing! Down at UWI, the girls have better taste.' He jiggled his eyebrows up and down. 'The girls there like them black and sweet. Like molasses!'

Once he had chosen his bed, he demanded a 'family discount' on the price. I instructed Suzanne to give the bed to him at the cost price. When my sister Indra came to do her Christmas shopping, she too got the family discount.

Suzanne sucked her teeth after Indra had left. 'I was mad not to give her no discount. All she do is criticise everything in the store. I does work my liver-string out in here, and I have to watch my Christmas bonus go in her pocket!'

I thought Suzanne had a point. We had four employees now, and if it weren't for them the store would never have become the success it was. They acted like the business was their own, taking every burden they could off my shoulders, making suggestions for improved organisation, dusting the shelves like furies when they weren't busy. I declared that employees were to get the family discount as well.

'And what about neighbour?' asked the Chinese shopkeeper from whom we bought our stocks of salt prunes and pepper mango. 'Neighbour don't get a discount in here?'

'Mr Chang,' Suzanne leaned on the cash register to offer him a sight of her breasts, 'when last you give us a discount on salt prunes?'

Neighbour discount was set at fifteen per cent. Friend discount was ten per cent.

'So how that lady could get a discount and I can't get none?' demanded a heavy woman in the queue at the cash register one day.

'You's a neighbour?' Suzanne demanded. 'You's a friend?'

The woman plopped her arms on the counter, letting Suzanne have a view of a pair of breasts that made her own look like mosquito bites. 'No,' she said. 'I's a enemy! Look, girl, I's a woman with eight children to buy toys for! And I come all the way from Arima to shop here.'

She refused to budge from her occupation of the cash desk. The queue behind her started to grow longer. I was installing a fan on the pillar behind the cash desk for Suzanne, angling it so it would cause the occasional snowstorm in the nearest window display.

'Darling,' I said to the woman, coming down the ladder and plopping my own arms on the counter opposite her, 'you entitled to the best discount of all.'

I gazed from her face to her breasts and back again. She straightened up. 'What's that?' she asked.

'Enemy discount!' I declared, and instructed Suzanne to deduct five per cent from her bill.

Charlo put up a banner in the window. 'SARAN'S FOR DISCOUNTS', it read.

Ma, of course, disapproved. 'You will bust this shop!' she whined.

'Bust this shop?' I asked. 'Ma, I can't keep up with counting the cash every night. You know how much profit we does make on a suite of furniture? Over seventy per cent.' I had raised the prices I paid Mr Antoine for his pieces. I felt a hundred per cent profit was too much. But I was now administering the ordering of wood and its storage as well. 'Your bank loans paying off theyself,' I told Ma, 'and your bank account standing at —'

'Hush your blasted mouth!' Ma hissed. 'You know how much doctor bill I paying for your father?'

Pa had returned from the nursing home and spent weeks in bed at home. Gradually, he started coming into the shop. The first few times he only blinked, as though his eyes hurt from what he saw: big glass windows exposing all his treasures to the world of thieves and robbers. He was convinced Suzanne must be stealing from the till, and that Nerissa gave away items to the customers. Jason, a jovial young boy I had hired to help shift furniture, was the final straw. Pa took up residence in the glass-enclosed director's office at the back of the shop and trained his dim old eyes on every move the employees made. Charlo dubbed him 'The Watchman'.

'You have to give that man tonic, you know, boy,' he said. 'He will go cokey-eye trying to watch Nerissa and Suzanne at the same time.'

'I glad for him to be there,' I said. 'I could leave the shop and go and drink beers when I feel like it.'

'When you does ever leave this shop and go and drink beers?' Charlo asked. 'You bury in here. In a few years you will turn into your father.'

I snorted. The idea of me turning into my father was absurd. The shop was really just one shiny new toy. I had just turned eighteen, but I was unemployed till I could do my exams the following year, and so was Charlo. He had to wait for the brick factory to start production again before he could get building jobs, so he was happy to potter around making show-windows. I dubbed him my 'advertising manager' and paid him his usual builder's fees every week.

I'm convinced that the way to make money is not to set out to make money. That's why I feel such a fraud when I'm urged to give talks at business seminars. Once I had rescued the family from bankruptcy, I didn't care about the quantity of money that rolled in. All our bank accounts were in the names of my parents. Ma signed cheques and order bills, and, if she was unavailable, I forged her signature. Some of our suppliers thought my real name was Chandrawattee Saran, the way I signed orders with a flourish. They thought Ved was some kind of nickname.

Christmas turned into a frenzy at the shop. I had to hire still more staff. Nerissa managed them. I was kept busy ordering goods as they sold out, running into town to get them, supervising deliveries of furniture, checking receipts and trouble-shooting. Charlo had an old pick-up he used for transporting Carnival costumes which he now used to deliver furniture for customers at a fee. Soon, there was hardly time for the employees to take a break. I installed a cooler in the lunch-room we had constructed at the back, and instructed Jason to keep it filled with soft drinks as the girls couldn't find time to go and buy their own. I started buying cakes so they could have a snack when they could snatch a moment; I bought roti and doubles for everybody at lunch-time.

'You spoiling the workers,' Ma snapped.

'The workers spoiling me,' I snapped back. 'When last you see Nerissa take her full hour for lunch?'

I couldn't do too much for them, I felt. They stayed behind on evenings to replenish shelves and help me unpack boxes of toys. Suzanne would complain about pains in her shoulders after the long days at the cash-register, and Nerissa would take a break from what she was doing to give her a massage. I would send Jason out to buy Chinese food for our dinner, and we would eat from cardboard containers, perched on cardboard boxes, the girls resting their tired legs on each other and on me. Then I would drive everybody home, joking and laughing along the way at the antics of some of our customers.

By Christmas Eve, we were wrecks. Nerissa had dark circles under her eyes; Suzanne's hair was no longer a smooth, well-oiled mass.

'Oh God, Ved!' Nerissa took a moment to prop herself up against my shoulder. 'That man over there want two dozen balloons. I know we still have some balloons in a box in the back, but it will be hell to get them out.'

'Forget balloon now,' I said. 'Tell him we don't have any more.'

She sighed. 'But he is a good customer,' she objected. 'He buy hundreds of dollars already for the season.' She set off to search for the balloons.

Jason wrapped goods in between moving furniture, making stupid jokes that helped keep everybody's spirit up. Nerissa's mother arrived with a huge pot of warm pelau and installed it in the lunch-room. We rushed there between sales to gobble up a few mouthfuls. The last straw was a child who insisted she wanted the Santa Claus doll from the display window. I waved my arm wearily and said she could have it, since it would be of no use the next day anyhow. She asked what the price was but I couldn't be bothered to work out the price on a used Santa Claus.

'Well if that going free,' said another woman, moving towards our second window, 'I want the skaters.'

'Wait, wait, wait,' said Charlo. 'Allyou will mash-up everything. I will take it apart.'

Charlo ended up like Santa Claus in the window, handing out decorations to greedy hands. He poured fake snow on the kids as he gave them gifts. People passing by came in to get their share of the free-ness, then remembered the last piece of gift-wrapping they needed, and discovered a sweet little vase they could give to their mother-in-law.

Pa exited the store. This was too much for his heart, this wild giving away of goods. Ma came in and stood in silence, gazing at the madness. I handed her a shoebox in which I had been stashing hundred-dollar bills that afternoon. Let her go and count and stack.

On Christmas Day, I refused to get out of bed. This was worse than a hangover. Not a single muscle wanted to move. Pa brought me orange juice in bed at about noon. I drank it and turned over to go back to sleep. He brought me some fried chicken the next time I woke up. I ate it, wiped my greasy fingers on the sheet, and turned over again. Charlo turned up with a bottle of poncha crème in the evening, and we slouched on the verandah drinking it idly with ice, hardly saying a word to one another. When he left, I ate a big hunk of rum-soaked Christmas cake and went back to bed.

On Boxing Day, my sisters and their families arrived. I barricaded myself into my room, but the children broke down the barricades and plumped themselves all over me. I pushed them off. In the pillow-fight that ensued, we destroyed not only the pillows in my room, but broke a lamp. One of the little girls got a cut from stepping on a piece of it, so I tore the sheet from my bed and bandaged her foot till it was twice the size of everyone else's. After that, the other children wanted bandages as well, and we finished off the sheet. The room began to look like the contents of one of our display windows. Stuffing from the pillows floated everywhere like big snowflakes, covering toys the children had brought in.

'Ved!' my sister Queen said, coming in and surveying the mess, 'when will you ever grow up?'

'Never!' I said, balling up a blanket as tight as I could and flinging it at her with my pace-bowling arm.

She rocked back from the impact and nearly fell over.

'Bull's-eye!' one of Indra's children shouted, and they all began flinging things at Queen. She had to retreat.

'It's Ved who has a bad influence on the children,' I heard Indra intoning in response to Queen's complaints. 'He's so irresponsible and lazy! Ma said he never got out of bed yesterday. And we had it so busy, with all the cooking and entertaining and wrapping gifts!'

I had an urge to suggest to the children that we go and smash up what was left of the shop.

On the day after that, the employees all turned out for work. I had hoped that they would go AWOL and I could leave the shop closed and head for Lopinot river. I had an image of myself lying prone among the clean pebbles while the water washed over my tired skin. But no, Nerissa arrived at the usual time and began to nag that we had to do stock-taking. I sat on the cash desk, surveyed the mess around me, and couldn't face the task. 'River,' I croaked, and let my body flop to lie on the desk with my limbs dangling over the sides. 'Just pick me up from here and carry me and dump me in Lopinot river.'

'Get up, Ved,' Nerissa said in a weak voice. 'We have to do the stock-taking before we can open the store again.' Her skin was ashy from exhaustion, but she still tried to lever me up by my arms.

'Stock-taking?' I groaned, making my body as limp and heavy as possible so when she let go of me my arms flopped down at the sides of the desk again.

Suzanne leaned against the counter, her breasts sagging. 'I not taking up work again until Mr Antoine make a new chair for me,' she said. 'That one wear out. My bottom going straight through the padding.'

'That is because your bottom too big,' Jason told her, but she didn't even respond.

Nerissa tried tickling me. I just closed my eyes, tightened my muscles and remained inert.

'Water flowing over me,' I murmured as she tried tickling me. 'Nice cool water, fresh from the mountains. Lopinot water . . . Jason, go and call Charlo to conduct the last rites. I know where to get holy water.'

Charlo arrived. I sat up. 'You ready to go Lopinot?' I asked him.

'Ved!' Nerissa's eyes were big and round and hurt. 'You really going to leave us in this mess and go river?'

'No,' I said, bending my knees and advancing on her in a menacing way. 'I going to kidnap allyou and carry allyou Lopinot.'

I declared that day Recovery Day. Everybody else would be back at work, moaning and groaning from hangovers and indigestion, and not getting a bit of work done. We would have the whole river to ourselves. Jason went into the stockroom to plunder some antique boxer shorts no one had ever dared buy, and proposed the girls use them as bikini bottoms. I knew Nerissa would never expose herself in her bra, so I unearthed an old box of T-shirts.

'What about the store?' Nerissa asked.

'What about the store?' I argued. 'You ever hear anybody does buy toy on the day after Boxing Day?'

'Me,' said a voice.

It was our enemy, the woman who had bought toys for eight children. She had forgotten the ninth.

'She say she want a blue car, like the one her brother get,' the woman informed us.

'You see we have any more blue car?' Suzanne demanded.

'Look it have a blue car here,' Jason said, wheeling a big object out of the stockroom, a tricycle disguised as a car. 'It have a dent so we couldn't sell it.'

The woman leaned down to examine the tricycle. 'I only pay $7.95 for her brother car,' she said. 'That one is $77.95.'

'Sweetheart,' I said, taking stock of her cleavage again as she leaned over, 'what is a little seventy dollars between enemies? You entitled to the Stale-Drunk Discount, six hundred per cent. Lopinot river waiting for us. Take your car, drive it back to Arima, and save yourself taxi fare.'

The woman squinted at me suspiciously. 'How the hell I supposed to get this thing to Arima?'

Charlo laughed. 'I will put it in the back of my pick-up and drop you. Just take a seat in the front, where I could keep an eye on that nice T-shirt you wearing.'

'But Arima is further than Lopinot!' Suzanne pointed out. 'She going to keep us back.'

'Nah!' Charlo said. 'We kidnapping this lady too. I will drop her after we go to the river.'

'The lady must be have things to do at home,' Suzanne muttered. 'She have nine children.'

'Who tell you', the woman demanded, pushing her bosoms up to assert her superiority over Suzanne again, 'that I have nine children?'

It turned out that Sybil, as she was called, was childless. She just bought gifts for poor children in her neighbourhood. She had nothing to do on Recovery Day, and was happy to accompany us to Lopinot.

Nerissa found a gigantic cooking pot among the stock, and we stopped off at a grocery, bought supplies for cooking at the river, and made a wood fire on its bank. Charlo went into Lopinot Village and came back with a duck purchased from a woman who had poultry running around her yard. I invented a recipe for curried duck that day that immediately became a legend. We all lay among the clean stones of the river letting the spirit of Christmas Past fade.

It became a Saran tradition. The day after Boxing Day, when the store business was at its lowest ebb and employees in other businesses were wasting time, was dubbed National Stale-Drunk Day by my employees. It was a holy day, we decided, when you had to get re-baptised in the river after committing the sins of gluttony, covetousness and showing off during the Christmas season. It was more than holy, Charlo was to say in later years, it was sacred. As he lay in the river bed, his mind became free of window displays and he began dreaming up the theme for his next Carnival band.

Chapter Two

You mightn't believe it was so easy to start a multi-million-dollar business. Luck was a primary factor. Trinidad had oil, and the prices of oil had just gone up. People would buy virtually anything with the money that flowed from the oil. 'Any damn fool could make money here,' my mother said. 'Except your father.'

And except Charlo, I realised.

After Christmas, the shop was at its lowest ebb, so I spent a lot of time over at the mas' camp, and began to notice that Charlo priced the costumes he made too low. I started importing the materials he needed and giving them to him at cost price. He only cut the prices on his costumes further. When Mikey, the steel-band's leader, said all other bands had uniforms and he wanted some for his pan-men as well, I gave him the rest of the old T-shirts in our stockroom and Charlo started designing a logo to print on them. The official name of our steel band was 'Symphonia', so for days Charlo played with the letter 'S', turning it into a long snake that curled into a steelpan. When his design was finally ready, I discovered that he had dubbed the band 'Saran's Symphonia'. I stared at him in surprise.

'Ain't you sponsor the costume?' he said.

I chortled. 'A few old T-shirt I wanted to get rid of?'

'Well I's the advertising manager of Saran's. I advertising. Saran is the sponsor of this band.'

'But when band have sponsor, they does sponsor all kind of thing,' Mikey pointed out. 'Look at Amoco. They give their band new pans, trailer —'

Charlo stood up straight and glared at him. 'You know who is Amoco? The . . . American . . . Oil . . . Company. You want to compare Saran's to Uncle Sam? Why allyou black people so greedy, eh? Look, take the T-shirt and say God is Love. When Saran get big like Sam, you will get trailer and thing.'

Charlo put me in charge of building the costume for the King of the Band. It was to be a massive mythological bird but I made it more massive than he had intended. He claimed it would overbalance, but I didn't listen. Much to the merriment of the spectators on Carnival day, Charlo proved to be right. To overcome my embarrassment, I took a few extra gulps of rum from the flask a guy carried in his pocket and just decided to have a damn good time.

We all did. Our wining girls even ended up on the front page of the next day's newspaper. Unfortunately, Carlene had dragged me into their midst, so I was there as well. 'SODOM AND GOMORRAH!' roared the head-line. The Catholic archbishop made us the focus of his Ash Wednesday sermon in the cathedral and my mother had fuel for complaints for months.

To escape her voice, I retreated to Ashok's bachie, and we started playing tennis together on the university campus. I quickly got a taste for the game, but the courts were always crowded and we spent more time waiting to play than playing. I grumbled at the waste of time.

'But look at the view you does get!' Ashok consoled me, his eyes trained on the plump thighs of a girl in a short tennis skirt. 'The problem with you is you don't appreciate the finer things in life. That is poetry in motion, boy.'

I suggested we join the St Augustine Tennis Club, a members-only establishment nearby, where we could book a court.

'That does cost money,' Ashok demurred.

'I have money,' I said, jingling my pockets. 'Money is no object.'

We had only seen the St Augustine Tennis Club from the outside. That is, we had only seen its ten-foot-high privet hedge. 'Waaay!' Ashok exclaimed the first time we went inside the hedge. 'It's wall-to-wall white people!'

The place turned out to be a hideout for the elite. There were a few black and brown people, but they were doctors and such-like. White inside their skins. More white than the whites. While the local white people tried to behave as boisterously as blacks, the blacks at the tennis club spoke in moderated tones, like they had just exited from Buckingham Palace after an audience with the Queen. The clubhouse itself was like a scene from the British Raj, a low bungalow with a large verandah framed in white fretwork.

'You have to have escutcheon and thing to come here, boy,' Ashok gasped.

'I don't give a fart,' I replied. 'I come to play tennis.' But Ashok never just played tennis.

'You ain't see that Thing, boy!' He gestured with his neck at a blonde girl on a chair, her knees drawn up and her tennis skirt falling away to give glimpses of her crotch. 'On a clear day, you could see for ever.'

'She want you to see for ever,' I replied sourly. 'She making style for these two coolie boys. Watch but don't touch.'

I had learnt this in high school. The white girls at the convents in the city had only been interested in the white boys at the Catholic colleges. The black boys from QRC had had no chance with them. But Ashok hadn't gone to high school in the city.

'You could dig out you eye to spite your face,' he said. 'Anytime I get a free show, I watching.'

We would drink beers at the bar between games. Ashok always wanted to linger and leer at the girls, while I was in a hurry to get back on the court. I grew to love tennis. It wasn't like cricket, where you had one turn to bat and then had to sit out the match. You could be slamming those balls for ever, drawing back your arm and shoulder, trying to time the stroke perfectly, feeling the satisfaction of seeing the ball arc gracefully over the net. I became a fanatic and began playing with other fanatics. Ashok turned into a barfly with the other barflies. Alcohol invokes colour-blindness.

'Well played!' a girl congratulated me one evening after I had won a hard-fought match.

I had noticed this girl. She never played, just sat on the verandah with a drink. She chatted with a lot of people but didn't draw much attention to herself. Now, when I went to get myself a drink, I offered to bring back one for her as well.

'Thanks,' she said, and smiled a brilliant smile at me. 'I'd love a gin and tonic.' She had a strong English accent.

I brought back the drink and we got talking. Her name was Janet Stevenson. She had bright blue eyes and wavy brown hair with reddish glints in it. Tallish and slim, in simple tennis shorts. She wasn't playing nowadays, she told me, because she had torn a tendon. 'It's totally frustrating,' she sighed. 'I'm going to turn into an alcoholic sitting here. I can't even drive. My neighbours come here every evening, so, instead of going batty sitting alone in the house, I join them. But they inevitably get sloshed and stay late. So I'm always stuck till I find someone else going my way.'

I put her down as about twenty-four. She lived close by, at Santa

Margarita, a hill behind St Augustine where a few lavish houses had been built into the hillside. So when I was leaving, I offered her a lift home. She beamed her smile on me again.

'That would be very nice of you.'

Her house was nearly at the peak of the hill. It was dusk and lights were flickering on down below. 'You must have a wonderful view,' I remarked.

'Come in and have a look,' she suggested.

I parked the car and followed her in. The house was magnificent. Balconies all around, with french doors that opened onto a view of a huge expanse of the Caroni plain. I exclaimed at it. She shrugged. 'It feels very lonely with just me up here.'

She explained that she was separated from her husband. He was a prominent black lawyer she had met when he was studying in England. Now, she was waiting for the divorce to be concluded before returning there. I realised she must be older than twenty-four.

I sipped the beer she had handed me while she went over to a turntable on a bookshelf. Joni Mitchell's voice filled the room. I turned around and went over to look at the other record albums on her shelves. Most were of jazz or classical European music. I asked her to put on a Miles Davis album I hadn't heard since leaving high school. Janet quietly went into the kitchen and emerged with a tray of crackers, cheese, pickled onions and horseradish.

When I was leaving, she thanked me again for bringing her home. I felt it was I who should be grateful for the lovely hour and a half. I offered to close the gate to the driveway behind me. She laughed. 'That gate has a mind of its own. Only I can close it. Don't bother, but thanks for the thought.'

This extreme politeness made me determined to be courteous as well. I tugged at the gate and it fell to the ground with a clunk. She laughed again.

'You see what I meant?'

I bent down to examine the gate. The screws had come off the hinge. 'You just need a screwdriver to fix this,' I said.

She made a rueful face. 'My husband took custody of the screwdriver.'

I offered to lend her one and Sunday morning saw me driving up to Santa Margarita again with my toolbox in the trunk of my car. There was a lovely breeze on the hill, and the sunshine sparkled on the lush vegetation. The gate took no time at all to fix. Janet offered me a cup of coffee and we went inside.

'Actually,' she said hesitantly in the kitchen, 'there's another thing I would like to ask you to do. Since you're already here with your tools.'

There was a dripping faucet. It needed a washer and the hardware shops weren't open, so I promised to do it another day. I insisted Janet tell me what other little repairs needed to get done. There was a reading lamp whose switch didn't work. I unscrewed the base and cleaned the contacts. Then a jammed door. Janet looked at the clock. It was after twelve.

'I think the sun is over the yardarm, whatever that means. Want a beer? I can't even offer you lunch to thank you. There's no food in the house. With this injury, it's difficult to get to the grocery.'

'So what are you going to eat?'

She shrugged. 'I can probably find a can of soup somewhere.'

I studied her. That was all she would have on a Sunday? 'Would you like to go out and get something?' I asked.

'What a good idea!' she said, with her brilliant smile. 'It'll be my treat, to thank you for all the repairs.'

She directed me to the western part of the city, to Woodbrook, where she knew a tiny restaurant hidden among trees in a residential suburb. The food was fantastic. Crab-backs for starters, which I had never had, shrimp in a spicy sauce, coconut cream for dessert. Over the meal, I learnt that Janet was twenty-eight and had a degree in anthropology. She was planning to go to art school when she returned to England. When she went to the loo, as she called it, I quietly paid the bill. She was upset when she learned this.

'You can pay next time,' I said with a smile, not really expecting there to be a next time.

But the following evening, after I closed the store, I diverted to her house before going to the tennis club and offered to drive her to the grocery. 'How thoughtful you are!' she exclaimed, and I felt pleased with myself. She insisted I stay for dinner and eat some of the lamb chops she had bought. I was delighted. I played her records and gazed at the view while she cooked. Then we sat at a little glass table on the verandah, set with place-mats and colourful cloth napkins, and ate as the lights twinkled below.

The following weekend, I fixed Janet's dripping faucet. When I was done, I offered to take her for a drive to get her out of the house. We drove to the west of the island, over the blue-green mountains of the northern range, and down to Las Cuevas beach. Janet spread her arms wide, inhaled the sea air, and smiled her brilliant smile at me.

'Another time,' she said as we were leaving, 'we should start early and go all the way around the north coast to Balandra.'

I was exhilarated. There would be another time. I loved being with Janet, with her quiet reflective manner and her inevitable politeness. It was suddenly like having a lovely older sister to treat me gently. I saw people glance at us when we were out together and knew what they must be thinking. I was glad. I felt proud to be escorting this beautiful, refined lady all over the place.

One evening, she suggested we go to a play together. It was staged in a little theatre on the western side of the city. All the cultural elite were there, white socialites and the black arty-farty crowd. Janet wore a long, batik-printed dress in shades of deep blue and turquoise. It was simple, of cotton, with little straps that tied around her neck. With her bright blue eyes, it looked stunning.

'There's Geoffrey over there,' she said, when we were settled in the theatre.

Geoffrey was her ex-husband. He was pretty nondescript, but the creature with him was not. She had very light-coloured skin and wore an elaborate dress in African print with a tall turban to match. As we left the theatre, they came up to us. Geoffrey chatted with Janet, his eyes swivelling repeatedly back to me, but Janet omitted to introduce us. I felt left out. I thought she was making an effort to indicate that I was not her boyfriend. I moved away a little and pretended to be studying posters for other plays.

'Coming to Smokey for a drink?' Geoffrey asked her.

'Maybe.' She smiled her brilliant smile at him.

I felt a bit jealous, a bit put in my place. I was a little boy, after all, not part of this sophisticated crowd. Janet moved towards me and jerked her head in the direction of the door. We went outside to the pavement. All the way, people were greeting Janet, kissing her cheek and saying they hadn't seen her for a long time. 'We could catch up on the news at the Pelican,' suggested a white guy with a little pot belly.

Janet shook her head. 'I'm not really up for the Pelican tonight. I'll catch up with you another time.'

We made our way down the dark street to where my car was parked. Once Janet got inside, she flopped into the passenger seat and heaved a deep sigh.

'I hope you didn't feel bad that I didn't introduce you. They would only have started chatting at you and I really wanted to escape.'

She didn't smile her brilliant smile at me. She looked at me seriously. I smiled at her instead. 'It's OK.'

'I'm sorry,' she said, touching my hand. 'I know I was being rude, but I couldn't bear to be held up listening to gossip. Do you mind if we just have a drink at my house?'

But when we got to her house she was rather subdued. I decided to leave after one drink. Then she put a record on the turntable that I particularly liked, so I sat in my usual big blue and white chair that faced the view. After a while I heard her voice.

'Ved,' she said, 'I want to ask you something.'

I looked over to where she was sitting in her usual chair. 'Sure.'

She was silent.

'Well?' I asked.

I thought this must be a big repair job she was going to ask me to do since she was hesitating so long. Her next words came out in a rush.

'Would you like to sleep with me?'

I froze. 'Sure,' I said finally.

Silence. She was looking at me gravely, her blue eyes violet in the dim light. Something in my stomach did a lurch.

'Sure,' I said with a little laugh. 'Who wouldn't want to sleep with you?'

The record ended and she got up to put another one on. It must have been a sort of theoretical question, I decided. Just to know if she still had pulling power, like her husband. Then I heard her quiet voice.

'So,' she asked, 'do you want to sleep with me or not?'

I looked at her and nodded. She continued looking at me. I held up a finger. 'Gotta go to the loo,' I said.

In the bathroom, I thought about what to do next.

When I got back to the living-room, I didn't return to my chair. I made myself cross the space between us and go to stand in front of hers. I held out my right hand towards her. She took it. Her fingers felt tiny and helpless in my hand, so light I could hardly feel them properly. I crouched down and stroked the back of her hand with the forefinger of my left hand. She just looked at me. I raised my left hand and brushed the hair back from her cheek, interlacing my fingers in the strands. She remained perfectly still, her eyes on my face.

'Your hair is so light,' I murmured. 'Like feathers.'

I kept brushing my fingers through it, feeling its delicacy. But that couldn't go on for ever. I tugged at her hand.

'Come,' I said, lifting her to her feet.

She rose and followed me into her bedroom.

The weeks that followed were glorious. We spent a lot of time on her big bed with the spectacular view and the music drifting in from the living-room. It's not that I wanted to have sex with Janet all the time, but it just happened like that. I always wished to touch her, to feel the connection between us, to hold her slim body in my arms and nuzzle my face in her neck where the hair brushed it. But one thing always led to another. And I loved it when her super-polite, lady-like manner sloughed off like a snake's skin and she turned into a writhing mass of desire. My own feelings took second place to the pleasure of watching her face and body glow as she reached for satisfaction. I never tired of watching her body, slim and unmarked and somewhat innocent. Where black women had pools of mystery, Janet had a smooth pinkness that invited touch. It was an experience I had never had before, wanting to be with a woman, not to have sex with her, but just to be in her presence, and then having desire creep up on its own.

I learned a lot about timing then. Maybe it was Maria Callas's influence. Janet would put on a record of Puccini's arias as the sun began to set and we would sit on the balcony with a glass of port and almost watch Maria's voice soar over the hills. I would hear her whole being build to a note, but she would delay over the phrase she was singing, caressing it, savouring every millisecond in her throat, and I would be in a state of longing by the time she reached her crescendo.

'You know what she's singing?' Janet asked one evening, her face seeming to be in another sphere of existence.

I shook my head.

'"*Non voglio morire*",' she said. 'I don't want to die.'

My own breast filled with the emotion. No one was threatening me with death at that moment, but I was suddenly full of the wonder of life,

45

desiring every moment that I had among these hills, desiring to fill them with feeling and beauty.

Death came soon, though. In May, Janet's divorce papers came through. She had registered to start art school in September. Before then, she had to put the house on the market, sort out and ship her things, fly to London, find a place to live and get herself settled. Arrangements for her departure overtook us and my wish to spend as much time as possible with her. I forgot about the exams I was scheduled to take. When I remembered, I swore to myself I would take them the following year.

'You will come and visit, of course,' Janet urged.

'Not till next year,' I said regretfully. 'The business will get very busy in the next few months.'

She smiled a crooked smile. 'You'll probably have a girlfriend by next year.'

I shrugged.

'You can bring her,' she said. 'I think you must definitely get a taste of life outside Trinidad. I won't make things difficult.'

I folded her into my arms, wishing I could squeeze her essence into me.

After Janet left, every day felt like Ash Wednesday, the day after carnival, when the savannah is dusty and dry and littered with beer bottles, a reminder of the previous day's intoxication. I lay on my bed for hours in a state of lethargy. I drove around blindly. Nothing had any charm for me, not tennis, not the shop, not conversation, certainly not other women.

If only I had done my pre-university exams, I reproached myself, I could have gone to England and started studying there. At least I would have been able to see Janet sometimes. Then I remembered that I would have had to apply to English universities long before I met Janet, and I was able to put that regret aside. But it gave me a goal. I would organise the business so it could run without me, take my exams the following year and go to London to study engineering.

The first problem was getting a constant supply of furniture for the store. We were always short of stock. Saran's reputation had spread far and wide, and people were often disappointed when they came from the other end of the island and couldn't get what they wanted. Mr Antoine simply couldn't keep up with demand. His son, Bernard, had never gone back to his job after the previous Christmas, and they now employed three young men on a regular basis. But the work was labour-intensive, so I suggested they hire yet more.

'And put them where?' Mr Antoine asked. 'On my head?'

The shed in his yard was overcrowded with furniture in various states of completion.

'I could rent another cocoa-house next door,' I said. 'That could make a great workshop.'

'Ved,' Mr Antoine said wearily, 'you think I could put up with any more of these young fellas around me? If rain fall, they don't come out to work. If they stale-drunk, they don't come out to work. If some girl leave them and they get tabanca, they does go on strike.' He shook his head. 'I not able with this younger generation, nuh!'

I perched on a table and let sawdust drift through my fingers.

'You know,' Bernard put in, 'the best thing would be if my brother would come and work full-time. He real good in this but he have a big job with McLaren's.'

'You think he would give it up to make furniture?'

Bernard shrugged. 'This have plenty more money. Why you don't go and talk to him? If you could get madman de la Guillame to rent you his cocoa-house, maybe you could get Tony to leave his job.'

I headed out of the valley and along the Eastern Main Road, to where the biggest commercial firm in Trinidad had its headquarters, a three-storey building next to one of its subsidiaries, which sold agricultural equipment. I walked past showrooms full of mustard-coloured tractors, went up in an elevator, and was directed to the accounts department.

Tony was in a little glass-enclosed office to one side, wearing a white shirt and tie. He rose to shake my hand. He was taller than his father, and had an energetic air. He looked to be in his late twenties. I explained the situation.

'We could sell a lot more furniture if you were in the business,' I said. 'That would mean a lot more profit for me and for allyou guys.'

He laughed. 'You don't know the half of it,' he said, raising his eyebrows. 'Since you make teak so popular, plenty other store owners does come asking my father to make furniture for them.'

'So what you think?' I asked hesitantly.

Tony laughed again and shook his head. 'Boy, I think it's a doomed case. You can't really fulfil that demand with my father's methods. That man in the nineteenth century. I glad you come along and revive the trade for him, but I don't feel you could do much more.'

He got up and went to a filing cabinet, then returned with a couple of catalogues. 'Here's what you need,' he said, leaning over the desk and pointing to a picture of a mechanical lathe. 'You know how many chair legs that could turn out in a day? Look here.' He pointed out electric saws, bevelling machines, various other apparatus. Then he went round the desk and dropped into his chair again. 'You could see my father using those things? The first thing he will do is saw off one of his fingers because the electric machine going too fast.'

I propped my elbow on Tony's desk, my face in my fist, and stared at the pictures. 'How much those things does cost, boy?' I asked.

He started checking price lists and quoting numbers. Then he drew an adding machine towards him. The total was high, but we still had money in the bank from the loan intended for building Ma's concrete palace above the store.

'Of course, you will need a bigger workforce,' Tony said, raising his eyebrows. 'Production will speed up. You'll have to calculate in a serious wage bill.'

'About how much?' I waggled my hand to indicate I wanted an approximation.

Tony started punching in numbers, looking up and squinting his eyes in thought now and then. When he was finished I looked at the figures he had produced. We could afford them from the extra earnings at the store.

'Would you be interested in managing an operation like that?' I asked.

He looked up at the ceiling for a while. 'Depends on the terms,' he said.

He wanted the same salary he earned at McLaren's at the beginning, plus fifteen per cent of the profits. Once the business got going, he would raise his salary demands. I found that fair.

'What about your father and Bernard?'

'Bernard would be glad to do things this way. I'll work out a good salary scale for him as production supervisor. The old man will go along if I am running things. He don't like doing business and dealing with employees.'

I smiled. 'We could give him the title of "Master Craftsman",' I suggested. 'And then there's your mother . . .'

'I'll put together a total set of cost projections for you.' Tony leaned back in his chair with a contented look on his face. 'We could supply all the furniture stores in Trinidad, and let my old man design special pieces for the President and people like that.'

I smiled broadly.

'You think I joking,' he said. 'My father could make real good stuff, you know. If you see the kind of bed he used to make for them big shots long ago. Not them kind of joke furniture you selling, you know.'

'When can we start?'

'I have to give one month's notice here. In the meantime, we could order the machines. If I put in the order as an employee, I get ten per cent discount.'

I shook his hand and went home to face my mother.

'Ma,' I said, 'about that loan for your house –'

She started ranting about the interest she was paying.

'OK,' I said, 'right now you paying fourteen per cent interest on the money. How would you like to make sixty per cent on it?'

'How I will do that?' She squinted sourly at me. 'What happen? You running pyramid scheme now?'

I laughed. 'No, I would like to invest the money in the business.'

'In the business? Why I want to invest more money in your business? You always studying the business. You never studying how I living in this old house with rat and cockroach running all round my foot.'

There were no rats or cockroaches in our house. They wouldn't have dared cross my mother's doorstep. But there was no point in mentioning that once my mother was in rhetorical flow. I let her rave for a while. When she ran out of steam, I put on my sternest voice.

'So you not interested in making money on that money? You content to pay interest till the brick factory ready?'

She raised her voice. 'How the hell I will be interested in making money unless you tell me how I going to make money?'

I explained.

'I don't like teak,' she stated flatly. 'I like mahogany. That have class. You ever hear Queen Victoria eating from a teak dining-table?'

'Ma, Queen Victoria ain't living in Trinidad,' I pointed out. 'Queen Victoria ain't even living. The people who living in Trinidad dying for teak.'

'Damn stupid people, if you ask me! Trinidadians don't have no class!

And when allyou run out of teak, then what? You always saying the importers don't have enough in stock.'

'We not going to run out of teak,' I said. 'I going to Guyana next week to start importing my own supplies.'

'Guyana?' her voice rose again. 'Who tell you to go Guyana? You going to leave me here with your sick father and go running round Guyana like a crazy dog? Suppose the man get a next heart attack?'

'I will get Ashok to come and stay with allyou.'

'Ashok? That locho? He will give your father the heart attack.'

I left her in mid-stream and went to the travel agent to buy a ticket.

Guyana only made me miss Janet more. The giant forests, the huge rivers, the sense of a continent barely touched by man . . . I could imagine her looking at it all and then turning to smile at me. I consoled myself with the thought that I would soon see her. Once I had got the production system organised, I could leave the business to run on its own.

Importing the wood turned out to be easy. Teak was going at rock-bottom prices. I would make a killing just by cutting out the importers' fees. By the time I got back home, Tony had identified a score of workers. He had found some of the equipment we needed in McLaren's stockrooms and ordered the rest. He handed in his notice, and, having holidays due, quit showing up at the office. He was deep in account-books and ledgers, preparing the administrative side of things. I was impressed. This man knew how to set up a business in the correct way. I noted some of his procedures for implementing in the shop.

What was it the man said? Some are born great and some have great-ness thrust upon them? I know the feeling well. I had greatness thrust upon me by a man who didn't want greatness for himself. One Charlo. When I went to visit him after my trip to Guyana, I found the steel band practising in his yard. He was making a series of radio jingles to adver-tise Saran's: 'Saran's, the only place for furniture and appliances'.

I laughed. 'We don't sell appliances,' I pointed out.

He stared at me. 'So you not going to sell appliances? No fridge and stove and thing? When you ever hear a store does sell furniture alone? You will mess up my jingles!'

'Charlo, where the arse I going and put appliances? On my head? You don't see the shop full already?'

He raised his eyebrows. 'So we not going to expand the shop?'

I stared at him. 'What we going to expand the shop with? You have a thousand brick in your back pocket?'

'Brick?' he sneered. 'Who talking bout brick? You didn't just go and buy out half of Guyana forest? Teak is hardwood, boy. Them Japanese does build temple out of teak that does last for centuries. Let me show you.'

Charlo had a heap of illustrated books that he banned anyone from touching. They were filled with pictures of Ancient Rome, Zulu tribes, Polynesian civilizations, Maya empires and the like. He rifled through them to get inspiration for his Carnival bands.

I studied his pictures of wooden pagodas in Japan. I began to see his idea taking shape in my head. 'But building does take months to build,' I pointed out.

'Who talking bout building building?' Charlo asked. 'We building a Japanese temple to furniture and appliance. Ved, a furniture store ain't no big set of building, you know. It's just a shell. One big room. Why we can't build that?'

'You does have to have plan, boy.'

'So, we will get plan. Mikey will draw the plan.'

Mikey, our band-leader, was a quiet, serious guy, a loner who never talked or wined. Charlo maintained he was a musical genius struggling to be born. His day job was as a draughtsman, working with the government's Town and Country Department.

'Mikey ain't no architect,' I pointed out.

Charlo stared at me. 'What the hell we want architect to confuse we for?' he demanded. 'They does want to challenge God and gravity, building building that ain't supposed to build. Mikey does listen to what you want, sit down quiet-quiet with a sheet of paper, and bam! You have plan, and Mikey back in the pan-yard beating he pan. You know how much plan Mikey draw for people? Half of the Croissee is house Mikey draw.'

'But plan does take months to pass,' I pointed out. 'You does have to submit it to one set of office and hope you get it back before you dead.'

Charlo sucked his teeth. 'What set of office? Not Town and Country, where Mikey working? When Mikey finish draw a plan, it does go through that office like a dose of salts.'

'That legal, boy?'

Charlo stared at me. 'You think I will tell Mrs Saran's son to get himself involved in anything that not legal?' He waved his hand back and forth in denial. 'You overestimating me, boy. I fraid that woman worse than twenty Tarzan.'

I went across the street to talk to Ma.

I had only just started my sales pitch when she stopped me dead in my tracks. She had had enough of being persuaded into my ideas, it seemed. 'I was wondering when you would have noticed that!' she spat.

'Eh?' I crinkled my face.

'It obvious to any fool. Furniture don't sell without appliance. You take so long to come to that conclusion? Boy, I only went to school till third standard, and I could have tell you that a year ago. But no, you so harden and own-way, you want to do everything the way you feel it should do. I don't tell you nothing. I does leave you to make mistake and then come crying to me.'

'So you agree to building an extension?'

'You should have build that extension since January. But no, you prefer to go and wine your backside on the savannah stage like a old-nigger. Let everybody else build extension and sell appliance. You building costume . . .'

So said, so done. As my first shipment of teak hit the docks, we swung into action. Tony started churning out chair legs; Charlo and I churned out our Japanese pagoda. Of course, I'm being silly here. The building was no pagoda. It was a very simple structure, a long addition to the store that extended all the way along the side-street. Again, our front was made up of huge glass panels. But now they were flanked by warm teak columns.

It required furious work to get everything completed before the end of November when the Christmas sales began. I fell into bed exhausted every night, sometimes without eating or having a shower. I would push aside thoughts of Janet for the whole day, waiting till I got to bed to start rewinding my mental tapes of the months with her. But before I could reach Scene Two, I was asleep.

Years later, I realised that had been the point of the whole project. 'I never see a man who could take on a tabanca like Ved!' Charlo would say. 'Tiger don't phase he. Hurricane don't worry him. Getting condemned to hell by the archbishop does roll off he back like grease off a hot frying pan. But let one white woman leave him, and he does dry up and shrivel and look like one of them people in a German concentration camp.'

'Charlo, you does exaggerate!' I would protest.

'Exaggerate?' His voice rose in indignation. 'Boy, you never look in a mirror in those days? I nearly order funeral clothes! You look like one of them malaria victim, walking round in a daze like you shivering inside. I see corpses in the mortuary that look better.'

I think, now, that Charlo and my mother had got together and planned the expansion while I was in Guyana.

'We could have the Grand Opening now!' Charlo announced when our pagoda was finished.

'Grand Opening?'

He stared at me. 'But we have to have Grand Opening! What kind of advertising manager I would be if I don't have Grand Opening? Symphonia going to play. You will buy rum. Nerissa mother going to make roti. We going to invite dignitaries. Who we going to get to cut the ribbon?'

We settled on the MP for our area. He was a big man with a greying moustache who spoke in a fake Oxbridge accent and had a dignified bearing. He would cut a ribbon at the opening of Hell if there was rum and roti to follow. Other than him, we knew no other dignitaries. We appointed Mr Antoine a dignitary. We appointed Mikey a dignitary. We tried appointing Ma a dignitary, but she would have nothing to do with stupidness, she said. We called up the university lecturer who had bought our first dining suite and asked him to make a speech. Then we issued our first radio jingle, announcing that Saran's was having a Grand Opening Sale of its appliance department with a ten per cent discount.

Crowds turned up. And where there's rum and roti, the Trinidad Press turns up. Photographers took pictures to publish in their papers, and their editors called me later to ask if they would get higher discounts for promoting Saran's. Symphonia played on the pavement, so there was no room there for the girls to wine. They took over the street, causing a traffic jam. The police came to clear the traffic, but smelled the roti being served by Nerissa's mother. They decided to stick around and exercise crowd control. This attracted more people, who, seeing police cars and traffic jam, rushed to the scene expecting a fire or robbery or some such entertainment. They came to goggle and stayed to guzzle.

Saran's advertising manager jumped up on a big crate and shouted for silence. Charlo hadn't remembered to put anything on over his sleeveless vest, but he could still make a big noise with his mouth. He called on the Guyanese lecturer to speak. The lecturer droned on about the significance of furniture in post-colonial development. Man and his landscape had to develop a symbiotic relationship for a new civilization to be built here, he intoned. Using the wood that flourished in our midst was a move towards our birth as a people.

The word 'wood' had only one meaning to that crowd. A smutty one. 'Allyou men hear what the professor say?' a raucous female voice shouted. 'Use the wood in allyou midst!'

I never imagined that a man so black as the lecturer could blush, but he managed it.

Symphonia played 'Dashing Through The Snow', and we dramatically unveiled that year's Christmas window display. Santa's sledge began moving down from the North Pole towards Trinidad, along a wire we had strung under the first layer of snow. Unfortunately, snow had been falling in the window all that day, so the first two reindeer hit a snow-drift and started rolling backwards on the wire. We ended up with an eight-reindeer pile-up and mass collision involving sledge and Santa and presents and dwarfs. Then we started looking for our MP to cut the ribbon. He was run to earth in the lunch-room at the back of the store where the drinks were. He rushed out towards the pavement to do his duty, but used the door where the ribbon had already been strung. The ribbon broke under pressure from his big belly and he sprawled forward. Luckily, Charlo and I were there to catch him before he hit the pavement.

'That pagoda well and truly open!' Charlo assured him. 'I never see a pagoda open so good in years. In Japan they does hire sumo wrestler to open pagoda in the self-same manner.'

And Saran's had another bumper Christmas.

In the last week, when the tempo of work in the shop neared breaking point, I heard the girls talking about how they were longing for Recovery Day. Lying in the water of Lopinot Village became a dream we all dangled before our eyes to keep us going. The girls asked if they could invite their families this year, and, when I nodded, Nerissa began counting numbers for the roti she would ask her mother to make. I put a quick stop to that. Every big company had a Christmas party and provided all food and drink. Saran's would do the same, but after Christmas.

I went to Santa Cruz, invited the Antoines and their employees, then proceeded to Lopinot Village to ensure I would get four ducks for making curry on Recovery Day. The woman who raised the ducks asked me if I wanted wild meat as well. Lopinot was an isolated village, and the men went hunting in the surrounding hills for tattoo and lappe. I didn't have a clue how to cook tattoo and lappe. The woman offered to cook them for me. We sealed the deal over a glass of her home-made cashew wine. I asked her to provide a dozen bottles for our celebrations. With my next glass of wine, things started to get out of hand. The woman's neighbour made home-made bread and meat pies. I ordered substantial quantities. Her husband offered to cut down a branch of peewah from a tall palm and boil them for us. Someone else had a balata tree. By the time I went back to the Croissee I was half drunk on home-made wine, and had ordered a lavish menu of country delicacies.

On Boxing Day, Jason came over and we selected a bunch of unsold toys to distribute among the children of the employees. Charlo collected the styrofoam mouldings that protected appliances and gave them to the kids the next day to use as boats on the river. The girls commandeered some of them to use as floating trays for the peewah and balata. Bernard Antoine started a men's wet T-shirt competition, and we awarded a prize for the man with the biggest belly. Tony invented a form of water-polo, using the clumps of bamboo that arched over the river as goals.

I lay in the river, and suddenly realised how many employees we had. Saran's was now a substantial business. Things were more secure. I could spend the next six months organising my own life. Real life, the life of a bright young boy heading for a professional career and a relationship with the most beautiful, wonderful Englishwoman. My brother Robin had sent me forms for the University of London, where he was studying, and I had got provisional acceptance to enter the following September. Final acceptance would depend on my exam results, but I intended to study hard and get brilliant results in June.

In January, the letter from Janet arrived. We had been corresponding regularly and she had been saying she missed me and had had difficulty readjusting to English life, English weather and student existence. I hadn't mentioned that I intended joining her. Now she was in a different mood. She had met Somebody. He reminded her of me, though he was older. He was of Indian extraction but had grown up in England. She sounded dizzy with happiness.

I kicked the letter across the room. So what had I been to Janet, just a bimbo? A stupid, ignorant little boy, only good for one thing? I sighed and hung my head as I sat on the bed. What did I expect? Janet was an accomplished woman studying for her second degree. What would she want with an uneducated boy?

I settled into a kind of depression, but then Charlo's Carnival band began to pick up steam. Never mind, I told my aching heart, forget Janet. I could throw myself into making the most impressive King of Carnival Trinidad had ever seen. This was going to be my last Carnival. I would leave in a blaze of glory.

'I want to make the big bird again,' I said.

'What?' Charlo asked. 'I didn't hear that. Say it again.'

I said it again.

'Ved.' He stopped what he was doing and stared at me. 'You ain't have no shame? You want the same costume to topple over twice on the savannah stage? You don't find you should build something new to topple over?'

'It not going to topple over this time,' I insisted. 'I figured out the engineering principle.'

'Well why you don't apply the damn engineering principle to another costume? Make a big fish or something, so people could forget about last year.'

'Nah,' I said. 'I have unfinished business with that bird.'

I was right. My bird didn't topple over this time. What happened was much worse.

I made a giant head out of lightweight papier mâché and yellow feathers, and attached it to a long neck made of PVC piping. Charlo said it looked like Big Bird from *Sesame Street*. Unfortunately, Gordon, the guy who wore the costume, could hardly feel the head, it was so light. While he was bouncing up and down on the stage, it got caught in a little tower the television crew had erected. Gordon remained with his legs dangling about a foot above the ground. A titter went through the crowd as he struggled to get free, then waves of laughter.

'Fly!' shouted spectators. 'Flap your wings and fly!'

Gordon made a supreme effort. Raising his hands from under his wings, he grabbed the neck and yanked. There was a crack, then a horrible ripping sound and Big Bird collapsed on the stage. Minus head. There was a hush in the bleachers. The giant yellow head slowly fall from the tower onto the stage. It bounced several times, rolled to the edge, and gently toppled off. The crowd collapsed with laughter. Disorder reigned for nearly half an hour.

'I nearly pee myself,' Charlo said afterwards.

As before, the only antidote to ignominy was rum, so the rest of Carnival became a drunken haze. I squeezed myself between the girls, who were too busy wining to make Big Bird jokes. I took comfort in the softness of the women; I didn't want to hear a word from the men. We chipped through the streets, arms around each other, Carlene's bosoms jammed into my armpits. By late afternoon, my hand was under Carlene's boobs. They were large and round, and bounced against my hand deliciously. When she bumped me with her hips I bumped right back. She moved ahead of me and wined her fleshy bottom against my penis. When evening fell, we found ourselves in a side-street, in a doorway. I lifted her up to the stoop so she was closer to my height, and buried my face in her bosoms. I decline to give further details of what ensued, but I will agree it was a most undignified situation.

On Ash Wednesday I felt marvellous. No, that's not quite true. I felt like shit. Worst hangover of my nineteen-year-old life. But after I had poured about two buckets of water down my throat, I started to feel this incredible sense of well-being. It was like someone had swept out all my veins with a cobweb broom, a long, flexible cobweb broom made of PVC pipe, like Big Bird's neck. I had a vision of that great yellow head bouncing and rolling on the savannah stage and started to laugh.

'You don't have no shame?' my mother asked, 'associating yourself with a quack like Charlo?'

I winced at her voice. She showed me the newspaper. I had captured the front-page photo again. Well, not me, but my beheaded King, horizontal on the savannah stage.

'From the time I see that picture, I knew it was Charlo's quack-work,' Ma went on. 'I shouldn't let him build my house, you know. Next thing the upstairs breaking off and rolling down the Eastern Main Road.'

I wandered over to Charlo's, even though the hot sun hurt my head. I was eager, now, to hear jokes about Big Bird's decapitation. The first person I caught sight of was Carlene. She was on the porch, leaning over the railing, a tight tube top offering a beautiful view of her physical delights. I instantly recalled the sensation of her breasts smothering my face the day before. As she moved around, my eyes followed her. Man, that body was nice! Plump everywhere. Once you got your face enveloped in it, it was like revelling in a mountain of jello.

'You want to go for a drive by the beach?' I asked her.

'Who driving? You? You mad or what? You look more dead than alive.'
I had to agree.

'Your eye too long for your stomach,' she said, which is what people said when you took too much food on your plate.

'It's not only my eye that long, Carlene,' I drawled, hooking an arm round her waist. 'I could show you something longer.'

'Like Big Bird neck,' spluttered Charlo.

I don't know what happened to me after that. Everywhere I looked I saw breasts. Where there weren't breasts, there were bottoms and round bellies. 'Nobody ain't tell you it's Lent, boy?' Charlo asked. I didn't hear. These were my last few months in Trinidad. Why let all these good, healthy breasts go to waste?

'Nobody was safe in those days,' Charlo would tell people later. 'Not your grandmother, not the old, the lame or the cripple. I see Ved make a play for a woman without a tooth in her head. Once the heart was beating, Ved was fornicating.'

Fornicating was the archbishop's word.

In the intervals between fornicating, I built my mother's concrete palace above the shop. The brick factory had finally reopened. 'I feel to build the house back to front,' Charlo muttered. 'Just to hear what your mother will say.'

The plans were identical to all Indian nouveau-riche houses of the day, with a big open verandah in front overlooking the busy Eastern Main Road. If we built it back to front, as Charlo proposed, the verandah would face our large expanse of land behind it. 'You could look out on your gardens,' Charlo said. 'Palm trees over here, flowers, plants over there, swimming pool in the corner.'

We stripped our old house of its handmade white fretwork and sent the pieces to Mr Antoine for restoration. We made slender wooden columns and painted them white. Then we fitted the fretwork in arches between the columns and had a graceful, old-fashioned, Spanish-style verandah. The only thing was, it was at the back of the house where no one would see it.

Ma got her revenge by refusing to use one stick of Saran's furniture in the house. She went to a store in the city and came back with the biggest, ugliest, most overstuffed velvet living-room suite she could find, in a hideous shade of maroon.

'I didn't know you was opening a funeral parlour,' Charlo commented.

She wreathed the living-room windows in thick white lace, installed a gigantic gilt chandelier in the centre and a huge mahogany sideboard along one wall. I didn't utter a word. I never intended to set foot in her living-room. I had chosen for myself the bedroom furthest from it, at the back corner of the house. It had a set of french doors leading to the balcony and an en-suite bathroom. 'I don't even want to imagine the kind of fornicating that going to take place here,' Charlo said. 'With you having your own back door and bathroom. The archbishop will turn in his grave.'

'He not in his grave,' I pointed out. 'He not dead . . .'

'Yet,' Charlo added. 'If he only get the full scoop on you, he will kirk-itay and dead with he four foot up in the air like a cockroach. And mark my words, one of these days it will happen. You know how you have a habit of exposing your exploits on the front page of the newspaper.'

Once the building was completed, Charlo announced that it was time to build the swimming pool.

'Swimming pool?' Ma put her hands on her hips. 'Who ask you to build swimming pool, Mister Man?'

Charlo squinted at her. 'You not going to build a swimming pool?' he asked in an astonished tone. 'You mean all them stupid Indian down in the country building swimming pool –' He waved his arm towards the south of Trinidad '– and the great Saran family not going to have a swimming pool? But what the hell is this?'

Ma began to simmer down.

'Why you want to build swimming pool, Charlo?' I asked when Ma moved away a little.

'It's not swimming pool I want to build, boy, it's fountain. You don't remember them fountain in Ancient Rome? With naked woman here, and naked angel there, and water coming out of fish mouth?'

'Charlo, that will look damn stupid in Trinidad!' I told him. 'Plus my mother wouldn't want no naked woman standing up in her backyard.'

He sighed. 'Well, let us build a simple swimming pool, then. If you had a pool here, maybe you wouldn't go chasing down skirt every night. I build big, big funeral parlour for your mother. Why I can't build a swimming pool for you?'

I was touched. But I wasn't planning to stay in Trinidad to swim in any pool. 'I don't have time for more building right now,' I told him gently. 'I have to study for my A-level exams.'

By the end of June, I was sure I had done well in the exams, so I broke the news to my parents that I was planning to abandon them in September. Ma demanded to know why I needed to go to England to study engineering when there was a faculty of engineering right on our doorstep. 'Suppose your father have a next heart attack?' she asked.

To my surprise, my father spoke up. 'I not going to have a next heart attack,' he said. 'Let the boy go if he want to go.'

'I going to get Vijay to come and stay with allyou,' I said.

Vijay was my cousin from San Fernando. I had recently hired him to manage the lumber-yard in Santa Cruz. He was stolid and humourless, less fun than a plank of wood in the lumber-yard. But he was highly dependable.

'Vijay?' Ma screeched. 'Who say I want Vijay here? He more stupid than your father! What I will do with two stupid idiots in the house?'

I came close to getting angry with her. I turned, left the house, and went out fornicating.

But in August Pa did have a second heart attack. It was a mild one and I recognised the symptoms straight away and got him to the hospital well in time. Still, it shook me. He looked so weak and helpless. Once again, it occurred in the middle of the night and he resisted going to the hospital, saying his father had died there.

'You didn't die there last time,' I reminded him. 'If you had stayed here, you would have died.'

I picked him up bodily and took him to the car in my arms, leaving my mother at home. It was the first time in years that I had touched my father, and I wanted to hold him closer, to bury my face in his chest.

At the hospital, he gripped my hand. 'Don't leave me, Ved,' he begged.

I looked into those old, faded eyes and my throat closed up. 'I not leaving you, Pa,' I said. 'I going with you.'

They let me stay next to the bed as they attached drips to his body. I kept hold of his frail old hand with one of mine, and stroked his forehead with the other. He closed his eyes and drifted off.

Once they were sure his condition was stable, they sent me home. I went and lay in the hammock on the balcony outside my room, unable to sleep. Somewhere in those hours my decision was made about my own future.

Charlo arrived the next evening. I had just come back from visiting my father in the hospital. I hadn't had any sleep for two days, but still couldn't rest. I was sitting on the verandah gazing blankly out on my incipient gardens.

'I feel he was worrying,' I muttered. 'He kept telling me, Go to England, but he was frightened to stay alone with only my mother in the house.'

'I would be frightened to stay alone with your mother too,' Charlo grunted.

I sighed and scratched at the arm of my chair with a finger. 'I can't leave him, you know, Charlo,' I said, and was surprised to hear that my voice had a quaver in it.

'You can't stay with him for ever, Big Bird,' Charlo replied. 'He will die one day. Everybody born to die.'

I looked up into his clear eyes, and, to my shame, I felt tears pop up in my own. 'I can't leave him, Charlo.'

I turned my body around to rest my head on the back of my chair. I heard Charlo sigh. 'It's not really fair,' he said. 'A nineteen-year-old boy with so much responsibility.'

Without looking up, I shook my head from side to side. 'I don't feel it as responsibility,' I said, wiping my nose on my sleeve. 'I does feel we does just be having fun.' I turned to look at him. 'We don't be having fun, Charlo?'

He nodded. 'That might be even more dangerous,' he said. 'Come. Let us go out and drink some rum. It getting to be time for your evening fornicating.'

I shook my head. 'I don't feel like fornicating today.'

He sighed again. 'You see?' he said. 'If you did let me build the swimming pool, you could have been taking a swim all now.'

I smiled at him, wiping my nose on the edge of my T-shirt. 'Build the damn swimming pool,' I said. 'I know you is the one who will dead if you don't build that focking swimming pool.'

Chapter Three

It took many years for me to realise that Charlo had been right that night. I was setting myself on a dangerous course. Those easy successes made me believe I could do more than I was capable of. The old Peter Principle tripped me up eventually: I rose to my level of incompetence. If I had had to pay the price, I wouldn't have minded, but Anji was to be the victim of my folly.

In the meantime, I seemed to be right. We just had good clean fun. Sometimes not as clean as the archbishop would have liked, but still. This is what makes me feel such a fraud when I read references to myself in the Press. Feature-writers have described my bumbling actions as illustrations of 'foresight' and 'keen business judgement'. They were nothing of the kind. Things happened outside of my sphere of influence. I just reacted.

After my father's second heart attack, for example, I realised I had not registered to enter the local university that year. I would have to wait another twelve months. So I just continued running the business, which kept speeding up on me. Oil prices rose and executives from foreign firms started flying into Trinidad to discuss joint ventures with the government. The Hilton Hotel needed more beds – teak beds – with teak side-tables and matching teak dressers. The Holiday Inn responded with an extension involving a teak staircase and balustrades. A smaller hotel was being built in Polynesian style. What kind of décor did they want for their interior? I was shuttling between the docks, the hotels, government bureaucracies and our lumber-yard, which expanded to occupy all the unused buildings on Mr de la Guillame's property. I had to rush back and forth to Guyana to ensure I had a steady supply of good-quality wood.

'Good wood?' the guys in the pan-yard asked. 'So you not sure you have good wood? What the hell you does be doing, running down all them woman, if you don't have good wood?'

I only shrugged. Somehow my fornicating frenzy had abated after my father's heart attack. Not that I had turned into a priest, don't get me wrong – I still had blood in my veins. But I got a new perspective on breasts. They were, when all is said and done, just globes of flesh, charming to play with sometimes, but not the entire solar system.

And Charlo turned out to be right in predicting that a swimming pool in my backyard would slow me down. When he rented a backhoe to start the digging, however, a tremor ran through my family.

'Your doctor advise you to take up swimming?' my brother asked my father when he came to Trinidad to visit.

'No,' Pa muttered. 'But I used to be a good swimmer in my young days.'

'Then why you building a swimming pool?'

'I can just see Ma lounging in a bikini next to the pool,' my sister Indra commented in her spiteful voice.

'Ved will swim in the pool,' Pa said. 'Not so, Ved?'

He was now stationed on the verandah during the day, recuperating on a lounge-chair. In between working on the pool, Charlo came up to listen to his tales about his hunting days in Dorado. When Pa brought out his rusty old shotgun, Charlo examined its workings intently, told him it was an antique that was probably worth money, then got some oil and cleaned it. Ma bitched at Charlo constantly, but was forever nagging him to eat at our house. To listen to Ma talk, you would think Charlo had signed a contract to eat all his meals with us.

'What does Charlo know about building swimming pools?' Robin asked. 'That's a specialist business.'

'Charlo could build anything,' Pa said. 'That man real talented.'

'Talented, my backside!' Ma snapped. 'Charlo talent is making Ved do whatever he want. He only trying to make more money out of Ved.'

'The swimming pool not costing much,' Pa argued. 'If we had to hire somebody else to build it, then it would cost money.'

My sisters grew uneasy. Before this, they had just dismissed Charlo as one of my bad habits. Now the habit was spreading to my father. They began to treat Charlo as a potentially fatal bad habit, like alcohol or drug abuse.

'What are you doing now, Mr Charlo?' Queen demanded, when the pool was completed.

'What I doing?' Charlo looked up at her. 'You can't see what I doing? I planting a tree. And you don't have to call me Mr Charlo. You could call me Charlo like everybody else.'

'So now you are a gardener?'

He shrugged. 'Nah, I is a health consultant. I don't want your children getting sunburn while they swimming. I trying to make shade.'

Queen began referring to Charlo as 'The Bumptious Negro'. Indra shortened this to 'The Negro'. 'What on earth is the Negro doing down there?' she would ask.

As soon as the pool had been filled, my sisters discovered what it was for. For their children to swim in every weekend. They arrived either on Saturday afternoon and overnighted at our place, or before lunch on Sunday. Charlo had planted a frangipani tree that would eventually spread light-green, shuttered leaves in a wide arc over the pool and produce sprays of orange flowers. But he didn't stop there. He bordered the pool area with oleander shrubs, fragrant jasmine and tuberoses. He surrounded his plants with white gravel, unusual rocks and bits of driftwood. When the light started fading in the evenings the tuberoses began to wake up and give off their potent scent.

I started swimming every night, floating for about an hour on my back watching the stars. The fragrance of the tuberoses made me feel a bit stoned, and as the water caressed my skin, my mind moved into another tempo. By the time I got out, I had lost the urge to go to a dingy bar and have inane conversation with drunken Trinidadians, far less engage in the routine rituals of seduction. The spirit was willing, but the flesh was weak. And I always knew I had a lot to do the next day. New challenges were always cropping up and I was on a treadmill of activity.

One day, I went to the sports shop in the city to buy a new tennis racquet. There was only one sports shop and it was expensive. It was an old business run by a Portuguese family called Pereira. I asked the attendant, a young, light-skinned guy in a tie, to let me heft all the racquets in the store. Some of the racquets were placed high up and he was reluctant to take the trouble to reach them. I figured he had looked at me and seen a coolie, someone who couldn't afford the best. I told him he could shove the racquets up his arse and walked out. I knew I could buy a racquet in Miami – I went there occasionally to order goods for our store and had noticed that racquets cost a fraction of what they cost in Trinidad. But my pride was hurt. I went home in a bad mood.

'What happen, Ved?' Nerissa asked when I went into the store.

'I need a new tennis racquet,' I replied.

'Sorry,' she said. 'We don't sell racquet here.'

'Why not?' I asked sourly.

She shrugged. 'The boss didn't give us any to sell.'

I banged my fist on the cash desk like a troublesome customer. 'Fire that boss!'

A few weeks later, Nerissa presented me with a racquet. She had ordered a few out of a catalogue.

'I want a new cricket bat too,' I said.

She glared at me. 'You getting impossible, you know! I going to ban you from coming in this store. Why you don't go out and look for woman?'

'I not looking for woman. I looking for cricket bat, football, cricket glove . . . Right here in the Croissee. People in the Croissee don't play tennis. They does play cricket and football.'

Nerissa organised a sports department in Saran's, and Charlo organised a Grand Opening. We applied our usual mark-up on sporting goods, which made them far, far cheaper than at Pereira's. We offered discounts to schools and clubs, and donated cricket bats as prizes at schools' sports days. Then sports teachers demanded trophies for their sports days, so Nerissa started ordering them. Basketballs were requested, hockey sticks . . . Players at St Augustine tennis club bugged me for discounts and I got permission to set up a little display cabinet there. Soon, the word about our prices spread to the city's country club, and its members started coming to the Croissee for tennis equipment.

When a five-day cricket test match between Australia and the West Indies approached, the newspapers came to us offering advertising space in their special supplements. Charlo wanted to buy space on the cricket ground as well. That was expensive but he argued that, as advertisers, we would get seats in the members' stand for free. Pa instantly went out and bought a bottle of tonic. He was not going to miss seeing a test match from the best seats in the Oval even if it killed him.

'Imagine,' Pa said, when the day arrived and he was settling into his seat and gazing at the banner across the field that read 'SARAN'S FOR SPORTS GOODS', 'people all in Australia seeing my name on their TV.' He turned to Charlo. 'Charlo, you is a boss, you know. Let me shake your hand!' He poured himself a drink from a bottle of rum Charlo had brought. I glanced at him. Was Pa allowed to drink rum? 'This will prevent any heart attack when the Australians start to bat,' Pa reassured me. 'Them Australians dangerous, you know.'

But that was only the beginning of Saran's lurch into fame.

Charlo had offered the services of Symphonia on the cricket ground, so our entire steel band would get to watch the match for free. When Gary Sobers hit his first six, Symphonia led the crowd into a frenzy of wining and the TV cameras switched from the players to the crowd gyrating around the band. The Saran's Symphonia banner featured in shot after shot.

Ma was Not Amused. 'What Mr Antoine was doing, a old man like he?' she asked when we got home in the evening. 'I couldn't believe my eyes when I was watching the TV. I thought I must be seeing things. This short little white man wining in the Oval with them worthless girls from the Croissee! Ved, you and Charlo could corrupt anybody, you know! Just don't let me see your father tomorrow on that screen, you hear! I will get a divorce.'

Tony and Bernard had asked Charlo to bring Symphonia T-shirts for them the following day: their wives wanted Symphonia T-shirts, their children wanted Symphonia T-shirts. Charlo and I worked till dawn to create a new design and get it printed. 'GO WEST INDIES', it read on the front; 'SARAN'S FOR SPORTS GOODS' on the back.

The T-shirts went like hot cakes. When Sobers hit his century and the entire Oval went into a ten-minute paroxysm of wining, the Minister of Sports, Education and a Few Other Things sent an emissary from her box to request a T-shirt.

By the end of the second day, the Australians were struggling to get our batsmen out. On the afternoon of the third day, with the score at 376, West Indies declared.

'No!' Pa bawled, louder than I'd ever heard him before. He glanced from me to Charlo, his old eyes wild. 'Allyou don't know them Australians dangerous?' he demanded, as though we were responsible.

The Australians didn't just prove to be dangerous. They were torturous. They started making runs slowly, staying in the wicket and wearing out our bowlers. Nothing our guys did could winkle them out. On the last day, they let loose. Their score started climbing. At lunch time, it was 321. Our boys grew desperate and made mistakes. The Australians started making fours and sixes. 'Go West Indies,' the crowd shrieked desperately.

But it was only a matter of time. By three-fifteen in the afternoon, the Kangaroos had kicked our asses.

There was silence in the Oval. I fell into my seat and put my face into my hands. 'I did tell them not to declare!' Pa sighed.

I heard the crowd start shouting again and looked up to see the

Australian team running over to where Symphonia was stationed. When those big red guys got there, they dropped their bats, opened their arms wide and wined in a most obscene fashion at our Croissee girls.

'But they worse than Trinis!' Charlo muttered.

The Australian players kept waving their arms at Symphonia, taunting them to play. There was only one response possible. Symphonia struck up. And the Croissee girls never let an opportunity to wine go to waste, so they joined the Australians. Charlo disappeared from the members' stand and the next thing I saw was the Australian players wearing Saran's T-shirts, which Charlo had swapped for their winning cricket bats. 'Go West Indies!' they chanted, pointing away from the cricket field.

I took a heart-broken Pa home, leaving Charlo in the Oval to help with getting Symphonia' pans back to the Croissee.

At about five-thirty, I was back at the store when I heard sounds of a disturbance on the Eastern Main Road. Nerissa, Suzanne and I went out to the pavement. An immense traffic jam was building up. We heard the thrill of steel band. Symphonia was coming down the Main Road, still playing, which was against the law except on Carnival days. At the front of a huge crowd was the Australian cricket team, their arms wrapped around the Croissee girls. Police were clearing the way for their advance as the Croissee population piled out onto the pavements, waving at the Kangaroos like they did when royalty visited.

'Rum, boy, rum!' came a voice in my ear. Charlo had appeared at my side. 'Saran's sponsoring the victory celebration!' he shouted.

'What victory celebration?' I demanded. 'We lose the match.'

'Who lose what match?' Charlo asked. 'Them stupid West Indies players lose match! But Saran's win.' He put his mouth close to my ear again. 'We have to be gracious in defeat, boy. We entertaining visitors from Down Under. When last we entertain visitors from Down Under in the Croissee?'

Even Pa went over to the pan-yard. 'These is international celebrities,' he told Ma.

'International hooligans, you mean!'

As I stood in the pan-yard doling out rum and Coke, a stiff-looking white guy came up to me. He was from the Australian High Commission. 'Can't we close this thing off?' he asked. 'The players are expected at a dinner at the High Commissioner's residence.'

I shrugged. 'Talk to the players.'

He got nowhere with the players. They had official dinners every night of the week; they didn't have the Croissee girls. The entire street between the pan-yard and our back-gate was jammed with people. It was Carnival in the Croissee.

'Is there a telephone somewhere that I can use?' the stiff man asked.

I took him over the street to our house. Another embassy official arrived in a car, then two guys from the West Indies Cricket Board of Control.

The Australian guy looked around our garden. 'I wonder if we could get the caterers to deliver the food here?' he asked.

'They will mash up my plants!' Ma exclaimed.

I shut Ma up.

By the end of the evening, I was well on my way to having a contract to supply equipment to Trinidad's national cricket team and furniture to the Australian Embassy.

There was no retreat now from sports goods. Sybil, the woman from Arima who bought gifts for other people's children at Christmas and toyed with Charlo's heart in between, came up with a new demand. She said the oldest boy had grown out of tricycles, and she wanted a bicycle for him at her usual discount. Without saying a word to me, Nerissa started ordering bicycles, so now we had to erect a second floor on the pagoda to store stock. Charlo created a suite of offices there for myself and the bookkeeper, and I turned over the director's office to Nerissa. I had an elevator installed at tremendous cost, to make it easier for Pa to come downstairs, and hired four new employees, raising Nerissa's wages to match the increase in her responsibilities. I installed a second cash desk upstairs, and made Suzanne deputy store manager. 'I don't want to see the two of you ever looking for goods for customers again,' I said, wagging my finger in their faces. 'Make Jason and the other girls do it. Your job is not to deal with customers. Your job is to deal with staff.'

A young schoolteacher who was responsible for sports at his primary school kept coming back to the store over and over. He was a small skinny guy who looked very serious. 'Serious?' Nerissa snorted. 'He serious about Suzanne, you mean! It's just excuse he does make to come here. You never see how he does be watching her when he talking to me, like he cokey-eye? Always finding something to complain about! My cricket balls not good, he want them changed; does Saran's have any bigger netball rings for training?

Next thing you know, the man will come and ask if we selling slingshot!'

Suzanne's cheeks grew rosy. I bet Jason ten dollars that she would never go for a man as scrawny as this schoolteacher. I lost my money. 'Hypolite not like allyou,' she said to Jason and me. 'He don't talk all the time. He know better things to do with his mouth.'

In no time at all she was pregnant. 'Hypolite jump the gun,' she said. 'I have to have a talk with Charlo. We planning a Opening Ceremony.'

What she meant was she was getting married. Hypolite had decided that it wouldn't be seemly for him to have an illegitimate child. But Suzanne refused to get married without a white dress and church and wedding cake, so by the time the banns were posted and the white dress was made she was nearly eight months pregnant. Her breasts and belly were so swollen that, as Jason put it, she looked like one of the bunches of white balloons we hung in the pan-yard for the reception.

I refrained from getting drunk at the wedding. A lot of my employees were there, and I wanted to preserve a dignified demeanour. It was a good thing. In the middle of the event, when Hypolite's school principal was waxing boring in a long, long speech, Suzanne began to get labour pains. 'Your child take after me,' Jason said to her later. 'When the headmaster start to talk in school assembly, I used to look for the first window to jump out of.'

I had to rush Suzanne to the maternity ward of the hospital. It was a bit worrying, this premature birth, and I got tense. But it was over relatively quickly. While Symphonia was still playing back at the wedding, the baby was conducting his own opening ceremony in the filthy maternity ward.

I sat on a bench with Suzanne's mother, Hypolite and Nerissa, and got a good dose of that hospital's laxity. Women who had just delivered were kept two to a bed. There was a shortage of sheets. Can you believe it? The country was awash with oil money, but none of it was going into the health system. My sisters had had their children at private nursing homes, so I had never experienced it firsthand.

'You going to stand godfather, Ved?' Suzanne asked when it was all over. She looked like she had done nothing more than usual: completely composed, just happy. Her husband, the famous sex machine, looked pale under his dark skin.

*

I was moved that Suzanne had asked me to be godfather to her child. But I felt ashamed that she had had to give birth in such circumstances. Tony Antoine had told me big companies offered their employees private health insurance, so I got some forms from an insurance company. The forms had to be signed by my mother, but I assured her that the cost came out of our taxes. The insurance scheme also included pension provisions. Then I brought up the subject of a profit-sharing scheme for the employees. It was something I had read about in a business magazine.

'That wouldn't come out of the tax!' Ma snapped.

'It would come out from my salary,' I retorted. In fact I took no salary from the business. What did I need a salary for? I lived at home with my parents. If I needed cash, I sent Jason down the street to the bank with a forged cheque in my mother's name. If I bought a car, it was a company car.

Ma stared back at me. I held her eyes. She knew what I meant. If she had to pay me to manage the business she owned, the cost would be high. She grumbled and complained, but signed those papers as well.

With all of this busyness, I missed the deadline for applying to university again the following year. It wasn't all my fault. I had been in Guyana that March, up-country in the teak forests with Tony, when a tropical storm blew up. A bridge broke, we were stranded for a couple of weeks, and the application had to be submitted before the first of April.

We were searching for the best quality teak for a national convention centre at the time. Its architect, an Englishman I instantly liked, had shown us his plans. He wanted very strong, lightweight wood to be turned into modernistic chairs and tables in our factory. In the end, the convention centre was a bit of a disaster. The acoustics were lousy and the roof leaked onto our beautiful furniture. But who cared? Saran's Symphonia played at its opening ceremony, the players in white dinner jackets that cost me a fortune. I was a quasi-dignitary.

At the cocktail party afterwards, I found myself in a group that included the Minister of Justice and Legal Affairs. He was an Indian guy with shiny black hair slicked down with pomade and a top lip that curled in continual contempt. I took an instant dislike to him. He waxed expansive about the plans he was drawing up to construct a new High Court in the centre of the city, across the street from the parliament building.

'Of course,' he said, looking at me, 'we wouldn't use teak.' His lip curled. 'We have to uphold the dignity of the law. We would want mahogany interiors.'

The other people in the group glanced at me. I fished around for something to say. 'My mother would certainly agree with you,' I said.

'Oh!' the minister said. 'You deal in mahogany as well? Why don't you have a word with the Minister of Works?'

I had no intention of doing any such thing. I had enough work. I drifted over to my steel band. 'Horse derves, boy!' Charlo exclaimed, holding out a silver tray of canapés. 'You taste these horse derves?'

'This champagne drinking nice, Ved!' Carlene had stuck herself in her sister's long white wedding dress and she looked awful. 'Only thing is,' she said, 'the glass and them too small.'

'Allyou will get pissing drunk,' I warned, 'and allyou have to play again.'

'But we does play best when we drunk,' one of the guys answered.

The guests were no better. They guzzled champagne and whiskey like they had just trekked across the Sahara. When Symphonia started to play again, the Minister of Health started calling for them to play calypsos. Mikey had practised the band for months with Beethoven's Fifth, 'Amazing Grace' and other stuff like that, but the band acceded to popular demand. Suit jackets got trampled as dignitaries forgot their dignity. The Junior Minister of Culture, Tourism and Community Development rolled her vast bottom in a movement that challenged conventional principles of engineering. 'That woman have ball-bearings in her waist,' Charlo swore. The Minister of Works, Transportation and Infrastructure unbuttoned his shirt to let air cool his gigantic belly. The English architect passed out on the stage, tried to rise to his feet later, and vomited on the expensive velvet curtains. The archbishop, who had blessed the convention centre, turned on his heel and walked out. 'If His Grace could have unbless that convention centre, he would have do it,' Charlo commented. 'But the centre was well and truly bless by that time.'

The next day I mentioned my conversation with the Minister of Justice to Tony Antoine, seeking sympathy about the insult to our teak. Tony's response surprised me. We should try to get the government contract to supply mahogany furniture for the High Court, he insisted. At a certain stage in business, you had to focus on government contracts. Private clients were too small. That's how the conglomerates had become conglomerates.

I had no ambition to become a conglomerate.

'Get real, Ved!' Tony snapped. 'If one of the big companies get that contract and start importing mahogany, you think they will only bring down mahogany? They will bring down teak as well, and you will lose your monopoly.'

I didn't care about any monopoly. But Tony did. He had abandoned a good career with the largest conglomerate to make his mark here, and he wasn't going to be stopped by my snivelling hesitations. He would have given his life and soul for that furniture factory. In fact, he had already given his soul to it. I suppose, being a poor white boy growing up in Trinidad, where white meant rich, must have had its effect on him. From my chats with the Antoines, I had come to discover that their Corsican artisan background had little currency in French Creole circles.

'I will get my father to make initial sketches for the Chief Justice's throne,' Tony urged. 'There isn't another furniture-maker in Trinidad who could do that. They would have to order it from England at many times the cost.'

I got the contract for Tony.

The government's architect proved to be an idiot. Thinking that the dignity of the High Court was directly related to its cost, he had hugely overestimated the budget. Mahogany shipped directly from Guyana was much cheaper than he had imagined, and furniture made locally was a fraction of the cost of that produced in England by craftsmen who usually worked for Her Majesty the Queen.

Thus Her Majesty Mrs Saran made a huge profit on each foot of mahogany the High Court required.

For the Grand Opening, Mr Antoine's wife upholstered a suit for him that made him look like something out of Dickens. The hat she created for herself was so elaborate it blocked everyone for two rows behind her. Tony and Bernard showed up in dark suits, while I wore my father's white shirt-jac, my garb for all formal occasions.

The whole thing was boring in the extreme except after the ceremonies, when Mr Antoine turned into the hero of the event. Everyone exclaimed at his workmanship, and he gave them his spiel about making furniture for Marie Antoinette's relatives back in the eighteenth century. Newspaper reporters scribbled furiously, and Tony smirked at all the free publicity. Then a man in a navy-blue suit appeared at Mr Antoine's side. The reporters switched their gazes to him, their pens poised in the air.

'The Prime Minister would like a word with you, sir,' Mr Blue Suit said.

'Oh, certainly,' Mr Antoine said, as though he was accustomed to dealing with prime ministers on a regular basis. Tony jerked his head at me and we both trailed behind his father towards a group in a corner.

'I wanted to ask you a question, Mr Antoine,' the Prime Minister said, with all the gravity of his office. He was a burly man with a face like a mile of bad road: bumps and potholes in a thick layer of soggy-looking black skin.

'Certainly, Mr Prime Minister!' Mr Antoine did a little movement like he was clicking his heels.

'I wanted to know,' asked the PM in an accusatory tone, 'how you could do this to me?'

'Do what, Mr Prime Minister?'

The PM leaned over the little man. 'How could you, Mr Antoine, build this magnificent furniture for my junior when you have built nothing for me?'

Mr Antoine took a step back. 'I was just practising on these things, Mr Prime Minister,' he said, waving his hand dismissively at the High Court, 'till you were ready for me. You know, of course, that I am always at your service.'

The PM regarded him carefully. 'I hope so, Mr Antoine,' he said. 'Because I'm planning to refurbish the parliamentary chamber across the street, and I expect to get a higher grade of wood panelling than you have given my junior.'

It was the way he said the word 'junior' that reminded me. The gossip around Trinidad was that the Minister of Justice was a competitor for the prime-ministerial post. Bad vibes were said to cross the street non-stop between Parliament and the High Court.

'Of course you will get a higher grade of wood panelling, Sir!' Mr Antoine did his heel-clicking again. 'But for that you will have to talk to my colleague here.' He gestured at me. 'Mr Saran is the man with the wood.'

The PM put back his head and roared with laughter. He liked to think of himself as macho. That meant being alert to any possibility of sexual innuendo. 'Mr Saran is the man with the wood, eh,' he said, looking me up and down. 'You hear that, Robert?' he called to the Minister of Works. 'Young Mr Saran here is the man with the wood.'

The Minister of Works laughed as though it was not a tired old joke. He repeated the line to others around him. All kinds of junior ministers glanced my way. The female Minister of Education, Sports and Something Else looked me over from top to toe. I stood there with a fake smile plastered on my face, feeling foolish.

'Well, Mr Saran,' the PM said, 'I would like to see you in my office on Monday to talk about your wood.'

After work had started on the parliamentary chamber I began to hear rumours that the Minister of Justice was saying I was a thief. The overestimation the government architect had made on the High Court contract hadn't been a mistake – it was to cover the bribe I was expected to hand over to the minister. But since the Prime Minister didn't speak to Mr Justice, he hadn't heard the talk before he issued the contract for the parliamentary chamber. 'Thief from thief does make God laugh,' Charlo said.

God could laugh, I reckoned, but the Minister of Justice had no sense of humour, and was known for his viciousness. I figured he would get me for the slightest infringement of the law. I took a decision that nothing in Saran's operations would infringe even the smallest sub-regulation of the smallest sub-section of the shadowiest article of the legal code.

I told my mother I felt bad about the extra money we had made on the contracts. That was taxpayers' money. 'I is a taxpayer,' Ma snapped.

I raised wages in all Saran enterprises. 'The workers are taxpayers too,' I told Ma.

I was getting too damn own-way, she said. 'Two man-rat can't live in one hole,' she warned darkly.

'I's not a rat,' I informed her. 'And you's not a man, as far as I know.'

Soon, every little boy who thought he could hold a hammer came begging Tony for a job. I encouraged him to set up an apprenticeship shop and give those young guys some training. We kept the best of them in our factory, and let the others peddle their skills elsewhere. Our factory soon housed all the best woodworkers in northern Trinidad. Other employers in the building industry didn't like this at all. They snubbed me at Chamber of Commerce functions and I stopped going. I didn't like Chamber of Commerce functions anyway; I only went because Tony dragged me.

I felt compelled, however, to go to the Grand Opening of the parliamentary chamber. This was even more boring than the High Court opening. The Prime Minister waxed abstruse in his speech about the

supremacy of Parliament, which made the laws the courts merely implemented. He looked over his reading glasses, down his huge nose, at the
Minister of Justice. He never glanced Mr Antoine's way and we received
not a single compliment on the superb wood panelling we had installed.
As attention shifted to the parliamentary library where drinks were laid
out, we huddled together in a corner, a miserable little group of small fry
among the political big guns. Mr Antoine decided to leave early.

I had come alone in my own car, and was following the Antoines to
the door of the chamber when I was accosted by a pair of chic young
women. They asked me if I knew where the drinks were being served.

'Right here,' I told them. 'If you stay right here, they will be served
to you post-haste.'

I went to the library, commandeered a bottle of champagne, and
returned to the girls. They were both recent law graduates hired as
researchers at the Office of the Leader of the Opposition, and were excited
to be able to access political gossip firsthand. I forgot about being small
fry; with girls, I could play big shark.

'Are you flirting with us jointly or severally, Mr Saran?' one of the
girls asked. She was called Sharon Lee. She had big oval eyes that danced
at you.

'I plead guilty, your Honour,' I said. 'Jointly, severally, upside down,
inside out, back to front, sideways, with handcuffs on, wig off, swinging
from a rope, with the cat-o'-nine-tails . . .'

The Prime Minister bustled by on his way out. He paused to smile at
the girls, looking like he was thinking up something to say to them. Then
he noticed me. 'Mr Saran, eh,' he said. 'The man with the wood.'

'Mr Prime Minister!' I did an echo of Mr Antoine's heel-clicking. 'I
hope you're satisfied with the wood you got in the members' chamber.'

The girls smiled at the whiff of double entendre. The PM did not. He
just stared at me for a long minute. 'You're very young, Mr Saran,' he
said, in a voice full of prime-ministerial authority. 'So you take a lot of
pride in your wood. But good wood improves with age, you will discover.'

He swept out, leaving the girls giggling. I could have bitten my tongue.
The PM must have thought I was crowing about screwing him on the
contract; the word 'wood' could also be interpreted that way. I wanted to
kick myself. I really hadn't intended to antagonise the PM, corrupt son
of a bitch though he was. I had just gone overboard showing off for the
cute young lawyers.

The PM was right to think I was young and cocky. I was really playing outside my league. I started looking out for any unexplained obstruction from the authorities that had to approve my import applications, tax returns and other things like that. I phoned Sharon Lee at the Opposition office and asked her where I could get information on Trinidadian law. We made a lunch date. After lunch she took me to the government registry, and I ordered a complete set of the laws of Trinidad and Tobago, twenty volumes bound in red leather. I took to studying sections related to business activities I was involved in, and became a bit addicted to those law books. I even got gripped by family law. It was fascinating to discover how many ways a hair could be split.

Soon, when bureaucrats turned officious with me, I turned bush-lawyer, quoting them regulations they didn't know. I discovered that it was easy to convert them into stuttering idiots. Playing little power games, you might think, but what else did I have to play at? Tony was a superb manager and I didn't have to make any day-to-day decisions regarding the furniture factory. Nerissa kicked me out of 'her' store if I dared to intrude. Only Vijay's stolid management of the lumber-yard left room for intervention in the mundane elements of the business. For the most part, I was tied up in the back-room logistics: getting trucks licensed and insured, ordering machinery, things that kept me busy in offices in Port of Spain.

You had to play power games in Trinidad, I realised. The alternative was bribery, and I had no taste for that. Perhaps it was my mother's influence. Ma Saran, as Charlo had taken to calling her, would never stoop to begging anybody for anything. She would never dream of letting anyone even think they had something she wanted. 'Who is he?' she would ask about a senior government official. 'His grandmother used to wash clothes for my mother.' I never heard Ma utter a moral injunction in her life, far less a condemnation of bribery. It was just beneath her, like the murky drains around the Croissee I had fished in as a boy, evoking warnings from her that I would catch every manner of disease. Pride was my mother's morality, and I think I inherited it. Once the government had declared me persona non grata, I returned the favour; I would sink or swim on my own strength. But that meant I had to be strong. I conducted all my business with great deliberation and watched my back constantly.

Sometimes, though, impetuosity got the better of me.

One afternoon, while helping Vijay get clearance for some lumber on the docks, I called Nerissa to get a piece of information I needed. Nerissa's voice was breathless on the other end of the line. A worker had been badly injured in our lumber-yard and had been taken to the Port of Spain General Hospital.

Vijay's car was locked into a parking space behind a row of freight vehicles, so I went to the hospital in one of our trucks that had already been loaded with logs of mahogany. The casualty department reminded me of the TV series *M.A.S.H.* Moans and groans were emanating from patients crowded together on broken-down benches that lined the stained grey walls. The waist-high wooden counter that separated them from the medical staff was pitted and grimy. An aged lady was sobbing in a wheel-chair. A child was shrieking somewhere else. There was a smell of old disinfectant and neglected body-parts.

The guy from our lumber-yard was lying on a bench, one shoulder and arm wreathed in bandages. He was a massive column of a man called Thomas. He had a gigantic head, and his large face was like a mass of grey-black lava, shifting in its proportions as he groaned in pain. He had got his sleeve caught in an electric saw and it had yanked his arm so hard he had wrenched it out of its socket. They had reset the arm in Casualty, stitched the wound that had caused him to lose a lot of blood, and told him to wait for painkillers.

'You ever hear fockeries like this, Ved?' a thin Indian guy named Mukesh, who drove the forklift at our lumber-yard, asked. 'All these people here can't get no medicine because one kiss-me-arse doctor gone for lunch with the medicine-cabinet key.' A recent newspaper report had said hospital personnel were stealing supplies. The Ministry of Health had announced it was instituting new security measures.

'Security, my backside,' a fat woman shouted in a hoarse voice. 'Them police helping to thief more!' She shouted this in the direction of a young policeman guarding the door.

Mukesh was pacing up and down. When he got to the counter, he gave it a bang with his fist and a young doctor standing behind it jumped. The policeman moved swiftly towards Mukesh. 'Get away from there!' he said.

'Kiss my arse!' retorted Mukesh.

'You want me to arrest you?' the policeman said.

'Arrest your mother!' Mukesh returned.

'Obscene language is a charge, you know,' the policeman warned.

'What obscene language the man use?' the fat woman asked, raising her voice to throw it at the benches. 'Anybody here hear this man use obscene language?'

'No!' a couple of voices shouted from the benches.

'Like your ears not clean, Mr Police!' the woman said. 'How you going to arrest the man when all the witnesses will say he didn't use any obscene language?'

'I will go to court and swear I didn't hear no focking obscene language!' a man shouted out.

I went to the counter and drew Mukesh away from the policeman. 'You don't have anything you could give this man?' I asked the doctor, indicating Thomas.

He shook his head. 'Everything locked up in the cabinet,' he said, waving towards a tall metal cupboard at the back of the room. 'The registrar must have fallen asleep when she went for lunch. She worked a double-shift, since last night. The doctor who was supposed to replace her didn't turn out, so she took the key with her when she went for lunch.'

'You can't break the lock on the cabinet?' I asked. 'I will replace it. I can't sit down here and watch my employee suffer like this.'

The doctor shrugged. 'It's the nursing sister who in charge here,' he said, indicating a short woman with an extended bosom in a purple uniform.

I looked at the sister questioningly. 'I will replace the whole cabinet,' I offered. 'I will give you a cheque right now to cover the cost.'

I reached into my back pocket for my cheque book. Sister folded her arms over her bosom. 'Your employee should have been more careful,' she boomed in a deep, placid voice. 'He made that accident himself. You want us to get in trouble, damaging government property, just because he was careless?'

I felt a surge of anger somewhere in my throat. 'Your job is not to take care of people?' I asked. 'Or it's to judge people?'

'My job is not to break open cabinets,' she said, turning away from me.

I glared at her back for a minute. She was an immovable force.

'Well,' I said finally, 'my job is to break open cabinets.'

I placed my hands on the counter, levered my body up, and swung my legs over.

'Constable!' the sister bellowed.

My mind was not on her. I was examining the lock on the cabinet. It was a simple lock, easy to release, but I had no tools. I felt a heavy hand on my shoulder. It was the policeman. I shook him off, moved backwards, then took a step forward and gave the lock a good hard kick. The lock gave way and the door eased open.

The policeman grabbed my shoulder again. 'Don't touch me!' I snapped. 'If you arresting me, arrest me,' I said. 'But don't touch me. I have all these witnesses here to prove that I never resisted arrest. So don't you frigging touch me!'

His hand dropped from my shoulder. The fat woman leaned over the counter. 'Arrest the Indian boy, nuh!' she bawled at the policeman. 'Allyou does only like to come up Morvant and arrest black people for smoking a little weed. This man mash-up a whole medicine cabinet in front of all these people. Arrest him! Let us see how you does arrest.'

The sister's voice rose behind me. 'I don't know who arresting or not arresting,' she said. 'But I know I resting. If you think I am going to treat that man just because you come in here and get on like a hooligan, you could think again!'

I turned round. She walked to a desk and plonked herself into a chair. I became stiff with fury. 'No,' I said, marching to the desk and shaking my head. 'I don't think you going to treat that man because I behave like a hooligan. You are going to treat that man because it's your obligation under the Nursing Authorities Act.' I glanced at my watch.

'You have already delayed treating Mr Thomas for two hours due to negligence in the management of keys. If you continue to delay, I have three employees here who can testify that it was deliberate negligence, malicious negligence, or even criminal negligence.' I wasn't sure whether there was any such thing as malicious negligence in the law-books. But I was under the influence of my own bush-lawyer antics by then, and it sounded good.

'Criminal negleegee!' the fat woman bawled, thumping the counter with her fist. 'I always say them nurse is criminal. They does jook you hard with injection, just for spite.'

The sister still didn't budge. But the young doctor was already shuffling through the medicines in the cabinet, and a ward-man started wheeling a stretcher towards Thomas. I noticed Vijay in the crowd around him; apparently he had finally got his car out of the parking space.

'Constable!' a man yelled from the public waiting area. 'You arresting the man, or you not arresting the man? Hurry up, nuh! You keeping us in suspense. I want to go and pee.'

Thomas was being wheeled into a treatment room to the left of me. I started to follow.

'You come here!' the policeman shouted at me.

I stopped and looked at him. 'No,' I said, shaking my head. 'I not going anywhere. If you want to arrest me, arrest me. Let it come out in court that a room full of people couldn't get treated because a doctor went to lunch with the key for the Casualty medicine cabinet. I sure the newspapers will like that story.'

The policeman hovered uncertainly.

'What happen?' the fat woman asked him. 'You don't know how to arrest people? They ain't teach you to arrest yet?'

The policeman had had enough. He came towards me and grabbed my belt at the back, pulling my trousers up into my crotch. I didn't resist. He frogmarched me to the little treatment room at the side of the counter that led out into the public waiting area, and out the front door. Then he let me go.

'So what happen?' I asked. 'You not arresting me? You grab me like a fowl-thief, and bring me out here, and now you not arresting me? You have to arrest me, man!'

'I don't have to do nothing you say,' he replied, putting on a pout like a child. He took up his stance at the doorway again, composing his face into impassive policivity. The crowd that had followed us parted as I walked back through the doorway and returned to Casualty. The policeman gazed straight in front of him as I went by, as though he was in another world. I flopped onto a bench. The crowd continued trying to needle the policeman, but the incident was over. Or so I thought.

When Thomas had been given an injection, we put him into Vijay's car and sent him home. I was following in the truck, with Mukesh behind us in his car. We got to the exit gate to find a red barrier across the roadway. Our friend, the policeman, was standing at its side. Another policeman came towards our truck. 'Get out!' he snapped. 'We have to search this truck.' He slapped the bonnet in an affectionate manner.

This policeman was older and looked meaner, more vicious. I opened the door on my side of the cab and stood on the running-board, my arm on the open door. 'What you searching for?' I asked. 'Woodlice? You can't see that this truck just full of wood?

Mukesh left his car and came to stand next to me. 'Don't let him search that frigging truck, nuh, Ved,' he said. 'When police search, they does find anything they want to find.'

'That truck not leaving this compound until it get searched,' the policeman said.

A horn tooted behind Mukesh's car. Its owner wore a white coat. After he had waited for a couple of minutes, he reversed his car till he could turn it at the curve leading to the Casualty entrance, and then sped away along the side of the hospital towards the ambulance entrance.

'You can't search my truck without a search warrant,' I said to the policeman. He ignored me. Other horns began tooting as a line of cars built up behind us. Drivers got out to enquire what was going on. I motioned to my truck driver to switch off the engine and hand me the keys. Then I got out of the cab, pressing the lever on the door so it locked when I closed it. The driver did the same. The two of them followed me to Mukesh's car, where we got in.

'Reverse,' I told Mukesh. 'Go on the pavement.'

Mukesh moved the car forward a little, then wrenched the steering wheel sharply and went into reverse onto the wide footpath that ran along the side of the driveway. He screeched backwards alongside the line of cars that had stopped behind him, alongside the hospital building, and then to the ambulance gate. 'Police don't have a wrecker that could move a truck full of mahogany,' he laughed as he swung out of the gate. 'They will have to call out the army. And them two rusty tank the army have probably not working.'

We drove to my lawyer's office, where I filed an affidavit detailing what had happened, and sent it with an official letter to the Commissioner of Police threatening legal action for the hold-up of our business.

I left the truck there for three days. It blocked the hospital's main exit, forcing the police to regulate incoming and outgoing traffic at the entrance on the other side. Only after the hospital director himself called me and begged me to move the truck did I do so.

My mother wasn't pleased. 'I tell you leave the truck there till the Commissioner of Police call,' she said. 'I have a few matters well that I want to discuss with him.'

'The Commissioner of Police wouldn't call me,' I told her. 'He would contact my lawyer.'

'Well, why you didn't wait for that?' she asked. 'The longer that truck stay there, the more compensation I was going to ask for from the police.'

I ignored her and started walking away. That didn't go down at all well. 'I tired telling you two man-rat can't live in one hole,' Ma warned.

'Well then, jump out of the hole,' I advised her.

Charlo laughed when he heard the story. 'How you always fighting with cabinet so?' he asked, shaking his head. 'I hope you can't only fight cabinet, you know. Because the day them police bounce-up with you on a lonely road, it will be thunder.'

Charlo knew the police well. His father was a policeman, although Charlo hadn't seen him since he was sixteen and his father had taken off his belt to beat him, telling him to drop his pants. 'I don't drop my pants for any man,' Charlo had replied. 'Only for women.'

Now, his words disturbed me. I felt an implied criticism of my actions. 'You think I should have let the police search the truck?' I asked.

We were sitting on his front porch at the time. He shrugged. 'I don't know. I only know I made a mistake the day I answer my father back and leave his house. I should have take my licks like a man. Then I wouldn't have had to leave high school and find work.' He shook his head regretfully. 'But when you is that age,' he said, 'and you screw two-three woman and get in a few fight, you does feel you is man.'

I had never heard Charlo talk like this before.

'You know what I wanted to be?' he asked, looking at me.

I shook my head.

'A teacher,' he said. 'A art teacher. I was real good in art in school. Look at me now. I always building house for people and I don't even have a house myself.'

I sighed. We sat in silence for a while.

'It only have three rules for living in Trinidad, Bird,' Charlo finally said. He held up a forefinger. 'Go brave.' He raised the next finger. 'Be strong.' He raised the other two fingers of his hand. 'Live good with people.'

Chapter Four

In the weeks that followed, I thought about Charlo's words. Living good with people seemed to come naturally to me. Old Mr de la Guillame in Santa Cruz, for example, had turned from a monster to a benefactor. Perhaps it was the fact that I took him a bottle of rum when I went there, and when Mr Antoine pointed out that I was becoming a danger to the old man's liver, added packets of biscuits, tins of sardines, salmon and bread.

One day, I had found Mr de la Guillame shaved and almost didn't recognise him. He was wearing a wrinkled cotton shirt that was sort of clean, and it made him look thin and pathetic. He was going to the bank. 'The fockers want to take away my place!' he had mumbled.

It had turned out the property was mortgaged. De Verteuil hadn't paid his instalments for years, and the bank was ready to foreclose. I looked around my bustling lumber-yard and furniture factory. What the hell would happen to us? I asked Mr de la Guillame how much the loan was. Twenty-two thousand dollars, he muttered. I asked whether his children wouldn't pay it for him. He growled in his throat like one of his dogs. 'And then throw me the fock out! Them son of a bitch will throw me out tomorrow if they get a focking chance. They does say I ill-treat them when they was young. Just because I wanted them to work in the cocoa –'

'Mr D,' I had asked gently, 'if I sign a paper that you could live here for the rest of your life, would you sign over the mortgage to me?'

He didn't even blink. 'Why not?' he snapped. 'It's better than them son of a mother-cunt get the place!'

I hadn't asked whether he was referring to the bank or his children. I just went home to talk to my mother.

Living good with Mr de la Guillame had certainly paid off.

I was also pretty strong. I liked hefting big planks of wood in the lumber-yard, feeling my muscles tighten and release against forces that could prevent a man from doing what he wanted to do. But could I fight? I didn't know.

I signed up for a course in karate and grew to like it a lot. Unlike the sports I had played so far, where you were constantly moving and had to make split-second decisions, karate involved a focusing of the body and mind. You concentrated hard on what you were doing. You didn't just respond according to reflex. But your reflexes got sharpened as well.

That paid off too. My reflexes eventually came in useful dealing with Sharon Lee, who was turning into a major addition to my social life. If I was in the city, I would drop by her office to get out of the hot sun in between encounters with petty officials in the nearby government departments. I provided Sharon with better excuses for looking in her law-books than her bosses in the Opposition, who didn't seem to have any zeal for government and had given up on the idea of ever coming to power. I paid for Sharon's legal advice with lunches at the sleaziest places in the city. She claimed the best food in Trinidad was served on the wharves, at the Breakfast Shed, where fat women cooked huge meals for the stevedores. She also liked the company there. It was like window-shopping, she said. 'I like my men big and black.'

She herself had spice-coloured skin, curly hair and the most beautiful figure. She came from Moruga, a settlement on the southernmost tip of Trinidad, where the local Chinese shopkeeper had had a penchant for getting black women pregnant. Sharon's mother hadn't escaped, and she was a primary schoolteacher with aboriginal blood in her veins. 'Carib, Spanish, Scots,' Sharon boasted. 'I have everything in me except Indian.'

She made it clear from the beginning that she thought little of Indian men. The Opposition office was studded with them. One day at lunch, I tried to brush away a fly that had landed on her shoulder and she slapped my hand hard. After that, any fly could land on Sharon if it wanted. It wasn't my business. My business was to console the other legal researcher, Roshni, who was having an affair with a married MP.

'Roshni is a ass,' Sharon said one day at the Breakfast Shed.

'She just didn't realise what she was getting herself into,' I replied. 'She will grow out of it.'

'You mean he will grow out of it,' Sharon retorted. 'He will leave her backside right there and move on to some other little girl. You just waiting round to pick up the pieces. To consume the leftovers.'

'Well,' I said, 'I've had worse leftovers.'

'You like leftovers?' Sharon picked up a glass half-full of sea moss, a thick milky drink the stevedores claimed was an aphrodisiac. 'Here's some leftovers.'

She made to pour the sea moss over my head. I held her wrist and propelled her arm back to her side of the table. When I let go, the glass toppled over and sea moss dripped onto her dark skirt. She started to laugh. 'Now you have me looking like Roshni,' she sputtered, indicating the milky liquid splashed against her crotch.

I took her home to change her skirt. She had a flat in St Ann's, in a crook in the hills north of the city. I took one look at the area and didn't like it. There was no sunlight; big trees leaned over from the hillside, creating a damp, brooding effect. Sharon lived above her landlord, a tall man whose build reminded me of my Carnival character, Big Bird. The house was like an echo of his strange physique. She led me up a long flight of stairs that seemed to have been tacked on as an afterthought, while a collection of Alsatian dogs barked at us from an enclosed area of the yard.

Inside, the flat was even uglier. A fake marble counter in sickly green divided the kitchen area from the living-room. A sofa was covered in gritty flowered plastic. Sharon went to the counter and held up a bottle of rum. I shook my head. She poured herself a drink and some water for me, sprawled on the plastic couch and kicked off her high-heeled shoes to reveal the ugliest feet I had ever seen. They were long and misshapen, bony in parts and bulgy in others where corns had turned permanent.

'So?' I asked. 'You going to change the skirt?'

'Feeling lazy,' she said, sucking on an ice cube. 'It too hot.'

'It's them clothes you does wear,' I said.

She tended to wear nylon blouses — murder in that climate, but they looked nice on her. You could make out the points of her nipples under her blouse and bra.

'This thing really hot,' she said, unbuttoning the top button. She leaned back and let the ice cube tumble from her luscious bottom lip to her collar-bone. 'That feels good,' she said.

As the ice melted, water ran down into the crease of her breasts, creating a transparent patch on her blouse. She motioned to me to pass her the ice cubes in my glass. I held one above her so it dripped directly onto her nipple and went to the fridge to get more ice. Then I returned and helped her turn her entire blouse transparent. Eventually we shifted to her bed.

The encounter lasted not more than four minutes. No, less. Sharon was trigger-happy in bed. Within seconds she was nagging me to enter her. She started bucking and heaving like a cement mixer gone mad, while the cheap bed banged and clattered till I was afraid it would fall apart. Sharon moaned so loudly the dogs downstairs started barking. I blocked out the noise and prepared to restart. My plan was to get the engine idling nicely and then gradually rev the motor, but Sharon pushed me off her. She propped herself up on her elbow and studied me.

'Not too bad,' she said, 'for an Indian.'

'What you have against Indian?' I asked, sitting next to her and admiring the graceful sweep of her body. She had pear-shaped breasts and the most succulent pear-shaped bottom to match.

'They too much like Chinee,' she said.

'What you have against Chinee?' I put out my forefinger to trace the curve of her breast. She slapped my hand away.

'That!' she said. 'They too fast-hand.'

'But you's a Chinee,' I pointed out.

'No,' she said. 'My father is a Chinee. A Chinee ram-goat. I's a chigger. Chinee and nigger.'

'I feel you inherit some of the ram-goat part, yes!'

She laughed. 'We will see, then,' she said. 'It will be ram-goat versus ram-goat.' She planned, she said, to sue her father for past child-maintenance payments. All eighteen years of them.

The thought of her father's neglect made me feel bad. Sharon entranced me, those dancing oval eyes and matching oval breasts and bum. She proposed we go all the way over the hills of the Northern Range to the beach, just to eat bake-and-shark sandwiches. I was willing to go anywhere with her. She showered and put on a pair of shorts that were a threat to public safety, a semicircle of her luscious bum was hanging out. The T-shirt she wore was even worse than the shorts. She had cut it off just below her breasts so you felt she only had to raise an arm and they would be dangling in front of you. I tested it by raising my own arm over my head when she had finished her sandwich and wanted some of mine. I was right.

I asked her if she ate so much because of being deprived as a child.

'Nah,' she laughed. 'My father used to pack up boxes of groceries from the shop and send them to us in the delivery van. I used to give him my book-list every year and my school books used to arrive. He used to bring dolly for me for Christmas.'

'So why you want to sue him?'

She shrugged.

'He paid for you to go to law school in Barbados, and you want to use that to sue him?'

She laughed. 'That will be sweet, eh! Ir-on-y! I going to give him some irony in his backside!'

At some point in her childhood, Sharon's father had gone to China and brought back a bride. He now had nine legitimate children. 'I not waiting for him to dead to squabble over inheritance with all his chinkey-eye children,' she explained. 'I getting mine in front. Every penny of it. And later, when he dead, I will also put in a claim for a share of the inheritance as well.'

I felt out of my depth. All this deep dark revenge stuff was beyond me.

But I liked the way Sharon took life by its throat and squeezed every possible drop of enjoyment out of it. She was completely contradictory and self-driven, absolutely original in her tastes and attitudes, which she would fight for if necessary. Sometimes if it wasn't necessary.

The next time I went to the Opposition office, she stamped on my foot with her high-heeled shoe. That was, she explained, because I had looked down Roshni's blouse while examining a document with her. I hadn't really. Well, maybe a quick peek. I couldn't avoid it. It was there for me to see. 'Go to Casualty,' Sharon advised when I complained about the pain in my foot. 'And pass by my house after that.'

I didn't go to Casualty, but I did go to her house. I went armed with an electric fan.

It didn't really improve things in Sharon's bed, though. Even in the cool of the evening, she was as explosive as before. Slam, bam, move your bam-bam, I joked, but it was a terrible pity. Her skin was totally hairless, smooth and unmarked. It really felt like silk. But the only way to get to touch it was to wrestle with her. I would sneak up on her and she would fight with me, and ours grew into a relationship that depended on fighting. If we were at the beach, she would kick me on the shins because she had caught me watching some other bikini. That would give me an excuse to grab her in a tackle and roll around on the sand. She would tickle me in the crotch all the way back to her apartment, but the minute we got there it was like a military campaign, one of those quick and dirty operations American army personnel refer to on the news. Get in, unload your ammunition, and get out fast before the enemy organises itself for resistance.

And Sharon's fighting wasn't limited to private occasions. When I escorted her to a wedding, some big-breasted Syrian woman who had had plenty to drink got hold of my hand and started raving on about how she loved the furniture I sold. Sharon scraped back her chair so abruptly, it toppled over onto the floor. She turned and headed for the door. I extracted my hand from the woman's and went after her. 'Go back and fock the woman,' she flung over her shoulder. 'That's all you didn't do so far.' She flounced out the door and I followed her. She headed out of the hotel and down the driveway. As we got to the dark roadway, I grabbed her arm. She turned round swiftly.

'Let me go, you coolie mother-cunt,' she said. She gave me a push in the chest. I slipped on the grass verge of the road and found myself falling backwards. I landed in the filthy ditch with Sharon on top of me. She shrieked. 'I think I twist my ankle!'

'Good for you!' I said. 'I tired telling you about them high heels you does wear.' I got myself out of the ditch and hauled her out. 'You want to go for a walk now?' I asked, putting on an inviting tone of voice.

'I lose my shoes,' she said, giggling.

I helped her to my car and took her home.

'You're ruining your feet with those shoes, Sharon,' I said, as I applied ice wrapped in a towel to her injured foot. I ran my finger along the bumps and swellings. She kicked me with the other foot. I grabbed that one, held it tight, and kissed the instep of the injured one. As she struggled, I moved my lips along the injured leg all the way up her thigh.

'Stop that, you nasty coolie!' she cried.

I raised my head briefly. 'You want to see how nasty this coolie is?' I asked.

I figured she would relax and enjoy it after a while. And she did. But once I let her go, she kicked me with her good foot and turned her body to the wall. I pried her shoulder away from her face and saw tears trickling from her eyes.

After that, Sharon grew even more possessive. I couldn't talk to another woman. I told her no woman could compare with her. 'You should see my mother,' she replied. 'She looks just like me, but with bigger boobs. And Lee Song still went and find a chinkey-eye woman who can't talk one word of English.' She opened her oval eyes wide. 'You could imagine that? She can't talk one single word of English. That is what man does want, deep down. Woman who can't answer them back.'

I argued that it didn't make sense that I came to her house nearly every evening if I wanted other women. I was crazy in love with her. But she remained a volcano, ready to erupt at the slightest provocation.

'I waited whole night for you last night,' she griped when I stayed away a couple of days. I had been at the mas' camp. The Carnival season had begun. 'Playing the fool with them jammette who does hang around mas' camp!' Sharon added.

That wasn't at all true. The girls at the mas' camp didn't hassle me any more. Carlene had had a baby that year and now had a steady – or rather unsteady – relationship going. To the younger generation of hot young things, I was a senior, like Charlo. They didn't dare bother me, the rich businessman and band sponsor. I had bought trailers for Symphonia, had the pans chrome-plated and paid for our soloist, Mikey, to attend the St Lucia Jazz Festival.

When I went to the mas' camp in the evening, now, it was just to design and build the costume for the King of the Band. The King was my preserve. Not that our King, Gordon, ever won any prize. I insisted on making a big bird every year. That was my private tradition: I wanted to build a big, beautiful bird that could suggest flight. Whatever theme Charlo chose for his band, I found a bird that could fit with it. The year before, the theme had been 'Treasures of the Nile', and I had made our king Ra, the Egyptian bird-god. Unfortunately, the costume was too restrictive and Ra couldn't dance. He had not impressed the judges or spectators.

This year, the band's theme was 'Wealth of the Rainforest'. I had read somewhere that scientists had discovered a flying frog in the highest hills of Trinidad's Northern Range, the line of violet-blue mountains that was always in sight. Whenever I drove into Port of Spain, or east to the tennis club in St Augustine, or north into the Santa Cruz Valley, or to the beaches on the eastern or western coasts, those hills accompanied me. Those were the hills that protected Trinidad from hurricanes and left us to prosper in peace. And there, in that one set of hills, only in that one place in the entire world, lived this recently discovered flying frog. It had deep red eyes and a very weird green face. I decided to make that flying frog our King, a cross between frog and bird, a creature that could leap from tree to tree, overcome its evolutionary frog-background, and fly a little. It must be a frog that turned into a bird when challenged by the highest trees of its homeland.

But, as I got more and more involved with the costume, my quarrels with Sharon grew more intense. I suggested she come with me to the mas' camp one evening. That turned out to be a very bad idea. Sharon disap-proved of all the wining and lasciviousness of Carnival. She went to the beach on the Carnival days. 'What wrong with that lawyer-girl?' one girl asked. 'Why she have her nose wrinkle up like she smelling shit all the time?' 'She smelling she top lip,' Carlene said.

When the band started playing and Carlene started wining, she deliberately jostled Sharon. Sharon put on her sternest expression, like she was calling on a judge to give the prisoner maximum sentence. She had worn her shortest shorts, but they cut no ice here, where short shorts were almost a dress code. She informed me that she wanted to go home. I left what I was doing and sped with her back to St Ann's. When I pulled up in the driveway to her house, I left the engine running and waited for her to get out.

'It look to me like you too busy for me, with all this Carnival in your head,' she said. 'I will see you on Ash Wednesday.'

I thought that a good idea. I reached over to kiss her. She slapped my face. 'You have a lot of your possessions here,' she hissed. 'You better come and get them.'

'I don't need them,' I said. 'Leave them there.'

'I going to throw them out the window,' she said. 'Those dogs downstairs could use some toys.'

My possessions included a few long-playing records. I went with her to rescue them. Inside the house, however, she began to revile me, pushing and pulling at me to start a fight. As I picked up the records, she hit me hard on the back. Louis Armstrong slid out of his paper sheath and smashed to the floor. I shoved Sharon away from me. She fell onto the plastic sofa, pulling me down with her. I heard a crack. The sofa had got smashed. I got up and examined my records. Two of them were also cracked.

Sharon remained sitting in the V where the sofa's wooden base had broken. 'My landlord wouldn't like this,' she said, giggling. 'Mashing up his pretty, pretty couch.' The stupid Alsatians were barking furiously from downstairs. I got mad and kicked the backrest of the sofa. I heard another crack. The wooden armrest splintered away from the main frame, and I kicked again till it fell to the floor with a satisfying thud.

'All right, Sharon,' I said, my chest heaving. 'You mash up my records, I mash up your couch. Now I getting out of here before I mash up your head. If you want somebody to fight and fock, the St Ann's madhouse right down the road.'

Sharon got up. 'You just using this as an excuse to go back with them jammettes in the mas' camp!' she shrieked.

'I could go back with who I focking want!' I shouted. 'I don't have to put up with a psychotic like you!'

'I psychotic?' she screamed. 'You have a Casanova complex!'

'I could have what I want!' I told her more quietly. 'And I going to damn well have whoever I want! And I could inform you that it's not you!'

I turned to leave. As I got to the door, I heard her coming up behind me, swearing. I turned just in time to see the wooden armrest of the sofa in her hand, her arm raised to hit me on the head with it. I put up my own arm to shield my face and suddenly felt a sharp pain.

I couldn't move my left arm. Sharon raised the sofa arm again. I grabbed it with my right hand and wrenched it out of her grasp. She cried out. I felt my arm: it was hanging from the shoulder-joint. Sharon was holding her right arm and bawling. I looked at it. It was dislocated too. I leaned against the room-divider and tried to get calm.

'All right,' I said, as my breathing slowed. 'We have to go to Casualty.'

We went down the stairs, with the Alsatians barking furiously at us, and got into the car. I gave Sharon instructions. I would steer the car with my right arm, she would manipulate the gear shift with her left. She obeyed, groaning, while I hoped I wouldn't be so unlucky as to encounter any of my old foes at Casualty.

My hopes were dashed the moment we entered the Casualty doors. The nursing sister I had fought with the last time was there. I decided I had to be stoic. The place was full, over-full with late-night decadence and misfortune. A big guy was groaning with pain from inflamed haemorrhoids, another guy had a bloody face from a motorcycle accident, while a child was screaming with toothache. An Indian woman was describing how her husband had come home drunk and beaten her, while the husband sat on a bench hanging his head and looking stupid. That woman had an injured little finger. She had wrapped it in a big piece of cloth that she displayed to everyone in the waiting room. She also displayed the tiny wooden stool that had been used to damage her finger, which she had brought with her in a big brown paper bag.

After about an hour's waiting, there was a flurry at the door. A chunky Indian woman came in wearing a white coat, a stethoscope dangling from her neck. 'Waay!' she exclaimed, surveying the waiting room. 'Allyou Trinis does really live at night, eh!'

She bustled through the door of the treatment room. From conversations between patients and a male attendant, I learned that this was the registrar in charge of Casualty. She wasn't supposed to be here, but her junior had called her at home to say he was having a hard time coping with all the patients. Things moved much faster after that. Dr Lopez came into the waiting room and chatted to the patients, ascertaining how urgent their needs were. She brought a cheerful air into the place, making jokes and chivvying everybody.

'How you get a dislocated shoulder this time of night, girl?' she asked Sharon.

Sharon pointed to me. I figured I was set down as yet another Trini wife-beater. 'She dislocate my shoulder too,' I pointed out.

Dr Lopez looked at my arm. 'But how she could dislocate your arm when hers was already dislocated?'

I explained. She started to laugh. 'So it was mutual dislocation!' she said. 'Allyou Trinis good, yes!'

She took Sharon into the treatment room to have her shoulder reset. The other patients started upbraiding me. 'Two nice young people like allyou, and it's so allyou does get on?' asked an old black lady who had forgotten to put her teeth in. 'This time of the night allyou should be loving up in the bed and making nice children instead of studying to dislocate shoulder!'

'It's she who start it,' I protested.

'So you had to finish it,' snapped a thick-set woman. 'You see why I don't keep no man in my house? Man is a curse! I bet you do something to get her vex enough to dislocate your shoulder. That look like a educated girl. She wouldn't just dislocate your shoulder for nothing. You must be do something!'

Dr Lopez came out into the waiting area again. Everybody looked up as she approached me. 'Resetting that arm going to hurt,' she said. 'Your darling want you to come and hold her hand.'

'But if he hold the next hand, he might dislocate that one too!' a man pointed out.

I followed the doctor into the treatment room. She gave me an injection and got the nurse to fill out a card for me, so she could reset my arm after she had done Sharon's.

'Saran?' Dr Lopez asked, looking at my card. 'You is the man with the wood?'

We got chatting. Dr Lopez seemed determined to get every laugh she could out of the hell-hole that was Casualty. 'I just buy some wood from your lumber-yard,' she said. 'I going to refurbish my house. You know a good builder?'

I shook my head. 'I don't know a good builder. I know an excellent builder. Best builder in Trinidad. But he does only work for people he like. He kind of choosy that way. He does have to interview you first and decide whether he like you.'

I promised to make an appointment for her with Charlo. Dr Lopez, whose first name was Sarojini, was a really nice woman of about thirty-five. No ravishing beauty, but a solid person with a strong appreciation of the absurd. She insisted that I shouldn't drive with my dislocated arm, and made us wait till she was finished helping out in Casualty so she could drive us home. She lived quite near to Sharon, on a pleasant hillside called Cascade, so she and Sharon delivered me to the Croissee and then went back home together.

The next day, I took a vow not to go back to Sharon's house till Carnival was over. I had Jason go in the van to deliver a set of furniture to her apartment to replace the one I had destroyed, and to pick up my car from the hospital parking lot. Then I tried to forget Sharon as I finished my frog-bird.

That became a real challenge. With my left arm in a sling, I was hand-icapped, but it only pushed me further. I used luminescent plastic to mimic the shimmering colours I had seen in photos of the flying frog. Our King, Gordon, would inhabit only the frog's torso, which would be tiny in comparison with the free-floating head and back legs. I built a very large, very green head, with huge, bulging red eyes. The legs were violet, very long and weirdly shaped, something like the legs of Sharon's landlord. Nature's frog was able to fly because of large muscles in its back legs; mine would have to depend on nylon strings. The legs folded in front of the torso, but when Gordon jerked the strings they extended backwards, their webbed turquoise feet opening into large fans that imitated wings. If Gordon synchronised his movements right, jumping while extending the legs and opening the feet, it would appear he was flying.

It required practice, and Gordon practised so hard on the last day, he fell and couldn't get up. I called Sarojini Lopez, and she met us at Casualty. Gordon had sprained his ankle and torn a ligament in his right arm. I gave in to defeat.

Not Charlo. He had a solution. The masses of our rainforest band would be dressed as trees. He proposed that Gordon be carried onto the stage by four of them. He wouldn't have to manipulate the strings that led to the legs and feet; they would do it for him. It was the best we could do. We never won anything anyway, but at least we could show off our beautiful frog-bird. I settled for that.

On the night of the competition, the night before Carnival began, we organised ourselves on the ramp that led to the stage. The guys lifted Gordon onto their shoulders while he groaned and complained at the pain. When we were announced, a ripple of sound flowed through the spectators. Symphonia's King was always a bird that got the lowest score from the judges. The crowd could relax, open a beer and prepare to jeer.

But when the translucent colours of our frog appeared on stage, there was a combined intake of breath in the crowd. 'Ooh!' thousands of people exhaled simultaneously.

That encouraged the tree-men. Ignoring Gordon's complaints, they danced to the edge of the stage so the spectators could get a good view of the frog. They got carried away with the crowd reaction and danced more enthusiastically. Eventually, one of them made a careless movement and the whole construction began to disintegrate. There was a titter from the crowd. My chest squeezed together. Gordon was going to fall, damaged arm, twisted ankle and all. The usual laughter began and I swore to myself in that split second that I would never make another King costume again. In his panic, Gordon kicked his legs hard as he began to fall, like a drowning person. But the feet propelled him forward and he soared into the air towards the spectators, the Webbed feet keeping him afloat like two small parachutes.

'Ooh!' went the spectators.

Gordon glided for about a minute, then drifted downwards slowly, ever so slowly, into the darkness below the edge of the stage.

'Ooh!' went the crowd again.

Then there was a long hush.

It had been a moment of pure magic in the savannah. That huge, hideously beautiful frog floating towards the spectators like a dream. A modernistic dream in translucent plastic, but a dream with its truth anchored in the reality of the rainforest and the mystery of nature. The spectators waited silently for the trick to be repeated. Commentators on the loudspeakers rushed into the silence, trying to capture in words what they had seen.

We hustled to the bottom of the stage, Charlo and I and some of the other guys, and discovered that Gordon was fine. Under the pressure of the moment, he had managed to compose himself while floating, landed on his one good foot, and let himself crumple into the darkness. The guys picked him up and took him to the side of the stage to dose him with rum. The commentators raved on about some intellectual theory of Carnival as Theatre, and other such blah-blah. Everyone thought what had happened had been deliberate and kept asking us to repeat the performance. But there was no way that would happen. Gordon was getting seriously drunk at the side of the stage.

When the results were announced, Gordon Campbell was awarded first prize – our Gordon, King of the Bands! Charlo got so jubilant, he slapped my bad shoulder. I was so jubilant, I didn't notice the pain.

Gordon wasn't jubilant at all. He was not moving from where he lay at the side of the stage, he said. No way was he going back on that stage to be crowned. This was the end of his Carnival career. He was retiring. We were going to kill him one of these Carnivals, what with heads breaking off and rolling about the stage and the other misfortunes he had suffered at our hands. He was quitting. 'Charlo going to carry you to collect the crown,' I begged. 'Not the other guys.'

Charlo looked Gordon straight in the eyes. 'Gordon,' he asked, 'you think I will let you fall?'

Reluctantly, Gordon climbed onto Charlo's shoulders. Charlo wrapped his arms around his legs and held him tight. I trailed along to manipulate the strings that controlled the legs and feet. I felt self-conscious at the sight we must have made, Charlo in his usual sleeveless vest, me in my khaki shorts and T-shirt. Between us, Gordon and I had multiple injuries that caused us to wince and groan all the way. But no one heard our suffering, and the roar from the crowd as we came onto the stage caused us to forget it. Trinidad rose to its feet in a standing ovation.

I jumped into a taxi afterwards and raced up to Sharon's house. I had to tell her my devotion had been justified. I pounded on her door as the Alsatians barked at me. She appeared in a thin cotton vest that showed off her glory. I stretched my good arm wide and advanced on her, wining. 'King of the Bands,' I said. 'You looking at the King of the Bands.'

She glared at me. 'What the fock you coming here for, this time of the night?'

She moved backwards. I advanced, picked her up with my right arm and whirled her round. She fought me off and rushed to the kitchen area.

She came back with a knife in her left hand – a big, long, butcher's knife. 'You feel you could just abandon me at Carnival and come back and fock me when you want, you nasty coolie shopkeeper?' Her body heaved. 'Come! I will show you what you will get! I will cut off that nasty prick and throw it downstairs for the dogs.'

I grabbed her wrist and turned and the knife loosened from her grasp. I took it away and flung it out of the open window. Then I grabbed her again and kissed her all over.

The next day I was on the front page of the newspaper again. But the incident with Sharon had taken my joy away. Knives were a step too far. Once I had sobered up, I realised that things could get really nasty with her. I had to break off our relationship. I called her and told her so. There was silence on the other end of the line. Then she hung up.

With Lent came a policeman to my door with a legal summons. I had committed dog-murder. Apparently, when I had flung the knife out of Sharon's window, I had stabbed one of the Alsatians and it had bled to death. I was being sued for property damage. I called Sharon's landlord.

'How much do you want to withdraw the charges?' I asked without preliminaries.

It cost me a lot. I didn't care. The matter was quickly settled.

Sharon attacked me, though. The landlord had given her notice to quit his premises. All the disorder and breakages she had caused had added up. She was hopping mad that I had escaped scot-free. 'Focking coolie cunt!' she barked on the phone. 'Allyou think allyou could buy allyou way out of everything!'

'That's all you have to say?' I asked, ready to hang up the phone.

'No! I have to tell you you have to pay for something else.'

'What?'

'An abortion.'

My heart stopped. 'I thought you were on the pill?'

'When you dump me for Carnival I dump the pills.'

I went to see her. I looked around the ugly apartment in this ugly part of St Ann's, and the hopelessness of the situation overcame me. I had thought of marrying her, but the house seemed to symbolise Sharon's mental condition. She was really too unbalanced for a long-term relationship.

'You really don't want to have the child?' I asked.

'No.'

Her face was closed. I took a deep breath. 'Sharon, I would be willing to take the child and bring it up,' I said. 'You wouldn't have to do anything. Just give the child to me.'

Sharon looked at me with a gaze full of hatred. 'What you think I am?' she hissed. 'A cow? Drop the young one and forget it?'

Eventually, I got up and went to see Sarojini Lopez. After I'd told her everything she sighed. 'I don't feel you need a doctor, you know. I feel you need a witch-doctor. How you so accident prone?'

She went to the telephone. Arrangements were made. The abortion would be conducted by Trinidad's best gynaecologist, in a private clinic run by the Seventh Day Adventists, who were totally opposed to abortion. Then there was nothing more to say. I didn't feel like talking. Sarojini invited me to stay to dinner and brought out a Scrabble board afterwards. I remained till after midnight, trying to beat her in one Scrabble game after the other.

On the morning of the abortion, I picked up Sharon and drove her to the clinic. We hardly spoke. Sharon went into the preparation room. I wouldn't see her till it was all over, till the anaesthetic had worn off. I had four hours to kill. To kill, I thought. Then I shoved away the string of thoughts that followed. I drove around a while till it was time for Sharon to wake up.

She sobbed helplessly when she did, as though her heart would break. I held her in my arms, feeling useless. I picked up some food on the way to her house. She didn't have any appetite to start with, but that changed as she began to eat. In the end, she finished everything. I put her to bed, watched her drift into sleepiness, and then left.

I went home and dropped into a chair on the balcony of our house. Pa came out and sat with me. I retreated to the hammock.

'You know, Ved,' Pa murmured. 'I want to go back to Dorado to die.'

I had heard these words before. 'You not going to die now, Pa,' I said absently. 'You have any pain?'

'No.' He shook his head. 'But sometimes in the night the traffic on the Main Road does sound like the waves in Dorado.'

I couldn't bear to listen to him. I got out of the hammock and went through the french doors to my room. I put a classical record on the turntable and lay on my bed. The music made me feel worse. I wanted to get up and switch the stereo off but I didn't have the energy. A figure blocked the light coming in through the doorway.

'You want some sweet rice?' Pa asked. He held out a bowl.

I didn't want any fucking sweet rice, but the look on his face was so humble, I took it. I couldn't eat rice pudding in bed, so I got up. I went back out onto the verandah, ate the sweet rice and it made me feel better.

After that, I avoided relations with women. Instead, I started dropping by Sarojini Lopez's house when I was in the city. Saroj came from a family similar to mine, but had ignored family feelings and married George Lopez, a man of mixed race, while studying medicine in Jamaica. Charlo was refurbishing her house then, building bookshelves along every wall. Books lay in tall piles everywhere, on the floors, on tables and desks, on kitchen counters. Novels, acres of novels. John Le Carré, Naipaul, Hardy, George Eliot, Graham Greene, Somerset Maugham, Paul Scott . . . Saroj read widely while George consumed airport novels by the dozen. I began borrowing books to read lying in my hammock on our verandah.

That verandah was a lovely place for reading. The garden below was wondrous. When Charlo had landscaped the area around the swimming pool, Ma had said she hoped he would maintain the plants he had installed. While trimming his oleanders one day, he pruned Ma's roses as well. She threatened to report him to the police, but the roses bloomed like they had never bloomed before. 'Charlo have a hand,' Pa had muttered. 'It have some people who could cut plants and they does grow. Other people, when they cut plants, the plants does dry up and dead.'

Now, whenever Ma wanted a plant trimmed, she just started whining that it was growing lopsided because Charlo had trimmed it wrong the last time, and he got out the pruning shears. Everything that went wrong in the garden was Charlo's fault, according to Ma. Rain never had anything to do with it, or drought. Pests and fungus were only figments of Charlo's imagination. The two of them bickered constantly, but the results were spectacular. Fuchsia-coloured bougainvillea covered the wall at the back; yellow honeysuckle climbed up the wall of our pagoda on the right. Young royal palms fringed the driveway that curved along the back of the pagoda to the stairs leading to the verandah. The lawn beyond the driveway was dotted with giant, velvety hibiscus.

Saroj took to coming over so her kids could use our swimming pool. One afternoon, she interceded in an argument Ma and I were having. 'But your mother right!' she asserted.

My mother had interrupted a pundit during a religious ceremony that morning to tell him he was misinterpreting one of the Hindu scriptures. I had had a ringside seat at the drama – since my father's first heart attack, he couldn't drive, so I had to accompany my parents to all social and religious activities.

'My mother just don't have any manners!'

'Why she should have manners?' Saroj returned. 'Them pundit does make money from talking shit.'

She lent me a Penguin paperback of the *Bhagavadgita*, translated by somebody called Juan Mascaro. The philosophy startled me. It seemed to me that Krishna was saying you should do what you believe is right even if your whole family is lined up against you, even if you have to destroy the entire existing world in the interests of justice. I got to know sections of the *Gita* by heart. I bought my own copy and read bits of it to Mikey, our steel-band leader. He was interested in stuff like that. He read the introduction to the book and informed me that the *Gita* had been Gandhi's bible in the Indian struggle against British colonialism. I began reading other books on Hindu philosophy. I bought a book on yoga and began thinking about things like duty, courage, discipline and strength.

Saran's had nearly fifty regular employees by now, and we hired a lot of extra labour in the months leading up to Christmas, so problems cropped up sometimes. I found myself challenging a labourer in the lumber-yard to a fight when he tried to bully my deadbeat cousin, Vijay. The guy was a very big guy, but I was fit, and I knew the other workers would have separated us before things got going. It was just theatre, a kind of theatre you have to be willing to put on to control the roughnecks who work in a lumber-yard.

Then one day in early December, I went into the store to hear Suzanne upbraiding Nerissa. 'Tell Ved,' she was urging. 'This is damn shit!'

Nerissa clammed up. She had a way of shutting down her face when she wanted to. Her eyes went dead, completely black. They seemed to get bigger till she looked like she was scared in her soul.

'Well I going to tell him!' Suzanne said.

Jason had cussed Nerissa out in the store that morning. In front of a lot of customers. 'If you hear how he get on, Ved!' Suzanne said. 'Effing this and that. And poor Nerissa never answer him.'

'If I had answered him it would have looked worse,' Nerissa protested. 'What people would say? Big quarrel in the middle of the store.'

'You should have picked up something and knocked him down,' said Suzanne.

That would have been absurd. Jason was tall and he had always been strong. That's why we had hired him in the first place, to move around furniture in the store. But he had always been awkward, making inappropriate jokes at times. We had grown around his faults, incorporating them into our work-style the way a tree grows to accommodate plants that feed off its bark.

I called Nerissa into the director's office. She stood in front of my desk silently, her body turned tight. But I could wait her out. I stared at her. She was wearing a pale-yellow blouse with an embroidered collar, and I didn't mind simply watching her for a while. She was a rather pleasant sight; she had put on a little weight, had lost her skinnyness.

Finally she sat down, and, with many sighs and hesitations, she began the story.

Turned out Jason had been stealing from the shop and she had spoken to him about it privately. He had denied it, but she had proof. She had suspected it for some time, and had laid a trap for him. The items he stole were small – batteries, tennis balls, and so on, negligible really – but who knew where it would lead? 'He was only playing wrong and strong when he cussed me,' she said.

I pointed out that she couldn't allow Jason to get away with cussing her in front of the customers. It would set a precedent for the other employees. 'You always telling me this is your store, and I does leave it to you to manage. You have to keep discipline.'

She sighed. 'It was just madness that fly up in Jason brain, you know,' she said. 'He is only eighteen years old.'

'Eighteen or no eighteen, Nerissa! You have to let your employees know who is boss here. They can't cuss you and get away with it. Jason has to know that if he don't behave he will get fired.'

She beamed her big dark eyes on me. Nerissa's eyes often had a hurt look, a bruised look, a worried look. I was never quite sure what Nerissa was feeling and never dared try to find out. The girls in the store had been strictly out of bounds from the very first day and I usually avoided Nerissa's eyes. 'I don't want Jason to get fired!' she said quickly. 'That boy have a hard life. He never had a father, and his mother depending on his salary.'

I shifted my gaze away from those eyes so I could think. 'All right,' I said, getting up. 'I going to solve this problem.'

She grabbed my hand. 'Don't fire him, Ved! I begging you. I will make sure he never thief again.'

I went out into the store. It was busy. 'Jason!' I called loudly as I approached him.

He looked up from where he was showing furniture to some customers. 'When you have a minute,' I said, leaning against a post to wait.

When he came up to me, his eyes were scared. I spoke loudly, so that everyone, staff and customers, would hear. 'I hear you cuss up Nerissa in this store today,' I said.

He started to excuse himself. I refused to listen. I cussed him roundly. I didn't use really crude words to offend the customers, but I was very abrasive. I saw tears spring to his eyes. 'Nerissa should have fired your arse!' I told him. 'If she ever come and tell me she fire any member of this staff, I not asking any questions, you know. That's her business. I not meddling. But I feel you should know how it does feel to get insult in front of a store full of customers.'

The customers stared at me like I was a beast. Jason's bowed head annoyed me. I felt he was seeking pity. And, once I had started letting myself get angry, the feeling just grew. 'Why you hanging down your head like a ripe breadfruit that ready to fall?' I jeered. 'Ain't you is a big man who could cuss up a woman who always treat you good? Why you don't get on like a big man now, and cuss me back?'

The other employees looked scared. Suzanne pursed her lips.

'If Nerissa don't fire you, that's her business,' I said. 'But if I hear anything like this again, I will wait for you outside the store and bust your arse!'

I turned and left.

Jason was quiet and withdrawn for a few days, and I didn't know whether it was sullenness or shame. But things were busy with Christmas coming up, and he soon bounced back. He seemed even more eager to please than before, and my heart went out to him. It was true what Nerissa had said about his background. I knew he depended on us all, Nerissa, Suzanne, the other girls and myself, for emotional sustenance. We were the closest thing he had to a family. He had always disturbed me because of this neediness, but I hadn't given it much thought before. I had just left him to Nerissa. I just hoped he would grow up and everything would be all right.

The other staff of the store began watching me warily when I came in. I guessed they had begun to see me as a nice guy but with an unpredictable temper. That was useful, I felt. In the Christmas season things could get chaotic. I didn't need any unnecessary problems. I had enough necessary ones.

Our customers' cars were causing traffic jams on the Eastern Main Road. I went to the guy who owned the lot where Symphonia practised and asked him if I could use the space as a parking lot during business hours. He charged me quite a fee, and I had to spend money cutting down the bush that surrounded the pan-yard and paving the space. But it was worth it. We made a lot of money that Christmas, and I was glad I had instituted the profit-sharing scheme. At the end of the year, our employees were in a jubilant mood, and our Recovery Day celebrations were spectacular.

This event had grown with the expansion of our workforce. We continued to hold it at Lopinot, on the grounds of an old cocoa plantation where the forest had been cleared and grass planted in a slope leading down to the river. I paid Lopinot villagers to tidy the grounds before and after our party, to cut the grass, trim the bushes and remove any debris caused by storm or erosion. They built bamboo tents and saved every rare country delicacy they had access to: wild meat, cascadoo fish, crabs, giant Brazil nuts, freshly roasted cashew nuts, you name it.

Lopinot was a really beautiful place, with bamboo arching over the river and giant forest trees to create patterns of light and shade. Symphonia played on the bank and people danced. The guys from the factory organised a cricket 'fete-match', which meant the team went in back to front, the worst players batting first while the better ones got drunk. As I had a reputation as a batsman, I had to wait till last. I hung out in the water, helping Charlo organise styrofoam-boat races for the kids.

At one point I began to get a bit uneasy about Jason. He had got hold of a liana and was playing Tarzan, swinging over the water from the branch of one tree to another. I shouted to him to ask if he was sure the liana could bear his weight. He called back something I didn't hear. I decided to take a look at the liana, but got distracted by a styrofoam-boat pile-up. Then I heard a gigantic splash, accompanied by shrieks of laughter from everyone. Tarzan had fallen into the river. I waited for him to emerge. He didn't. I dived into the pool. He was at the bottom. I swam to him and lifted him out. He was heavy, inert. I thumped his back and water came out of his mouth. He began to sputter and choke and cough. 'His head!' I heard Nerissa cry.

There was a cut in Jason's scalp.

'We have to carry him to Arima hospital,' said Charlo, picking Jason up in his arms. He led the way to my car. Nerissa wrapped a towel around Jason's head and sat with him in the back.

At Arima hospital, the doctor wanted an X-ray to be taken before letting the nurses stitch the wound, but the X-ray machine wasn't working. He advised us to take Jason to the Port of Spain hospital, my old stomping ground. We raced off again with Jason dozing off in the back seat. Nerissa put her arm round him and cradled his head against her.

To my dismay, my old foe, the nursing sister, was on duty. 'Your employees again!' she snapped. 'What kind of business you running, that you and your employees always getting injured?'

We were a dishevelled-looking lot. I had pulled my T-shirt on over my wet bathing trunks, and Charlo was in his sleeveless vest and drenched khaki shorts. Nerissa was wearing a dress over her bathing suit, but it was creased and damp, and bloody from Jason's head. Her hair hung in strings round her face. Jason himself was just wearing bathing trunks and the towel around his head.

We had to wait while other patients were treated. Many of them needed X-rays too. I left the others and raced up to Saroj's house. She dragged her white jacket on over the T-shirt she was wearing and followed me in her car back to Casualty. Jason was dozing on a bench when we got there. Saroj hustled him through a door and they disappeared.

They were away for a long time. One hour passed. An hour and a half. Two. It was after four in the afternoon when Saroj reappeared. Her face was blank. She shook her head as we approached her.

'Where Jason?' I asked.

'He didn't make it,' she said in a still voice.

'What you mean, Saroj?'

'He died before they started operating. He had been bleeding inside his skull.'

I just stared at her, unable to grasp what she was saying. I heard Nerissa's voice at my side. 'Died? What you mean died? You can't tell me Jason died!'

Saroj just stared at her. I suddenly heard a shriek.

'Doctor!' It was Nerissa's voice, but barely recognisable. 'You can't tell me that!'

Saroj's face remained a calm mask.

'No!' Nerissa screamed. 'No! Don't say that! How you could tell me that?' Her voice broke. 'How I could go and tell Jason mother that? How I could tell his sister?' She burst into sobs. Charlo put his arms around her and stroked her hair. I patted her back, feeling numb. 'How I could tell Jason mother that?' she sobbed, her shoulders shaking.

'Don't worry, Ner,' I said. 'You wouldn't have to tell Jason mother. I will do that.' Nerissa's whole body heaved and shuddered. I found tears in my own eyes as well, and wiped them away.

I became aware that we were surrounded by people. Other patients made sympathetic noises, uttering the clichés people use at times like these. I jerked my neck in the direction of the door and Charlo led Nerissa outside. Saroj found a vendor and brought us a couple of cans of Coca-Cola. We made Nerissa drink some sitting on the back seat of my car. Then we began that awful drive to Jason's house.

It was an old concrete house in Tunapuna, with broken steps and peeling paint. A little girl was sitting on the steps and I asked if Jason's mother was at home. She went and got her.

She was a slim woman in her late thirties, good-looking but with a face marked by hard times. 'Mr Ved!' Then a look of alarm replaced her smile. 'What happen?'

Nerissa started to cry again.

'Jason fell in the river,' I said.

She glanced around behind us. 'Where him?'

'We took him to the hospital,' I said.

Nerissa moved forward. 'Miss Grant. I'm sorry. I'm sorry, Miss Grant.' Her voice broke and she dissolved into sobs. Suddenly she and Jason's mother were clutching each other and weeping. A couple of neighbours appeared. Charlo and I explained what had happened. Jason's mother fell into a chair.

'Jason,' she kept muttering. 'Jason.' Then all of a sudden her voice rose to a shriek. 'Jason!' She closed her eyes and rocked back and forth in the chair. 'Oh God!' she groaned, tears streaming down her face. 'Why you have to take my son from me?'

I realised that tears had started in my own eyes again. I brushed them away.

'God!' Miss Grant wailed in a voice that didn't sound human. 'My son! Oh God! Why you have to do this to me? Jason!'

I leaned against a post and tried to collect myself. I felt a body against mine. It was Nerissa. I put an arm around her and she held on to me. I kept wiping my eyes only to find them wet again. The neighbours bustled round Jason's mother, soaking her head with Limacol, saying all the things people said on those occasions, about how you couldn't know God's will and so on.

Suddenly Miss Grant rose as though possessed. 'I have to go and see my son,' she cried. 'I have to go and see Jason! Oh, God, I have to go in the hospital to see Jason!' Her knees buckled and the neighbours caught her. One of them volunteered to take her in his car. As she was leaving, she stopped near me. 'Mr Ved . . .' she said brokenly.

My arms reached for her automatically, and she sobbed against my chest. 'Don't worry about anything,' I murmured. 'We will take care of everything. I promise you, Saran's will take care of everything.'

Once she had left, we three looked at each other blankly. What to do now? We were all still wearing damp clothes. Nerissa's house was locked up; her mother was still at the party in Lopinot. So we decided to go to my home. There, we found my father sitting on the verandah, at a dining-table near the door leading to the kitchen. Charlo began explaining what had happened. My mother and our maid Sylvia came out of the door to listen. I leaned against the railing and tears started in my eyes again. I turned towards a post and then couldn't control myself. I felt a hand patting my shoulder.

'Take it easy, son,' my father's voice said. 'Take it easy.'

I remembered that he shouldn't be allowed to have too much heavy emotion. I wiped my eyes and turned towards him. 'Pa . . .' Suddenly I was in his arms, sobbing against his shoulder.

'Here,' I heard my mother say. 'Drink some tea.'

Sylvia had made a pot of tea. Pa made me sit at the table and drink some. Nerissa's head was on the table. Ma grabbed Nerissa's shoulders and made her straighten up and drink some of the tea as well. Pa brought out a bottle of rum and Charlo poured himself a drink, then said he was going home to change. We would have to go back to Jason's house later, to the wake. Ma went inside the house and came back with a pile of clothes. 'My daughters leave these here,' she said to Nerissa. 'See if you could find something that could fit you.'

She took Nerissa off to the shower, and I went to the one attached to my room. By the time I had returned, Ma had arranged with Mr Chang, the owner of the shop next door, to bring over the food traditionally served at a wake. She made us eat something before setting off for Tunapuna again.

By the day of the funeral, I was calm again. Charlo didn't look like himself in the white shirt-jac he wore, similar to the one I had taken from my father's wardrobe to wear. Charlo's was a blinding white, with creases that showed it was new, and he looked nothing like a mas' camp leader or builder. He seemed remote in that garb, just a big, dignified black man.

We went to the funeral parlour and looked at Jason in the coffin. He, too, looked very handsome for the occasion. They had dressed him in a dark suit, and his slim face looked noble, somehow. Still and quiet for the first time, he made you aware of what he really was, despite the circumstances of his birth: a beautiful, intelligent young man. But he looked dead all right. His skin was an unnatural colour. I wished he could just be alive for a few minutes more so we could talk to him, let him know he was loved. I wanted to hold him in my arms, squeeze him, just for a few moments.

We drove behind the hearse to a church in the centre of Tunapuna. Together with some relatives, we lifted the coffin out and moved it to the door, where the priest was waiting in his long gown. He swung a censer, made the sign of the cross over the coffin, and began muttering some prayers.

I looked into the dimness of the church. It was packed. Saran's entire workforce had turned out. I spotted Mrs Antoine in a gigantic black hat. Her sons, Tony and Bernard, stood out from the crowd with their light-coloured faces and dark, well-groomed suits. I heard a sound and realised Symphonia was in the church as well, to one side of the altar. The guys were a mass of dark T-shirts hunched over their gleaming chrome pans. They launched into the Oscar Hammerstein song that was popular at the time.

"'When you walk through a storm,'" sang the choir at the back of the altar, "'hold your head up high, and don't be afraid of the dark . . .'"

I got a lump in my throat. As we started moving forward with the coffin, I had an image of poor Jason walking through the dark, accompanied by the fear that lay under his silly jokes. Tears came to my eyes at the image, and I couldn't brush them away because I was holding the coffin. I came as close as I ever had to praying, a deep strong wish that someone would hold Jason's hand on his journey.

"'Walk on through the wind,'" sang the choir as we moved up the aisle; "'Walk on through the rain, though your dreams be tossed and blown . . .'"

Tears started rolling down my face and I felt self-conscious. But then the music rose, the thrill of the steel band, my steel band, our steel band, Jason's steel band, the steel band of all the people in this church. As Symphonia launched into its crescendo, everyone joined in the chorus and I couldn't care any more.

'"Walk on,"' the church resounded, '"Walk on, with hope in your heart, and you'll never walk alone . . ."'

We set the coffin down. Out of the corner of my eye I saw Suzanne beckon to me, indicating a place next to her and Nerissa in the second row of pews. As I sat down, she slipped her hand into mine. I wiped my eyes and followed the service, believing, against all rationality, that our feelings here would be conveyed to Jason. He must be somewhere, I felt. He couldn't just vanish and cease to exist. I sang with the congregation, something I never did at religious events. I was willing to sacrifice disbelief to the faintest glimmer of the possibility that singing the hymns counted for something.

I noticed a familiar face in the choir. Could it be? Yes, among that white-robed, dark-skinned mass was Carlene, Symphonia's most famous winer-girl and sex-mate of my youth. Her hair was pressed till it barely existed, and skinned back from her brow. Her face looked narrow and repressed.

And then, at the end of the service, there was a solo, and I understood why the church tolerated this black bombshell in its choir. Carlene had a rare singing voice. She launched into the 'Ave Maria' and it was like a flock of white doves had been released over the black-clothed, dark-skinned mass in the church. Her voice soared and whooped like Mary Magdalene's spirit. I'm sure Carlene didn't understand one word of what she was singing. She was singing just to sing. But as her voice rose to the ceiling, it brought such joy and peace into the church that you knew, you just knew, that Jason's innocence would stand for him and that he would go to his destiny with the same swinging pleasure he had always done.

Charlo and I drove back to the Croissee in silence. As we approached the gate at the back of my house, I felt I had to break the silence.

'Thanks for arranging for Symphonia to play,' I said.

'I didn't do that,' he said. 'The boys do it themselves.'

I had never thanked Charlo for anything before. I stopped the car. 'I'm glad everybody turned out,' I said. 'I think it would be good for the mother. And for Jason.'

'The people didn't turn out for Jason or his mother, Big Bird,' Charlo said. 'They turned out for you.'

Our eyes locked. I nodded. He got out of the car and went home. I went up to the verandah of my house to contemplate this awesome thing I had created, this group of people who depended on me. I didn't feel it as a burden; I never had. It was just embarrassing to be treated the way people treated me, like I was somebody so special. I went into the shower, turned on the water, and found myself humming the 'Ave Maria'.

I became wrapped up in Jason's mother's problems after that. She wanted to go to the US and live with her daughter, but getting a visa was difficult. I had to put money into a bank account in her name to reassure the American embassy that she would be no burden to Uncle Sam.

So when the new year broke and the guys began to gather in Charlo's yard to plan the mas' band, I had no inspiration. A young guy who had been helping me suggested we construct a giant hummingbird and I told him to start it. Once Miss Grant had left, I figured it would be unfair to take over the guy's hummingbird, so I became involved in planning the tennis club's Carnival fete instead. This was the club's annual fundraising event and God knows we needed funds desperately. The courts were so full of potholes they resembled Trinidad's roads. I was nervous I'd break my ankle one day. I knew I had only been asked to serve on the fete committee so they would get Symphonia to play for free. The committee was really a collection of barflies that included my cousin Ashok, who had just graduated from university and was now working for an engineering firm in the city.

We had many, many meetings, each one more drunken than the last. Every time a decision was made, the committee forgot about it the next time it met. They failed to print tickets on time and I found myself running around to printers. They failed to get police permission to have the fete. They failed to do anything, really, trusting to some kind of fete god in the sky that everything would come out OK on the night. 'This is Trinidad,' Ashok reassured me. 'Hurricane don't come here. Tourist don't come here. God is a Trinidadian.'

The only serious committee member was a girl called Rosemary de Freitas. I think she had been invited onto the committee because of her boobs: she had a luscious pair. She and I ended up doing everything, and by the time the fete had taken place, Rosemary had invited me into her bed.

I grew bored with her very quickly, I have to tell the truth. The boobs were great, but I didn't feel comfortable with the company she kept. White people in Trinidad lived in their own little world, a world of weekends on boats and internecine gossip. I felt like an intruder.

Rosemary couldn't understand why I kept turning down her invitations. 'You only want to sleep with me!' she accused. I said nothing. I was really at a loss when it came to women. They would invite you into their bedroom, but then they would want you in their living-room as well. I was always shocked at the speed at which this transformation took place. You met a girl; she lured you on with her body; as soon as you succumbed, she started acting as though you owed her a full-blown relationship.

'Woman is pure trouble,' Charlo concurred. Sybil, the woman from Arima who bought toys for poor children, was threatening to take up residence in his house at that point. She had moved in with him while he repaired her own house, but was now delaying moving back. 'The woman say she going to make curtains for me,' Charlo said one evening. 'You could imagine me in a house with curtains?'

I burst out laughing. We were sitting on our verandah, so I could see Charlo's house in the street that backed onto ours. The thing was a ruin: unpainted concrete walls with big wooden windows that were always wide open. He said that was to let thieves see inside his house and know there was nothing to steal. It saved him having to buy locks and remember where he left his keys.

'Sybil don't realise I is a man who does live with the elements,' Charlo muttered. 'When sun come in my window, it's time to get up. She say my house don't have no privacy. What I want privacy for?'

I was relieved to listen to Charlo's problems instead of contemplating my own. The girls I got involved with kept making me feel guilty.

'I feeling like a crayfish,' Charlo muttered. 'Stick up between a rock and a hard place. One side is Sybil . . . next side is curtains for me. I could end up living in a funeral parlour like your mother, and getting heart attack every week like your father.'

'Just say no to curtains,' I suggested with a grin.

But Charlo was really bothered. Sybil was a very nice woman. Too nice. 'It does start with curtain,' he mumbled. 'Next thing it's furniture. And you know where furniture does lead?'

I shook my head.

'Decor, boy, decor!' He slapped my thigh. 'Next thing I, Thomas Nathaniel Charles, living in a focking glass case in your store.'

To cheer him up, I changed the subject. 'What you think about building another pagoda, Charles?'

'Where we going to build pagoda?' he mumbled. 'We don't have space for no more pagoda.'

'We have plenty space,' I told him. 'In Dorado.'

I had long been contemplating building a beach-house in Dorado for my father. The old man was forever saying he wanted to go back there to die. I figured a weekend house there might be a good idea. I had lots of wood, and he had the land he owned with his brother. Just put the two elements together.

'Dorado, eh!' Charlo muttered. 'Might be just the thing to teach Sybil who she dealing with. A building to build all the way in Dorado.' He paused. 'But Dorado does eat house, you know, Bird. That sea-blast is a killer. House does turn into ruin before you finish build it.'

'I studying to use materials they does use to build yacht,' I replied. 'Them thing does eat sea-blast.' Hanging out with Rosemary had given me some ideas. We could use boat paint, copper fittings, the works.

Charlo got up without a word, went home, and came back with a heap of illustrated books. His reference materials had grown over the years. Each time I went to Miami I brought back some additions. Now, he opened a book on Siam. 'Look how they does build wooden house in Thailand,' he said.

We leafed through the pages and grew more and more enthusiastic. 'I was thinking about designing it like one of them cocoa-house in Mr de la Guillame place,' I said. 'With a roof you could slide open and shut, depending on where the sun is.'

Charlo held up a finger. 'The very thing self!' He stared at me. 'But Bird, you turning into a genius! I knew if I wait long enough it would happen.'

The next Saturday, we drove up to Dorado with Mikey. The Saran estate started at the far end of Dorado Village and extended for a couple of miles along the wide stretch of beach to where the bay ended in a peak called Guayaguayare.

'Yes!' Charlo said, as he got out of the car. He stretched his arms wide and took a deep gulp of sea air. 'I think a little time up here will do me good. Get Sybil out of my lungs and them.'

We decided to build at the furthest point, where the beach was narrowest and the land beyond it sloped towards the road. There, you could escape the Dorado sand. Mikey said he would need an engineer to assist him because you had to cater for erosion. We contacted Ashok. Ashok was only too happy to get a private job on the side; his normal work was boring as hell. Then Charlo and I set off for Miami on a hunt for materials. Plastic nails and hinges, plastic window frames.

Normally I hated Miami and made my trips there as short as possible. But being there with Charlo turned out to be an entirely different experience. 'Wait, nuh!' He stopped in his tracks as we left the airport building. 'You think that old lady know her hair pink? Or she blind?'

Where I had found the inhabitants of Miami pathetic and irritating, Charlo found them an endless source of delight. 'You think it have apartheid here?' he whispered. 'Only people over ninety allowed in Miami? And they have to prove it by wearing two-tone shoes?'

Observing Charlo observing Miami was an education. He was absolutely non-judgemental. He just seized on every absurdity the human race had piled up in Florida and got the greatest pleasure possible out of it. He was like a kind of gentle god, gazing at the antics of America from an unshakeable Trinidadian perspective.

'They have a drink named Orgasm,' he said, examining the list in the cocktail lounge of our hotel as we watched half-dead old men tottering around with bouncy young girls. 'You think it's a substitute for sex? Them fellas does give them girls two-three Orgasm a night, and business fix?'

'Well, exchange is no robbery,' I shrugged. 'Where you think that girl get those boobs? Mother nature? I sure she have a bicycle pump under her bed.'

'You think we should order a Orgasm, Bird?'

I shook my head. 'You get me to try pina colada yesterday. Not me and no more American concoctions.'

'Concoction is right,' he replied. 'Drinking that pina colada was like sucking cock. But I feel I should order the Orgasm. Suppose it taste nice? You never know. Imagine when I go back home and people ask me what I was doing in Miami. I could say, "having orgasms", and the fellas in the pan-yard will start picturing me with a bus-load of chicks from *Miami Vice*.'

'Go brave,' I said. 'I sticking to a fruit punch.'

'I going brave,' he said, putting down the menu. 'I feel this could be a Rite of Passage.'

Before we had done anything else in Miami, Charlo had found a book-shop in the telephone directory and had bought an illustrated book called *Rites of Passage* that focused on tribes in Africa. He had kept me in the bookshop for hours while he went through every section, from Architecture to Tropical Plants.

Now, when he took a pull on his Orgasm, he made a face.

'How it taste?' I asked.

'Like a rite of passage.'

I tried a sip. 'Charlo, you damn lie!' I said. 'That thing taste like a wrong of passage.'

He sighed. 'Well, right or wrong, I going to have to drink it now that I order it. It's the black man's burden. Always having to undergo rites of passage.'

As soon as we got back home he moved up to Dorado.

'The plans ain't passed, yet, Charles!'

'I going and start planning the gardens,' he replied. 'I will come down on the weekend and report back.'

He took up residence in one of the broken-down old concrete houses on our estate that had been abandoned by the workers, he and a heap of his illustrated books. When he didn't return the next weekend, I drove up to Dorado. I found him diverting the river that flowed next to our site by digging a channel crossways at the back of where we planned to build the house. He was creating an ornamental pond, he said. 'Dorado nice, boy!' he said. 'Fish broth every day. I feel like a new man. Next weekend I going to come back to town and show Sybil a thing or two.'

Fish broth was reported to be an aphrodisiac.

'Sybil gone AWOL,' I informed him. 'She say you is a dirty dog and she don't want nothing more to do with you.'

I felt sorry for Sybil. To my surprise, neither my mother nor Sarojini did. 'Sybil too damned stupid!' Ma said. 'What she want with a man like Charlo? Charlo don't have two cents in he pocket. Charlo don't even have a pocket to put two cents in.'

'Sybil not stupid,' Saroj argued. 'Sybil smart. She thought if she stay long enough, Charlo wouldn't notice that she was there. She should have looked at Charlo and know he is not a marrieding kind of man. It have man who does married, and man who doesn't married. A big woman should be able to know the difference.'

'So what kind of man I is?' I asked.

Saroj tilted her chubby face and looked at me sideways. 'You? You is a marrieding kind of man. You could see that from the word Go.'

I laughed. 'That's not what the girls say.'

Saroj sucked her teeth. 'That's them kind of stupid girl you does be with,' she replied. 'The minute the right girl catch up with you, your dog's dead.'

I hoped she was right. My love life was depressing. It always ended up in tears. Tears, recriminations and resolutions about self-discipline on my part that never held up under the pressure of a pair of breasts. Ashok said the girls at the tennis club referred to me as 'Close Encounters of the Third Kind'. I began taking refuge in Dorado every weekend.

The house we had designed was extremely simple: a low, wide structure made entirely of wood, with windows opening onto broad patios front and back. 'You call this a beach-house?' my sister Queen demanded when she and her family turned up one weekend on a surprise mission of inspection. 'I call it a shack.'

'You don't have to call it nothing,' I snapped. 'It's just for Pa.'

'Pa?' she replied. 'Pa can't make this long drive.'

I got annoyed. I went to a car-dealer in the city and ordered the most comfortable car they had, a big Jaguar with leather seats and cherrywood dashboard that moved on the road like a hovercraft. With the windows rolled up and the air-conditioning turned on, you heard nothing. You could do eighty miles an hour and you felt like the engine was just idling.

'You going to take my car Dorado to get lick-up with sand and sea-blast?' my mother demanded.

'Your car?'

'Who car, then?' she asked. 'Who money buy that car?'

The beach-house progressed rapidly. We painted the walls a faint pink and laid the patios with big flagstones that absorbed the sun during the day and bathed Charlo's ornamental pond with a deep, red warmth. He left some spaces untiled and set small trees to grow in them. I asked Tony Antoine to produce the best teak kitchen cabinets he could think of, and he designed the counters out of beautiful blue and green Italian tiles. Charlo built a pizza oven in the front patio and made notches in the posts so I could hang a couple of hammocks. On weekends, after working on the house all day, the two of us slid back our cocoa-house roof and lay in the hammocks, watching the stars twinkle beyond the swaying coconut palms.

'That's the Big Dipper over there,' Charlo murmured.

'That's not no Big Dipper, Charles. That's just the oil-rig.' At that point, the Oil and Gas Company of America was drilling off Trinidad's coast. They had nearly exhausted our inland stocks.

'No, Bird,' Charlo insisted. 'The oil-rig is a little to the left.'

'Let's buy a dinghy,' I said. 'We could go and take a look. I never see a oil-rig.'

'The Yanks will shoot us,' he said. 'When Yankee on a oil-hunt they don't like black people around.'

We decided not to go visit the Yankees. Instead, the Yanks visited us.

'A white fella always hanging round here,' Charlo told me. 'He ask me who is the owner of this house.' He turned out to be the site-manager for the drilling platform. He caught up with me one weekend.

'Mr Sayran,' he called. 'Can I have a word with you?' He gave me his card: E. Duncan Rutherford, Operations Manager. E. Duncan Rutherford wanted to rent my beach-house.

'Sorry.' I shook my head. 'This house is not for rent.'

He offered a thousand American dollars a month. I shook my head again.

'How much would you want?' he asked.

'I don't want to rent this house,' I said. 'This house is for my father.'

E. Duncan was back the following weekend. The Oil and Gas Company was willing to pay two thousand dollars.

'Mr Rutherford,' I explained, 'my father is an old man who grew up in Dorado. He wants to spend some time here in his last days. I wouldn't rent this house for any money.'

'I have permission to offer you up to three thousand dollars on a two-year lease,' he said. 'I've convinced the company that it would boost efficiency if I lived closer to the site.' He had obviously spent time with Charlo in the course of the week.

'Rent the man the house, nuh, Bird,' Charlo urged. 'He living all the way in Maraval and have to travel more than four hours to get to work and back every day.'

I looked at Charlo.

'For three thousand US, I could build a better house than this one for your father,' he said.

'Charlo, you know how long my father going to last?' I asked. 'By the time you build a next beach-house, the old man might be kaput.'

'Your father going to live longer than you,' Charlo replied.

And with three thousand US dollars a month, I would recoup my expenses in six months.

'You crazy, Ved?' Pa asked me when I told him. 'Of course you should rent the house.'

My dream of spending every weekend in my hammock at the beach faded. It was Pa's land. He was jubilant that it was turning out to be valuable. 'I always knew it was a good idea to hold on to Dorado,' he told my mother.

In the end, I charged OAG over four thousand dollars a month for the house, complete with furniture, appliances and kitchen equipment from our shop. I pointed out to them that buildings on such a windswept coast were expensive to construct and maintain. They just had to look at other beach-houses in Dorado to see that.

We started building a second beach-house. That one was nowhere near completion when the Yanks stepped in again. 'OAG wants four more houses to rent in Dorado,' E. Duncan stated.

'What happen, E.?' Charlo asked. 'Allyou strike gold out there in that bay?'

'Not gold, boy,' the American replied. 'Gas. Natural gas.'

E. Duncan was beginning to talk like Charlo. The two of them spent a lot of time playing poker on the terrace of the first beach-house in the evenings. E. Duncan's wife was handicapped and fancied herself as an artist. She sat in a wheelchair painting the most god-awful beach scenes you could ever imagine.

'We're flying in a team of specialists from Dallas,' E. said. 'Things have got very complicated. We're talking about five-year leases here.'

'Duncan,' I said. 'I have one-and-a-quarter house on this beach. Where do you expect me to find four?'

'Ved,' Duncan replied, 'don't be an idiot. When OAG asks you for houses to lease, you don't let little things like the non-existence of houses stand in your way. You materialise houses.'

Charlo burst into laughter.

'Let me tell you what you do in a situation like this,' E. Duncan said. 'You ask for a million dollars up front. A million Trinidad dollars to build the houses. Then you organise a team and churn out houses, hell for leather.'

'Duncan,' I said, 'are you aware that I have a builder who doesn't build for three months of the year? Once Carnival time reach, your poker games are history, you know. Mr Charles here will be building Carnival costumes.'

'Who say I bound to build Carnival costume every year?' Charlo asked. 'You feel nigger only born to make mas'?'

I stared at him. 'You will give up making mas' to build these houses?'

'Why not?' he replied. 'This is a rite of passage, boy.'

Duncan raised his eyebrows at me. They were ghostly eyebrows, bleached white by the sun. Duncan was one hell of an ugly son of a bitch, but, as I had begun to discover, he was a very nice guy. 'OAG isn't going to move out of here for at least twenty years,' he said. 'You can keep increasing the costs of your leases every five years. You'll never have to work again. You could just lie in your hammock and fart at the stars. Meanwhile, you charge the company a whopping bill for maintaining the property. Make Charlo here head of maintenance, and I will take every penny he earns from him in poker.'

My life turned upside down. I set up a new company called Saran's Enterprises, of which I was the managing director and my parents were ordinary directors. We paid my uncle a fixed sum per year for his interest in the Dorado property, and then proceeded to plan for mass production of beach-houses. I made Charlo site manager.

'I want a business card,' he said. 'It must say T. Nathaniel Charles.'

'Haul your tail,' I replied. 'I want a holiday. You sitting down here playing poker in the moonlight while I catching my arse buying truck to transport building materials.'

I was having trouble sleeping at night. Things kept whizzing around in my head. I hired an assistant to help me in my office over the store, but she could only perform routine tasks. I had to try and keep everything in my own head: the various materials that had to be ordered, the equipment that was necessary, the workforce that had to be in place once Mikey and Ashok finished drawing the plans and got them approved.

'This is not going to work,' Ashok said one night.

'Don't tell me that,' I said. 'I sign contract already.'

'I quitting,' he said.

I looked up from the calculations I was making. He grinned. 'I quitting my job,' he said. 'You need a construction engineer.'

I was a little dubious about taking on Ashok full-time, but he turned into a godsend. He was actually a very good engineer, full of inventive ideas, who did everything with a zest that eroded obstacles. He could drink all night with the fishermen and be fresh as the contents of their fishing-nets in the morning. And he knew, more than anybody else in Trinidad, how sea-blast worked. He claimed to have sea-blast running in his veins. 'Dorado Beach is an Open Book to me,' he boasted.

Ashok could plot the movement of a crab from one point on the beach to another before the crab itself knew what it was going to do. I ended up leaving a lot of things to him, from deciding on the equipment we needed to searching for skilled construction workers in the villages around Dorado.

'Here,' Nerissa said as I sat in the office one day making telephone calls. 'Drink this.' She had brought me a glass of peanut punch.

'Thanks, Ner,' I said. 'You having any problems downstairs?'

'Not as much problems as you having upstairs,' she said, tapping her head.

I smiled. 'How you know I have problems upstairs?' I asked.

She sucked her teeth. 'Who wouldn't know? You don't even have time to make a little joke these days.'

'Pressure, girl, pressure,' I said as I drained the glass of peanut punch. Then I got up from my chair. 'Talking about pressure, you could hold on here for me while I go and take a piss? I waiting for somebody in Miami to phone me back with some information.'

When I returned, Nerissa was talking on the phone. I flopped down in a chair next to her, in front of a supplier's list. 'Ask them how much they will charge to ship three twenty-gallon water heaters to Trinidad,' I said. 'Must be heavy-duty stainless steel.' I scribbled while she repeated the information she got.

'How soon can they deliver?' I asked.

'Sixty days.'

'What's the cost on a five-hundred-gallon steel water tank?' I rested my head sideways on the desk and looked at Nerissa as she made the enquiries. 'A water pump that can handle those quantities?' I scribbled sideways. 'Tell them we'll call back.' She did. 'OK, now, dial this number and ask the same questions.'

My ear had been chafing from the pressure of the phone that day. Nerissa did the rest of the talking for me. The next afternoon, when the store was quiet, she left it to Suzanne and came upstairs again. I had to go to the bank to finalise line-of-credit arrangements. I compiled a list of materials I needed to order and left Nerissa to the telephone.

'Call Ashok and ask him how much copper piping we need,' I said the following day as I scribbled more lists. 'Shower fittings, stainless-steel fridges and stoves . . .'

'You should take a break, Ved,' Nerissa said. 'You have circles under your eyes.'

I sighed. 'I went up Dorado last weekend and all I could see is work.'

'Don't go Dorado, then. Go somewhere else. I will keep an eye on things here for you.'

I felt a sudden lump in my chest. I was so exhausted, my emotions were close to the surface. And Nerissa was such a darling. She was alert to the customers' needs, to the other employees' needs, to my needs.

Eventually, we were ready to begin the new houses. We were just waiting for the final stamps of approval on the first set of plans we had submitted. Charlo was building a series of wooden bridges at the back of the building site for an extensive water-garden he had in mind. 'Let us take a business trip,' I suggested.

'Where?' he asked.

'Anywhere. Where you want to go?'

'Thailand.'

We left Ashok in charge of the site and went to observe how they built with teak in Thailand. We took Mikey with us, and had the most wonderful holiday. 'Allyou Indian in Trinidad ain't no Indian at all!' Charlo stated. 'Allyou is a set of fraud. Allyou don't have a clue how to cook curry.' He had developed an addiction to Thai green curry. He ate it for breakfast, lunch and dinner.

'I tell you this beach-house thing was a rite of passage,' he said at the night market, his arms full of orchid specimens, lotus seeds, rare fruits. 'I now know what my historic mission in life is: to plant a mangosteen tree in Trinidad. Allyou bring over mango from the East, but forget to bring over mangosteen. I have to make up for the omission. This is the best thing I ever eat, next to Thai green curry.'

'Why you don't bring back a few fried cockroach?' I asked, pointing to a stall selling fried grubs and beetles.

'I bringing back the best and leaving the rest,' he said, waving his hand.

'I studying to import a few silkworm. Imagine me up in Dorado spinning silk? You don't find that will be a historic mission?'

I had bought silk blouses for all the girls in the store. They came in only one size, so I figured they must fit. I bought silk cushions for Suzanne and Saroj.

'What you think about that Chinee dress for Nerissa?' I asked, pointing to a cheongsam hanging in a window.

'Nerissa breasts wouldn't fit in that,' Mikey declared.

Charlo and I turned around and stared at Mikey. 'How you know what size breasts Nerissa have?' we asked.

He shrugged. 'Observation,' he said. 'Allyou fellas does talk. I does observe.'

'Nerissa, boy?' I asked. 'You does observe Nerissa? I does fraid to observe Nerissa. From the time she watch me with them eyes she have, I does forget what I does be observing.'

'You know why Thailand so nice?' Mikey opined. 'Because they never had colonialism here. Look at these dishes.' The Thai crockery was really beautiful, all blue and white curves, like fish-scales. I made a mental note to get some suppliers' lists from Thailand for the shop.

'Everything they make in Thailand have a aesthetic element,' Mikey nattered on. 'From the smallest tamarind ball to little plastic bags with curry in them.'

'I hate to disillusion you, Mikey,' Charlo said, 'but what I see in Patpong last night didn't have no aesthetic element.'

Charlo and I had taken a trip to the red-light district. It had turned our stomachs. We had watched a little Thai girl pull razor blades out of her vagina.

'This place is Sodom and Gomorrah,' Charlo went on. 'They does make nice tamarind ball, they does make nice flower garland, they does make nice curry. But this is focking Sodom and focking Gomorrah! When I see that girl pull that razor blade out her pussy last night, my balls shrink! I feel I going to join a monastery. I don't want nothing more to do with this nastiness called sex.'

Charlo's flirtation with celibacy was short-lived; it only lasted till we finished building the first of our new houses. We were celebrating that event at the rumshop in the village when fire broke out at the Dorado

Library. There was nothing anyone could do, since the village standpipe was broken, so, while the fire was growing, we helped Dorado's librarian rescue the books and take them to her house. By the following week, Miss Reyes, the librarian, had started dispensing books out of her living-room, so Charlo built her some shelves. The next thing we knew was that he and Miss Reyes were an item. 'I only ask the lady if she have a cookbook with a recipe for Thai green curry,' he explained. 'Next thing I know, she inviting me for dinner. Well, you know I don't back down from free food.'

Eighteen months later, our houses were completed and OAG was drawing up a new contract for us to build smaller cottages for its bachelor staff. Miss Reyes, now known as Cassandra, was still dispensing books from her living-room. I had workers sitting idle, so I offered to repair the library for free. Cassandra said I had to contact the Ministry of Education. They said I had to tender for the project. I got a form from the Government Tenders Board and offered to do the job for one dollar payable over five years. The Tenders Board informed me that I had omitted to fill in the tender number. There was no tender number for the Dorado Library.

We completed the bachelor accommodation, and Cassandra was still lending out books from her home. By that time, our compound had become Dorado's biggest employer. Its occupants hired housekeeping services from the village, and we supplied a maintenance crew for the grounds. Charlo's water-gardens had turned into something spectacular, with little waterfalls and windmills, ferns and orchids and bamboo and lotuses, every tropical creeper and flowering plant in existence, crabs and squirrels, bird-feeders and wind-chimes, and benches made of driftwood.

The bachelors started demanding a swimming pool, tennis court and recreation centre. We drew up plans that included a commissary, library and video-screening centre.

While waiting for these to be approved, Ashok took a crew over to the library and started rebuilding it. We received an official complaint from the Ministry of Education that we were trespassing on their property. We ignored it. I received a legal summons charging me with damage to government property.

By then, Charlo was planning his Dorado Community Library Reopening Ceremony. He invited the MP for Dorado to cut the ribbon. Symphonia performed and the Dallas cowboys who occupied our new houses jumped up and down in an attempt at dancing. Dorado's Catholic priest blessed the new building and the primary school's choir sang. The MP made a long,

long speech full of statistics about how much money the government had provided in the budget for education. Cassandra, who was sitting next to the MP, sucked her teeth in a rare display of vulgarity. The sound travelled over the crowd via the loudspeaker and she hid her face in her hands.

In this phase, we finally fulfilled our original plan: we built a beach-house for my father. My sisters promptly appropriated it. When I took Pa to Dorado on weekends, the place was full of their families, complete with servants, in-laws and hangers-on. When my brother came to Trinidad on holiday, he also took up residence in Dorado. Robin had been called to the English Bar by this time and when I arrived on weekends, I found myself in the dock.

'How you does get so much lawsuit?' he asked. 'The Dorado Library, now the Dorado standpipe. What you have against Dorado?'

'Look, I never damage no standpipe,' I said. 'Go and ask the stand-pipe. Our plumbers repaired the standpipe.'

'So why they charge you?' Robin persisted.

'They couldn't find anybody else to charge.'

The Dorado standpipe had been broken for months, with water spilling from its base while villagers couldn't get water during the dry season. It was located next to the market, so when Water Authority staff turned up three weeks after our plumbers, the vendors threw rotten tomatoes at them. Things got a bit heated and cabbages followed the tomatoes. There weren't so many cabbages around, but Dorado produced a lot of water-melons in the dry season and, with the drought that year, there was over-supply. Watermelons followed the cabbages, like dessert after a meal.

'You should have learned your lesson,' Robin said. 'Stay away from standpipe. Now why they charging you with stealing water?'

'Look,' I tried to appeal for sympathy, 'the Dorado people see us putting up big-big water tanks for the Yanks on our site, while they don't have water most of the day. They asked us to install one for them at the stand-pipe. The Catholic priest say they will pay for it.'

Robin heaved a sigh. Robin could heave a sigh like he was wearing a judge's wig. 'Boy,' he said, 'this kind of Mickey Mouse business you running here . . . You have no right interfering with Water Authority instal-lations. You didn't know that when you went putting up tank and pump?'

I sucked my teeth. 'I didn't even know I was putting up tank and pump. Charlo and Ashok do that.'

He stared at me. 'Ved, it's not a company you running, it's a republic! Your underlings throwing tank, pump, all kinds of expensive things around the countryside like watermelon in the dry season? What else you does install in Dorado unknown to you?'

'Ved doesn't deal with this building site,' Queen said. 'Just the rumshop.'

Convicted. No point in mentioning that I didn't drink at the rumshop, just hung out with the boys. Being at the Dorado rumshop was, in itself, a disapprovable offence in my family.

Eventually, I began staying instead with Ashok's family in their rambling old estate house near the village. Charlo was still theoretically occupying a dilapidated worker's house there, though he was often to be found at Cassandra's, conducting, as he put it, experiments in Thai green curry. To my surprise Pa chose to join me at my uncle's house, installing himself in a hammock made from a dingy old jute bag to reminisce with other crumbling Dorado geezers who dropped by. He only went down to the beach-houses occasionally to strut around and chat with the Dallas cowboys, letting them know that they were talking with the Owner. 'Ved? Ved is my son,' he would say. 'He is the one who does the business. But this land belonged to my grandfather. This, here, where we're standing, used to be a thriving coconut estate, you know. At that time, coconut oil was as valuable as the oil that you does now drill for.'

I had business under control by then. Or rather, my team had the business under control. Nerissa managed day-to-day operations at the Croissee headquarters while Suzanne ran the shop. Charlo and Ashok took care of things in Dorado. Tony had a beautiful operation going in Santa Cruz, supplying the beach-houses with cupboards and a new range of lounge furniture which had turned into an exclusive line that took the luxury resorts of the Caribbean by storm.

One day when I was going into the city to see my lawyer about the Dorado Library case, Pa put on his best shirt-jac. He had decided he was coming with me. As I concluded my business, Pa disclosed that he had business of his own to conduct.

'I want to make my will,' he announced.

The lawyer drew a fresh notepad towards him. 'How many children do you have?' he asked, looking up.

Pa shook his head. 'Don't mind that,' he said. 'I want to leave everything I own to my son, Ved Prakash Saran.'

'It might cause some problems with your other children, you know,' the lawyer pointed out.

Pa shrugged. 'How I will have problems?' he asked. 'I will be dead.'

Chapter Five

I was the one who started having problems.

These began, I believe, the day some arbitrary guy got his penis lopped off. This guy had nothing to do with me. I never heard his name, never met him, and don't even remember how he got the thing sliced off. At the beginning, he was just one character in Saroj's huge stock of penis stories. He got filed away in my mind with the other guys who came into Casualty with their pricks stuck in Coke bottles, etcetera. But this prick started haunting conversations at Saroj's house.

'The man wrap the penis in a handkerchief and make his wife put it in a cooler full of ice,' her husband George enthused. 'I salute that man. That was presence of mind!' George was the leading consultant surgeon in the public service. He had rushed to theatre and sewn the penis back on.

'That man have good tissue!' he exclaimed the next time I went to visit. 'If you see how the prick growing back. Nerves, blood vessels, everything.'

A couple of weeks later, when I arrived at their house, he sprang out of his lair. 'Put it there, Ved!' he said, holding out his palm for me to slap it. 'The thing working!'

'What thing working?'

'The prick, boy!' He put his fist to his crotch and made a rude pumping gesture. 'Good as new!'

He opened a bottle of champagne that evening. He sat back on the porch with a big, stupid-looking smile on his face. He had achieved an international first; no one had got a penis to resume action before this.

Unknown to the Trinidad population, George became a medical celebrity. He gave talks on his prick at international conferences. Within a couple of months he was offered a job to do medical research at a top institute in Boston.

'Brain drain,' Saroj commented the night they told me the news. 'The Americans want to drain George brain. He going to lead a team of prick-specialists. Had to be a Trini, eh?'

'If this blasted Trinidad government wasn't so shitty, I wouldn't have accepted the offer,' George said. 'But half the operating theatres in the hospital not working. I fed up.'

I was happy for him. But it led me to thinking about my own life. I was twenty-three by now, but was becoming aware that no one would ever invite me to lead a team of specialists anywhere in the world. I wasn't a specialist in anything, or was ever going to become one. I could have become a surgeon too. I had steady hands, and the academic part of the training was easy. 'Any dog-and-cat could be a doctor,' Saroj often said. 'You don't need brains for that.' But I had thrown away my chances of getting professional training. I had let my easy successes in business lure me into a pattern of life that was leading nowhere.

After Saroj and George left Trinidad, these thoughts began to haunt me. I sat on my verandah in the evenings cursing myself. All my old schoolmates were now doctors or lawyers or engineers. They could one day end up like George. When I met them I could sense a patronising attitude. What was I? Just a guy who made money.

And I didn't even do that properly, according to my brother Robin. He maintained that our business was leaking money like a fisherman's net. 'You think you is the government,' he said when he visited. 'In England, the government foots the bill for health insurance.'

'In Trinidad,' I informed him, 'foot does get chop off because the government hospital don't have tetanus injection. The day one of my employees step on a nail and dead in the casualty department, I have to go and pick up his hammer to keep production on schedule.'

Robin had grown heavy in England and whatever he said had the weight of international experience. He sparked a lot of complaints against me when he was in Trinidad. 'Ved don't have a clue what racket Charlo and Ashok running up in Dorado,' Ma told him.

'Ma,' I asked, 'you want to go up Dorado and check up on Charlo and Ashok? Be my guest. I busy holding down things here.' Ma had never been to Dorado in all the years we were working there.

'But I thought you said Nerissa does hold down things here?' Robin asked. 'That's why you paying her more than I making as a lawyer in London, with all that pension rights and profit-sharing.'

'Nerissa worth more to me than a lawyer in London,' I snapped.

I often urged Robin to come back to Trinidad and take over some of the responsibility for the business. It would make it a lot of fun, I figured.

When he wasn't playing lawyer, Robin was a lot of fun. He would go out onto the front balcony, open his arms wide, look over the dirt and grime of the Eastern Main Road, and inhale deeply. 'Bacteria, boy! I can taste the bacteria. Once you have third-world bacteria running in your veins, you never get rid of it.'

'Why you don't come back and eat bacteria full-time?' I often asked. 'That fish and chips not doing you any good. You will dead of a heart attack before you hit forty.'

He glanced at the house behind him. 'You think I could take on your mother and father full-time? They will kill me faster than fish and chips.'

Robin had never forgiven Pa his harshness when we were children. Ma had never changed. The two of them were more dangerous than bacteria, he maintained.

'That old man is a toothless tiger,' I urged.

'Toothless? That old man is a viper. He only playing dead to catch corbeaux alive. You see how he have you tie up in knots till you don't know whether you coming or you going? You escape him when you was small. He taking his revenge now.'

He caused me to remember Charlo's warning when my father had had his second heart attack. Why hadn't Charlo been more insistent, I asked myself. Then I remembered Jason's fall into the river. I should have been more insistent then, myself. I had always blamed myself for not taking a look at the liana and preventing that little fool from falling into the river. I still felt guilty towards his mother, who sent me a Christmas card every year, full of maudlin wishes that God would bless me for the help I had given her. They always made me feel bad. She had entrusted her son to me, and I hadn't gone that last mile to protect him from himself.

'What happen to you now?' Nerissa asked me one day. 'Love life again?'

I sucked my teeth. 'Ain't have no love life, girl.'

Looking back now, it's easy to see that she had put her finger on the problem. Charlo was enmeshed in Cassandra's arms up in Dorado while I was stuck in town, provoking arguments with my mother for entertainment. I was glad that Ashok came to town often, partially to bug Nerissa.

'Let us go out for lunch,' he would nag her.

'Me? Go out for lunch with you?' She would snort. 'For people to think I stupid?'

'What about if we get married?' he asked. 'If you and me get married, you will go out for lunch with me?'

'Me?' Nerissa would point at her chest. 'Get married? That and God's face you will never see.'

Nerissa's attitude intrigued me. Suzanne had told me lots of guys were after Nerissa, but Nerissa ignored them. 'You don't ever want to get married, Nerissa?' I asked her once during a quiet period in the office.

'Married?' she asked. 'What that good for?'

I shrugged. She screwed up her nose.

'I see enough people married to know that not for me,' she said, raising her eyebrows. 'You see what happen to Suzanne?'

Suzanne's husband, Hypolite, had turned out to be a womaniser of the worst sort. They had two children now and Suzanne rushed home every afternoon to look after them while Hypolite was screwing down the town, as Nerissa put it.

'I have three sisters,' Nerissa told me. 'If I had to live with any one of their husbands, it would be murder and suicide.'

'What wrong with their husbands?' I asked.

She stared at me. 'Nothing,' she said eventually. 'Nothing special. They just like every other man.'

'Man is such a bad species?' I ventured.

She chuckled. 'You should know for yourself. You's a man.' When I said nothing further, she leaned towards me. 'Ved,' she said, 'let me ask you something. When last you wash a plate?'

I shrugged. I couldn't remember ever washing a plate. We had a maid called Sylvia who washed plates.

'When last you iron a shirt?' Nerissa went on. 'When last you cook?' When I didn't reply she pointed at her chest. 'You see me? I just like you. I don't cook, I don't wash, I don't iron. I does work and support my mother. When I go home in the evening, I does take a shower, drop on my couch, and put up my two foot. You find I should exchange that for having some man hassle me?' She shook her head. 'Nah! If I have to get married, I will married my couch. I does get along good with my couch. At least I know where my couch does be twenty-four hours a day.'

I could only laugh. In a way, I admired her logical approach. Nerissa was an extremely busy woman. Apart from her work, she was now doing courses in accounting at the extra-mural department of the university. I had written her a strong recommendation to make up for the fact that she didn't have the required secondary-school certificates, and she talked the supervisor of the programme into letting her in. Saran's Enterprises paid her fees and I had promised her a whopping raise once she got her diploma.

'But you don't ever want to have a child, or something?' I asked her.

Nerissa tilted her head and considered me. Then she started to laugh. She laughed deep in her chest. Nerissa had a low voice, and everything seemed to come from deep within. 'I have a something,' she sputtered eventually. 'I have you.'

Nerissa didn't mean to hurt my feelings that day. She was a very kind person. But, in a way, that was the problem. Nerissa and Charlo treated me like I was a spoilt kid they indulged in spite of themselves. If I grumbled about some tedious form I had to fill out, Nerissa grabbed it out of my hands and filled it out for me. If I forgot to do something, by the time I realised it, Nerissa had done it. Sometimes I wondered if she deliberately kept me dependent on her. She came from a very poor family: her mother had left her alcoholic father when Nerissa was eleven, and had become a vendor at Tunapuna Market to support her children. As the oldest daughter, Nerissa had helped her, and she often quoted her market-vendor experience when we had difficulties in the business. 'OAG pushing their luck,' she would say when the oil company made requests we didn't feel comfortable with. 'They don't know I used to sell in Tunapuna Market. Tell them we will replace furniture As Necessary. Not every three years.'

As Necessary was one of the phrases she had learnt at the extra-mural department. In Due Course was another one. 'What you mean by In Due Course, Nerissa?' I asked, reading a letter she had composed for me to sign.

'In due course mean: When I Damned Well Feel Like Doing It.'

Sometimes Nerissa spoke in capital letters. You heard them.

We were building furniture for OAG's city headquarters then. The oil company had bought an old French villa in the poshest part of the city, near the Prime Minister's office, and were restoring it to its original state. The whole thing was wood. The architect on that job was the same eccentric Englishman we had worked with on the convention centre, and he had come directly to us. Mr Antoine was in paradise. He and the Englishman conducted endless squabbles over Louis Quinze and such-like. It took several bottles of rum to resolve their differences. Tony put together a special crew to supply the building with fretwork, columns, friezes, God-knows-what.

Everybody had their jargon nowadays. Tony had his friezes, Nerissa had her As Necessaries, Mr Antoine had his Louis Quinze. What did I have? 'I feel I getting to be de trop around here,' I said. 'I feel to leave allyou arse and go away somewhere.' I had begun thinking about university again. Where? To study what? I would figure that out later.

'Nah,' Nerissa said. 'We need you here.'

'For what?' I asked, hoping to hear something nice from her for once.

'For Grand Openings,' she said, flinging an embossed invitation at me. OAG was planning a Grand Opening of its new headquarters.

'Go in my place, nuh,' I begged.

She shook her head. 'You have to Show Your Face.'

I had to Show My Face at all ceremonial events. Showing My Face was a Pain In the Ass, but Nerissa wouldn't brook any argument. 'Try getting pneumonia,' she said. 'If you show me a doctor's certificate, I will let you stay home.'

I knew she was right. To OAG bigwigs in Trinidad, I was a favourite son: a Go-Getter, a Guy Who Didn't Let Sand Grow Under His Feet, a Puller-Upper by the Bootstraps . . . They trotted out these phrases to my face, not knowing that I cringed inside. I was a Would-Be Surgeon, dammit! I hardly knew what to say at these bloody PR events. The US ambassador's wife had taken to rescuing me, blabbing on about furniture for her residence.

'Don't fock up that embassy contract, eh, Ved,' Tony warned me darkly.

'Fock up contract?' I warned back, even more darkly. 'You think it's contract that in danger of getting fock up? Good thing I don't drink and lose touch with my eyesight any more. Otherwise we end up with a Diplomatic Incident on our hands.'

Tony was a right proper pimp. He sold me to the highest bidders in the guise of Interior Design. How did I become an Interior Designer? I certainly had no ambitions in that area. Interior designers didn't leave Footprints in the Sands of Time. That bullshit had started the night the Australian cricket team invaded our pan-yard and the Australian ambassador's wife had decided she wanted us to redo her residence. She then invited the US ambassador to dinner with his wife.

Now, getting caught in the sights of an American ambassador's wife is no easy matter. It's like contracting malaria: you never get rid of it. Every time you start to relax, another bout hits you. The US embassy held Fourth of July celebrations and served hot dogs and baseball caps. The caps tasted better than the dogs, I told Nerissa afterwards. Then they held Thanksgiving. They held Christmas and New Year. They even took it into their heads to hold a Carnival Party.

'Why you don't send me in your place?' Ashok suggested. 'I could handle Mrs Ambassadress. I don't find she so bad. She's only about sixty-five. I could always put a paper bag over her face.'

'Next thing Trinidad getting shelled by the US,' Charlo mumbled. 'Don't give them an excuse, nuh! You see all that natural gas out there? They will invade Trinidad at the drop of your pants.'

And, as a Single Man, once you slip onto one embassy invitation list in Port of Spain, it's hell to pay. Folks desperately need Single Men some-times, especially when they were hosting cocktail parties. There, all wives saw me as a conduit to eleegant decor. Give a woman from the upper echelons of Trinidad society two drinks, and her mind immediately drifts towards wooden furniture.

'Wooden furniture?' Ashok asked. 'Or just plain wood?'

I shrugged.

You see how this section of the book is declining into vulgarity? That's the effect of cocktail parties. Why do you think they call them cock-tail parties? You have to wake yourself up afterwards with some blood-and-guts-and-semen talk, just to know you're still alive. And the women on the cocktail circuit weren't the worst. At least they liked me. There were the men.

The local businessmen pretended I was invisible. I was an interloper, a coolie with a capital C. Whoever heard of a Coolie Construction Company? What did a Coolie know about Louis Quinze? And to the government officials, I was a Sharp Operator. Whenever I said to the OAG guys that we had to wait for official approvals, they got on the phone to the Minister of Energy, a lethargic little man who looked like he suffered from hookworm. OAG had no time for Banana Republic Bureaucracy. And the quicker natural gas could be pumped out of Dorado, the sooner the government would get its royalty payments. It all worked in my favour. Now, as Ashok said, the Town and Country Department was an Open Book to us. Our plans went directly to its Head. He sent them through the bowels of bureaucracy like a dose of castor oil.

This didn't endear me to government ministers. I had no reason to fawn on them at official events. When OAG's head honcho tried to draw me into the in-crowd by introducing me to the Prime Minister at the opening of its new headquarters, the Old Goat nodded without holding out his hand. 'I know Mr Saran,' he murmured distantly, like 'Saran' was local slang for Tuberculosis. 'The man with the wood.'

I wriggled out of that group. I was woodworm in these rarefied circles where power and kickbacks hovered in the air like spittle.

'But them fellas don't even do kickback good,' Charlo pointed out. E. Duncan had told us how much the contract for the exploitation of Trinidad's natural gas had cost OAG in kickbacks: a blonde for a night in a Montreal hotel. The Minister of Energy had flown up to New York to examine documents OAG had prepared. He let them know he wanted to proceed to Montreal for the night and they offered him use of a corp-orate jet and picked up the tab for his entire visit to North America. 'He specified a blonde.' E. Duncan nearly pissed himself laughing. 'A rent-a-blonde in a Montreal hotel. We'd have *given* him a blonde for that kind of contract.'

Corruption was now an Open Book to us, though I refused to let anyone in my company get near it; I didn't need money enough to be tempted into murky waters. Police stations within a radius of ten miles of the Croissee loathed my shadow. Businessmen were supposed to give policemen favours, but I operated a strict policy in my businesses. Any crackpot who came in with a donation list got a donation. Didn't matter if they were the Scouts, the Seventh Day Adventists or some madman trying to start a new political party. Let a thousand flowers bloom, I said to my managers. Let weeds bloom. If rocks want to bloom, give them a few dollars to do it with. The quantity of dollars was discretionary, but no beggar was to be turned away, just given a quick buck and asked politely to leave. But policemen didn't beg or bring in donation lists. They had a kind of leaky grin instead. Leaky grin wasn't on my list of reasons for giving away anything.

One day, Ashok came to my office with a proposal that we take a busi-ness trip to Germany. The Minister of Transport, plus entourage, had just been to Germany to buy buses from Mercedes Benz. We ourselves were buying a couple of Mercedes trucks at the time. Ashok said we would be well entertained by the Mercedes sales department if we went to the factory to buy our trucks. 'You know what they mean by entertainment?' he asked, jiggling his eyebrows. 'The marketing manager gave me a blow-by-blow account of the minister's trip. And I use the word "blow" in its broadest sense.'

He claimed he was overworked and could use a break. 'And you use the word "break" in its broadest sense,' I laughed. 'Break' was local slang for orgasm.

'Yes, boy,' he said. 'I feel a nervous break-down approaching. Let us go and fock some fraulein. Free. At Mercedes' expense.'

I frowned. Prostitutes didn't appeal to me in the least. And Ashok was just fantasising; he couldn't leave the site for a couple of months. And I was too busy at that moment to fantasise with him. Robin was arriving in Trinidad that afternoon, and I had big plans for his visit. 'If I want to fock fraulein free,' I said, 'I will go down by the German embassy. You will have to take your Break in a seaside resort named Dorado. Go there and fock jellyfish. Free.'

Nerissa came into my office with some papers. 'Not even jellyfish will let Ashok . . .' She dissolved into laughter.

'Nerissa,' Ashok held up a finger. 'You really don't know what you saying, you know. I have jellyfish lining up for me. Begging. I does tell them I saving myself for you.'

When I was finished with my work, I stopped in at Nerissa's room next door. 'You does really give Ashok a hard time,' I observed. 'He really like you, you know.'

She stared at me, her dark eyes like velvet in her face. 'I look like some fraulein?' she asked.

I rocked back in embarassment. 'You heard that conversation?'

'Ved,' she said, 'I does hear everything that does go on in your office. I think you should soundproof it. That Jamaican fraulein who does drop in sometimes have a real loud voice.' She looked down at the papers I had handed her. 'And I use the word fraulein in its broadest sense.'

I stared at her curly hair. She had recently had it cut and it fell around in nice shiny waves. 'Next time Miss Jamaica comes, tell her I'm not here,' I said, rushing out of the office to get to the airport, my mind quickly switching to my plans for my brother's visit.

Robin maintained that I had had it easy because I was the last child, the indulged one, the pet of the family. While he had been busting his ass in cold England, subsisting on the pittance Pa sent him while he studied law, I had been basking in growing Saran wealth. I had a swimming pool, a Jaguar, a hammock of my own and all the mangoes I could eat. I suspected Robin was torn between Trinidad and England. He would have to wait till he became a QC to enjoy the luxuries I did, and he could still never have the sunshine and the mangoes.

Robin longed for mangoes. He attacked them like a jaguar each time he returned. He dreamed of tomato chokha and fried bake. He spoke of pigeon-peas dhal like Ashok spoke of frauleins. 'What Sylvia cook today?' was his first question every time I phoned him.

'Dhal and rice and fried fish.'

'Oh, God, boy! Don't tell me that. You ain't have a heart? You could have tell me allyou fasting for Ramadan or something!'

'We ain't Muslim. We don't fast for Ramadan.'

'You could have lie! Ved, you don't know the truth could kill? Just don't tell me she make tamarind chutney to go with the fried fish. Do not tell me that, brother!'

Now, as I drove to the airport to pick him up, leaving Sylvia behind me developing a vast menu, I was planning my strategy. I was not going to get trapped into arguments about the business on this visit. I was going to trap Robin instead. His mango lust and curry nostalgia were my weapons. Robin and I were going to exchange places. Money was no object for the scion of the Sarans. I had learnt how OAG operated. You shrug off all the petty details. You put an offer on the table that undermines your opponent's expectations.

What I didn't take account of was that Robin could develop his own plans. It was these plans that would lead me to Anji.

Book Two

ANJI,
FINALLY

'The stripped man is driven back to that self-astonishing, elemental force, his mind. That is the basis of the Antillean experience, this shipwreck of fragments, these echoes, these partially remembered customs, and they are not decayed but strong.'

'The Antilles: Fragments of Epic Memory', The Nobel Lecture
Derek Walcott, 1992

Chapter Six

'Are you ready for some bacteria?' I asked, as Robin came out of the Arrivals area.

He slapped me on the back. 'Lead me to your bacteria!' He held up a thick, hairy finger. 'But first! Congratulations are in order.'

He had grown a moustache. It made him look like a crook.

'You,' he said, jabbing the hairy finger at my chest, 'might think you looking at a little coolie boy from Trinidad.' He paused for effect. 'But,' he put on a deep voice, 'you actually looking,' he pointed at his own chest, 'at the legal representative of the Duchess of Peale.'

He had got a place as a junior in one of London's top legal chambers. The Duchess of Peale would never see Robin; he would just be doing the research on her cases. But he didn't want to see her anyway, he said, she was ugly as sin and twice as bad-tempered. What he wanted to see were her Refreshers.

'You know what kind of refreshers these royal pains in the ass does pay, boy?'

'You will pay your own DHL bill in future, then?' I commented. I had taken to sending him fruit by international courier. It had started as a surprise for his birthday and cost me a staggering sum. He had nagged me into turning it into a habit, ringing me collect to inform me that he knew the sapodilla season had started in Trinidad.

'Sapodilla?' He waved his hand grandly in dismissal. 'What is sapodilla to me? I going to import sapodilla by the crate. Rabindranath Saran, Sapodilla Supplier to Her Majesty.'

'And the pigeon peas? Pigeon peas don't travel, you know. Her Majesty's legal representative will still be tied to Trinidad by his navel-string.'

He held up a finger again. 'I have a plan for the pigeon peas. All will be revealed in due course. But first! You ever hear about the Duchess's driving skills? Every week she in court on some bad driving charge. At two hundred pounds an hour.'

Scuppered. Plan A was in danger of being scuppered. Robin's career in London was looking up. I decided to let him settle down. After a few days of Sylvia's cooking, things might begin to look different. I had a whole six weeks to lead him to the slaughter. And I had a secret weapon. Coconut Chutney. I had recently discovered Sylvia's genius with Coconut Chutney. It would be Royal Refresher versus Coconut Chutney. The Battle of the Titanics. A Battle for the Soul of Rabindranath Saran – or, at least, for the belly.

I could have saved myself the scheming. The next morning, after Robin had consumed about twenty pounds of tomato chokha, he unveiled his plan. He was leaning on the door-jamb between the kitchen and the verandah, his usual stake out when he was in Trinidad, looking dazed from the tomato-chokha. Ma was picking rice at the table on the verandah. Nobody could pick rice clean enough to suit Ma, and by now she had enough cleaned rice in tins in an empty bedroom to feed the population of Tobago. But she never stopped. Other women knit; my mother picked rice.

Suddenly Robin shook off his tomato-chokha-induced somnolence. 'By the way, Ma,' he said, 'I want to get married.'

'To who?'

Ma's boxing gloves were out. You could hear them in her voice. I lowered the newspaper I was reading. Plan B was under attack. If Robin had contracted Love in London, my ass was grass. I was stuck with Saran's Enterprises till my dying day. I might as well give up and grow a belly and a moustache like his.

Robin shrugged. 'Don't know,' he said.

Ma's eyes narrowed. 'So this Miss Don't-Know living in England?' she asked.

'Nah!' he drawled. 'She living somewhere in Trinidad.'

'Oh, you been writing to her,' Ma said. 'Miss Don't-Know, Somewhere, Trinidad and Tobago.'

'Not Tobago,' demurred Robin. 'I don't want no big-bottomed woman.'

'Oh?' Ma resumed her rice-picking. 'You know the size of Miss Don't-Know bottom then. What else you going to tell us about her?'

He tilted his head back to rest against the door-jamb. 'She have hair down to her back . . . a shy smile . . . And she could cook a damned good dhal and rice and bhaji!'

Robin had decided that Ma should find him a bride. The specifications he gave her were actually a menu. Cachourie. She should be able to make a good crisp cachourie. Curried channa, fried alloo . . .

'You want me,' Ma pointed at her chest, 'to find a girl, engage she, and married you in . . . what it is . . . six weeks?'

'Well,' Robin replied, 'if you could manage it in four weeks it would be better. We could have a little honeymoon in Barbados before I go back.'

Ma pushed away the rice and trained her gaze on him. 'What the hell I does be hearing here?' she asked. 'Like England only get you more stupid? You get worse than your father. You know what it does take to have a Hindu wedding?' She started counting on her fingers. 'You have to check the Patra and make sure the horoscope match, get a good date for the wedding –'

'I not too fussy about the wedding,' Robin interrupted her. 'If push come to shove, we could get married in the registry. But the fry alloo must have the right degree of crispiness and the right degree of softness.'

Ma opened her eyes wide and took a deep breath. 'Registry?' she bellowed. 'You expect me,' she pointed at her chest, 'to married my first son in the Port of Spain registry like one of them nigger who don't have a khaki pants to cover he bottom? Boy,' she swept another heap of rice towards her with her hand, 'you didn't get stupid in England! You get mad! You put a foot in any registry and you don't ever cross my doorstep again.'

'Ma,' I said gently, 'Robin don't want you to married him. He want Miss Don't-Know to married him.'

She looked up sharply. 'Why the arse you don't mind your own business?' she spat. 'You always busy. How come you not busy now?'

'I take time off to spend with my brother. Boy,' I said, scraping back my chair and getting up, 'come with me. We will see if Miss Don't-Know lurking somewhere on Maracas Beach. If we don't find her, at least we might find a good bake-and-shark.'

Ma glared at us. 'Yes,' she called to Robin's back as we left, 'you pull your tail and go Maracas to eat bake-and-shark while I here looking for girl for you all over Trinidad . . .'

I clung to my hopes in the following weeks. I bided my time like a snake. Each time Ma and Robin returned from their bride-hunting expeditions they were enmeshed in argument. 'She wasn't so bad-looking . . .' Robin would plead. 'Not so bad-looking? You didn't only go mad in England! You went blind too! You didn't see the size of that girl nose? It was longer than my foot!'

She would get on the telephone to my sisters. 'Roopsingh granddaughter?' I would hear her saying. 'I see that girl in Sona funeral. She have two left foot! She nearly fall down on the coffin. I say the dead man would have end up on the ground.'

'Why you don't just marry Sylvia?' I asked Robin. Sylvia was fifty-four and had six grandchildren.

'Sylvia husband don't know the danger he in,' Robin muttered darkly. 'If British immigration regulations wasn't so stringent, I load Sylvia in a crocus bag and smuggle her out of the country.'

'Sylvia is a Jehovah's Witness!' Ma snapped. 'I don't want no Jehovah Witness daughter-in-law! Next thing my grandchildren trying to sell me *Watchtower.*'

Tension rose in the house as the weeks began to slip by. I whistled Christmas carols.

'That girl from Penal, Ma,' Robin urged. 'That girl from Penal. The one who invent cucumber chutney. That is a inventive sort of girl. Maybe she could invent curry apple.'

Ma sucked her teeth. 'You believe that story about inventing cucumber chutney? You don't know Penal people does lie? That girl grandmother make the chutney. I could see it all over her face. And you see the size of that girl foot? No, you wasn't looking at foot! You does let a little chutney get you stupid. I see the foot. It don't have a pair of shoes in England to fit that girl foot. You will have to import them from Penal.'

'You don't study thing like love, boy?' I asked Robin once when my parents weren't around.

'Love?' Robin asked. 'What is that? Since when Indian does study love? Look at your mother and father, they perfect for each other: a match made in hell. I know all about love. I know I could love any girl that could make a coconut chutney like Sylvia's.'

I whistled calypsos. Time was on my side. The only danger was that Robin would go behind Ma's back and marry the girl from Cunupia with the secret recipe for curried coconut jelly. But Ma had promised him he wouldn't inherit a penny of Saran money if he did, so I was keeping my fingers crossed.

'What about Nerissa?' Robin asked one morning after his daily dose of tomato chokha. 'She is a damned nice woman.' He made a curving gesture in the air with his hands. I sputtered into my tea.

'Nerissa is Muslim!' Ma snapped.

'Muslim does make nice sawaine . . .' Robin's face took on a dreamy look. 'You ever eat a Muslim paratha roti? And a long-water curry goat?' He turned to me. 'Nerissa have a boyfriend?'

I shrugged. 'I don't ask Nerissa her personal business. You will have to find out for yourself.'

The next day, Nerissa stopped me as I was going out of the office. 'Ved,' she said, her eyes troubled, 'what going on? Like allyou don't trust me, or what? Why your brother coming in here asking me to explain my accounting procedures to him?'

I felt bad. 'Don't worry about him, Ner. Just tell him any questions about the business should be directed at me.'

Her eyes followed me out the door.

The next day, she had a new question. 'What it is really happen to your brother? Why he always coming in here to chat? He don't know we have work to do?'

'He just idle,' I said. 'He on holiday.'

She narrowed her eyes and shook her head. 'He not just idle. He gone beyond idle. It have more in the mortar than the pestle. I could smell rotten fish from a mile. I used to sell in Tunapuna Market.'

'Why you don't tell him that?' I asked.

She eyes looked like pools of troubled water. 'I did tell him that. You know what that man tell me? He say, then I must know how to choose good pumpkin!'

I started to shake with laughter. She stared at me in puzzlement. I figured I owed it to her to come clean so I sat down on the chair next to her desk. 'Robin looking to get married,' I explained. You are one of the candidates.'

She began to laugh as well. 'And you didn't tell him my philosophy of marriage?'

I shrugged. 'Nerissa, girl,' I said, 'I never know how people does react when it come to things like marriage. Look at Suzanne and Hypolite. I was the one who offered to bet money that Suzanne would never take him on.'

Nerissa nodded thoughtfully. 'I think she only take him on because he was a schoolteacher,' she said.

I raised my eyebrows. 'And Robin is a lawyer. Not a pot-hound like me. He is a big-time lawyer in London.'

She looked at me and scratched her face, nodding all the while. 'Well,' she said. 'I want you to give your big-time London-lawyer brother a message from me.' She paused and leaned forward. 'Tell him I am not no Fraulein.'

Robin eventually grew desperate. 'I only have three more weeks in Trinidad,' he reminded Ma as they were leaving for the umpteenth time to conduct a bride-viewing. 'It's this one or none at all! If you can't find a daughter-in-law in Trinidad to suit you, I will just order a girl from India through a mail-order service in Bradford.'

'India?' Ma curled her lip. 'You will get one dose of diarrhoea in your backside, you will pack her up in her sari and post her right back to the banks of the Ganges! You ever eat the food them Indian does cook? All kind of ginger in the pumpkin and thing.'

The threat worked, though. Ma stooped to accept the latest girl on offer, even though, as she said, she was doing it over her dead body. 'Hurry-hurry work does always have to do over,' she warned. 'And when you married your children bad, you does dead bad.'

My hopes collapsed. I could only wish Robin well now.

The girl, Madhuri, turned out to be plump and pale and sallow-looking. Robin put his arm around her for a photograph after the wedding ceremony and she shrugged it off like he had leprosy. Even I had to agree that that wedding was not the most auspicious way to start married life. We had hastily gathered a few available relatives and headed to the south of Trinidad for the ceremony at the girl's house. My sisters criticised everything in less-than-hushed whispers.

The whole thing left a bad taste in my mother's mouth. After Robin left, she moved about the house looking like she had constipation, mumbling imprecations against her ungrateful sons. 'You work your liver-string out to mind them and grow them big,' she muttered, 'and then, baps! They running off and marrieding and leaving you to go on honeymoon without even a by your leave. Have me looking like a damn fool! Wedding in house, no hardie, no lawa, no nothing!'

If you don't understand this tirade, rest assured I didn't understand it either. But I never tried to understand Ma's words; I just tried to survive them. This only redirected her attention to me. 'And this one I have down here!' she started grumbling to no one in particular. 'He worse than the English jackass! He will probably pick up a big-bottom nigger and go and married in the Catholic cathedral!'

'The archbishop not going to let me put foot in the cathedral,' I consoled her. 'I get excommunicate years ago.'

Her nose tightened in contempt. 'You don't know them Catholic!' she said. 'Once they smell money, they will un-excommunicate Lucifer himself to get a share of it.' She was convinced everyone had their eye on the Saran millions, especially Robin's in-laws.

But I didn't have time for her problems. I had my own. Nerissa had gone to Canada on holiday. I called it a business trip so her flight could be paid out of a company account, then settled down to wait out her absence. Every bloody piece of correspondence that now came into the office had to be dealt with by me, every telephone call from the US embassy and OAG. I also had to order everything Ashok and Charlo needed. I didn't even have anybody to complain to before and after a cocktail party. I just had to grit my loins, stiffen my spine, and go and bear it.

I spent a lot of time staring out the window of my office. The dry season had started and Trinidad was rapidly growing parched. If I drove into the city in the evening to eat a roast corn at the savannah, the combination of dust and exhaust fumes made me feel I was choking. I thought of Nerissa having a nice time in cold Canada, like being inside a fridge surrounded by bottles of beer. Nerissa really had done well for herself: from selling pumpkin in the market to dealing with the most powerful company in the world. It was no wonder she was always so cheerful and impatient with me. She had got her diploma in accounting and had registered for a course in business economics. She was learning to drive. I had bet her she wouldn't pass her driving test on the first try. The stake was a company car.

I should follow Nerissa's example, I thought. Take things one step at a time. Register for a degree at UWI and give up on the dream of abandoning the business. I could do a degree while keeping watch on the Croissee office. Nerissa would handle most of the work. But what degree? Engineering had lost its charm. Ashok had studied engineering and he now worked for me. I didn't want to work for me. Maybe it was a good thing after all that I'd let Janet distract me from entering university all those years before.

I figured the area to get into was biochemistry. Now, there was exciting stuff! The scientific magazines I subscribed to were full of new discoveries concerning the nature of molecules. There was talk of something called cloning. The writers in those magazines babbled on about unveiling the secrets of life. The phrase intrigued me. A lot of diseases could be cured once some biochemical puzzles were solved. I could go one better than George Lopez. What was sewing back a penis? I would get guys to sprout penises like moles. Cutting into people's bodies didn't interest me – I would rather they stayed whole. But finding the cure for diabetes – I would feel like a god if I did that.

I would have to wait till the end of the year just to apply to UWI, though, and I could only start the following year. I would be over twenty-four. An old man surrounded by eighteen-year-olds. No problem. I would stroke my beard and appear wise to the eighteen-year-old chicks. In the meantime, I would prepare Nerissa to take over most of my tasks. Maybe I could even get her to go to some of the cocktail parties once she had a company car.

When she returned to the office with a big smile on her face, I almost jumped up and kissed her. I had gone in early to await her arrival and was skulking at the secretary's desk. She ruffled my hair and went into her room to put down her bag. I followed her.

'I was frighten you might decide to stay in Canada,' I said.

She dropped into her chair. 'I only have one thing to say about Canada,' she said.

I dropped into the chair opposite hers. 'What's that?'

'God bless Trinidad!' she said.

I burst into laughter and stretched out my legs. She leaned across her desk as if she was about to impart a secret. 'Ved,' she said in a serious tone. 'I want to ask you a question. Why they invent Canada?'

I shrugged. 'To keep the polar bear population in check?'

She shook her head gravely and waggled a finger. 'Nah, nah, nah. I see plenty polar bear in Canada. Downtown Toronto. They was pretending to be human beings, but they can't fool me. I could spot a polar bear from a mile.'

'I know,' I said, holding up a finger. 'You used to sell in Tunapuna Market.'

I started bringing her up to date on the state of things in the office. But what I really wanted to say was: Nerissa, girl, let's take the day off and go down to Carenage and sit by the water and drink a polar bear.

I didn't say it though. Knowing Nerissa, she would have refused. She might have told me she wasn't a Fraulein.

So instead, I revealed my latest plan to her. I was going to enter university the following year. In the meantime, I was going to enjoy the life of the rich and not famous. I was going to Travel.

My trip to Thailand had given me the idea. I had met an Indian archae-ologist on the plane who had been deeply curious about the Indian settle-ment in Trinidad. He wanted to know everything about us, whether we still practised Hinduism, whether we ate Indian food, how we thought about ourselves. I had sent him a book that had been published about Indians in Trinidad, and he had been very grateful. He sent back maga-zine articles about the work he was doing in a place called Moenjodaro, and, in letter after letter, urged me to come and visit.

'India?' my mother asked when I informed her of my plans. 'Why you want to go to India? You don't know people does dead from diarrhoea there? Why you don't go Switzerland instead and learn to ski?'

Where did Ma get these ideas? Switzerland? Skiing? 'People does dead from skiing, too. They does trip and fall in ravine.'

'Well, it always have Barbados.'

Ma herself had never left Trinidad. Ma never wanted to leave Trinidad. Not that she liked Trinidad, mind you.

It turned out Moenjodaro was in Pakistan. But what's a few thousand kilometres between enemies? My month in India and Pakistan was great. There was the diarrhoea, of course, but what's a little diarrhoea? I only lost ten pounds.

Rehan, my archaeologist friend, had a wide collection of associates, each more learned, more witty, more hospitable and generous than the last. Film-makers and feminists accosted me, demanding to know about Indians in Trinidad. Did they still conduct arranged marriage? Did they burn brides? And Rehan's own work was mind-boggling. His team was turning history on its head. The civilization that had existed in Moenjodaro before time even began in Europe was so advanced it had practised democracy while Plato was still swinging from trees. Now this was a field of study! Talk about unveiling the secrets of life? Man, those molecules were just molecules; left to themselves, they would still be molecules. They required civilization to bring out their potential. It was the study of human history that told you what molecules were capable of.

I wasn't too charmed by the dust and heat of the archaeological site – not for me the eternal brushing away of sand from artefacts. But in Pakistan you had coolies to do that for you, true coolies, not Coolies with a capital C, like us guys in Trinidad. Fellas who carried rocks on their heads. Moenjodaro might have discovered democracy, but Pakistan still had to discover the wheelbarrow. Anyhow, the coolies did the coolie-work and the research assistants did the cataloguing and filing of the artefacts. A fella like Rehan just did the turning of history on its head. I could see myself doing that, particularly with the aid of the female research assistants with their big sparkling eyes, saris dropping every which way over their shoulders revealing ballooning blouses, and long thick plaits bouncing against silk-clad bottoms.

Problem was, there was no department of archaeology at UWI. What did we have to archaeologise about? A few Caribs and Arawaks lying in hammocks. Hammocks don't make good artefacts. But no problem. To a dedicated archaeologist, the world is your oyster. I decided to start with a degree in history and geography.

By the time I returned, Nerissa had an admirer. She had been to a cocktail party in my absence. 'I don't find cocktail party so bad,' she smiled.

She was now full of business information she had got from the people she had chatted with there. It figured, I thought. While I irritated the cocks at the parties, a pretty woman like Nerissa would have them preening all around her. She had regular lunch-dates with a guy called Roger McIntosh, Scotiabank's business analyst.

'Ay, ay!' I said. 'I thought you wasn't no fraulein?'

'Roger not like allyou fellas,' she said. 'That man wouldn't know a jellyfish from a jub-jub. He is a polar bear. He harks from Canada.'

I was, frankly, jealous.

'What happen to you?' my mother asked. 'Like you want to get married too?'

'How I could get married?' I asked. 'Trinidad ain't produce a daughter-in-law you would accept.'

'Just don't bring none here from India for me, eh!' she said.

I had shipped boxes full of books from India. You got books there that you couldn't dream to acquire in Trinidad, such as Chairman Mao's *Little Red Book*. I had gone profligate. 'I hope you not planning to come out a pundit,' Ma warned. 'You know me and pundit don't get along.'

'You and me don't get along,' I returned. 'What difference it make if I come out a pundit?'

Ma decided to save me from the dangers of religion. Or so I thought at first. Suddenly, she upped her attendance at Hindu religious events. There wasn't a puja she didn't want to attend, a Ramayana Yagna she felt she could miss, a wedding that didn't require her presence. I was chauffeur and escort. I figured it was intended to give me a surfeit of religion so the appetite would sicken and thus die.

I decided to out-Ma Ma. I would approach these events like an anthropologist, learning all I could about Indian culture and history, ancient practice and cultural change. 'So why they does use mango leaf for the puja?' I would ask on the way home.

'Because mango leaf cheap,' my mother replied.

Ma was a hopeless guide to religion. She didn't think about the symbolic significance of things.

'Why the pundit throw camphor before turmeric on the fire?'

'Because that pundit damn stupid.'

All pundits were stupid according to Ma, except for her own pundit, Pundit Jagdeo. He was an ancient creature who smelled faintly of piss. He was half blind and half deaf. 'That prove he good,' Ma said. 'He don't have to read the books to recite the shlokas. He know them by heart. And he don't listen to the damn stupidness people does talk.' But, as Nerissa would say, there was more in the mortar than the pestle. If I had ever sold in Tunapuna Market, I would have smelled the rotten fish earlier.

'I tired giving people gift for their children wedding,' Ma grumbled one day while wrapping a present. 'I must have spent over ten thousand dollars in wedding gift already. It's time I get some back.'

'Ten thousand?' my father rumbled from his easy chair. 'You must be give away more than a hundred thousand in gift.'

'You want wedding gift, Ma?' I asked. 'Just take a trip downstairs. Half of Trinidad does buy wedding gifts in Saran's. I could offer you a family discount.'

I was anxious to drive them to this wedding, drive them back, and then head for the tennis club. With his heart condition, Pa couldn't stay long anyhow.

I dropped them off in front of the house where the wedding was being held, parked the car, and then hung around in the street outside where a group of fellas were drinking whiskey and coconut water from the trunk of a car.

After a short while, a cousin of mine came to look for me, saying my mother wanted me. I got slightly alarmed. Pa often complained about the heat and noise of weddings. I followed my cousin through the throng of dressed-up people.

Ma was sitting on a folding chair in one corner of the large garden. A fat woman in a noisy green sari was sitting with her.

'You remember this lady?' Ma asked.

The woman rustled her sari. I didn't have a clue who she was, so I just put on my best good manners. 'Seeta Raam,' I said, bringing my palms near to each other in a truncated Hindu gesture.

'This is your Aunt Goomatie sister-in-law from Claxton Bay. The one with the cement factory.'

'Oh, yes!' I said, as though this was exciting news.

The lady in green smiled broadly at me. She was sweating profusely, and her smile seemed to drip as well. She rustled towards a circle of girls standing behind her. 'That is my daughter, Meera,' she said.

I nodded at the girls, though for the life of me I had no clue which one of them was Meera. There were four of them dressed in saris and long, fussy dresses. They dissolved into giggles.

'But what these children laughing so for?' my mother snapped.

One of the girls started choking, putting her hands over her face and bending over to cough. The green lady's smile was replaced by a frown. 'Meera, why allyou don't behave?' she demanded.

Her glare was directed at a plumpish girl in a long yellow dress who had buried her head on the shoulder of one of her companions. The girl straightened up, bowed her head and began pawing the ground like a horse.

'She just feeling shy,' Mrs Green explained to my mother.

I glanced at my watch. 'Go and find your father,' Ma said. 'He heart can't take too much wedding.'

So. I had been placed on the Trinidad Indian marriage market. If the wood and cement industries combined with each other, it could shake the foundations of the construction industry.

But it was not to be. 'Shy!' my mother spat on the way home. 'Stupid, you mean! That bison of a girl they making so much fuss about? And as for the mother in that green sari, like a big fat avocado!' She sniffed. 'When people make a little money they does get too big for their boots!'

I told her she was making a fool of the people and their daughters by embarking on this fruitless enterprise. But you know Ma. She never had time for anyone else's opinion. Privately I predicted that her wife-hunt would take her the rest of her life. The creature she was seeking had yet to be born, a combination of beauty, grace, elegance and a certain *je ne sais quoi*. Indian families didn't produce *je ne sais quoi*. They produced bison. They mass-produced sheep. Don't doubt me. I been there.

'I thought you don't go to funerals?' I enquired when we were setting off for San Fernando after the death of the father of one of my brothers-in-law. 'You always say if you don't like somebody when they alive, you don't want to see them when they dead.'

'I want to make sure this stupid Narine-father dead for true,' she explained. 'He threatening to dead for twenty years. I can't believe he really manage it this time. With his dropsy, he could just be sleeping.'

On the way home, she gave her verdict. 'They say that girl could play sitar and sing!' she snorted. 'Well, I hope she could really play sitar. Because with that voice all up in her nose-hole, she can't talk, that's for sure. I could never have a girl with that parakeet voice in my house! I would give her two slap and send her flying!'

Indian families produced parakeets, flocks of them. Ma's wife-hunt would self-destruct under the weight of its own ambitions.

I had no time for worrying about Ma anyway. My mind was occupied with a project on the north-eastern coast of Trinidad. The eccentric English architect had struck again. Jeremy Jameson-Jones, for such was his name, had been commissioned by an international consortium of natur-alists' foundations to create a research station. Weirdos in khaki shorts and binoculars were to spend months at a time in Balandra observing trop-ical fauna and flora. I was preparing the ground for some new Charlie Darwin.

The northern coast of Trinidad is no Dorado. Dorado is flat. Dorado is beach. In Balandra, hills reach over sea. Blue-green Caribbean sea, the mistress of my dreams, who can still reduce me to a helpless love. Once you've grown up with vistas such as Balandra's, you're lost for ever. I am now a middle-aged man writing this, and am acutely aware of the power that sea has exerted in my life. I should know better than to let a body of water control my destiny. I have been through the age of reason. But reason doesn't stand up to Caribbean Sea.

Our site was on a curve of land jutting out over the water. If you sat at its edge, you became hypnotised by the movement of the tide. In and out, in and out. Crash at high tide, gurgle at low. Crabs teased your eyesight in the curves and crannies of the rocks beneath. Other crustaceans clung fast against the rocking of waves. Circular sea grape leaves bowed their backs over them. Sea-almond branches contorted themselves in a wild dance with the wind and got fixed into those positions by the salt. Plumes of sea spray drenched you when the tide rose high.

We had to reorganise ourselves slightly to take on this project. I would supervise the building crew in Balandra, with Charlo acting as my consultant. Jeremy wanted Ashok as engineer. He claimed Ashok truly understood coastal engineering. Ashok demurred. 'What I know about cliff?' He pointed at his chest à la Nerissa. 'I's a man accustomed building on sand.'

'What it have to know about cliff?' I asked. 'Throw some piles down into the cliff.'

He opened his eyes wide. 'Hear, nuh! Sea does eat cliff. You think seablast bad? Wait till you meet sea. Sea is sea-blast father!'

He proposed a trip to Portugal, to the Algarve coast, to observe the way buildings were constructed on the cliffs there. Like the Caribbean, it had been sea versus cliff for centuries. He and Charlo scheduled a three-week shut-down of the Dorado site in August, when everything slowed in Trinidad. We decided to take Mikey along for the hell of it. Then we discovered that the Antoines were also planning a trip to Europe. Tony wanted to attend a major furniture exhibition in Milan, while Mr Antoine wanted to visit his roots in Corsica and Mrs Antoine had business with the Pope. We planned to rendezvous with them in Rome.

I felt terrible that we had to leave Nerissa behind to keep watch on things. I told her Saran's would pay for a business trip to go anywhere she wanted in the world. She smiled. 'I going to hold you to that one of these days. Maybe I will be the first Saran's employee to take a trip to the moon.'

'You got it!'

'The honeymoon, I mean,' she said, still smiling.

Roger McIntosh had proposed marriage. I rocked back. 'So congratulations are in order!' I said.

'Could be,' she replied, with an alluring look on her face. 'I haven't given him an answer yet.'

I went round the desk to kiss her. 'That is one lucky polar bear,' I said.

Nerissa wore a lovely perfume. She screwed up her nose and shook her head from side to side, her worried look back in her eyes. 'I ain't really make up my mind yet,' she said softly.

'So don't put Symphonia on stand-by for wedding?'

'Don't you dare! I have mall to build. Mall comes before marriage.'

'Nerissa, sweetheart,' I said. 'That polar bear don't know what he getting. He don't really deserve you. I don't know a man who deserve you.'

She made a rueful face. 'That's the problem,' she said.

Europe only increased my thirst for the study of history. Charlo and Mikey argued from Portugal to the Pantheon. The architecture of Lagos had been built on the Backs of the Black Man, Mikey said. 'And who back the Sistine Chapel was built on?' Charlo retorted. 'A white man. Michelangelo was the slave of the Pope.'

Charlo bought heaps of books in Rome. 'Leonardo, boy,' he said, shaking his head. 'Leonardo was the man. That man didn't just make picture and statue and object d'art. He used to build war machine! What you think, Bird? You think we should go back Dorado and build a few war machine?'

'Who we going to fight?'

'Jellyfish,' Ashok put in. 'Let them jellyfish mount one more invasion! We will fight them on the beaches.'

When we got back home, I started filling out forms to enter university the following year. Then I hit a rock. Not a rock; a cliff. To enter the history department you had to have A-Level history. I had only done science and mathematics.

I put away the forms with a sigh, and joined Ashok and Jeremy at their conferences in Balandra. They conducted them with the aid of an assistant, they said. The assistant was a bottle of rum. 'The dining-room must jut out over the cliff,' Jeremy insisted. 'We are building out of raw wood so the rest of the complex is integrated into the terrestrial environment. But the ultimate environment is the sea. That's where we have to go. That's where this building has to lead.' He availed himself of a little more assistance from the assistant.

'Hear, nuh, Jeremy!' Ashok said. 'You feel building does lead. It's sea does lead. To rack and ruin.'

Jeremy waved away the objection. 'This building is a contemplation of nature,' he said, sweeping back a lock of dirty blonde hair from his forehead. 'People might think it is *for* the contemplation of nature. But it must *be* what it is for. It must lead thought, not house thought.'

'Them fellas coming here to watch bird and thing,' Ashok pointed out. 'Not fish.'

'We have to make them watch fish,' Jeremy returned. 'Fish is where birds began. The sea is the origin.'

I gazed at that raggedy-looking white man and understood why he had been selected for the job. Jeremy looked like a vagrant, according to Nerissa. He had never met an ironing-board in his life. His cotton shirts were always impeccably crumpled, his khaki shorts swung around his nonexistent bottom. But put a bottle of rum in front of Jeremy and he could make a building project sing.

Of course I had now begun to dream of an architectural career for myself. But I suppressed my dreams. I had changed my mind so often I now doubted my own thought-processes. I just became determined to make Jeremy's dreams come true. 'If we shave these posts holding up the roof at an angle,' I suggested, pointing at his drawings, 'it will draw the eye to the horizon.'

Jeremy stared at me. 'But Ved, you are turning into a genius!' he said. 'Have you ever thought of becoming an architect yourself?'

I shrugged off his compliment. Jeremy was gay, and under the influence of the assistant, he and Ashok swopped the most obscene stories of their past exploits.

But I was really happy to work on this ambitious project.

Too happy to be bothered by my mother's frustration as she hunted down the ultimate Indian wife. All those religious events brought her into greater contact with the stupidness the pundits talked. The weddings and funerals brought her into contact with the stupidness the rest of the Indian population committed. 'The more money people get, the more stupid they does get,' she railed. 'As soon as people get a little money they does get too big for their boots.'

'You should know,' I commented.

'What you trying to say?' she rounded on me. 'You see I change since we get money? I does do the same things I always used to do. I used to cuss pundit from ever since. I does wear the same clothes I always wear. I don't confuse myself with sari and jewels. Jewels is for putting in the bank.'

I realised that she was right. Ma had never changed. Since I had known her she had worn these old-lady dresses, very plain, always cut the same way, with a little belt made of the same fabric for tucking in her veil. It was always the same kind of veil, a simple piece of sheer, white fabric. To Ma, a coloured veil was vulgarity unbound. Her dresses were in delicate pastel shades and meticulously sewn out of fine cotton.

'What about when we build the swimming pool?' I challenged. 'You only do that because Charlo say it was good for your image.'

'You think I listen to that shit?' Her nostrils flared in derision. 'You and Charlo think allyou could really fool me? I hear Charlo saying that if we had a swimming pool you would keep your arse home when night come. You think I like to know my son does be knocking dog from pillar to post, in all kind of nasty places?'

I dried up. I was a bit ashamed of my sluttish behaviour in the past. Horrified as well. I could have caught diseases. These days, there was talk of AIDS. I had secretly gone and had a test. They screened me for all kinds of other things at the same time and I breathed a sigh of relief when I got my results.

I hardly had any contact with women nowadays. Wealth exacts its own price. When women looked at me they saw money and turned stupid, if they weren't stupid before. The bad old days with Carlene and the Croissee girls had been freedom days, actually. Those crazy girls hadn't wanted anything from me but what they themselves gave. Exchange is no robbery, including the exchange of bodily fluids, but I was now terrified of bodily fluids.

Still, if my mother thought I was going to have a marriage arranged by her she would have to think again. These girls she passed under my nose were the worst: simpering, silly, stiff as a flagpoles. I would rather marry Carlene. I would rather marry one of my sisters, I told Ma. At least they had gumption.

Ma's grumbling increased. The Trinidad Indian population was producing a bunch of nincompoops in the form of female progeny. I can't imagine why that surprised her. She had always dismissed the Trinidad Indian population as a bunch of nincompoops, and, as she herself said, mango trees don't bear guavas. Her wife-hunt went steadily downhill.

And then it hit rock-bottom. One day, the girl under review didn't even turn up at the puja we attended in Tacarigua. Ma didn't even have an object for rejection. Aunt Samdaye, who had proposed the connection, urged us to drop in at the girl's parents' house, which was just down the street. 'The mother expecting us,' she said. 'She wasn't feeling so well, so they stay home.'

I was directed to drive the two of them to the girl's home. I did so without a word. These encounters were all the same. Ma came, Ma saw, Ma condemned.

The family in question had a small corner shop. They lived upstairs. The approach to their house was on the side-street, behind a driveway wreathed in hibiscus and bougainvillea. My aunt bustled up the stairs to the verandah, calling Hindi greetings, jangling her many bracelets, and generally making commotion. Ma followed, her eyes retracted into their sockets in grim anticipation. I said I would wait in the car, but was nagged into getting out and joining them.

The girl's mother was a slim woman with a harassed-looking face. Her father was a bluff man with a jovial manner. Ma pursed her lips. 'Let me call Anjani,' the mother said, and went into the house with her brow wrinkled.

It took a long while for this Anjani to emerge. When she did, I glanced at my mother with a suppressed smile. This one made the previous candidates look like objects of desire. She wasn't just too ill to attend a puja; she was a candidate for a coffin. She was as skinny as a twig and appeared feverish. Her face was drenched in sweat and her hair was lank and greasy. She wore a voluminous dress that reached to her ankles. Her eyes stared fixedly into space, like she was sleep-walking.

I leaned back in a hard metal porch-chair and concentrated on observing a mango tree that was swaying gently against the bright blue sky.

'Come and see Mrs Gopaul's orchids,' my aunt urged my mother. 'She have a lot of unusual plants at the back!'

Ma wasn't at all interested in other people's orchids. As far as she was concerned, she had long won the world competition for the cultivation of orchids. But Aunt Samdaye insisted. 'Leave the young people here to converse,' she smiled, clinking her bracelets.

All the others trooped downstairs and went around to the back of the house.

Converse, I thought, glancing at the girl. Was this creature capable of conversing? I wondered whether there was psychosis mixed up in her illness. That stare was really unnerving. She looked like she was trying to hypnotise the mango tree. I shuffled my feet. That seemed to wake her up. She swivelled the stare in my direction.

'Ahhm,' I said.

She kept the haunted look on me.

'That's a julie-mango tree?' I asked.

She returned her gaze to the mango tree. 'No,' she said in a low voice.

What the hell was I saying? A julie-mango tree is a hybrid, and very short. Only a blind person could have thought that that was a julie-mango tree. The girl sighed and shifted the gaze to her feet. I decided to give up on the conversing business. She looked up at me again. 'Listen,' she said. 'I just want to tell you something.'

I nodded.

'I am not interested in getting married,' she said.

I nodded some more to indicate that I thought this was very wise. The greasy face contorted into a frown.

'It's not anything to do with you,' she said. 'But I really don't want to get married.'

I nodded harder. She continued glowering at me. I shifted my eyes to the mango tree again. 'It look like a rose-mango tree,' I opined.

'Ahmm,' she said.

I switched my eyes back to her.

'I just not interested in getting married right now,' she said.

Luckily, at this moment a car turned into the driveway and a guy in blue jeans got out. I kept my eyes on him. He looked to be a few years younger than I was, with a lock of hair that fell over his brow. 'Hey,' he said, leaping up the stairs and onto the porch.

'Hey,' I replied.

He caught sight of the creature on the other chair. 'What happen?' he asked.

'Nothing,' she said, keeping the stare on the mango tree.

He narrowed his eyes and tilted his head to peer at her sideways. 'You sick?' he asked.

She shook her head, her eyes on the mango tree.

'You're sure?' he asked. 'You look real sick to me.' He went up to her and reached to feel her neck with the back of his hand. She slapped it away.

'I tell you I not sick!' she said. 'Leave me alone.'

Psychosis. Definitely this problem was not all physical. He looked at me and shrugged. Then he held out a hand. 'Arun Gopaul,' he said.

'Ved Saran,' I replied, shaking his hand.

'Saran?' he enquired. 'As in Saran's Symphonia?'

I nodded.

'Waayy!' he said. 'That's my band! I like how them does sound too bad. I been trying to get tickets for the St Augustine Tennis Club fete next weekend, but they run out.'

'I could get tickets,' I said, relieved to be talking to a normal person. 'How many you want?'

'How many?' He opened his eyes wide. 'Well . . . me and some partners want to go. They does have some nice Sisters in them tennis club fete . . .'

'I'll see if I can get six for you,' I told him.

The older folks came back round the house and started bustling around our car saying farewells. My mother didn't even glance at the girl on the verandah. That was OK, because the girl herself didn't glance anywhere except at the mango tree. I took leave of Arun, promising to drop off the tickets the following Tuesday evening. It wouldn't be any trouble, I assured him, I'd be passing on the way from Balandra anyway.

It turned out I couldn't get six tickets for the fete after all – they were really sold out. The best I could do was two. I dropped by the Gopauls' with a plan for how Arun could get his friends in. The shop downstairs was open and I went through its wooden doors. Mr Gopaul seemed to half-recognise me. He waved me round the counter and sent me through a doorway at the back of the shop. I went up the staircase he indicated, and found myself at a door leading to the kitchen of the house. I knocked at the open door and Arun's mother called me in. A delicious smell rose from a pot on the stove. I could recognise that smell anywhere: pigeon-peas dhal. Mrs Gopaul said Arun was in the shower, asked me to wait, and opened the refrigerator door to get me a drink. She suggested I sit down in the living-room, waving at the space beyond an archway.

There were two girls at a dining-table immediately beyond the arch, bent over a Scrabble board. The older of the girls must have been somewhere in her teens. She had long, silky hair that looped around her ears and was pinned up at the back with a clip. The younger looked to be about eight, had two front teeth missing, and wore her hair in ponytails sticking out at the sides of her head. They both looked up and said hello. I felt awkward standing at the table watching them, so I dug in my pocket and found a little plastic bag full of tamarind balls I had bought from a vendor in Balandra that day.

'You like tamarind balls?' I asked, offering the bag to the little girl. She looked at me with grave eyes.

'Go on, Beena,' said the older girl. 'You can take them.'

'Thankth!' Beena lisped through the gap in her front teeth. She gave me a shy smile. The older girl also glanced briefly at me. She had the smoothest of brown skins, and her cheeks glowed faintly.

'I beating Anji,' Beena said conspiratorially, indicating the Scrabble board as she bit into a tamarind ball.

'But I have a seven-letter word,' the older girl warned.

I stared at her. This was Anjani? Standing next to the table, I watched her place her word on the board. Her hair cascaded to her neck from its clip in a glossy fountain, like the top of an ear of corn.

Arun came out of the shower and shook my hand.

'Arun!' Beena squeaked, 'Ar, thith ith a word?'

We all looked at the Scrabble board. Anjani had put down the word 'oxymoron'.

'Nah!' Arun said, towelling his head. 'She make up that word. Challenge her. If it not in the dictionary, she lose her turn.'

Anjani sat back and smiled, her cheeks like spots of low-burning light. She had little dimples that went deep into them.

I shook my head warningly at Beena. 'Yes,' I said. 'That's a word.'

'Thatth a word?' Beena frowned. 'What it mean?'

I couldn't remember. I stroked my beard. 'It mean somebody that really, really stupid,' I said.

'No . . .' Anjani drawled, looking at me and shaking her head slowly back and forth.

'Yes . . .' I drawled back. 'I know plenty oxymoron. People who moronic as a ox.'

Beena slapped the table. 'Thatth not fair!' she cried. 'Putting down wordth I don't know!'

'You don't know better than to play Scrabble with that beast yet, Beena?' Arun asked. He tapped Anjani at the back of her head. 'You ain't shame, taking advantage of your little sister?'

'She is the one who wanted to play!' Anjani protested. 'And I couldn't resist that word.'

'But now,' I warned, looking at Beena's tiles from above the table. 'Beena could massacre you.'

'How?' Beena tapped my arm impatiently. 'How I can mathacre her?'

Anjani's word had ended just before a triple-word lane, and Beena had an 'S'. She could get triple Anjani's earnings from 'oxymoron' and then a whole lot more. I crouched down beside her to show her what to do.

'Fix Anji!' Arun urged. 'She does beat up little children just because she studying English and thing.'

It turned into a fierce competition. I sat on a chair next to Beena to help her. At the end, we won the game. 'You finally meet your match!' Arun crowed, tapping the back of Anjani's head. 'You feel you could beat everybody in Scrabble.'

Anjani turned round to slap his hand. 'It's only because I was letting Beena win before he came along!' she said. 'If I was playing serious from the beginning, he was dead as a goat in a Muslim party!'

'Dead as a goat?' I raised my eyebrows. 'Who? Me?'

She looked me up and down. 'Yes. You.'

I shook my head and uttered the next line of the children's chant: 'Couldn't be,' I challenged.

'All right.' She began collecting the tiles together. 'Let's start over.'

Mrs Gopaul came out of the kitchen with a dish in her hand. 'No more Scrabble,' she said. 'Dinner.' She looked at me shyly. 'You will stay and eat something?'

Beena tapped my hand. 'She cooked peath dhal,' she said. 'My mother doeth cook the betht peath dhal.'

'Yeah, boy,' Arun added. 'Stay and eat.'

'And then get beat,' Anjani added, shaking the Scrabble box at me.

'Beat?' I said. 'You could beat me? Girl, go and put some Bay Rum in your hair, eh. You will be sicker than Sunday when I done with you.'

Arun burst out laughing. 'It wasn't Bay Rum, it was coconut oil,' he said. 'That girl look bad for truth, eh! With the oil dripping down on her grandmother dress.'

'It was her grandmother dress?' I asked. 'I thought it was a parachute. She was sitting down on one end of the porch and the dress was billowing all the way to the other end.'

Anjani tried not to smile, but her dimples gave her away.

'You didn't know the worries I had, eh,' I told her. 'You was only studying mango tree, but I was wondering: if a hard breeze blow and you start to lift off, what I would do? If I grabbed you and pinned you down in a tackle, your parents mightn't have liked it. They would have say that was going too far on the first date.'

She opened her eyes wide. 'I was studying mango tree?' she asked. 'It's you was asking oxymoronic questions!'

Mrs Gopaul went downstairs to help her husband close the shop. The rest of us started eating. The peas dhal was truly delicious and the hot sada roti opened in two spontaneously when you touched it. Mrs Gopaul could give our Sylvia a run for her money.

I explained to Arun about the tickets for the fete. I advised him to leave his friends at the tennis-club gate, come inside and look for me at the bar. I would come to the gate and let his friends in.

'You sure you could do that?' he asked. 'It's not a benefit for the tennis club?'

'I does organise that fete every year,' I reassured him. 'Who going to prevent me from letting in who I want?'

'You does organise fete?' Anjani asked. 'Then how come you letting your mother find girl to married you?'

She had perfect eyebrows, I noticed. Fine. Delicate little curves over her eyes. I had never noticed anyone's eyebrows before, but now I began wondering how eyebrows could be so perfect.

I laughed. 'I can't stop my mother from looking for girl. She could do what she want. But she will never find no girl to suit her. At the rate she going, I will still be a bachelor at the age of sixty-five.'

'Tho you don't want to get married?' Beena asked, swivelling round to look up at me, her ponytails dancing.

'Not unless you want to get married,' I told her, feeling an urge to tickle her under her chin. 'If you want to get married, I might change my mind.'

Arun started spluttering over his food. 'And Anji say she buff you and tell you she don't want to married you!' he cackled. 'Girl,' he tapped Anjani over the head again, 'you is the one who get buff!' He laughed so much he started to choke and almost fell off his chair. 'I always know nobody wouldn't want to married you,' he taunted Anjani. 'You can't cook, you can't iron, you could only read book and use big word in Scrabble!'

'Who say I want to get married?' Anjani retorted. 'What marriage good for?'

She was an echo of Nerissa.

Arun winked at me. 'It's the same thing I does ask myself. What marriage good for? The way how them young girls of today is, what's the point of getting married. Eh, boy?' He nudged me. I nodded gravely. 'Why buy a cow when milk selling cheap all over the place?' he continued.

'And sometimes it does be giving away free,' I muttered, 'if you know how to talk to the cow and them.'

Anjani glared at me. 'You really full of yourself, eh!' she said.

'You see?' Arun said to me. 'It's all right for she to say she don't want to get married. But let a man say he don't want to get married, and you will hear how he worthless.'

'But allyou worthless, yes!' snapped Anjani. 'Running down women all over the place!'

'Who say I ever run down women?' I asked. 'I don't ever run unless it have a ball running in front of me or a police running behind me. I does walk slow, slow, slow.' I shrugged. 'But some girls does want a little exercise, and they does take up jogging, and they does catch up with me.'

Their parents came upstairs and we changed the subject. Mr Gopaul was interested in my business activities, so I told him about the research station in Balandra. He asked about the exact location. 'That is Breakfast river,' he nodded. 'That river full of crayfish.'

'Yes, some of my workers does catch crayfish in it,' I said. 'They does offer me, but I never take any.'

Arun opened his eyes wide. 'You don't like crayfish, boy?'

I shrugged. 'I never eat it.'

'Boy, that is the sweetest thing on this planet! Better than lobster. Better than crab. Better even than peas dhal.'

'I'll drop some down for you next time they offer me,' I promised.

Beena nudged me. 'And tamarind ball. The lady in Balandra doeth make the betht tamarind ballth.'

Chapter Seven

I dropped by with the crayfish two weeks later. Mr Gopaul insisted I stay and eat some after his wife had cooked them. Anjani insisted I play a game of Scrabble with her in the meantime.

Beena was doing her homework at the dining-table, so Anjani set up the Scrabble board on a table on the porch and we sat on those hard iron chairs again. Arun lounged on the banister nearby, deriding the big words Anjani made on the board. 'She studying English and social science,' he said, looking at me. 'You could tell me what social science is?'

I shrugged.

'The science of how long it does take for a piece of gossip to go from one ear to another and eventually get in a book?'

It appeared to be an old argument.

'And what you study?' Anjani challenged Arun. 'How to count money!'

Arun was an accountant working at a firm in the city.

'And you?' Her eyes flashed at me. 'What you study, except parachuting and how to tackle women?'

'I study how to make money,' I said, 'so people like Arun could have something to count. Apart from my score, that is. Look! I putting down my last letters. Count your losses.'

I won the game but it was a close thing. Anjani grumbled that she was just not accustomed to my style of playing: blocking all the triple-word lanes. She would beat me next time, she promised. I sneered.

Her father had come upstairs and was watching us on the porch while her mother was laying the dining-table. 'You ain't see I bring up a bunch of educated asses?' Mr Gopaul asked, waving his hand to indicate his progeny. 'This idiot study accounting, so he could count somebody else money. I tell him go into business. But nah! He just want to earn salary and pension and thing. You have any pension?'

I shook my head and shrugged. 'I don't even have salary,' I said.

Mr Gopaul raised his eyebrows at his son. 'And he rich like Croesus!' he said, indicating me with his head.

'Croesus Who?' Arun retorted.

'You see?' Mr Gopaul directed the eyebrows towards me. 'They feel they educated but they don't even know who Croesus is. What kind of education they giving the children nowadays, boy? In my days we had to know Latin and Greek.'

'Greek Who?' Anjani asked.

Over dinner, I realised that Mr Gopaul was a bit like me. As a teenager, he had had to leave high school to run the shop when his father got too busy with the family cocoa estate up in the Balandra area. Now, he made up for this by provoking discussions with his more educated children. They quoted modern concepts at him, so he aggressively asserted the value of old-fashioned ones. He was an expert in outlandish statements; they could only defend themselves by resorting to outlandishness themselves.

I relished the wayward talk. A lifetime of argument with my mother had honed my skills in ridiculous arguments, and I could give any one of the Gopauls a run for their money. It was an uproarious cray-fest.

After dinner, Anjani insisted I play Scrabble with her again, so we settled down on the porch once more. The rest of the family gathered in front of the television in the living-room, but the news programme on the screen was just a stimulant to more absurd conversation. Arun argued loudly with each politician who gave a news conference; Mr Gopaul argued with Arun; Anjani yelled the occasional contribution from the porch; Mrs Gopaul told them to hush so she could cluck her tongue over the sad results of a car accident.

As the Scrabble game got more intense, Anji took a long time to make every move, her face still and guarded. That gave me the chance to do quick calculations in my head about the value of each of my options, so that the minute she made her play, I was ready with my own. Eventually, she held up one finger as though she had got inspiration. 'Brain food!' she said. 'I need some brain food!'

She went into the kitchen and came back to the porch with the bag of tamarind balls I had brought for Beena. She drew her feet up on the chair and hugged her arms as she bit into one. She was wearing a pair of orange slacks in a thick, embossed cotton. They were a bit weird, those slacks, but they looked nice with her slim figure. I took a tamarind ball too and ate it slowly, savouring its sour-sweet flavour. Arun came out to the porch to inspect our progress.

'You really feel one day you will beat Ved in Scrabble, girl?' he asked.

'You never hear that women brains half-pound lighter than men own?'

'Yes, I hear that,' she returned. 'But since three-quarter pound of men's brains does be in their crotch, it easier to be smarter than them. Look at this triple-word space.' She glanced up at me. 'I making your middle name on it.'

She put down the word 'sex' and got a lot of points.

I couldn't resist the banter. 'You forget one letter,' I replied, adding a 'y' and taking back the lead.

She decided she needed more brain food. She went back to the kitchen and came out with a little scrap of greasy brown paper. 'You like paynoose?' she asked, holding it out to me.

Of course I liked paynoose. Everybody liked paynoose except for my sisters, who said it was too messy to eat. It was a rare treat, an Indian sweet made only with the milk of cows that had just given birth. Arun followed Anjani to the porch and they squabbled over the last dregs of it. Anji licked the brown paper afterwards.

With all these interruptions, the game went on till nearly midnight. It was very pleasant to sit in the cool breeze of the porch, stretch my legs out under the table and wait for Anji to struggle with her extensive vocabulary. The mango tree swished with a breeze now and then, and crickets and frogs chirped and croaked in the vegetation below. Eventually, the rest of the family went to bed, with Mrs Gopaul asking me to lock the gate when I left.

A couple of weeks later, I was back at the Gopauls' bearing gifts: two rum bottles full of milk from a cow that had given birth near our building-site in Balandra. I was warmly welcomed.

'Ved, why you think them pundit does talk so much stupidness?' Mrs Gopaul asked, as we sat down to dinner. She had been to a Ramayana reading the night before. 'I really feel Pundit Mohun does be sitting down on he brains when he reading the Ramayana, you know.'

I shook my head. 'It's not his brains he does be sitting down on,' I said. 'It's his piles. They does be jooking him, and he does shift about and lose his place in the text.'

Arun cackled. 'Boy, you worse than my father!'

'You think I making joke?' I said. 'Ask anybody! All them old lady who does go plenty puja does be whispering in the back about Mohun piles. If he do the puja quick-quick-quick, they does say the piles swell up that day.'

Mrs Gopaul's brow was still wrinkled. She didn't want to join in her husband and children's religious scepticism, but the pundits made that difficult. On another visit, I brought her a book by Krishnamurti. Mr Gopaul started calling me 'Pundit'.

To my surprise, Anjani read the book along with her parents. As we talked about it later, her face grew serious. With her smooth unblemished skin and heavy hair parted in the middle, she looked like a Madonna in a Christian picture. She listened in a most attentive way, her eyes fixed on the face of the person talking. Then she spluttered out her objections in an excited fashion, going instinctively for the logical flaw in the reasoning. She could grow fierce if your thinking was weak, and it could be bruising to argue with her. I resorted to wisecracks to throw her off.

'How you could say you like Ramayana readings?' she sneered. 'The Ramayana is pure rubbish!'

'How you know?' I challenged her. 'You ever read it?'

'I don't have to read it,' she replied. 'Everybody know. After Sita get kidnapped by this monster Ravana, they put her on a big fire to prove that she wasn't unfaithful to her husband. That is all they were concerned about!'

'Well, why not?' I asked. 'She was the queen. Suppose she had produced an heir a few months later, and it had come out with three nose-hole or something? Son of Ravana would have inherited the whole kingdom, and the monster would have got his way after all.'

'You does only talk stupidness!' Anji brushed me off.

'You find that is stupidness, girl?' I persisted. 'This Son of Ravana might have made a law that only people with three nose-hole could own property or something –'

'Yes!' she pounced. 'That's what matters, eh! Property and inheritance. That's all Indian culture is about. Land and son to inherit. You notice you didn't say if an heiress was produced?'

'Well,' I rejoined, 'a girl-child with three nose-hole would have been a worse tragedy. At least if it was a boy he could grow a big moustache and hide one of his nose-hole.'

I guess it was a power struggle I was involved in, now that I come to think about it. Anjani was the scholar of the family. Arun and I were always trying to take her down a peg or two, since she treated us with the scorn due to a pair of Neanderthals with their brains in their crotches. She lived in a world of books and theories, only emerging to engage with her family. She was dangerous, with her smiles and her sweetness. She seemed to love her mother deeply, and she doted on her younger sister, always buying her little things, making up games for her, helping her with her homework and telling her stories. I think Arun teased Anjani so much because he secretly adored her. If she was in her room studying when I arrived, he would poke in there to try and provoke her till she came out and joined in the conversation.

The whole bunch of them were intensely hospitable and generous. Mrs Gopaul was always cooking and baking and offering delicacies. She had a shy manner, but was very kindly, and interested in the world at large. Mr Gopaul did not make much money, and they were certainly not rich, but they seemed to enjoy life far more than anyone in my family did.

I took to dropping by once a week on my way back from Balandra. There was always something to bring them, countryside treats that were scarce in the town: sweet balata fruits that only grew in the deep forest, chilli bibbi, peewah. They called these things by the collective Hindi word 'gajar-bajar'. Apart from Mrs Gopaul, they all liked eating silly little things. They would cut up green rose mangoes from the tree in the yard and douse the pieces in salt and pepper and garlic. When their mouths got burnt from the pepper, Anji would rush to the kitchen to find a tin of condensed milk and pour pools into everyone's hands so they could get some relief. Mr Gopaul would go and get a saucer and a handful of biscuits and start eating bits of biscuit with the milk and the rest of us would join in. I remembered that I liked eating gajar-bajar myself. I had got the habit from the girls in the store in the early days, but it had died in recent years since I had got so busy with the business.

One evening, Anjani had an essay she was doing for a history course. She discussed it with us. 'Who said Indian civilization began with the invasion of the Aryans from the west?' I asked.

She shrugged. 'All the books.'

I shook my head at her. 'It's not true.'

'All the major scholars agree on this,' she insisted.

'What major scholars?' I asked.

She rolled off a list of names.

'All European scholars,' I pointed out.

'So?'

'So they're lying. Indian civilization began in India.'

'Ved! You too prejudiced!' she cried. 'Indian this and Indian that. You just like one of them pundit, for true.'

'I not prejudiced,' I rejoined. 'It's the historians who prejudiced. When Europeans began researching Indian history, they couldn't believe that such an advanced civilization could be created by people who weren't white in colour. So they made up a myth.'

'How you could say that?' she challenged.

'Because I saw the evidence myself.'

'What evidence?'

'The ruins of Harappa and Moenjodaro.'

'You saw Harappa and Moenjodaro?'

I nodded.

'You went to India?'

'Well, they're in Pakistan now, but yes.'

'Wait, nuh!' Mr Gopaul put in. 'You ain't just a pundit. You's a sadhu!'

We all laughed at the thought of me being a monk. But I did live something of a monk's life then. Apart from the occasional adventure with one or other woman I met in my dealings with the city bureaucracy, I lived my life among men. I went to Dorado on Friday evenings and hung out with Charlo and Ashok. They each came to Balandra occasionally and we hung out there, sometimes with Jeremy. I passed by Santa Cruz to check on the doings of my cousin, Vijay, and discuss new furniture orders with Tony. For the rest, Nerissa and my mother were the only women I related to on a regular basis. Nerissa was intensely busy managing most of the business now that I was so occupied in Balandra, and managing her up-and-down relationship with Roger McIntosh. My mother was no fun at all – the wife-hunt was a constant source of aggravation to her.

So it was a real pleasure to enjoy some of the cosy family atmosphere the Gopauls offered. I invited Arun to visit the Balandra site, and he came one Saturday with Anjani and Beena and we walked on the cliffs sucking chennettes from their shells. It was on that day that I admitted to myself that, though I enjoyed spending time with the whole Gopaul clan, it was Anji who was really the focus of my attention. She wore a silky blue dress that day, with red flowers splashed on it. It eased down off her graceful hips and swung around her thighs. She had slender legs that ended in a pair of strange red sandals the like of which I had never seen before, but which suited her perfectly. I was disappointed that she hadn't brought a bathing suit. I would have liked to see what she looked like without her clothes. She had tiny breasts, I had noticed from the first, and a slim, delicate torso.

I had realised that, though it was fun to chat and laugh and argue with all the Gopauls, the high point of my visits to their house came afterwards, when Anji and I settled down on the verandah to play Scrabble. Arun and his father would drift by and start conversations in between, but they would eventually meander back inside the house to watch television or read. Anji would sit quietly, looking at me guardedly as I made my moves. I would tease her as her brother did. I liked to see her face tense with determination, and always tried to beat her. Then she would want to play another game, and we would end up playing till the entire family had gone to bed and we were stranded in the dimness of the porch, with the sound of crickets and the cool night air. I tried to teach her the position of the stars, but she wasn't interested. I forgot about that. It was enough to see her rise and dance off to the kitchen to find some gajar-bajar.

One day, Arun informed me that he and Anji were going shopping at our store the following Saturday. 'Beena's birthday coming up,' he said. 'We planning to buy a bicycle for her, and everybody say Saran's is the place to buy bicycle.'

That Saturday, I stuck around the store. Suzanne narrowed her eyes at me. 'What you doing here?' she asked. 'Why you not in Dorado?'

I made some excuse about having to do something in town, then went out and bought a cake and installed it in the lunch-room.

'It's somebody birthday today?' Suzanne asked.

Anjani and Arun arrived and took their time looking round the shop.

'I thought you did grow out of woman-chasing,' Suzanne muttered to me.

'I not chasing no woman, girl.' I tapped her on the back of her head the way Arun did to Anji. 'These are good friends of mine.'

'Friends, eh!' she muttered. 'I hope my friends don't be watching my bottom the way you watching hers.'

Once they had picked out the bicycle they wanted, Suzanne proposed to give them the friends discount. I instructed her to give them the family discount. Anjani objected, insisting that they were not my family.

'Family-to-be, maybe,' Suzanne said, and Anji blushed furiously.

'Give them the friends discount,' I said.

Suzanne did the calculation on the adding machine.

'And then minus another ten per cent for peas-dhal discount,' I instructed her.

'Peas-dhal discount?' Arun asked. 'Allyou does give peas-dhal discount here?'

'And another ten per cent. That's fry-fish discount. And another five per cent. That's mango-chow discount.'

'Ved!' Anji stared at me. 'Don't be ridiculous!'

'I being ridiculous?' I asked her. 'Who paying for this bicycle? You? Since when you working somewhere? Girl, hush your mouth, eh! This is a transaction between me and your mother.'

The bicycle was stored away till the actual birthday. Then, I was supposed to bring it over to the Gopauls' as a surprise.

But the following week, when I was visiting their house, a political discussion blew up. The government was about to nationalise the banks and Mr Gopaul predicted the banks would go bust.

'Foreigners making huge profits from our banks,' Anji argued. 'Why shouldn't we keep the profit inside the country?'

'You think we will make profit when black people running the banks?' Mr Gopaul asked. 'You don't know black people can't do business?' He turned to me. 'Pundit, you ever see a black person run a successful business yet?'

I thought. I recalled the practices of Charlo and Mikey. They didn't save a cent. I never knew where their money went, although they were handsomely paid. I thought about Nerissa's attitude by contrast. I shook my head.

'You see?' Mr Gopaul said. 'You get it from the horse's mouth. From a man who know what it takes to make money. Black people does spend all their money on Carnival costume.'

'And even those who making the costume don't make money on it,' I added with a laugh. 'They does be broke at the end of Carnival.'

Anji's eyes flashed at me. 'And you feel making money is the be-all and end-all of life?'

'I didn't say that,' I responded. 'But you have to have money –'

She pounced. 'Spoken like a true Indian! All allyou does do is dig out people eye and help allyou family and not the rest of the society. How you could give your family so much discount in your store? Because you digging out other people eye with your prices.'

'Who eye I dig out?' I challenged. 'Name the person. I will personally pay for a eye transplant.'

Her nostrils flared. 'Yes. You could pay for everything. People eye, people heart, people liver-string.'

I laughed. 'Well, I don't know the going price of a liver-string,' I said. 'But eye transplant does cost about twenty thousand dollars. I could manage that.'

'Yeah,' Anji sneered, going off to the bathroom. 'Twenty thousand dollars is nothing for a capitalist like you.'

After dinner, when I thought we were going to play Scrabble, Anji went off to her room.

'Anjay!' Arun hollered through the door. 'Ved waiting for you to play Scrabble!'

I went out to the porch. I thought that, if she had to study, I might as well go home and read a book. She emerged into the dim light of the porch. 'I ain't feeling to play no Scrabble,' she said.

She was wearing her blue dress with the red splotches. It hung perfectly still, silhouetted against the light from the living-room.

'You can't take licks tonight?' I teased.

'No,' she said. 'I just don't like the way you does play. Always these little tiny words that does block up the board for everybody else, just to get points. That ain't no fun.'

'Since when it's not fun to play Scrabble with me, girl? Just because you lose an argument?' I tilted my head and smiled at her encouragingly. 'Come on. I'll let you win this once.'

That was the wrong thing to say. 'You think you is always the big winner, eh!' she snapped.

I raised my eyebrows and tried to dispel her bad temper with a challenge. 'Well, I does always win.'

That was also the wrong thing to say. 'Yes, Mr Ved Saran,' she sneered. 'You does always win! You think so much of yourself, just because you could make money out of people who not so money-minded as yourself!'

I perched on the banister. 'I was just talking about Scrabble, Anji.'

She came towards me. 'And about women!' she said, poking her head out aggressively towards me. 'About how you does always win with women. Ain't that is your next claim to fame?'

I stroked my beard a while. 'I does just be joking.'

'People does talk true thing in joke,' she said.

I rocked back on the banister. There was a short silence as I thought how to break this deadlock. 'All right,' I said. 'I am a boastful fella. But I am also your best Scrabble opponent. You don't have to take me seriously, just try to beat me, as you always do.'

Her eyes narrowed. 'Take you seriously?' she asked. 'I would ever take you seriously? Who would ever take you seriously, with your racist views.'

My head jerked up. 'Racist, Anji?' I asked. 'I am a racist?'

'All that bullshit you does talk about black people can't do business, and Indians build the most advanced civilization, and all that crap . . .'

Her voice tailed off. I sighed and tried again. 'You shouldn't take all that old-talk seriously, Anj. You should just play Scrabble with me, and talk and laugh and treat me like a worthless sexist pig, like you always do. I am quite contented with that.'

'Yes,' she sneered. 'You are quite contented to go about with people despising you, just as long as you make plenty money.'

That hurt. I suddenly felt empty inside, like there was a desert in my stomach. I felt I was losing something, that I had already lost it, that it had drained away when I wasn't looking.

'You despise me, Anji?' I asked softly.

She didn't answer. I remained sitting on the banister, looking at the wall opposite me. I shifted my gaze back to her. 'You despise me, Anji?' I asked again.

It was the only thing I could think of to say.

She still didn't reply. I felt a heaviness in the pit of my stomach. I got up off the banister. 'OK, then,' I said, and, without saying goodbye to her parents, I went down the stairs and left.

The next two weeks were terrible. Anji's words rang in my ears like cymbals. I had not imagined that people's misunderstandings of me could go so far as despising me. I felt sorry for myself. After all, I had been trapped into this life I led, trapped by my father's invalid status. Then I reminded myself that I liked my life, liked building buildings and making furniture. But now, the pleasure was absent when I went to Balandra. The sea lashing against the rocks only reminded me of Anji standing there, her blue dress blowing against her slim thighs. I felt like I was eating sawdust when I stood amidst the lovely teak wood, whose reddish glow was like Anji's cheeks when she got angry.

I grew angry myself. How dare she judge me like this, just because I never went to university and learned all that bullshit theory her head was full of? She knew nothing of life, nothing of the struggle to make things work, to make a building come to fruition despite all the hassles and red tape and sea-blast and erosion. She didn't know the troubles I had with Symphonia, to get those guys to keep some discipline and rise to their true potential as one of Trinidad's leading steel bands. She had never asked about my life. She had never asked what I felt about anything. I knew everything about her and her family. I thought about them. She had never thought about me. She only looked on the surface, took my flippant remarks and turned them into a monster of a theory. All she knew was a pack of words in books, educated ass as she was. She was just as stupid as all the other girls, letting money and shit-talk blind her to reality.

When I passed through Tacarigua on my way back from Balandra, I kept my hands gripped on the steering wheel of the car. I felt that if I didn't, the car would turn into the street where Anji lived of its own accord. I went home, ate Sylvia's dinner, and lay on my bed, reliving that last, awful scene. I tried to drag myself up to take a swim, but the most I could do was go down to the pool and idly sit by the water, watching it and thinking of all the old times over the Scrabble board. I didn't want to see a tamarind ball, a pepper plum, a sugar cake.

'What happen, Ved?' Nerissa asked. 'Your father not feeling well?'

'Nah,' I said. 'He OK.'

'Well, how you looking like you seeing a coffin in front your face all the time?'

'Worries,' I said.

'Woman worries?'

I nodded. I sat on the edge of her desk and swung my legs.

'Well, if it's any consolation, I have worries of my own. This man pressuring me to marry him.'

'Nerissa, girl,' I said, 'why you don't just married me instead and put me out of my worries?'

She smiled, her eyes velvet with our combined troubles. 'Over your mother's dead body,' she said softly.

I remembered a cute little Portuguese girl who worked in OAG's housing department. There were a couple of details still to work out in one of the contracts, so I put on a nice cotton shirt and made my way to the restored French villa. Just walking through the driveway improved my self-esteem. Big frangipani trees shaded the broad entranceway with its wide, curving stairs. The girls behind the reception desk greeted me with the respect due to a company associate and asked me to wait a few minutes till Miss Almandoz could see me. Miss Almandoz herself was all smiles. She was a very small girl with curly hair and big breasts. She had a somewhat bouncy manner for someone in such a senior position. I found the combination attractive. She called me Mr Saran.

'The name is Ved,' I corrected her.

She smiled.

When we had done our business, I sat back in my chair and regarded her for a moment or two. 'What do you do in your spare time?' I asked.

She smiled again. 'The usual. Go to the gym, watch TV, go to the beach.'

'I was wondering if you'd like to have dinner with me one evening.'

She smiled even more broadly than before.

I made a reservation at a little Italian place near the Savannah. Trisha, as Miss Almandoz was called in her spare time, wore very high heels and put her hair up with a sparkly clip at the top of her head. Her curls cascaded around her face and she looked really nice.

The meals were served outdoors, under fake grapevines. Tricia and I ordered a bottle of red wine.

'How did such a young guy like you get control of such a large company,' she asked as we waited for our food.

I shrugged. 'It wasn't so big until OAG started leasing everything we built.'

'Oh, and what do you do in your spare time?' she asked.

I shrugged again. 'Read, swim, play tennis . . .'

She laughed. 'That's why you look so fit! You're the sporty type.'

We talked about our interests for a while, but it got to be hard work. There wasn't much you could say about swimming or tennis or cricket – you just did those things. And Tricia hadn't registered the reading part. She didn't talk politics or bullshit. She was thoroughly integrated into the off-white scene of Port of Spain: the evenings at the Pelican, the mas' playing with an expensive Carnival band, Sundays at Scotland Bay. I had nothing to add to her litany of the joys of the elite life. But, still, she seemed to like me. And there were the breasts to consider.

I suggested we go down to a club in Chaguaramas for a drink after dinner. Chaguaramas was a dark, uninhabited peninsula that had the right atmosphere for what I had in mind. The club lay on a bay and had big balconies where you could look out over the water.

But once we got there, conversation got even tougher. A few glasses of wine weren't able to turn me into the senseless beast of the bad old days. We admired the pools of light playing on the bay, and I thought of subjects to talk about. But as soon as she began to speak, I found my mind drifting off. It was all so uninteresting, her attendance at the Tobago boat race and the fete afterwards. I tried to focus on the breasts, but I just couldn't bring myself to make the next move. I knew she expected it and wouldn't resist, but I started feeling too tired to be bothered. My mind began wandering off to things I had to do the next day, and I decided to throw in the towel.

'I have an early start tomorrow,' I said. 'I should get going.'

The next day, Arun rang to remind me that it was Beena's birthday on Friday. I told him I hadn't forgotten and would come over in the evening with the bicycle. Then I found myself looking forward to Friday. I told myself I would just drop off the bicycle and my own gift for Beena, and then leave. I reminded myself of the terrible things Anji had said to me. But still, I kept wondering what she would say when she saw me. I pictured these scenes in my mind with Anji wearing her blue dress with the red splotches. In these scenes, I was very cold towards her. Icy. Frosty. Short. Cutting.

I trimmed my beard carefully on Friday evening. I looked at several of the shirts in my cupboard and chose a light-blue one. I even thought of wearing shoes, but decided Anji wasn't worth shoes, and put on my old beat-up sneakers instead. That idiot would regret the way she had dismissed me. She would realise I was a man with dignity who didn't care a damn about an ignorant little educated ass of a girl.

I got a jolt when I saw her. It wasn't anything she did, but just seeing her caused something to lurch in my chest. She was wearing a cotton dress that was caught by a band on her hips. Those dresses always danced around her thighs so nicely, setting off the slender curves of her legs. Her glossy hair was brushed back and some of it was caught in her silver clip, so that the rest hung to frame her face. I kept my own face straight. I chatted with the rest of the family, ate birthday cake, but she never directed a word my way.

In my mental preparations for the showdown with Anji, I had forgotten that the World Heavyweight Boxing Championship was due to take place that night. 'Sit down, nuh!' Arun urged. 'By the time you reach the Croissee, the fight will already have started.'

I sat down to watch with them. I didn't really want to go home. Anji went to the kitchen to help her mother wash up. I began to feel let down. I hoped she would try to talk to me later, so I could put her in her place. I saw her leave the kitchen and go into her bedroom. My heart sank. There would be no final farewell scene, then.

The boxing went on late. Anji came out of her bedroom and went to the porch with a book. The action on the screen heated up. I tried to make remarks and appear normal, but my mind was on the girl sitting outside on one of the hard porch chairs. At every moment I expected her to come in and go to bed. I was on tenterhooks, worse than the people who had betted hundreds of dollars on the boxing match.

When the bout was over, I got up and stretched. It was after eleven. Mr Gopaul and Arun talked for a while about the match. We had a last drink. There was nothing to do but say my goodbyes. Arun walked me to the porch.

'Ay,' he called to Anji, who was sitting in a dark corner. 'Ved leaving.'

She looked up. I inclined my head in her direction. She said nothing.

'I gone,' I said to Arun. 'Don't worry about the gate. I will close it behind me.'

I went down the stairs, aware that Anji's eyes might be on my back. I didn't turn. When I got to my car and began to open the door, I heard her voice finally.

'Ved!' she called. 'Wait.'

I straightened up and looked at the porch. She was leaning over the banister. I waited. She moved towards the stairs and I saw Arun go back inside. Anji walked down the stairs with her head bowed as though she had to be careful, and came to stand facing me at the car. Her eyes were big in her face.

'I'm sorry,' she said.

I didn't answer.

'I'm sorry for the things I said.'

I shrugged. 'It's OK,' I said. 'You just told me what you thought about me. You're entitled to your opinion.'

She furrowed her brow. 'I don't really think those things,' she said.

I crossed my arms over my chest. 'So why did you say those things, then?' I asked.

'I don't know,' she murmured softly. 'I was just vexed with you.'

'So if you get vexed with somebody,' I asked sternly, 'you does just say horrible things to them? What kind of girl are you, Anjani?'

She hung her head. I leaned against my car, my arms still crossed over my chest. 'I'm sorry, Ved.' Her voice was thick. 'I'm really, really sorry.'

I heaved a deep sigh. 'OK,' I said. 'I got that. You're really sorry.'

She took a little step towards me. 'So you'll come back?' she asked in a small voice.

'Come back where?'

'Here,' she said. 'Come back and play Scrabble and chat sometimes.'

'I don't know,' I said.

Her eyes were very still as she gazed into my own, and I began to feel a kind of thickness in my chest. 'Why you don't know?' she asked.

I crossed my legs as well, angling them so I leant more comfortably against the car. 'I don't know if I should take that risk,' I told her. 'If you get vexed with me again, who knows what other home truths you might decide to lob at me? I don't want to experience that again.'

'I won't insult you again,' she said. 'I promise.'

I didn't reply.

'Will you come back?' she asked in the little, scared voice.

'I'll think about it,' I said.

'Please don't think about it.' She looked up at me with those imploring eyes. 'Please come back.'

I tore my eyes away from hers and looked at the ground. 'I said I'll think about it,' I said. 'That's the most I can say right now.'

She reached out and grasped my wrist. 'Don't think about it,' she begged. 'Just say you'll come back again.'

I didn't answer. She shook my wrist and moved closer to me. I moved to one side to avoid the pressure of her voice and her nearness. She moved too so that she blocked my view of the rest of the world. I looked into her eyes and something sank in my stomach. She was so close. To escape that gaze I would have to push her away. I reached out, and somehow she was in my arms.

'Anji,' I whispered into her hair, 'what are you doing?'

'Please say you'll come back.'

Her voice was muffled in my chest. I stroked her hair, giving myself up to the pleasure of feeling her body against me. She raised her face and looked at me beseechingly. I bent my knees to bring my face closer to hers and kissed her closed lips. She pressed herself closer to me. I slid my arms lower to circle her waist, picked her up and sat her on the bonnet of the car. She immediately put her arms around my neck and locked them together so I couldn't move away. I breathed in the fragrance of her hair and skin. I drew my head away and looked into her face.

'Smile,' I said. 'Let me see your dimples.'

Her lips widened in a cautious smile.

'That's better,' I said, kissing a dimple and then sliding my mouth towards hers.

When I went back two days later, it was like old times again. I had dinner with the whole family and then played Scrabble on the porch with Anji. It was better than old times, really. All evening, my consciousness of Anji was heightened. It was like I had an extra eye that stayed on her even when I was speaking with her father, like I was breathing her in with every breath.

After her parents had gone to bed, she leaned over the Scrabble board and looked at me seriously. 'Ved?'

'Yes Anji?' I tilted my face to look into hers.

'You have a girlfriend?'

'Not apart from you.'

She straightened up and a dimple started to form in her cheek. 'So I am your girlfriend, then?' she asked.

I shrugged and leaned back in my chair. 'Well,' I said, raising my eyebrows, 'no other girl don't ambush me the way you did the other night.'

'I didn't ambush you!' she said. 'You ambush me.'

'You didn't give me any other option,' I pointed out. 'I needed mouth-to-mouth resuscitation after you started strangling me.'

She sat back in her chair and smiled her mischievous smile. I reached over the table and took her hand. 'So what you think?' I asked. 'You could bear having a capitalist for a boyfriend?'

She just smiled at me more.

She came over and perched beside me on my chair. I slid an arm around her shoulders. She swung both her legs over one of mine, and I buried my face in her neck. After a while I heard some movement inside the house.

'Get up, Anji,' I said. 'If your mother comes and finds you on my lap, she will throw me out.'

Chapter Eight

Two weeks later, her mother made her move.

'Ved,' she said, as Anji and I sat playing Scrabble on the porch, 'I have to ask you something.' She sat down on a chair near to me and drew a deep breath. I looked into her worried face. 'What are your intentions?' she asked.

I kept my eyes on her face. 'I want to marry Anji,' I said, without skipping a beat.

She sat back in her chair. 'So I better go and see my pundit then?'

'OK.' I nodded.

There was a squeal from Anji's chair. 'Who say I want to get married?' she asked, her eyes looking wild.

Her mother ignored her and said to me, 'Let me get a piece of paper and you can write down your date of birth and your Rasi name.' This was for the pundit to check whether our horoscopes matched.

She went inside to get paper and pen. Anji stared at me, her mouth open. 'Who tell the two of allyou I want to get married?' she asked. I shrugged. Anji got up and followed her mother inside the house. 'Ma, who tell you I want to get married?' she demanded.

'So what you want to do then?' her mother asked in a sharp voice. 'Stay in my house and make amchar?' I laughed at the expression. Her mother was asking if she wanted to stay home and turn into a pickle.

Mrs Gopaul returned and I wrote down the information she needed.

'But I don't want to get married!' Anji squeaked.

Her mother turned to her irritably. 'Girl, if you think I going to have boy coming and sitting down in my house year-come and year-go, you must be mad.' She turned back to me. 'I will see the pundit on Sunday and get him to check the Patra.'

She went back inside. Anji watched her walk through the door, then turned to me, her fountain of hair whipping round her face. 'Why did you tell my mother you want to marry me?' she asked.

I shrugged. 'What else you expected me to tell your mother?' I asked. 'That was the only answer I could give her. Otherwise she will show me the door. You think she don't know what does be going on out here when she gone to bed?'

'Well, that don't mean I have to get married! I am only nineteen. I still have a year to go in university.'

'OK,' I said. 'You playing Scrabble?'

She folded her arms over her chest. 'No.'

I raised my eyebrows. 'Don't worry about it,' I said softly, leaning over the table. 'Everything will come out all right.'

'But I don't want to get married off like some stupid Indian girl.' She looked at me imploringly. 'Ved, do something!'

I opened my palms in a helpless gesture. 'Honey, I can't do anything. The whole thing is in your hands. If you insist you don't want to marry me, your parents will ask me to stop coming here and staying up late at night with you.'

She twisted her face to one side and regarded me. 'So you don't mind getting married, then?' she asked.

I shrugged. 'I'm twenty-six. I can get married.'

'But you don't want to get married.'

I shrugged again. 'I like the way things are going. I want them to continue. I knew from the moment I kissed you I had to be prepared to marry you.'

Her eyes narrowed. 'Then? Down there by the car?'

I nodded. 'It was a split-second decision I had to make. I had to push you away or marry you. I didn't have the will-power to push you away.'

It was easy to cheer her up. Just kiss her and cuddle her like the baby she was to me. I didn't let myself think of having sex with her, just of holding her in my arms and having her close.

By the following week her mother had a date for the engagement cere-mony. The pundit had checked the Patra, confirmed that our horoscopes matched, and determined that the seventeenth of June was a good day for people to get engaged.

'Engaged!' Anji squealed. 'Ma, I still going to university!'

'Your exams ending in June,' her mother said. 'Didn't you tell me so?'

'But I have another year to go,' Anji spluttered. 'What you want to do? Make me leave school to get married, like your mother do you?'

'Who talking about leaving school?' her mother asked. 'Ved, you hear me say anything about leaving school?'

'Ma,' Anji pleaded, 'this is not right. You can't make me get married.'

'I not making you get married,' her mother insisted. 'The pundit will come, and Ved parents will come, and we will have a little engagement ceremony, and you will go back to school in September, and go on just like before. Not so, Ved?'

I didn't answer. I was torn between the two of them.

'Anji,' I said later when her mother was out of earshot, 'your mother only wants to make sure I won't run off again if you annoy me. We can get engaged, so your mother can breathe free. I won't hold you to it if you want to break the engagement later on.'

Then I went home to face my own mother.

'Ma,' I said to her in the kitchen, 'I getting married.'

She adopted her combative stance. 'You have a next Miss Don't-Know in your pocket?'

'Nah,' I said. 'This is a Miss Know.'

'You go and get some girl pregnant!' she said, staring up at me. 'Look, boy, I tired tell you I don't want no picky-haired grandchildren in my house.'

I laughed. 'You wouldn't get no picky-haired grandchildren. It's a Indian girl you know. Hindu. And she not pregnant.'

'So how all of a sudden you decide you getting married?' she demanded. 'Without a by your leave. Without consulting the Patra. Without nothing.'

'Patra done consult,' I told her. 'The horoscope match.'

'Who say so?' Her eyes narrowed.

'The girl mother pundit.'

'Girl mother pundit? What girl mother pundit?'

I shrugged. 'I don't know the pundit.'

'So Pundit Don't-Know planning to married my son without my say-so?' She sniffed. 'That is a nice pundit, man! Pundit who does married people son without them knowing anything about it.'

'You know about it,' I said. 'I telling you now. And you introduce me to the girl yourself. The girl from Tacarigua.'

Her eyes narrowed again. 'That girl who suffering from mirasme?'

I nodded. 'The very same.'

'You ain't play you have bad taste, nuh, boy!' she said. 'And after you done consult your quack-pundit, you coming to tell me? You expect me to accept that?'

'What you going to do about it?'

She put her hands on her hips. 'What I going to do about it?' Her voice grew shrill. 'What I going to do about it? I going to throw your arse out of my house. That's what I going to do about it.'

'No problem,' I said. 'I don't want to bring no wife into your house anyway. But I will need a salary, so I'll set that up.' I paused. 'Or you planning to fire me from the business too?'

She ranted and raved, but eventually had to accept my decision. I informed her that Anji's parents were coming to see her the following Sunday. 'Coming to see me?' she asked, pointing to her chest. 'Why they coming to see me? Ain't you marriering yourself? What kind of people does go and see people after they make arrangements with the son without consulting them.'

'They coming to make arrangements with you. Next Sunday.'

'I not available next Sunday.'

'Where you going? You hire a driver?'

'I ain't going nowhere. I taking a rest next Sunday.'

'Rest from what?'

'Look!' she said, in a tone of finality. 'I can't do no entertaining next Sunday. All those curtains in the living-room have to take down and wash.'

'The people not coming to see curtains. They coming to see you. You don't have to entertain them. I never know you to entertain anybody in your life, except me with your bad behaviour. But you better be on your best behaviour next Sunday. Else I moving out and paying myself a salary for running your business, and you could find a chauffeur to take you where you want.'

Ma didn't have any best behaviour. She had bad behaviour, extremely bad behaviour, and viper-mode. She was simply on 'bad' when Anji's parents came.

'I don't trust any and every pundit,' she informed Mr and Mrs Gopaul right at the start. 'Half of them does can't read the Patra and does make up horoscope for people.'

Mr Gopaul's eyes lit up. 'You're perfectly right!' he said. 'Most of them pundit does be quack.'

He could have taken the words straight out of Ma's mouth. She narrowed her eyes. Mrs Gopaul's face got a look of strain. Ma took another breath. 'I will have to consult my pundit myself,' she informed the gathering.

'But Ma,' I put in, 'your pundit blind as a bat. He doesn't know if the Patra upside down or inside out.'

'Blind or no blind,' Ma said in her sourest voice, 'Pundit Jagdeo does read Patra better than anybody else in Trinidad.'

'Oh,' Mrs Gopaul laughed. 'Pundit Jagdeo is your pundit too? I didn't know that. He say the horoscope match perfectly.'

All Ma's ammunition was now shot. Pundit Jagdeo had set the date for the engagement, and all my family had to do was to turn up at the Gopauls' home on the appointed day. I hustled them out of the house as quickly as I could.

Two weeks later, my father called me into the living-room. He opened a little box to show me its contents. A gigantic diamond ring flashed at me. 'Where you get this, Pa?' I asked, touched by the gesture of acceptance.

'I bought it from Gajadhar,' he said. 'I got a real good price on it.'

I was less touched. Gajadhar was an old family connection, a jeweller. Pa must have decided to use him to minimise costs on the engagement. I examined the ring. There were diamonds everywhere. Anji would hate it for its ostentation. Pa put it back in its box carefully and locked it in the safe in his room. I realised I had to buy a ring for my girl and discussed it with her mother the next time I was in Tacarigua. We arranged that I should pick her up at the university a couple of days later and take her into the city.

I met her outside the library. She was standing talking to two other girls when I came up behind her. She blushed as she introduced me. 'Oh,' said one of the girls, a black girl with big eyes who reminded me of Carlene. 'So this is the mysterious boyfriend!'

I smiled and took a stack of books out of Anji's arms.

'You didn't tell us he was so good-looking, Anjani,' the girl said, smiling up at me flirtatiously.

'He not good-looking,' Anji grunted. 'He only look good-looking!'

I laughed. I was in a very good mood at the prospect of driving with her to the city under the bright blue sky.

We went to Ross's and I asked to see engagement rings. Anji made a face as she studied the cases full of glittering diamonds. A slim, dark girl with a lot of white talcum powder on her face grew impatient as she directed Anji's attention to one case after another. Mrs Ross kept watch from the cash register, her blonde hair piled in rolls that went high up over her head, her ample bosoms bedecked with rubies and emeralds like one of her own glass cases. Anji's figure began to sag. I asked if she liked any of the rings she had seen. She shook her head. I told her we would go to another shop. The sales-girl shut the engagement-ring cabinet with a loud snap. Anji began drifting round the shop looking at other things. She stopped in front of a case for a long time. I peered over her shoulder. She was gazing at a ring with red stones. The girl behind the counter came up and looked too.

'That's much more expensive,' she said. 'Those are rubies and sapphires.'

'You want to try that one, Anji?' I asked.

She nodded, still looking down at the ring.

The girl behind the counter made no move to open the glass case. I stared at her for a couple of seconds without saying anything. She opened the case and handed over the ring, keeping her eyes on me.

The ring looked perfect on Anji's slim hand. She smiled as she held it up for me to see. 'You want that one?' I asked.

She nodded. I took out my wallet and placed my credit card on the counter without looking at the sales-girl.

'You want to wear it now?' I asked Anji.

She smiled up at me mischievously and nodded. I kissed her nose.

We went to lunch at the restaurant Janet had first taken me to. By now, I was well known there. Anji liked the crab-back hors d'oeuvre so much, she ate a second one as her main course, and then two coconut creams for dessert. Afterwards we drove down to Carenage and sat on a bench under a spreading sea-almond tree and watched the sea for a while. Anji snuggled up to me and I put my arm around her shoulder. 'See?' I said. 'It's not so bad to be engaged. You get to go out alone with me.'

She didn't argue. She just snuggled closer.

On the day of the engagement ceremony, she looked beautiful. She had refused to buy a new dress for the event and wore one of her mother's saris. I was transfixed as she came out of the house, her slender figure wrapped in deep-blue silk.

'Blue is for when you pregnant,' my mother hissed in her carrying voice. I turned round to direct a stony glare at her. I had promised to retaliate in front of the entire gathering if she embarrassed me that day. I had never threatened anything of the kind in the past, so she was unsure whether I would keep my word.

Luckily, the ceremony was very short. The night before, we had built a bamboo tent in front of the Gopauls' house and installed a table there. The pundit sat at one side of the table; Anji's father, my father and I sat opposite him, while the relatives sat on folding chairs around us. I was in the middle, and Anji had to sit in the vacant chair next to me. She looked bemused and frail as she approached the table, and I got up to help her into her chair. I wanted to take her hand, which was shaking as the pundit put a twisted piece of mango leaf on the ring finger and said a few mantras. Then he asked whether we had a ring. I dragged Pa's ring-box from my pocket and took out the diamond-covered monstrosity. Anji looked up at my face, her eyes opened wide. I couldn't explain at that moment, just took off the mango leaf as the pundit instructed and slid the diamond ring onto her finger. She kept staring at me with distressed eyes. I closed her hand and kept mine over it so she couldn't see the ring. Then her mother was instructed to lead her out of the bamboo tent, and I saw Mrs Gopaul wiping away a tear with the end of her sari. I felt a bit sad myself. Anji looked so pitiful and docile, not like her usual self at all.

After the ceremony, a meal was served and I had to sit with the men. My father was on one side of me and Ashok was on the other. The pundit was on the other side of my father, so Ashok and I had to behave solemnly. In any case, I wasn't in the mood for jokes. I wanted to see Anji and re-assure her that everything would be OK. I also felt I had to behave like a man among men that day, since I was taking on the responsibility of a woman. All eyes were on me, most of all the eyes of Anji's relatives, who would be assessing me as potential bridegroom.

I felt a touch on my back. Beena was standing beside me. I put an arm around her. 'Ved,' she said in my ear, 'Arun say to come. Anji crying.'

I scraped back my chair, muttered something to my father, and went up the stairs. Eyes were on me all the way. I saw a knot of women and girls in front of the closed door to Anji's bedroom. Arun was guarding the door. His eyes were worried as he told me he had chased all the women out of the room to give Anji privacy. I moved through the throng and knocked softly on the door.

There was no answer.

'Anjani, what you crying for?' a thick-set woman in her forties called through the door in a raucous voice. 'Look at the good-looking husband you getting.'

I knew this would only make things worse. I tried the door. It was unlocked. I opened it slightly, slipped in and closed it behind me. Anji was lying on one of the single beds in the room, her face in a pillow. I went and sat on the bed and took her into my arms. She dabbed at her eyes with the end of her mother's sari. I reached into my back pocket, found my handkerchief, and gave it to her.

'If you hear the stupid things they saying,' she muttered in a choked voice. 'About how many Mercedes Benzes there are outside, and how you look like a prince . . .'

'And only you know the prince will turn into a frog if you kiss him,' I said, my mouth close to hers.

She opened her mouth to let me kiss her. Then she struggled away again. 'And what is this?' she asked, holding up her finger with my father's ring on it.

I laughed and took it off her finger. I dug her ring out of my pocket and explained about my father's purchase.

Her mother bustled into the room. I didn't move away from Anji the way I would have done the day before. I had paid Mrs Gopaul's price, and now I would claim my pound of flesh. She looked flustered as she complained that I hadn't eaten my meal. She said she would send some food upstairs so I could have something to eat before I went home.

'You take back the ring?' the thick-set woman asked when Anji and I sat down at the dining-table upstairs and she glimpsed my father's ring on my little finger. 'You can't do that!' she said. 'The ring is to show she engaged!'

Anji held up her hand to show the ring she had chosen.

'But that don't have no diamonds!' the woman exclaimed. 'Engagement ring must have diamonds. You never hear diamonds are for ever?'

'That's why I like my ring,' Anji answered. 'This is just for now.'

Ashok's face appeared in the front doorway. 'But how you could do that to me?' he asked, coming into the room. 'Abscond and leave me with one mile of geriatrics! I myself start to feel my prostate hurting after a half an hour talking with them. And you find yourself up here with the girls!'

I introduced him, and Anji offered him a glass of fruit juice.

'Juice?' he asked, jiggling his eyebrows up and down. 'After what I just went through? I sitting down there, and all them old lady sizing me up to see if I is the next marriageable Saran on the list. Squeezing my shoulder like I is some piece of fish they choosing in the market. Girl, I need some-thing stronger than juice after that!'

Arun got a beer and poured it into a coffee mug. 'What about a nice cup of tea?' he offered.

'That is the damn thing self,' Ashok said, taking the coffee mug and drawing up a chair, 'that is the damn thing self! A nice cup of tea. Just what the doctor ordered!'

One of my cousins came into the room to tell me that my father was ready to leave.

'Leave?' Ashok asked, his eyebrows shooting up in horror. 'Well, your father could leave if he want! It have a whole line of hearse parked outside. One of them could take him home. Boy, you stay here, eh! Tea party now start. I have to get to know my new family and them. What you say, girl?' He turned to Anji. 'You think Ved should go and fulfil he filial duties when you here in your nice, nice blue sari?'

Anji agreed with him.

'Okay, boss,' I said, tapping the back of Anji's head the way Arun did. 'I'll go and get rid of the geriatrics.'

By the time I had persuaded my mother to go home with my brother-in-law, the tea party had moved to the front verandah. Ashok was in full stride.

'When he start calling you boss, that's when you have to get worried,' he was telling Anji as I climbed the stairs to the porch. He looked up at me. 'I giving my sister-in-law here lessons in Ved-management. The poor girl don't know what she let herself in for.' He switched his attention back to Anji. 'If I was you,' he said earnestly, 'I would back out now. If you have to married a Saran, choose the lesser of the two evils.' He pointed at his own chest.

I perched on the banister behind Anji's chair. She turned to smile at me, her dimples showing. Arun offered to bring me a beer as well, but I shook my head. Somehow, the day was sacred to me and I didn't want to spoil it by drinking. The old Hindu traditions seemed to have reawakened in me. With my mother no longer around to create unpleasantness, I began to feel mightily relieved and content. I leaned against a pillar, stretched out my legs on the banister, and closed my eyes. I could sense Anji on the chair just in front of me. I felt her nearness somewhere in my chest. It was like there was an elastic band holding us to each other.

Ashok continued his warnings. 'Get out while the going good,' he urged Anji. 'That man does get on quiet, quiet, and then . . . Click! The trap shut on you. Look, Ved tell me I was only going to work on three houses in Dorado. Three houses! Now I find myself in permanent exile among the jellyfish, building recreation club, beach pavilion, research station! I say, let's you and me make a break-out now. We could get a boat and leave the country. Wash up in Venezuela, and *habla Español*, away from that man influence.'

'You will really frighten the girl,' I said. 'Anji, don't listen to any of that nonsense Ashok talking.'

'Don't listen to Ashok?' he repeated. 'Ashok is not the only one who will tell you this. Ask Charlo. Charlo will give you the full scoop on that beast you marrieding.

'Who is Charlo?' Arun asked.

'You don't know Charlo?' Ashok's voice went up an octave in mock-surprise. 'You marrieding your sister to this animal here and you don't know Charlo?' He paused for effect. 'But that is gross incompetence! You mean to tell me, you marrieding your sister to a man and you don't know he father?'

'Charlo is Ved father?' Anji asked. 'But he was just here.'

'No, no, no!' Ashok cried. 'I don't mean that kind of father! I mean he real father. Not the contributor to he DNA. He spiritual father. He guru. You never meet Charlo, Anji? Big black Creole fella without a nose-bridge? But how the hell this could happen? Next thing, you will tell me allyou didn't consult the Patra!'

Anji tapped me on my leg with her hand. 'Who is Charlo, Ved?' she asked.

I had an urge to grab her hand, haul her onto my lap, and kiss her all over her face even though there were so many people around.

'Saran's builder,' I replied, with my eyes still closed.

'Saran's builder?' Ashok asked, his voice rising still further. 'That is how you does refer to Charlo, Ved?' He paused and I heard him shift in his chair. 'Look, I will tell allyou who is Charlo.' He paused again for effect. 'Charlo is another name for God. That is who Charlo is. If Charlo say jump, Ved don't ask how high. Ved does quietly go and start importing uranium to build a rocket-ship so he could reach Mars when he jump.'

Beena was leaning against my legs as I sat on the banister. I reached over, picked her up, put her to sit on my legs and put my arms around her.

'What allyou doing next Sunday?' Ashok asked. 'Bring the family up to Dorado, and we will make a cook, and allyou will meet Charlo. Them fellas will catch manicou and lappe and all kind of wild meat if they hear the forthcoming Mrs Saran coming up.'

Arun responded enthusiastically to the invitation. Mr Gopaul joined the group and they began making plans. I closed my eyes again. For me, everything was OK now. My team was even taking over my personal life.

It's a long, long drive to Dorado. You go through a five-mile corridor of coconut palms, with the surf pounding your eardrum on one side and the sway of louvred green branches to hypnotise you. Everything you were thinking about gets blown out of your head by the breeze of the Atlantic, which smells only of itself and, here and there, of fish. By the time you arrive in Dorado, you've forgotten there's an existence beyond Dorado. Here, you can just pick up little shellfish on the beach and cook them to eat. You can squelch into mangroves beyond the village with the teenage boys at full moon and come back with a crocus bag full of big blue crabs, or help the fishermen pull in their nets at dawn and get as much fish as you want in return. You can collect dasheen leaves and make a wonderful soup with crab and coconut milk. You can boil the dasheens themselves, and the bananas that spread their suckers through the village. The juiciest of little mangoes litter people's yards; gigantic yellow bread-fruit fall from great fans of leaves to bang on their tin roofs. You can time the drop of a mamee-seepot, another great cannonball of a fruit that hangs immobile on corky stems and then crashes to earth, denting the asphalt of the road. You can slice off the top of a green coconut and drink water that melts kidney stones, then scoop out its delicate jelly and replace the essential ions of your body if you're tired. You can grate coconut flesh, mix it with shredded cassava, pumpkin and brown sugar, and end up with a dessert called belly-full. You can drink the water in which the fishermen boil little black barnacles they scrape from rocky outcroppings, and get a hard-on when you want a hard-on. You can drink the water in which fishermen's wives boil soursop leaves, sleep like a stone, and forget you had a hard-on. You can drink milk in which sea moss has been boiled, and claim you always have a hard-on. You can pry oysters from mangrove roots that grow above the murky swamp and suck them out of their shells with a mixture of herbs, lime juice and pepper sauce. You can boil conches till they turn into something like boiled truck-tyres, taste of nothing at all, and then support the villagers' lie that it is the tastiest dish on earth.

Everything tastes better in a sea breeze, I swear this. Maybe the scientific community hasn't noticed the phenomenon yet, but, like everybody else, they need to go to Dorado to discover some important truths about life.

I discovered one truth the Sunday after my engagement ceremony: that it was better to go to Dorado with my two girls in the car than with anyone else in the world. Anji and Beena drove with me, singing all the way, while Arun drove his parents in their car.

'When I dead and go to heaven, I hope it will be like this,' Mrs Gopaul said when we finally arrived. It sounded like she was giving a warning to God.

'What you want to go to heaven for, Moms?' Charlo asked her. 'That place will only be full of pundit. Stay alive and come up here. I will build a better house for you than any of these.'

Few people had seen our compound at this stage; Guayaguayare was too far away for seaside visitors. But people staying at the beach-houses strung along the Dorado coast took drives to have a look; it was becoming an exclusive form of entertainment. The compound was now a large bowl of flowers and greenery carved into the earth on the far side of the village, outlined by a curve of coconut palms, white sandy beach and blue sea. The houses were dotted around the curve, each wooden structure the centre of an extensive garden that climbed up its walls or flowed through its patio into its interior.

'But Ved, you is not a pundit!' Mr Gopaul commented. 'You is a genius! I never see house like this in Trinidad.'

'It's not me, it's Charlo,' I told him.

Ashok jiggled his eyebrows at Anji. 'You see what I tell you?' he asked. 'According to Ved, Charlo is more God than God himself.'

'And who is the devil?' Mrs Gopaul asked, jiggling her own eyebrows in imitation of Ashok. 'Where it have a God it must have a devil. I have a feeling it's you.'

It was Charlo's landscaping that made the place. With each house, he dreamed up a new garden the way he had created his Carnival band every year. That year he had had his Filipino phase. He had put together a miscellany of wind-chimes out of polished bits of coloured glass, shells and wood-chips, and tiny steel pans. I had been afraid that the sound would be cheap and horrible, but somehow those chimes created an aura of peace among the muffling fronds of banana and bamboo. Near the recreation complex, he had built various sizes of windmills that generated electricity to create a completely unpredictable light-and-sound show in the evenings. His water-gardens were full of fish, crabs, tortoises, and a pair of lobsters he called Adam and Eve. Workmen on the site brought him parrots and parakeets they caught in the forest behind the beach, monkeys, and once even a crocodile they trapped in the nearby river. He had only let the croc go after eliciting a promise from me that I would import a pair of peacocks from India for him.

Arun and his father were sampling Ashok's Dorado lime punch on the patio of the last house we had built. 'Let's go in the sea,' Beena begged, pulling at Anji's arm. She had already put on her bathing-suit. But Anji felt shy to take off her shirt with all the guys around the building site. Mrs Gopaul had deliberately not brought a bathing-suit. That wouldn't be proper in front of her future son-in-law, she said.

I went down to the beach with Beena. The two of us lay in the surf, letting the tide pull us this way and that. I liked to feel the drag of the undertow, the immense hidden power of the ankle-deep water that could lure someone of my weight into depths from which there was no escape. That paradisical landscape was really a dangerous place to bathe.

Anji came from the house with a handful of nuts. I tickled one of her feet as she bent over to pop some into my mouth. When she raised her foot to escape my fingers, I grabbed her other leg and pulled her forward to make her topple on top of me. She was soon prone next to Beena and me, her thin white shirt plastered over her bathing suit, her trousers drenched, and her hair dripping in strands at the sides of her face.

I could have lain there for the rest of the day, just watching tiny shellfish get disturbed by the waves and dig themselves back into their holes. Beena and I scanned the beach constantly to see if we could encounter a crab or two. Anji piled wet sand up and watched it settle into fat clumps that slowly dissolved back into formlessness.

'Ved,' she murmured, putting out her forefinger to trace the hairs on my chest.

'Yes?' I asked.

'Nothing,' she said.

But the smile in her eyes made me feel as though the undertow had crept up beneath my body and was sweeping me away into the depths. I had to tear mine away to pay attention to Beena again.

When we went back to the patio to eat, Mikey was in a far corner of the front garden with his tenor pan, playing a bleak melody that became a storm of sound at times, then died down and became bleak again.

'What's that tune?' Anji asked.

'He does call it "The End of the World",' Ashok replied.

On our trip to Portugal, we had driven along the coast to a place referred to as the End of the World. The name had tickled our imaginations. It was the most south-westerly point of the European continent, the curve on the map where the Atlantic and Mediterranean met. It had turned out to be a desolate promontory high up over the sea, miles away from the nearest human habitation. The water there was a deep but transparent turquoise, with streams of jade and sapphire where the tides of the ocean challenged the sedate Mediterranean. You could feel that turquoise in your throat, in your veins. Mikey hadn't wanted to leave. He had made us go back twice with him, just to stand on that edge of the continent and let the high winds whip his dreadlocks in wild arcs round his head. 'This is where our history began, Ved,' he kept saying, in a voice that seemed to contain tears. Africa was to our left, invisible to our eyes, but visible in the Moorish architecture of the towns. There, where we stood bracing ourselves against breezes that threatened to launch us into the ocean, Henry the Navigator had paced six hundred years before. It was in Henry's dreams that we had been conceived. That Atlantic horizon on which we then gazed was where ships were supposed to tumble over the edge of the ocean into the nothingness of nothingness, into the end of the known world. Crossing that horizon was to mean the beginning of our journeys to this other Atlantic coast, called Dorado.

'He will go on so for three days non-stop,' Ashok was saying. 'When Mikey catch a soor, he does beat that pan till he fall down from exhaustion.'

'The complete thing is called "Lost at Sea",' Charlo added. 'That is Columbus travelling in the *Santa Maria*. Just now, he going to get catch-up in some weeds and can't move . . .'

Mrs Gopaul was not concerned about Columbus and his troubles. 'So Mikey don't eat when he playing?' she demanded.

'Eat?' Ashok asked. 'Mikey don't sleep. The man does get like something possess him.'

Mrs Gopaul put on her worried look. 'But that not good for him,' she said. 'Look how thin he is! All that hair sucking him.' Indeed, Mikey's locks were as thick as his body.

'That is why I does cook this thing you eating here,' Ashok said. 'Mikey is a vegetarian. We does have to force-feed him when we get a chance.'

To accompany his stew of wild meat, Ashok had thrown chunks of breadfruit, green bananas, ripe plantains and herbs into an old vegetable-oil tin and let it simmer over a wood fire with a few crabs in coconut milk. He claimed the barbeque we had built for the residents of the house could not create the same flavour as authentic not-home cooking.

'When Mikey get lost at sea, I does cook Found on Land,' he explained. 'I does throw in everything nourishing I could find.'

I left my food and went across to Mikey. I knew he wanted me to listen to the latest progress on the tune, the little refinements he had added. That was one of my tasks when I came up to Dorado. In some way, I felt that this was why I had been born in the Croissee, to listen to Mikey's compositions and give him encouragement. The melody eventually veered into its familiar pattern. Mikey had long succeeded in getting his pan to imitate the sound of waves. I touched his shoulder and went back to my lunch.

Ashok had given the guests the claws of the crabs and Anji was struggling with the thick carapace. Charlo reached into his back pocket, pulled out a shiny new pair of pliers, and set it down in front of her. 'Try that,' he said.

She didn't know how to manipulate a pair of pliers. Charlo took them from her and demonstrated, then handed them back to her. She was still ineffectual.

'Use the muscles in your hand, girl,' Charlo urged. 'You have muscles in your hand, you know. You have to grip the pliers firmly. Don't be afraid. You is the boss over the pliers.'

I glanced at him. Those were some of the first words he had uttered to me when he had taken me under his wing all those years before. He had told me that the first lesson in life was how to hold a pair of pliers. Once you could use a pair of pliers properly, he said, you could take over the world. Now they were our kitchen implement of choice. We crushed garlic with them, nutmegs and cloves and anything else that needed to be crushed. I sometimes disintegrated tiny cardamom seeds into tea with them to make Indian chai for Charlo. Ashok picked up hot pots with them, bits of coal to regulate the temperature of his wood fires, and pieces of chicken when he was grilling Jamaican jerk. He claimed he was waiting for one of us to break a tooth on a crab leg so he could practise his dentistry with them.

Mr Gopaul borrowed the pliers next, and the others followed. Although we had supplied the house with nutcrackers and special implements made in France that were cast in the shape of lobster claws, they only made a mess of broken shell and bits of flesh. I had even got tongs and picks designed for opening up the backs of lobsters and winkling snails out of their shells, but the pliers worked better if you held them correctly.

'I could keep these pliers as a souvenir, Charlo?' Arun asked. 'They have a nice design on them.'

They were stamped with the insignia Charlo had originally designed for Saran's Symphonia, a long snake of an S, its tail curving into the form of a steel pan. We marked all our tools to prevent them getting stolen, which only caused them to get stolen.

Charlo shook his head at Arun. 'That's your sister's pliers,' he said.

'That's your dowry, girl,' Ashok told Anji. 'If you behave good, we will give you a bread-knife next,' he said, pointing to a ragged-toothed saw.

The smile she gave him swept me off my feet again. Her hair was tangled around her head and shoulders, and her clothes were drenched and awry. That smile was like sunshine penetrating the dampness of a mangrove swamp.

As we finished our meal, Mikey swung into a Castillian movement. Columbus was approaching Santo Domingo. Ashok got two dried coconut shells and clicked them like castanets. Then we listened as French waltzes took over Haiti.

'It's a symphony he playing?' Anji asked, looking at me with her mother's puzzled eyes.

'Yeah,' Ashok said. 'The unfinished symphony. The way he going, writing that symphony will kill Mikey.'

We all lay slumped in our chairs on the shaded patio, listening as Mikey beat out the history of the Caribbean on his tenor pan. Charlo argued that Mikey wasn't really doing a good job of depicting slavery, that he needed a bass for the voodoo and shango.

The earlier movement, which was about the eradication of the indigenous peoples, had been masterful, full of shrieks and screams and blood and disorder.

Mr Gopaul picked up a Sunday newspaper that was lying nearby and began reading it. He looked up from an article. 'Ved,' he asked, 'how come you not supplying teak for the new Central Bank building?'

Ashok chortled. 'Who say Ved not supplying the teak?' he asked. 'Where anybody does get teak in Trinidad except from Ved?'

'But this *Sentinel* say Chong Ping is the supplier of the interior materials. Look, they have a big article praising the elegant teak interior in the boardroom.'

'Chong Ping have shares in the *Sentinel*,' I told him. 'He advertising. You ever hear about Chong Ping doing woodwork before? Chong Ping is a pothole specialist. He does lay all them bad roads in Trinidad.'

'So how he get that contract?' Arun asked.

Ashok raised his eyebrows. 'How anybody does get contract in Trinidad? Bribe.'

'How you know that?' Anji challenged.

'How I know?' Ashok opened his eyes wide. 'But everybody in Trinidad know! Where you living?'

'I submitted a tender for that contract,' I explained to Anji. 'My tender wasn't accepted. Now, Chong Ping buying teak from my lumber-yard at the same price I would have charged the government. He must be charging the government a higher price for the teak, or he wouldn't take the contract. What that smell of to you? Not bribe?'

'And what you doing about it?' Anji promptly demanded.

I opened my eyes wide. 'What I doing about it?' I pointed to my chest. 'I selling Chong Ping teak.'

'But that's tax-payer's money wasting,' Anji spluttered.

'What you want me to do about it?' I asked.

'Tell the Press!' said Anji.

Ashok chortled. Charlo smiled. I myself was forced to smile at her naiveté.

'The name of the Press,' I told her, 'is Chong Ping. And Associates. It have other associates with other contracts.'

Anji shook her head gravely. 'And all allyou does do is laugh,' she said.

'What you want us to do, Anji?' I asked. 'Cry? We don't have time to cry. I busy from Balandra to Dorado to Santa Cruz to Port of Spain–'

'Ved,' Anji asked, her brow darkening, 'all you does study is making money?'

'Anji!' her mother cried. 'Don't start that again!'

Charlo turned to Mrs Gopaul with a surprised look on his face. His face had broadened in the last few years and was now a matt black that seemed to absorb light and sound. 'Why not, Ma?' he asked. 'Why the girl shouldn't start what she want to start?' He turned to me. 'Answer the girl's question, nuh, Bird. You does only study to make money?'

I shrugged. 'I does study the contracts I have to fulfil. I have to deliver a research station and recreation centre.'

'And make more money!' Anji pounced.

I got slightly annoyed. 'You know how many people depending on this company for work, Anji?' I said. 'I should get myself distracted by the arseness that does be going on between the government and Chong Ping?'

Anji shrugged. 'Usual capitalist story,' she said. 'You providing survival for a few people and the rest could go to hell. And you making the real money.'

'Anji!' her mother said. 'Stop that!'

I took Anji's hand firmly in mine under the table. 'If I wanted to make real money,' I said, 'you know what I would do?' She shook her head. I squeezed her hand. 'Sell Saran's,' I said. 'Sell the whole business right now. All this land. You know how much that foot of ground you sitting on worth, with OAG drilling off this coast?'

'But why would you sell the land?' Mr Gopaul asked. 'This land is a goldmine. Every grain of sand on that beach producing pearls for you.'

I laughed. 'It have bigger pearls in the sea. If I sell my property and put the money in the New York Stock Exchange, I would be reaping pearls of the highest price without moving a finger.'

OAG had recently discovered the world's second largest deposit of natural gas off the coast of Dorado, I explained. They hadn't let the Trinidad government in on that. They were in the process of drawing up contracts to exploit the gas on terms that our local idiots would think lucrative. But E. Duncan and the engineers who had made the discovery hadn't been able to keep their mouths shut after such an amazing find. They were begging us to build a golf course for them, knowing they were stuck here with Adam and Eve for at least five years more.

It was E. Duncan who had advised me to buy OAG stocks right away. They would sky-rocket once the news of the find emerged. I had followed E.'s advice, but this talk of selling the company to buy stocks was just late-night meandering with Ashok and Charlo. What would I do with more money?

And, as Charlo had pointed out, we had the peacocks to consider. We had spent over a year battling with Indian bureaucracy to get permission to buy those peacocks. The correspondence I had been conducting with

Indian officialdom had taken on legendary proportions and was beginning to constitute one of our own epics, complete with mythical flourishes. Knowing how things worked, Charlo argued, the decision might come through another year from now. Even if we didn't want the peacocks by then, those Indians would say procedures were procedures, the forms were already filled out, and the peacocks would be dispatched. We had to guarantee housing for them.

'Peacocks?' Arun asked. 'It's peacocks you studying, Ved?'

'Well, who will study the peacocks?' I asked. 'You know how much Indian regulations I battle with over those peacocks already? Indian regulations longer than the Indian scriptures, you know. In the old days, educated Indians used to write holy books. Nowadays, they does write government regulations. The Indians say peacocks is their natural heritage I trying to thief. I offer to send them a sample of my DNA to prove we thief it already. They say it's their cultural tradition. You ever notice how many peacocks Indian pictures does have?'

I felt something rubbing against my ankle. I glanced down. It was Anji's foot. I smiled at her and started stroking the palm of her hand under the table.

'You know how much peacock they have walking around on the highway in India?' I asked. 'They wouldn't give us two measly peacock, but bus running over peacock every day in Rajasthan. Screech! And a next peacock hit the dust and end up in road-kill heaven.'

I was a major palm stroker. At the risk of being immodest, I must inform you that I knew palm-stroking like . . . well, like the palm of my hand. Anji smiled at me in a seductive manner. She didn't know it was a seductive manner, but anybody could see seduction writ large in her dimples. I wondered whether I should stop with the palm-stroking – her mother might get embarrassed. But then I decided, what the hell?

'I tell Ved we should mount a commando raid and thief a couple of peacock,' Ashok put in. 'Just fly in on an Air India jet, anaesthetize a couple of peacock, put them in a suitcase, and fly back.'

'Nah,' I shook my head, 'next thing some Minister of Peacock in India have two birds unaccounted for,' I said. 'He will say it's Pakistan thief the peacock, and war will start. I going legal. If it take me till my next reincarnation, I going to reunite with my peacock brothers from the subcontinent.'

Anji was stroking my palm now. 'But allyou should really inform the government about what going on with OAG,' she said more quietly.

'Why you don't inform the government?' Charlo asked her. 'We have enough worries with the Indian government.'

'The government wouldn't believe me,' she answered.

'Ved will give you the proof,' Charlo said.

I had obtained a copy of the OAG engineers' report from one Miss Trisha Almandoz, who was always trying to get me to go boating with her. I'd told Trisha I had a girlfriend, but that just caused her to waggle her breasts harder during our meetings. Trisha now had a constant stream of excuses for calling me. OAG wanted a suite of offices in Dorado. They wanted accommodation for some office staff. They wanted a heliport to fly their staff back and forth from the drilling-platform – landing their helicopters on the beach only caused sand to go up in their nose-holes. They wanted a company dining facility.

'Nah,' Ashok objected. 'Trisha will get fired if that report come to light.'

I shrugged. 'Trisha *should* get fired.'

'Oh gosh, Ved!' Ashok exclaimed. 'Your heart make out of stone! Trisha will do anything for you. She came up here last Saturday because I mentioned you does be here on Saturdays. Meanwhile, you was in Tacarigua building tent for your engagement. She say she have to inspect the furniture to ensure it accord with what in the agreement. I tell her I not too sure the beds good. Maybe we should test them out.'

Anji stopped stroking my palm. I felt a bit irritated with Ashok. 'If you give away confidential company information, you think I wouldn't fire your arse as well?' I asked him.

'But Ved!' Mrs Gopaul said. 'You are a terrible fella! You will fire your own cousin?'

I think she was worrying about what she was getting her daughter into.

'Why I wouldn't fire him?' I returned. 'You think I have time to check up on the people who running this company? If they go giving away my secrets, why I shouldn't fire them?'

Anji tilted her face and stared at me. 'You have secrets?' she asked.

'Who don't have secrets?' I turned to her. 'You denying that you have secrets, Anji?' I held her gaze.

'What secrets I have?' she asked, blushing.

'You tell me.' I shrugged. 'They are your secrets.'

She sat looking at me speculatively. Let her look, I thought. Let Anji wonder what I was referring to. I knew one of her secrets, the reason why she had agreed to get engaged to me. It could be summed up in three small letters. S-e-x. I hadn't fooled around with so many women not to know the signs when a girl desired me. But that was going to remain my secret. I could have led Anji straight down the path to her own deflowering, but I wasn't going to do it. It was a hold I had over her. And I knew, too, that despite all her protestations, she was impressed by my wealth and power. That was hard to resist.

But I wanted her. For some reason, I wanted her at a very visceral level. Everything Anji did was lovable to me – the way she moved, the way her eyes flashed, the way she ate gajar-bajar, even the physical clumsiness she sometimes displayed. There was a dynamic surrounding her that affected me like electricity. Sometimes she made me uncomfortable though. I wasn't used to being forced to defend myself. I could return the favour if I chose.

'So who is Trisha?' she asked on the way home. Beena had fallen asleep in the back seat as soon as we left Dorado.

'The woman in charge of housing at OAG,' I replied.

'Why she give you that report?'

I shrugged. 'She stupid.'

Anji kept her eyes trained on my face. 'That's all, Mr Saran? Or it's what Ashok was suggesting?'

'I have never laid a finger on Trisha Almandoz,' I said. 'You can ask Ashok if you like. Ask Charlo. They know everything about me.'

'They will never give away your secrets!' she said. 'You think I don't know how fellas does operate?'

'What you know about how fellas does operate, Anji?' I laughed. 'You didn't even know how to kiss a fella before you met me. I had to give you instructions.'

'You feel I real naive, eh?' she asked.

All I could do was shake my head and laugh.

'Ved, you want to marry me because I am this innocent Indian girl, don't you?' she asked. 'After you screw around with all kinds of women, you ready to settle down with the virgin goddess?'

I glanced at her. 'Stop it, Anji,' I said quietly.

I think my tone of voice frightened her. She was quiet. When I glanced at her again, she still wasn't looking friendly. I decided to concentrate on the road ahead of me.

Chapter Nine

Over the following months I could feel Anji watching me and wondering what I was really all about. I just let her. What was the point of arguing? I myself wondered what I was about. I kept wondering if I shouldn't get serious some time, get some professional training and stop the playing around with this company. But then the company would come up with some new challenge that would engross me again, like the research station. I truly loved working on Jeremy's concepts, trying to make that beautiful teak wood speak to its future inhabitants, tell its stories of slow growth in the forest among a miscellany of other vegetation, and birds and squirrels, and the rustle of snakes and dead leaves. I loved being there all day with the sea and the wind and the forest, and then taking a shower on the site and changing and driving down to Tacarigua to play with Anji in the evening.

So I could understand Anji's doubts. How would she explain to her university friends that she was involved with a businessman? Businessmen were scum, according to that campus, according to Mikey, even according to me. I knew scum well by this time. Scum was an Open Book to me. I myself was just an Accidental Businessman. I didn't put the world's second-largest quantity of natural gas on my father's doorstep. I didn't even buy the land. I was compelled to be a businessman. OAG was hustling me all the time. If I hesitated over something, they threw more money at me.

But despite Anji's doubts, we had a wonderful time together. We didn't have to play Scrabble on the porch any more. She was now allowed to go out with me, provided she was back before eleven – her mother said she couldn't go to sleep with her young daughter out of the house. We went to the savannah to eat roast corn sitting on a bench. We went to the movies. We went out to dinner. She always held my hand, or my arm, and I liked that. I liked her clinging ways.

'You have muscles!' she said.

'Oh? I was wondering what that was.'

'Do this.' She flexed her biceps. I refused. What's the use of having muscles? All the guys in the lumber-yard had biceps twice the size of mine. But they didn't have much muscle in their head. Girls always liked to feel your biceps, though, particularly intellectual types like Anji.

'Ved,' she asked, 'You could fight?'

'Cabinet and wall,' I replied. 'If you see me demolish a wall that built bad, I am a champion wall-fighter.'

'You can't fight?' She looked disappointed.

To be able to fight effectively in Trinidad, I explained, you needed to be able to use a gun. Armed robbery was on the increase, I don't know why. Some people said it was the rapid growth in wealth that caused it. Mikey argued that Trinidad had always been a violent society: it was born out of the violence of slavery. My brain couldn't quite wrap itself around that argument, and I gave up trying. I just took precautions like everyone else. Bad guys in Trinidad were really bad. They never committed robbery without rape. In the old days, you could park your car on the look-out at Lady Chancellor Road and indulge in some sexual frenzy. Nowadays, you were liable to get held up by bad guys and have both your car and your lady-friend stolen. I understood Mrs Gopaul's concern that her daughter should be home by 11 p.m., but it certainly put the brakes on any inclinations towards sexual frenzy.

Not that I was getting any ideas about sexual frenzy, mind you. I was on my best behaviour. Better than my best behaviour. I could have been a hero from one of those old Errol Flynn movies. Romance, a little kissing, nothing more. Girl home, safe and sound and hymen intact, in mother's house. I patted myself on the back. Maybe those self-restraint exercises had a delayed effect – I seemed perfectly capable of restraining the beast.

'How come you don't ever try to have sex with me?' Anji asked one night as we sat on the porch of their house.

'What? On this porch?' I replied. 'On these hard chairs?'

'Well, anywhere else,' she said.

'Name the place,' I answered. 'Where we does be that I could try to have sex with you?'

She stared at me out of the corners of her eyes. I patted myself on the back. This girl would discover that I was no Neanderthal. I adopted an airy unconcern about all things physical. Who me? V. P. Saran? Try to create opportunities for sweating and gasping? Naah! You must be mixing me up with some other denizen of the Croissee. I was strictly a candle-light-and-roses kind of guy. I could have starred in a Hallmark greeting card.

But every now and then, my past caught up with me.

One Sunday afternoon, I told Anji I had to leave her house at four.

'Where you have to go on a Sunday?' she asked. 'People don't do business on Sunday.'

'What you know about business?' I replied. 'Plenty business does do on Sunday. I have an appointment on the golf course.'

She looked at me askance. I laughed. Her worst fears realised: not just a businessman boyfriend, a golf-playing businessman boyfriend. Soon, I would be exploiting little boys by having them lug around my clubs while I only lugged around a gigantic belly.

'I have to go to a christening party,' I explained. 'One of the workers in the lumber-yard.'

She screwed up her face. I had only been there about an hour, and I hadn't touched her. She wanted to be cuddled. I suggested she come with me. We could go somewhere for a drink afterwards. She changed into a cotton dress with a little lace at the neckline and asked if she looked OK.

'Beautiful, as always,' I replied, Errol Flynn style.

As soon as we got out of the car in Santa Cruz, the father of the baby called me over to where he was hanging out with a group of guys. He was a mountain of a man with a big scar down the side of his face. His name was Jacob and he liked fighting. In fact it was Jacob I had once challenged to a fight. Since then, we had become good buddies.

'Ay, Ved!' he called. 'I thought you wasn't coming.'

'I nearly didn't come, yes!' I replied. 'I tired coming to christening by you. How much children you have now?'

That's the way you talked to lumber-yard guys. No niceties.

'This is only the sixth,' Jacob replied. 'I now getting started.'

'Why you don't pack it in, boy?' I asked. 'You don't find you getting too old for this kind of thing?'

'Old?' he replied. 'People does get too old for this thing? What happen to you? The older you get, the sweeter it is. You ain't learn that yet?'

'This is Anji,' I said, introducing her. I had never brought a girl into these circles before. They all fell over themselves to shake her hand.

'Anji, girl,' Jacob said, keeping her hand in his huge paw, 'when this young boy here start saying he getting too old, get in touch with me. I know some good tonic.'

Anji blushed all over her face. I slapped Jacob's hand away from hers. 'You embarrassing the girl,' I said.

'Ay, ay!' Jacob took a step backwards. 'So for that you want to fight?'

'Yes,' I said. 'You want to see me bust your ass here today?'

Those were the words I had used years before in challenging him to fight. It had become a joke between us.

'So this tonic?' Anji asked, her head on one side. 'What it is?'

If I knew Anji, she was thinking about Jacob's tonic as a topic for her final-year dissertation. That was on her mind a lot.

'Like Ved need the tonic already!' one guy crowed. 'The girl selling out your secrets, boy.'

I had to stay silent. If Anji hadn't been there I would have given the appropriate response.

'Hear, nuh, Anji,' Jacob said. 'This tonic does really work, you know. You sure you want Ved to take this thing?'

'I sure I don't want him to take it,' she said firmly.

'Whoo!' the guys hooted. 'The old Ved!' They started slapping my back. 'You have the girls and them frightened!'

'You know what Ved does say,' Jacob cackled. 'When you handling wood all day, you does build up an appetite.'

I hustled Anji away to more decent company as fast as I could. I headed in the direction of Mrs Antoine's hat. Mr Antoine kissed Anji's hand and proceeded to give her his lecture on Furniture-making From a Historical Perspective. She was riveted. Her eyes shone as she heard about Antoine's forebear who had made chaises longues in the court of Louis XIV, but had been exiled to Corsica because of some dalliance with a prince's wife.

Then Tony put his bloody foot in it. 'Talking about chaise longue,' he said to me, 'you inspect Her Excellency chaise longue yet?'

The American ambassador's wife had ordered chaises longues for her Residence. It was the first time Tony had had to build the things, and they had been a pain in the ass.

'I so busy, Her Excellency can't catch up with me,' I said.

'You better go, eh,' Tony said. 'Just put on your chastity belt first.'

Everybody burst out laughing. Anji looked from one face to another.

'Ved never tell you about his girlfriend, the American ambassador's wife, Anji?' Tony asked.

'The woman is about seventy-five and she does look like ninety-five,' I informed Anji. 'She does wear this red, red lipstick dripping down the sides of her mouth like Bride of Dracula.'

'And she always trying to get her fangs into Ved!' Tony added. 'The woman spending thousands of Yankee dollars on furniture, just to try and trap our boy on a chaise longue.'

When we left, Anji was quiet in the car. I drove down to Chaguaramas, to the club on the water where you could have a drink and watch the lights and ripples. Anji made a little conversation but was very subdued. This got me worried. Anji was thinking, and Anji's weak point was thinking. She could think herself into some major theories about me.

'So?' I asked. 'What's the problem?'

'I was just thinking.'

I knew it! Danger ahead! Keep your eyes on the road and a firm grip on the steering wheel.

'What you thinking about?'

'Well,' she said, looking out over the water, 'those lumber-yard louts probably thought I was another one of your playthings.'

'No,' I said. 'They definitely didn't think that. They never saw me with a plaything before. If I brought you there, they must know it's serious.'

Silence. I shifted nearer to her on the semicircular bench. 'Anj, don't take all that old-talk seriously.'

'It's not just old-talk,' she said. 'Someone told me Jacob doesn't have six children. He only has six children with his wife. He has others with other women all over North Trinidad.'

'That's Jacob,' I replied. 'Anji, that's the way lumber-yard guys are. You are the one always talking about working class. That's the working class in Trinidad.'

She looked at me. 'When you with them,' she said softly, 'you does behave just like them.'

'I have to, honey,' I replied. 'Those guys are my biggest business problem.'

Our lumber-yard was the foundation of all Saran activities, I explained. A lumber-yard is highly inflammable, so alienated workers can cause massive damage. And Jacob was also highly inflammable. He was the leader of the lumber-yard bunch and his status was built on his huge size and overactive penis. Sometimes he could be really troublesome. So I kept an eye on him, hoping that, sooner or later, the police would pick him up for indecent relations with a minor, or some such thing. That's why I had thought it necessary to attend his umpteenth christening. I always acted like I admired Jacob's sexual prowess and was awed by his size. He and I colluded in the myth that he would have beaten me to a pulp the day I had offered to fight him. But he was just a big lug, like a wall or cabinet. His own weight would have defeated him.

Anji didn't seem impressed with my explanation. 'So you does be putting on act depending on who you with?' she asked, looking at me out of the corners of her eyes again.

I sighed and scratched my head. 'Half of life does be an act . . .' I opened my palms helplessly. There was a silence. I tried again to make her understand how important it was to strike the right note with the labourers who worked for us. 'My cousin Vijay, who manages the lumber-yard, doesn't really know how to deal with those guys,' I said. 'They wouldn't do anything extra for Vijay, but they will do anything I ask them.'

'Not just the guys in the lumber-yard, it seems,' she replied. 'The American ambassador's wife, Trisha —'

'I never asked the American ambassador's wife or Trisha to do anything for me,' I broke in. 'I have never asked any woman to do anything for me. Except you.'

'What you ask me to do?'

'Don't dump me,' I said.

She looked into my eyes for a little while and then reached over and took my hand.

She was very attached to me, Anji. She was demanding and wilful, but I think she was just testing me. When we were alone, she would just curl up in my arms and feel my muscles.

'What you have with my muscles?' I asked.

'Well, if I going out with a Neanderthal, at least it must be a strong Neanderthal,' she said. 'It's survival of the fittest with Neanderthals.'

'You want to see survival of the fittest?' I would pick her up and spin her over my head till she begged me to stop. Then I would pretend I had injured my back. Anji loved that kind of clowning. She would gurgle like a baby.

I figured my patience would win out in the end. I was a patient guy. I had even come to regard bureaucratic bullshit as a game to be played. And I was extremely patient with people I loved. When my father wasn't well, I would get up a couple of times a night to check if he needed anything. I almost never grew angry with my mother. I just gave her back-chat because she needed it. I figured I had been extremely lucky in my life: I had been given so much, I could afford to give wholeheartedly. I always got back more than I gave. Look at the people who worked with me, Charlo and Nerissa and the others. They were just a joy to be with. What we did together wasn't work. It was play. And yet the money just kept rolling in.

'What happen to you?' Nerissa asked one day in the office.

'What happen to me?' I repeated.

'Why you always in a good mood so? I not accustomed to you being in a good mood. You trying to throw me off, or what?'

I grinned. 'And what is that you wearing on your finger?' I retorted. 'That is not an engagement ring, by any chance?'

Nerissa blushed. She went crimson. She put the hand with the ring behind her back. 'It's only to keep him quiet. Get him off my back.'

I shook my head. 'Why you so unromantic, Nerissa? I don't know how that man does put up with you.'

'This is not man we talking about,' she said. 'This is polar bear.'

'Well you always say you don't want no man. You say man is a sin against God!'

She sighed. 'When I get tired of him,' she said, 'I will just put him in the fridge. I going to buy one of them big, big deep-freeze we selling downstairs and park him in there. You know how Dracula does park up in a coffin in the night?'

I shook my head again. 'You and Anji is the spitting image of one another,' I said. 'Always saying allyou don't want to get married. I thought it was man who not supposed to want to get married. What wrong with the two of allyou?'

She made her rueful face. 'I don't know. Maybe we have the same disease.'

I wished Nerissa would settle down and put her fears aside. I had grown to love Nerissa. She was such a beautiful woman, but she denied herself love. I would have given her anything she asked for, but she never asked for anything. I gave anyway. She was so efficient, and threw herself so totally into getting the best for Saran's Enterprises, I kept on raising her salary and increasing her benefits. Eventually, I gave her the post of general manager, so she could sign company cheques when I was away.

This caused outrage among my sisters. 'Nerissa!' Indra exclaimed. 'But Nerissa never even went to high school.'

'You ever went to high school?' I retorted.

I found it annoying when my sisters tried to intrude into my business affairs. None of them had ever done a stroke of real work in their lives. They had just married professionals at an early age, and, as their husbands rose in the ranks, put on more and more airs.

'I went to St Joseph's Convent in Port of Spain,' Indra said, with her nose, literally, in the air. 'I have eight O levels.'

'Nerissa went to the University of Tunapuna Market,' I said. 'That is the best qualification for running this company.'

When Nerissa went to Miami to order stock for the store, Ma gave her a shopping list of things she couldn't get in Trinidad, things like Four-Seven-Eleven eau de cologne, which nobody except Ma bought any more. Ma had a huge stockpile of Four-Seven-Eleven in a cupboard, but she always wanted more. Nerissa urged her to come with her to Miami, but Ma wouldn't set foot in a plane. 'Plane does have germs,' she said one Sunday when I mentioned this in my sisters' presence. 'It just like bus. You does have to sit down close-close with nasty people.'

She had only ever seen the interior of a plane on TV. I don't think she had *ever* seen the interior of a bus.

I tried arguing with her. If she was ever to see anything beyond Trinidad, this was the best way to do so. Nerissa would look after her. 'You don't have to sit down close to nasty people,' I said. 'Nerissa does fly business class. You could go first if you want.'

'Business class?' Queen sniffed. 'I don't fly business class.'

'You don't do business,' I replied.

'Ved treats Nerissa as though she is his wife,' Indra said. 'Are you sure you're not having an affair with her?'

I stared at her. 'Are you sure you're not having an affair with your gardener?' I asked. 'You does treat him just as bad as you does treat your husband.'

While she digested that, Queen took up the cudgels. 'And what about this famous wife-to-be of yours?' she asked. 'When are you getting married?'

I shrugged. 'When Anji feel like it. The girl have final exams this year.'

I beat a hasty retreat before they got too deep into that subject.

Anji really was studying hard, but had dropped a bombshell on me. She was trying to get first-class honours so she could get a scholarship to do her masters degree abroad. What was it with all these women I fell in love with? Why did they always go abroad? But Anji planned to take a year off studying before she went abroad, so I had nearly two years to win her over.

I contented myself with that. I felt I was making steady progress. Anji couldn't really do without me, I thought. She complained if I went abroad myself for a week or two.

I suggested she come with me on a trip I was planning to Guyana to buy land. The latest contract being drawn up with OAG would involve such a large cash deposit that I had to dispose of money somehow. She accused me of trying to colonise Guyana, but it wasn't quite that. There was a lot of talk nowadays about ecology and destruction of rainforests. I was guilty as hell. Land was dog-cheap in Guyana, so I figured I'd better buy some and replant teak and mahogany, expiate some sin.

I was sure Anji would love Guyana, all that jungle and far-flung villages and rivers and suchlike. I promised I would get separate hotel rooms so she didn't have to worry about my Neanderthal ways. She asked me whether I wanted to give her mother a heart attack. I tried to give her lessons in mother-management. Just leave a note for your mother, I said, explaining where you are. She doesn't care what you do as long as the rest of Trinidad doesn't find out. Mothers don't want to know the bad news. She might complain when you come back, but it won't last. The deed will already have been done.

Anji listened thoughtfully, her head tilted to one side and her eyes a bit narrowed. I felt she was tempted. Then she shook her head. Her mother was not like mine, she explained. Her mother lived in terror of public opinion. Her in-laws had been awful tyrants, from a very strict Hindu family. Not being able to control their son's scepticism, they had taken it out on their daughter-in-law. She had had a nervous breakdown when Anji was nine. Anji still remembered her mother lying in bed for months staring up at the ceiling.

The expressions that crossed her face as she related the story touched my heart. She looked down at her feet, she spoke quietly, she hesitated. She wasn't the usual terror of a girl, tormentor of my existence. She said she knew that she was the greatest source of fear in her mother's life. Her mother was the kindest, most considerate person she knew. The only time she had ever been harsh with Anji was when she insisted that she get engaged to me.

My heart sank a bit. 'So that's why you let it happen,' I said.

She looked at me. We were sitting on their porch at the time, side by side on the broad banister. Her eyes looked troubled. She turned and slid her arms around my neck. 'But also', she said, 'because you are my favourite Neanderthal.'

When Anji pressed her body against me like that, she was open to me. It would have been easy just to keep kissing her, slide my mouth down her neck to her collarbone and then lower. I didn't. What was the use getting myself frustrated? Might as well just fool around with her at a superficial level.

'I'm always trying to protect my mother, even against myself,' Anji said, holding on to my hand. 'She is so soft, Ved. You can't imagine how vulnerable she is. When I started going to university, she was scared I might get involved with a black guy or something. She never said so, but I know it. She says I am my father's daughter. I just try not to do anything to worry her unnecessarily. I come home early every evening and stay in the house. I only have a big mouth, but I don't like to make her worry. That woman is the biggest worrier in the world.'

'Okay, honey,' I said, putting my arm around her and stroking her hair. 'We won't do anything to worry your mother.'

She looked up at my face. 'You are the besth Neanderthal in the world,' she said, in her imitation of Beena.

'So you don't like any of the non-Neanderthals on campus?' I asked softly.

She wrinkled her nose. 'Them?' she asked. 'Them is worse Neanderthal than you! They only have big words.'

I laughed. She opened her eyes wide like Ashok did when he was going into shit-talk mode. 'You know what it is to have a Neanderthal with big words jam you in a corner of the library, Ved?' She raised her finger. 'The only thing to do is take cover in the toilet. "Excuse me, I have to pee." My standard getaway line.'

We went with Arun and Beena to Dorado again, and had the 'besth' argument ever. Charlo introduced them to Santa Claus's Sleigh, a little car he had painted red and green and filled with toy cars for the Christmas window displays.

'Santa Claus's Sleigh?' Anji commented. 'Allyou realise allyou is real Mimic Men? Thai garden, Filipino wind-chimes, dashing through the snow . . .'

Charlo offered Anji the Sleigh so she could come to Dorado on her own and she suddenly changed her tune. It was tiny and very cute, a curiosity in Trinidad where no other such car existed. It was one of those Citroens that used to be called Ugly Ducklings, the ugliest, cheapest car ever built, with windows that fold halfway down to save on a winding mechanism. We had found it on the estate in Santa Cruz. It had been imported by one of Mr de Freitas's profligate children and abandoned when some part ceased to work. We had made a replacement part and got it running.

I thought it was an excellent idea for Anji to take the Sleigh. It couldn't go very fast, and was made of heavy steel: perfect for an inexperienced driver. But Anji's mother absolutely refused to let her accept such a large gift from the Sarans. Anji pleaded that it wasn't a Saran gift, but a Santa Claus gift, a found object, a gift from Charlo. Mrs Gopaul wouldn't hear of it.

Anji got her revenge by driving a real Saran car, my car, when we went out, denting it several times in the process. She was a terrible driver, no instinct for spatial relations, always too busy in her head. To her mother's horror, I just laughed about the damage. We had fleet insurance that would cover the cost of repairs. Mrs Gopaul kept insisting that I was spoiling Anji worse than her father did, but I found Anji's ineptitude charming. I indulged her any way I could. Why not? I indulged anyone I could indulge.

But then disaster struck.

Anji decided she wanted to go to the Breakfast Shed for lunch. She had heard about it from other students; it had become chic to go slumming there. I took her and she fell in love with it. It fitted in with her ideology.

Then this apparition appeared before my eyes: my old girlfriend Sharon. She had put on a little weight, and, as you would expect from Sharon, it was all on the boobs and bum. She was wearing one of her sheer blouses, except that this wasn't nylon, it was silk – white silk, shimmering against her shimmery skin, with a white bra underneath that was mainly lace. The nipples were in evidence, just the hint that Sharon was so adept at arranging. The skirt was of some brown silky fabric, elasticised somehow, so that it clung. The shoes were the usual weapons of destruction. The hair was as bouncy and shiny as ever, the smile seduction itself.

'Hello, stranger!' Sharon said, stopping by our table with a tray of food. I was genuinely glad to see her. I liked Sharon, even though she was as mad as a hatter. I was glad to find that there were no hard feelings about our parting.

At the Breakfast Shed, you don't have separate tables. You sit at long trestles. It was crowded. Sharon was looking for a place. What could I say? Sit here.

I introduced Anji as my fiancée deliberately, to warn Sharon not to start any nonsense. She glanced at Anji but squeezed in beside me. As she sat down, she bumped her tray and her drink tilted. I grabbed at it, but it spilled. Sea moss. Right on the crotch of Sharon's brown skirt.

'Aaa-gain!' she exclaimed, laughing and looking down at the stain. 'Ved, you ain't lose your touch! The aim still as good as ever!'

'It wasn't my fault,' I protested. 'I was trying to stop the glass falling.'

'That's what you said last time too!'

'It was true the last time too.'

She shook her head from side to side, smiling a sweet smile. It was a very amused smile, a smile full of mischief and memories. Oh God, oh God, please don't let this happen, I prayed inside. I will cease all my evil ways. I will never cut another teak tree down.

'Really?' Sharon asked, raising her eyebrows. 'If I recall correctly, it ended up with my skirt off.' She shook her head again. 'The old Ved, eh! Always protesting innocence.'

God, did you hear me? Anybody there?

'Sharon does only talk crap,' I told Anji.

Sharon began eating. 'Crap?' she said. 'Boy, the list of damages to my clothes alone that I could charge you for could keep me busy in the courts for months! Not to mention the couch, the dog . . . and then there's the bodily injuries . . .'

She didn't mention the abortion specifically. Thank you, Jesus. Thank you, Allah. Thank you, Thousand-and-One Hindu gods. I will believe in all of you jointly and severally for the rest of my days.

'So how are you?' I asked, trying to drag the conversation towards the present. 'How the Opposition going? They wake from the dead yet?'

'They going. And I going. But, by the way . . . Remember your old girlfriend Roshni? The one you used to lust after while you was going out with me? Well, I have a surprise for you. The MP leave his wife and shack up with Roshni.'

'Really?' I tried to ignore the jabs and concentrate on the main gist. 'So you was wrong in your predictions!'

'Not all my predictions,' Sharon said, the smile reappearing as she ate. 'Don't forget my prediction about you.' She inclined her head towards Anji.

'What prediction was that?' Anji asked, speaking for the first time.

'I always tell Ved that he will screw around with twenty thousand nigger woman, but he will end up marrying a nice little Indian baytee.' She skewered something on her plate. 'It's the shopkeeper in him. Always keep the resources in the community. Play outside, but keep things safe for the family.'

'Sharon,' I said, looking at her seriously, 'you being rude.'

She put on a puzzled face. 'Rude?' she asked. 'Since when you know me to be anything but rude?' She started to laugh. 'I never know you to object to rudeness. You does still hang out in the mas' camp with the jammette and them?'

'Sharon,' I said, 'you going to cause trouble with Anji. Stop talking stupidness.'

'No,' Anji piped up, 'don't stop talking stupidness, Sharon. Ved used to hang out in a mas' camp?'

Sharon opened her eyes wide. 'So you don't know Ved was the father of the Croissee mas' camp? Croissee jammette was Ved specialty.'

'Charlo had a mas' camp behind our house,' I said to Anji. 'I used to build the King of the Band.'

Sharon winked at Anji. 'Ved used to *be* the King of the Band. In a certain sense.'

Anji was absolutely silent after we left the Breakfast Shed. I was supposed to drop her back to the university library and go back to work myself, but I drove straight past the library and headed for Santa Margarita. It was the only place I could think of where we could talk privately. I drove up the hill to a quiet spot, stopped the car and switched off the engine. Janet's house was just below us.

'Anji,' I said. 'Talk to me.' She looked at me.

'I don't have anything to say.'

'You believe all that crap Sharon say?'

'Ved, why everybody always talking crap, and you are the only one not talking crap?'

'Sharon is a total madwoman, you know.'

Her voice rose. 'Ved, I really don't appreciate that!' she snapped. 'You were involved with the girl and now you calling her a madwoman! That's despicable!'

'It might sound despicable to you,' I returned, 'but it's true. I have medical records to prove it. Sharon tried to kill me twice. She dislocate my shoulder . . .'

'According to her, you dislocate her shoulder . . .'

'I dislocate hers after she dislocated mine . . .'

This wasn't sounding good. I tailed off. Anji heaved a sigh and when she spoke again it was in a despairing tone.

'What you doing with me, Ved? Anybody could see I don't fit in with you. Look at the kind of women you used to be involved with —'

'Used to be. Past tense.'

Her voice rose. 'I feel like a real ass sitting there, you know that?' She glared at me. 'A real ass. Ved Saran. King of the Carnival band, with jammette and Sharon, sexpot supreme, and me, sitting in the Breakfast Shed hearing all kinds of revelations.'

'Sharon's revelations are not true, Anjani. Sharon's revelations are Sharon's imagination.'

'Everybody imagining things! I imagining things. Sharon imagining things. Jacob imagining things. The US ambassador wife imagining things. Only Ved Saran not imagining things.' She leaned closer to me. 'What Sharon said only reflects reality. You screw around with twenty thousand nigger woman and now you want to settle down with the good little Indian baytee. That is reality. Anybody could see that from a mile.'

I ran my fingers through my hair. What could I possibly say? She stared out of the window at Janet's house.

'Anji,' I said. 'I don't know about reality. All I know is that I love you and I want to be with you.'

Her voice was quiet when she turned to me. 'You ever thought you might be imagining things, Ved?'

I had no answer. I was lost. We both looked at the view for a while. What to do? There was no point sitting there in silence for the rest of the afternoon. I switched on the car engine.

'What you doing?' Anji asked.

'Going to drop you back to the library,' I said.

She reached over and switched the engine off. 'Ved,' she asked, 'why are you such a dishonest creep?'

I felt like somebody had hit me. 'Anji,' I said. 'I am not a dishonest person. Be careful what you saying to me. You accused me of all kinds of things before. You said I was racist. Don't go overboard and annoy me again.' I switched the engine back on. She reached over and switched it off again. 'Anjani,' I said, 'please stop playing games.'

'I'm not playing games,' she said. 'You playing games. Whenever you get in a corner, you does run away. Put on your big-man voice and tell me to shut up.'

My chest was filling up. With what I don't know. 'Anjani,' I said. 'I have nothing more to say to you. It's true what Sharon said. I fucked twenty thousand nigger women and now I want to settle down with you. I can't change that. You will make your decision about what you want to do. I can't do anything about it any more, and I don't want to do anything about it any more. I'm tired of this. I'm tired of the whole thing. Now, let me drop you back to the library and I'll go back to my office.'

'No,' she said. 'You not getting away today. I want to know something. What do you think you want from me?'

I stared at her. 'What I think I want from you? I know what I want from you. I want to marry you. It's you who don't know what you want from me.'

'But you don't want to sleep with me,' she said. 'You want to sleep with girls like Sharon.'

'Sharon?' I was genuinely astounded. 'I want to sleep with Sharon?' I let my mouth stay open in shock. 'Why I would want to sleep with Sharon, Anji?'

'Every single man in the Breakfast Shed want to sleep with Sharon,' she said. 'You didn't see the agitation when she came in?'

I started to laugh. 'That is Sharon's tricks,' I said. 'That's Sharon's specialty.'

'Why you laughing so?' Anji asked.

I had to let her into the joke. 'Anji, Sharon is practically frigid. The other guys in Breakfast Shed don't know that, but I know.'

She stared at me as though she didn't believe me. I couldn't help continuing to laugh.

'Anji, I glad this come up. Because I never really saw the funny side of it before. I felt bad about the break-up with Sharon and I just blocked it out. But, boy, the crazy things Sharon get me into!'

I told her all about the double dislocations, the dog murder, the ditch Sharon dragged me into. I told it in my best storytelling manner, better than in this book, in full dialect and cinemascope.

'You sound like you enjoy it yourself!' she accused.

I considered. 'It was good for a time,' I said. 'Come to think of it, I wouldn't have missed it for the world. It was fun, like riding motorcycle. You never know when you going to crash.'

She stared at me in a bemused way. 'You say she is a madwoman,' she said. 'You sure you are not a madman? Perverted?'

I started to laugh again. 'Anj,' I said, taking her hand, 'that was good stuff for a twenty-year-old boy. Make you feel you is man, as Charlo does say. You could wrestle this wild beast named Sharon into subjugation. You know what an ego trip that is? And all the fellas looking at Sharon and wishing they could be me. Only I know you have to be more Neanderthal than Neanderthal to deal with Sharon. You have to be able to grunt real good.'

'You could grunt?' she asked. 'How come you don't grunt by me?'

I laughed again. 'You can't take grunt. One grunt and you will run off and shut the cave door.'

'Ved,' she said, her eyes narrowed, 'I don't feel you attracted to me at all. I feel it's just a mental image you have in your mind. I am just like Beena to you. But you really like wild beast.'

I stared at her in shock. 'That's what you think?' I asked.

She nodded, then bent her head. I bent my head too, to look into her eyes.

'You really, really think so, sweetheart?'

She nodded again. She looked sad. I reached over and pulled her into my arms.

'But you are the wildest beast I ever meet,' I murmured in her ear. 'A mental wild beast. I know how to deal with the physical ones. I just trying to develop some weapons against the mental ones.'

She wriggled to get more comfortable against my chest. That was all I needed. 'You really think I'm not attracted to you?' I asked, and took her hand and placed it against my penis.

She pulled it away like she had touched a hot coal. I dissolved into laughter.

'Anji,' I said, 'you are the jokiest person I ever meet. That's why I want to marry you. Charlo say that too. He say, with that girl around you don't need TV. Electricity could go off, and you could still switch her on. Just give her some capitalist talk. Tell her you going to rip off the masses or something.'

She glared at me out of the corner of her eyes. But she wanted to smile.

I could see the dimples winking on and off. 'Allyou does only laugh at me!'

'Sweetheart, we does laugh at weself more than we does laugh at you,' I said. 'You ever hear Charlo on the subject of my mother? Charlo say my mother only have to growl at him and he does get an erection. He swear the only woman he will ever marry is my mother.'

She was smiling now, so I continued to entertain her. 'Ashok say the only woman he will marry is Nerissa. Nerissa don't even have to growl at him and he does get an erection that don't go down for days. He say only jellyfish juice could cure that. I used to say I going to India and kidnap a feminist and bring her back here to give me erection. Them Indian feminist could insult man! The things they used to accuse me of! You would think I burning bride every Monday morning. You think all that peacock talk is just about peacock? Half the time we talking about peahen. I spend a month in India with a hard-on from Indian woman insulting me.'

Anji was smiling now. I moved into pure shit-talk mode. 'People think I lose weight from diarrhoea. It wasn't diarrhoea at all! It was masturbation. I tell the boys since the Indian government wouldn't let me import no peahen, I going to content myself with the next best thing. You.'

'Allyou does just spend allyou time laughing at everybody and everything,' she said, but not in a hostile manner.

'Anji, seriously,' I asked. 'What you want us to do? You ever went to Port of Spain General Hospital, casualty department?'

She shook her head.

'Well,' I said. 'I know that place good. Partly from my days with Sharon. Partly from experiences with employees. Anj,' I said, something sinking suddenly in my stomach, 'I watched a young boy die in Casualty. A young boy that I knew well. One of my employees. A boy I threatened to kick-up a month before. You know what that is, Anji? To watch a young, strong boy die because of the incompetence of the health system in this country? Then to go and have to tell his mother the news? To see my best friend leave this country because of that casualty department? To see the finest medical mind abandon Trinidad because he can't even get a functioning operating theatre to work in? Because he have to sit down at home and read airport novel while he should be cutting open people?' I shook my head and ran my fingers through my hair. 'I don't know what else to do but laugh, baby. Laugh and be strong, as Charlo says. Go brave. Grand charge. Pretend that you know what you doing, even though you guessing half the time.'

It was a relief to be able to say these things. I had never said them to anyone before. Everything was understood between Charlo and Ashok and Nerissa and my mother and me; we never had to explain ourselves to each other. We went brave, with bullshit as cover. But what I learned from Anji that day, from that little, inexperienced girl, is that you have to explain yourself to yourself sometimes. I needed her, as I had known from the beginning. I needed her to complain to about the things that grieved me, but which I could do nothing about, so I just blocked them out of my mind.

'Grace under pressure, as the man said,' she murmured, tangling her fingers in my hair.

I liked the feeling of Anji's hand in my hair. I wished she would do it for ever. 'Grace under pressure?' I shrugged. 'Sometimes it does be disgrace under pressure. I would be ashamed to tell you some of the things I do.'

'Like what?' She squinted at me. I sighed.

'You does call me Neanderthal. You don't really know what Neanderthal is, you know. I fucked a girl in broad daylight in the middle of the street in Port of Spain already. Anybody could have come along and see. I didn't care. A newspaper photographer could have come along and take pictures. My arse would have been on the front page of the newspaper, for all my employees to see. When I think about it now, I shudder. The embarrassment I would have caused my mother!'

'Why? Why you do that?' She was grinning. It just seemed to amuse her. I raised my eyebrows.

'Alcohol, girl! The name of the beast is alcohol. I was so anaesthetised by rum, I could have done anything.'

'You used to drink?' She looked shocked.

'If I used to drink?' I raised my eyebrows. 'Ashok couldn't drink with me. He used to be vomiting all over the place while I still trying to get more anaesthetised.'

'Anaesthetised from what?' she asked.

'From what?' I shrugged. 'You know what it is to be seventeen years old and be facing a mountain of debt?'

She shook her head.

'I don't know myself. I used to drink myself into not knowing. I didn't even know then that was what I was doing. Only as I'm talking now, I realise it. I thought I was just playing man. Fellas drink. I used to drink too. But fellas didn't have to sit down outside the intensive-care unit for hours, wondering if their father was going to live or die, and at the same time wondering if the topics they prepared for their A-level physics exam had come up. That was like a bout of schizophrenia. One part of my mind doing exam, answering questions, inventing the questions and answering them; the other part wondering if they trying to rescucitate the old man. That is the only day in my life I ever remember touching my mother. I tried to hold her hand. She pushed it away.'

I laughed at the memory. Anji started caressing my neck and shoulder. I liked that too. 'So you used to drink to escape your worries,' she said.

I held up a finger. 'I used to drink to escape arithmetic. I used to have all these pieces of paper by my bed. Full of arithmetic. How many thousands we owe this bank? What is the interest rate on that figure? How much is the shop bringing in each month? How can I pay Nerissa and Suzanne? Arithmetic drive me into the arms of so much jammette you wouldn't believe.' I held up a finger again. 'One thing with fucking. You can't do that and do calculations at the same time. I try it.'

Anji was silent for a long time. Eventually, I pointed at Janet's house. 'See that house down there?' I asked.

I told Anji the story of Janet and me, the story of Janet who had rescued me from bewilderment when I found my life had changed beyond my control. I didn't care that I was dominating the conversation. I didn't wonder if Anji was only pretending interest, if she was disgusted, or upset or what. I just felt like talking about these things for the first time in my life, and I almost didn't care if no one was listening. I was listening to myself tell myself the story of my life. I hadn't known it till then. I hadn't dared face all the fear I had faced. And the longing afterwards. Missing Janet. Knowing there was no one in Trinidad like her, and that I had probably lost her for ever. I told Anji about painting broomsticks at Charlo's mas' camp, about the unborn child that I felt terrible about disposing of, about the business community that snubbed me, about the government officials that hated me, about OAG that loved me, about the jellyfish on Dorado beach. I entertained her and entertained myself, reliving jokes and revisiting bullshit. I swore that one day I would take her to Patpong, to Thailand's red-light district, so she could see for herself a girl pull razor blades out of her pussy. I didn't use polite language. I'd given Anji all the polite language I was capable of and she still mistrusted me. Fuck you, Errol Flynn.

Then I announced that I wanted to go home. I had exhausted myself and the shadows of the mountains were beginning to lengthen on Santa Margarita. I didn't care what Anji did. I would drop her home, drop her at the library, drop her anywhere she wanted to go.

'I want to go with you,' she said.

'What? To encounter the Beast from the Black Lagoon?' I asked. 'You don't know my mother, Anji.'

'What will she do to me?'

I shrugged. 'Insult you. Ignore you. Depends on her mood. Depends if she wants to rip somebody to shreds for entertainment. She likes to watch people squirm.'

'She worse than me?' Anji asked.

I had to laugh. 'You only specialise in ripping me to shreds,' I said. 'My mother is omnivorous.'

'That's what you think!' Anji boasted. 'You never see me in a tutorial. I does dig out the liver from educated asses and eat it raw in front their face.'

'You calling numbers you can't play, Anji,' I said. 'We are talking here about a woman who does make pundits stutter from the moment she enter a Ramayana Yag.'

She opened her arms wide. 'But I am not no pundit,' she said, the Anji I loved.

Chapter Ten

I was worn out from argument, from defending myself, from explaining myself, from talking. Otherwise I would never have taken Anji to my house that day. I just wanted to get home, take a shower and retire to my hammock. But she insisted that she wanted to stay with me.

'Last chance for retreat,' I said, holding up the electronic device that opened the gates at the back of our compound.

'Electronic gate and thing!' she exclaimed. 'Let me press it. I never open a electronic gate before.'

'All right,' I said. 'Say your prayers. We are going into the jaws of hell.' I drove forward.

'Wow!' Anji exclaimed as she surveyed the garden. 'You sure we in the right place? This look like something from a movie.'

'A horror movie,' I warned.

My mother was watering plants. 'Ma!' I called, when we got out of the car. 'Anji's here.'

'I could see that,' Ma snapped. 'I not blind.'

I raised my eyebrows at Anji. Then I led her up the stairs and went into the kitchen to get drinks. 'Tea, juice, Coke?' I asked.

'Whatever you having,' she said, gazing at the kitchen. 'Look at all these gadgets!'

'Then it's whiskey and soda,' I said. I poured a tiny amount of whiskey into a glass for her and topped it up with soda. Then I led her over to my part of the balcony. 'Now,' I said. 'I'm not going to talk. You wanted to come, so you have to accept my conditions. We are going to lie in that hammock silently.'

'What will your mother say?'

'Absolutely nothing. My mother don't talk to other Indian people. She say they too stupid to talk to. And she don't give a damn what you do. Never say a single word while you in this house, and everything will be fine. Trust me. I am the world expert on my mother.'

I held the hammock open for her and she sat down gingerly. It was a big hammock, a Brazilian hammock. I sat next to Anji. Then I swung my legs into the hammock, knocking hers in as well. I placed a cushion behind her head and one behind my own. I closed my eyes and rocked with my toe against the wall.

'What?' I asked.

'Nothing,' she said. 'You said don't talk, so I didn't say nothing.'

I swung my arm around her and pulled her against my chest. 'You're comfortable?' I asked with my eyes closed.

'Yes.'

'Sure?'

'Yes.'

'OK.' I pulled her a little closer. 'Go to sleep now.'

I could have lain there for hours. I can usually lie in my hammock for hours, so Anji's presence wasn't the reason. I thought about Nerissa saying she would marry her couch, and thought maybe I'd marry my hammock if Anji wouldn't have me. I began to visualise the ceremony and found myself chuckling. Lying in my hammock with my eyes closed sometimes did that to me. I began to indulge in the most absurd fantasies. But starting to chuckle at the thought of the pundit performing the wedding ceremony between me and the hammock made me aware of Anji's presence once again. I had been stroking her hair absent-mindedly, enjoying the weight of her head against my chest, the scent of her against me. Then I realised her head was moving up and down and wondered how long I'd been laughing.

'You OK?' I asked.

'Yeah,' Anji murmured.

'You need anything?'

'No.'

'Water, juice, tea?'

'Mm-hm.'

'Want to feel my muscles?'

'I thought you said not to talk?'

'I changed my mind. You could talk.'

'Where's your father?'

'Don't know. Shooting wild animal maybe. In his dreams. Whenever you miss him, he shooting wild animal in his dreams.'

She giggled.

'I think my father drive a good few species extinct in his dreams already,' I said.

'If you wait long enough,' I kissed her hair, 'he will tell you what he catch today.'

She was shaking with the giggles against me. 'Ved,' she gasped, in the middle of a hiccup, 'I love you.'

'What?' I sat bolt upright, nearly spilling her onto the floor. 'Girl, you want to give me a heart attack here!' I said. 'You mustn't spring these things on me so.' I kissed her neck. 'Lead up to it gently.' I kissed her collarbone. 'First, say, Ved, you have nice hair.' I kissed her jaw-line. 'Ved, you have a nice Adam's apple.' I kissed her ear. 'I like your car, or something.'

'But you don't have no nice Adam's apple,' she giggled.

'Lie, girl, lie,' I murmured against her neck. 'You don't have no imagination?'

'Well, I tried,' she gasped. 'With your muscles. But you never take me on.'

I stopped kissing her. 'You mean you was lying all the time about my muscles?' I asked. 'And here was I, planning to enter the Mr Universe competition. I done order the steroids.'

Naturally, my mother had to choose this moment to butt in. 'You does eat cascadoo, girl?' she called, approaching the hammock.

I tried to shoo her away. 'Who don't eat cascadoo?' I asked. 'Of course Anji does eat cascadoo. What happen? Pa catch cascadoo today?'

Anji put her hand over her mouth to suppress her giggles. Ma glared at us. 'Sylvia cooking cascadoo,' Ma said.

'Thylvia doeth cook the betht cathcadoo,' I told Anji.

'I have to call my mother if I staying for dinner,' she said shyly, shifting away from me in the hammock.

'Well, we have phone!' Ma snapped. Anji looked at me in a sort of scared way. I think the full extent of my mother's charm had finally penetrated.

'I should really go home,' she said. 'I need to take a shower before I eat.'

'Well, we have shower!' Ma snapped. 'What you think? The Croissee ain't get running water yet?'

'You can take a shower here,' I said. 'Go on. You know you love cascadoo.'

'Come,' Ma said, and turned on her heel and walked off.

Anji made a face at me and got out of the hammock to follow my mother.

I went to my own bathroom to shower as well. When I returned to the verandah, Anji was sitting at the dining-table with my mother. 'Hindi easy, you know,' Ma was saying. 'It not like Chinee. I try to learn Chinee from Mr Chang newspapers, but I give up.'

I realised that Ma was giving Anji the story of how she had secretly taught herself Hindi and Sanscrit when she was a little girl. I got myself a drink and settled down with them. I had heard the story before, but Anji's eyes shone as she listened. Ma's stories about her childhood opened up another world, a long-lost world, when the area just south of the Croissee was still almost rural. She described how her parents had spoken Hindi as a secret language there. The other children only knew English, but Ma managed to decode the Hindi.

'If my father tell my mother something and I see my mother go and get a towel, then I know that one of those words mean towel,' she said.

Anji kept plying my mother with questions. Give that girl a little dose of oral history and she was as happy as a pig in shit. And I have to admit that Ma had a good line in oral history.

The motivation behind Ma's thirst for knowledge, she revealed, was self-preservation. She wanted to know when she was going to be punished, so she could go and hide in a big breadfruit tree. Her misdemeanours were many: playing cricket with the boys, going fishing in the river, reading her father's Sanscrit books. Her father was a pundit, and his books were holy. Girls were not supposed to read holy books. There weren't any other kind of books in those days, except school books in English.

'English books? What is that?' Ma said. '"Dan is the man in the van." What kind of book is that?'

The Sanscrit books were full of stories. Demons and gods and bad guys and magic powers. Ma's father related parts of the stories at religious ceremonies. Ma wanted to know the rest, so she stole the books when he was resting in the afternoon and read them in the breadfruit tree. She taught herself to read Sanscrit in that breadfruit tree. Being in the breadfruit tree itself was a deeply punishable offence for a girl, but they didn't discover her hiding place till she was fourteen because her perch was too high even for her brothers. Nobody thought of looking there for her.

'I coulda beat all my brothers in cricket, you know,' she told Anji. 'That's why they didn't like me. They used to tell on me. Then I used to beat them in fight.'

My father emerged and dinner was served. Anji switched the conversation back to Ma's childhood. 'So you used to really beat up all the boys?' she asked.

'Of course!' Ma said. 'I was a kick specialist.' She pointed at me with a piece of roti. 'Look, that damn fool there. He gone by the Chinese Association to learn how to kick. One set of money he spend in karate lessons. I could have teach him how to kick. They used to call me the Grasshopper. Ask him,' she indicated my father. 'I put one good kick on him the first day I get married.'

Anji asked her why she had kicked my poor father. Ma sucked her teeth dismissively. 'You can't see that he need a kick?' she asked. 'He is a Saran. But then, you is a damn fool yourself. Only a fool would married a Saran. You know what Saran is short for?'

Anji shook her head.

'Saran is short for Stupid. I would have never married a Saran if I had my way.'

'You would have never married anybody if you had your way,' I said.

'Correct!' she snapped. 'What married good for?'

'You didn't want to get married, Ma?' Anji asked.

Ma slipped into storytelling mode again. By the age of nine, she said, she had already decided that she was not going to get married. Her brothers were fools, her brothers-in-law were fools, her uncles were fools, and her father was already married. He was the only one she respected because he read the scriptures correctly. But he was a tyrant, and he walloped her ass regularly for her misdemeanours. It was the battle of the tyrants when she was a kid. Ma figured out from his secret Hindi questions to her mother that he planned to marry her off the moment he discovered she was menstruating. She managed to keep her menstruation a secret for two years. But then she was found out and he started finding boys to marry her. The first time a candidate came to their house, she hid in the breadfruit tree. A snake ran over her leg and she fell out of the tree just as the guests were passing under it on their way back to their car. She didn't escape the walloping that followed, but she escaped the marriage. Being in a breadfruit tree was a strong reason not to accept her as a bride. The second time a candidate for her hand showed up, she vomited all over his feet. She had drunk mustard water to achieve that effect.

The third candidate was my father.

'I get married because of Saran stupidity,' she said.

My father never came to view the prospective bride. He was too busy hunting wild animals in the forest. Dorado was too far away to travel from just to view a mate-for-life. So he didn't get a dose of Ma's anti-bridegroom tactics and agreed to marry her sight unseen. 'Why I shouldn't kick him?' Ma asked.

Anji was staring at Ma like Moses had stared at the Promised Land. Now here was a woman worthy of a dissertation, I could hear her thinking. Ma had her eyebrows raised.

'You think that coconut oil fool me?' she asked.

'What coconut oil?' Anji murmured.

'The coconut oil you bathe in that time when we come by allyou,' Ma reminded her.

Anji started to blush. Anji looked very pretty when she blushed. Her cheeks lit up and her dimples showed.

'You think I don't have nose?' Ma asked. 'I could smell coconut oil from a mile. And you think I can't see when somebody put on their grand-mother dress?' She sucked her teeth derisively. 'You was playing mad. You think you could play mad like me? In my days, I used to play mad until every dog run under the bed and hide.'

Anji and I grinned at each other while Ma concentrated on her cascadoo.

'I was only sorry you didn't drink some mustard water and vomit on Ved shoes,' she added. 'It's a long time I telling Ved he should buy some new shoes.'

Within two weeks, Anji and my mother were as thick as jam on bread. Why did this surprise me? After all, my last, best girlfriend, Sarojini Lopez, had been a great fan of my mother's. And Saroj was a nuts and bolts kind of woman, grounded in the blood and guts of Casualty. To a fly-away like Anji, Ma was feminist icon. 'Tell That Girl if she want to taste Sylvia's coconut chutney,' Ma would say, 'today is the day to come.'

I had turned into a conduit for gracious dinner invitations. 'Now, just remember who you engaged to, eh, Anji,' I warned. 'Not my mother. Don't waste the whole night talking with her.'

She looked at me out of the corner of her eyes. 'I engaged?' she asked.

Why didn't I go with my original instincts and have a lobotomy performed? I could have been happily married to Donna from Dorado, instead of getting back-chat left, right and centre.

'Let me tell you, you engaged,' I said firmly. 'I know an engagement ceremony when I perform one in a hammock.'

'You engaged to about twenty thousand nigger woman, then,' she said. 'Why you don't married them first?' It must have been Anji's new fixation on 'Cultural Change' that did it. Before she got involved with me she would never have used the word 'nigger'.

I myself was involved in some cultural change. Since Anji had interpreted my gentlemanly conduct as disinterest in her body, I had decided to switch gears. Every time my parents' backs were turned, I grabbed her and subjected her to some seduction techniques.

After a while, I was not even needed as a conduit for invitations. I arrived at home for lunch one day to discover Miss Anji sitting at the table discussing Durkheim with my mother. Durkheim who? Durkheim, the founder of modern sociology. According to my mother, Durkheim was an ass. He didn't understand Cultural Change. Cultural Change was primarily motivated by stupidity, not adaptation. 'You think them pundit does do wedding wrong because they want to do it wrong?' Ma asked as she illustrated her point. 'It's because they don't understand what the book tell them to do.'

Anji was torn between Durkheim and Ma, her two authorities. As I listened to the two of them, I discovered that they were mapping out the argument for her dissertation.

'Next thing I going to start getting lawsuit from the Hindu Maha Sabha.' I predicted.

Ma dismissed the Hindu authorities with a wave of her hand. 'Bunch of crooks!' she snapped. 'They only formed the Maha Sabha to get their hands on the money the government gives out to religious bodies. You know how long I want to sue them? They does get money for every head of Hindu born in this country. Like we is cow. They getting money for me, every year.' She slapped the table. 'I want back my money with interest. I done calculate how much it is.'

Anji took notes.

I had no time to engage with Durkheim that day. I had OAG on my back, trying to push me into speeding up arrangements for building their heliport. I was not going to be pushed, or so I told them. They tried pulling, with cash. Nerissa determined how much pulling they could afford and gave me instructions on playing hard to get. I followed her instructions while she ordered cement and another truck, and trained a new accounts clerk in preparation for the heliport contract. I had given Nerissa instructions that OAG's gas-lust was not to intrude on the time we spent shit-talking on the beach or in the office. She would have to reorganise our production systems so as to keep shit-talk time sacred. These Americans thought work was supposed to dominate your life. Give you a hint of a promotion and you would work night and day for them. 'When night come, I going in my deep-freeze and shut the door,' I had told Nerissa. 'OAG have thousands of slaves all over the world, with PhD and thing, that they does control with promotion and career. I don't have no PhD and no career. I ain't no slave. You got that?'

So that first day Anji turned up at our house unannounced, I had been deep into my un-favourite things. A meeting with my lawyer to insert as many 'as necessaries' as possible into the draft contract OAG had sent us, some telephone calls with my banker, a visit to the lumber-yard to check how many girls Jacob had got pregnant that week. I had retired to the verandah for a quiet lunch and hour-long communion with my hammock.

Pa was sitting next to Anji, trying to interest her in the effects of his heart pills or something. I sat across the table next to Ma, where I could get a good view of Anji's neckline. She was wearing a blouse with a frill at the neck and I thought I could detect a little bruise just below. That would have been from our last encounter. I had nothing to say about Durkheim, so I concentrated on watching this beautiful girl who was mine, all mine. Anji wasn't like Nerissa, who could squelch sexual desire with one bolt from her velvet eyes. Anji's eyes sparkled as she swung from Ma to Pa to me, giving me little glances that she probably didn't know were the most seductive things on earth. She was trying to get me to join in the conversation, but I had only one desire: to sweep her up into my arms and take her off to my cave.

'What are you doing here, miss?' I asked, crouching down next to her chair after my parents had gone off for their afternoon naps. 'Trying to wreck my life?' I put my arms around her and pulled her up out of the chair. 'What are you trying to do to me?' I muttered, my mouth buried in her neck at the back of her hair. 'You shouldn't do this to me, Anji.'

I was more or less talking to myself. But once the words came out of my mouth, my hands couldn't stop themselves. Anji shouldn't have come here and caught me with my guard down. She was so slender, I couldn't feel her properly with my arms, and I had to reach for the places where there was flesh to satisfy this driving need.

'Ved, your parents!'

'One of them dreaming about catching wild animal,' I murmured, 'the other one dreaming about catching the Maha Sabha.'

Anji and Ma eventually launched their Field Research. What was Field Research? Going to Hindu weddings every Sunday.

Now, if there's anything you don't want in your life, it's a woman who makes you go to Hindu weddings. I had two. Or so I thought.

'I am not taking the two of allyou to any wedding,' I stated clearly. 'Occasional wedding is bad enough. Every Sunday for a month? Forget it. I have tennis to play Sunday mornings, swimming with my nephews in the afternoons, and romance with my baby Sunday evenings. I am all booked up.'

Anji's face fell. I started feeling sorry.

'Who ask you to carry us wedding, Mr Man?' my mother piped up.

'So how you going to go then?'

'Ain't She could drive?' Ma gestured at Anji.

'Who car?' I asked. 'My car will be at the tennis club on Sunday mornings.'

'So?' Ma asked. 'You is the only person with a car?'

Ma and Anji were going to use the Jaguar.

'You could drive that big thing?' I asked Anji.

Anji's eyes looked scared.

'Why she can't drive it?' Ma snapped. 'If you could drive it, why She can't drive it? I could drive that Jaguar! I see what you does do. I just don't drive because I don't want you to get more summons to appear in court.'

Actually, the Jaguar was the easiest car in the world to drive. It moved like a dream. Power-steering, automatic transmission, power brakes, the works. I gave Anji some practice and she was soon moving around the Croissee like the Duchess of Peale on wheels.

But. You have to understand that no human being had ever been allowed to touch that cherrywood steering-wheel except Yours Truly. Mrs C. Saran did not permit mere Other People to drive her automobile. Indeed she had created a purpose-built chauffeur for her needs. She had raised him, fed him, watered him and changed his diapers. Now his purpose in life was to take her out occasionally so she could cuss pundits.

My sisters went be-serk!

On the first Sunday Ma and Anji went off on a Field Trip, I picked her up, brought her to our house, and let her loose on the Jaguar. I went and had a couple of games of tennis, then returned, had a shower, and settled down nicely in my hammock with Durkheim for company. Anji had left him behind and I thought I'd choose a few quotes out of his mouth to confuse her with when she came back.

My sister Queen arrived, complete with the Band of Terrorists, a.k.a. her children. 'Toilet!' I snapped. 'You, you and you.'

Terrorists had a tendency to jump into the swimming pool and then remember they needed to pee.

'Ved.' Queen put on her long-suffering tone. 'How many times have I told you that's not the way to talk to children?'

I looked around me. 'I don't see any children,' I said. 'I only see brats.'

That was perfectly true. Those kids were brats, and I had a strict policy of truthfulness about them, part of my resistance campaign against my sisters. But I loved the brats and they loved me. They loved Truth, a good fight of any kind, and money. I gave them all of the above. They regarded me as their rich uncle and practised ritual extortion. If I asked them to pass me the butter, they demanded twenty-five cents in payment. They offered me every possible service on earth at a price, including tying my shoelaces and putting toothpaste on my toothbrush. I therefore charged them for my services, such as providing Truth. They were all sex maniacs. They had reached that age, and those who hadn't were getting a jump on their classmates at posh schools in South Trinidad – their imaginations were lurid in the extreme. I tried to tame them with Truth – it's the only weapon you have with rich kids.

Queen enquired after my mother and father. Pa was counting his cartridges, I informed her. He had realised that they no longer made cartridges to fit his gun, so he was very concerned about how he was going to kill off the last manicou in Trinidad. I hoped he wouldn't have another heart attack from the worries.

'And Ma?' Queen demanded.

'Gone wedding,' I replied.

Before Queen had a chance to get into details, Sylvia emerged from the kitchen. Queen began interrogating her as to what she was cooking that day. Queen's interrogations of Sylvia could last two hours. Each of her terrorists had special dietary demands that she flagrantly indulged. So I returned to Durkheim.

Then Indra's car, a little red Honda, swept into the driveway. When Indra's car swept into a driveway, the driveway knew it was being swept into. She swept in, complete with husband as well as her own terrorists. Queen's terrorists immediately launched a water-attack on Indra's terrorists. Normal chaos began.

I returned to Durkheim again, knowing that it was only a matter of time before I got drafted into chaos. Or, worse yet, into conversation with my brother-in-law, Krishna. He was a chartered surveyor working at OAG's oil installations in Pointe-a-Pierre, and therefore thought we had something in common. I hoped to God that we didn't. Krishna was a little shrimp of a guy who could bore God into dropping a hurricane into Trinidad just to get him to shut up a bit. The threat of conversation with my brother-in-law often drove me into the arms of the terrorists.

The next thing I knew was that Anji was sweeping into the driveway in the Jaguar, nearly running over a plant pot in the process. I got up and went over to the top of the stairs to receive her.

'Who is that driving Ma's car?' Queen's eyes were a-goggle. I didn't reply. She would find out soon enough.

Indra pushed her sunglasses to the top of her head and peered down as Anji emerged from the driving seat. 'Is that your fiancée?' she asked, wrinkling her nose.

'I not sure,' I replied, going for accuracy.

Terrorists swarmed around Anji. They had been waiting to get better acquainted with her for months. 'Hands off!' I barked over the verandah railing.

Anji looked up.

'They were just going to lure you down to the swimming pool and push you in,' I explained.

Twelve-year-old Shreshtha put on her most winning manner. 'Well, we could just talk to her then?'

'You?' I asked. 'The Embodiment of Evil? You will only corrupt her.'

'Suppose we pay you a dollar?' thirteen-year-old Narvin asked.

'Make it five,' I replied.

'Two dollars.'

'Two-fifty,' I said. 'Two and a half minutes with my girl for two and a half dollars.'

'A dollar a minute!' Narvin's voice was breaking and went into its wildest squeak. 'Uncs, you's a killer!'

I turned around to Queen's expostulations. 'But you don't even let my husband drive your car!' she was saying to Ma, who had climbed the stairs.

'Your husband can't drive!' Ma snapped, going into the kitchen.

I had to suppress a smile. According to Ma, Queen's husband couldn't do anything. He was a doctor from Chaguanas to whom Ma attributed every flu epidemic that swept Trinidad. She claimed he mixed up the injection needles and gave people flu germs instead of antibiotics.

'I better go and monitor what those hooligans saying to my girl, yes,' I said. 'If she only know the truth about the kind of family I come from, she might never marry me.'

'You and your precious girl!' Indra said, sitting at the table and dangling a high-heeled slipper from her pedicure in her most eloquent manner. Indra had perfected the art of dangling high-heeled slippers. It was one of her key skills. She believed she was Trinidad's answer to Marilyn Monroe. Her relationship with *Vogue* magazine was like Anji's relationship with Durkheim. Indra should have married *Vogue* magazine, I had recently decided. But she wasn't going to affect my marriage plans. I was going to let her know that now.

'What about me and my precious girl?' I asked, pausing on the third step.

'Nothing,' she replied. 'I was just admiring her dress.'

Anji was wearing her best dress, the little cotton dress with the lace at the neckline she had worn at Jacob's latest christening. I felt hurt that anyone should laugh at Anji's clothes. I liked Anji's clothes. They were always very distinctive.

'Indra,' I said in my quietest voice, 'if you say one off-key word to Anji, you will hear my mouth today.'

I proceeded down the stairs in the direction of the terrorist camp. I was forestalled with a request that I kiss Anji for Terrorist Education Purposes. I proposed a dollar in payment. We settled on fifty cents and I kissed her cheek. Loud protests. I was supposed to know what kind of kiss they meant. That would cost them six dollars, three for me and three for Anji. We settled on two, and I kissed her on the mouth. Outrage! That amounted to a dollar per second! I offered a deal. Twenty dollars for a kiss that would knock their socks off. They didn't have twenty dollars, I knew.

Anji was scandalised, of course, both by the petty capitalism we routinely practised as well as by my willingness to provide practical sex education. We, terrorists and I, jointly and severally, informed her that their sex education was well advanced. They had a private instructor in the form of their next-door neighbour, who habitually imposed himself on his young maidservants. The terrorists had an educational aid in the form of a telescope I had given them to study the stars. I was merely trying to instruct them in Romance, even though I knew it was a lost cause – I had been a thirteen-year-old boy once.

'I should go and pay my respects to the ladies,' Anji said, looking up towards the verandah.

'Disrespects, more likely,' I muttered, and escorted her into the lion's den.

'Well,' Queen greeted her, as we came up the stairs. 'You finally deign to come upstairs.'

She actually said that, I swear. This was typical Queen: catch them off-guard and let them know who was setting the pace of the batting.

'She was getting a crash-course in juvenile delinquency,' I explained sweetly. 'She don't know if she might end up as a social worker in the Prisons Service.'

That was calculated to shut Queen up. I regularly predicted that my nieces and nephews would end up in prison. Ravi had already been expelled from two private schools.

'Social worker?' Anji turned to me. 'Boy, you mad? After today? I going and blow Durkheim out of the water!'

'How the field trip went?' I asked her, smiling, my arm around her as we leaned on the verandah railing.

'Field trip?' she replied, smiling back at me. 'What field trip you talking about? It was a circus I went to.' She started laughing. 'Your mother was like a lion-tamer. The poor pundit didn't know what to do, go for the chair or run from the whip.' She started imitating my mother's voice and the pundit's reactions.

Indra blew on her sunglasses, polished them meticulously, and adjusted them just so among the curls on her head. Queen studied the end of her nose. Obviously, Anji needed training in the Modern Saran Approach to Indian Weddings. Indra's was to act as though she was dropping in on them on her way to an appointment in Paris. She got dressed up in her *Vogue*, put on a particularly deep shade of nail polish she reserved for such occasions, handed over her gift, intimidated the bride, and swished off. Queen did something similar except that she looked like a buffalo on the loose doing it.

Sylvia emerged from the kitchen bearing a big chocolate cake. Anji's smile widened till the dimples threatened to swallow her face.

'You didn't tell me you were making chocolate cake this afternoon,' Queen said to Sylvia.

'I wasn't making chocolate cake this afternoon,' Sylvia replied. 'I make it since Anji came this morning. I was only going to make the frosting this afternoon. Quick,' she said to Anji, 'take a big piece. Once them children spot this cake, it finish.'

Sylvia didn't know she was playing with her life. Or maybe she did. She was taking liberties with Queen because she had seen Ma permit Anji to drive her car.

And the revolution had only just begun. Anji laughed so hard as she related her own part in the wedding comedy, she got frosting on her nose. When Ma proceeded to deliver a blow-by-blow analysis of the pundit's errors in her usual stentorian tone, Anji started shaking with suppressed laughter. She had dropped her pen and it had rolled under a woman's sari.

Anji didn't notice the glances my sisters were exchanging; her attention was focused on me. But I knew what was going on behind those two sets of raised eyebrows. What woman with any culture would drop a pen under somebody's sari? And if, by some wild stretch of the imagination, they did, would they come back and tell the story? And get frosting on her nose in the process? This situation was far worse than Queen and Indra had ever imagined it would be. They might condemn me to kingdom come, but they had expected better from their prospective sister-in-law. They expected her to strive to be A Saran. Everybody knew you couldn't really become A Saran, you had to be born one, but you could give yourself ten nervous breakdowns trying. They had looked forward to assisting in the process.

'Weren't you embarrassed, Ma?' Queen asked, her tone more frosty than the frosting.

'You ever know me to be embarrassed?' Ma replied.

Ma had simply instructed the pundit to stop the proceedings until Anji found her pen, saying this was going in a book so it was important. The poor bride and groom were stranded mid-way through walking round the sacred fire while Anji scrabbled under the woman's sari. Ma told the woman with the sari to get up, asking her if she didn't have any sense, didn't she see the girl was looking for her pen? It turned out the pen wasn't under the sari at all . . .

'I told you to bring a tape recorder,' Ma snapped at Anji. 'But you too damn harden!'

'Ma,' Anji spluttered, 'if I could create so much commotion with a pen, you could imagine what I will do with a tape recorder?'

'She would have plug it in the wrong socket and knock out all the electricity,' I told Ma. 'People wouldn't be able to hear the pundit on the loudspeaker. They would only hear you.'

I heard Queen sigh. Indra's high-heeled slipper dropped to the floor with a thud. This girl would undermine Saranhood. Sarans sewing wild oats like me was bad enough. But Saran womanhood had a sacred duty to avoid a sense of humour at all costs.

Anji got so engrossed in her reminiscences, she didn't even pay attention when the terrorists launched an attack on the chocolate cake. 'Ved,' she said, holding on to my arm, 'by the time we were leaving, I was laughing so hard I nearly reverse into the pundit. Your mother say I should have do it. She say, car could fix but that pundit can't fix.'

When she finally got hold of herself, I had a chance to watch cultural change happen right in front of my eyes, and so did my sisters. The last piece of chocolate cake was just vanishing into a terrorist's mouth. Anji's own mouth dropped open as she watched ten-year-old Vani pick up the empty plate.

'Where you going with that plate?' she asked.

'We carrying it down by the pommecythere tree to lick it,' Vani informed her.

'So you feel only allyou does lick plate?' Anji demanded.

Queen turned her eyes to the ceiling as though imploring God for help. The terrorists recognised a business opportunity.

'Five dollars,' Ravi demanded, blocking Anji's view of the plate.

'I didn't bring no money with me,' Anji said. 'I didn't know I was going to have to buy frosting.'

Shreshtha tapped her arm. 'You could borrow money from your fiancé,' she suggested. 'He loaded.'

Anji glanced from the plate to me. I sent one of the terrorists off to fetch my wallet.

'Now,' I said, putting the wallet down on the table, 'I am willing to lease this object for fifteen minutes. What's it worth to you, Miss Anji?'

'Tell him twenty kisses,' Gayatri suggested to Anji. 'He does pay ten cents a kiss.'

'That wouldn't be enough,' Anji told her.

'He will pay more for quality,' Narvin urged. 'And we will give you a discount.'

I folded my arms across my chest and waited. Anji studied my face with her eyes narrowed. I could see her thinking, OAG-style. She was going to come up with an offer I couldn't refuse.

'I'll marry you,' she said.

I didn't want my sisters to know Anji was still dangling me, so I immediately pushed the wallet towards her. 'Not a second more than fifteen minutes,' I said, just to save face.

The terrorists immediately upped their price. 'We want the gold credit card,' they chorused.

Anji specified that she didn't want the plate of frosting, just rights to determine where it should be located during licking operations. The terrorists seized on that suggestion. They were faster lickers than Anji, they knew. They agreed on two-fifty, and went into the implementation phase.

'So,' Queen looked at me and tried to take back the initiative, 'what about these famous wedding plans?'

Anji licked frosting from her index finger. 'The twenty-sixth of June,' she said. 'That is the best wedding date in the Patra.'

Queen and Indra looked at me in surprise. I controlled my own surprise. 'Your mother consult the pundit?' I asked Anji.

'My mother don't have to consult pundit,' she replied. 'Your mother read the Patra. Pundit Jagdeo too blind to read. Your mother does read the Sanscrit upside down and tell him what to say. That's why she believe in Jagdeo.'

Queen and Indra started complaining that the twenty-sixth of June was too soon.

'You know something, Anji?' I said softly, fixing her with my eyes and touching my wallet. 'You is a dog. You know that?'

She licked her finger once again. 'Thylvia doth make the betht frothting,' she replied, smiling blissfully.

I retired to my hammock. I knew Anji would follow me once the frosting was gone.

'Clunk!' I said to the two terrorists who had trailed me. 'Force-field in place.' They knew better than to cross the boundaries of the two-foot force-field I sometimes established around the hammock.

'Why you didn't tell me allyou consult the Patra?' I asked Anji when she came and stood by the hammock.

'I tried,' she said. 'You say your hammock is not for talking in.'

I took her hand and pulled her into the hammock.

'All your family here,' she protested.

'That's why you coming into this hammock,' I replied. 'This is the safe zone.'

Terrorists ringed the force-field, peering interestedly through its transparent shield. I instructed Anji to close her eyes and pretend she was asleep; those terrorists couldn't stay still for long. They tried to outmanouvre us by installing a look-out to alert them if Anji and I did anything interesting, and the rest went to create carnage somewhere else. But they outmanouvred themselves. They put eight-year-old Kiran in charge of the survelliance operation and Kiran had an attention span of zero. He was soon busy trying to wreck the nearby swings.

'We can't get married in June,' I informed Anji.

'Your secretary say you don't have any big plans for June,' she informed me.

'Anji,' I asked, 'where would we live?'

I had been intending to buy two parcels of land next to each other in St Augustine and build two houses side by side, one for my parents and the other for Anji and myself. I would screen them off from each other with a hedge higher than the Great Wall of China, so Anji had absolutely no need to deal with my family, while I was able to keep an eye on my father. I had it worked out to the last detail. I would hire some poor hapless male to live in my parents' house to assist my father, and visit every day. It would take some effort to get my mother to move out of the Croissee, but ultimately she would have no choice. I had all my arguments well prepared: the shop would extend upstairs, I wanted to create a book department, plus I had plans for a recording studio for Mikey and Symphonia.

The problem was that I hadn't found the right land in St Augustine so far. The university owned almost all the property in that area and my need for two plots side by side made things difficult. And they had to be large. Ma would want a garden at least the size of the one she now enjoyed, and I didn't want to move without my swimming pool. I was considering

Valsayn Park, but Valsayn had a smell of *nouveau riche*. I wasn't keen on it.

In any event, buying land in Trinidad took months. They had to do these legal searches and a whole lot of other crap. Then there were building plans to prepare and get through Town and Country. If I knew my mother, getting the plans through her approval process would take more time than getting them through Town and Country. Then there was the building process itself. I had no crew available at the moment; all spare capacity was on standby for OAG's new installations. And I would want Charlo to be involved in building my own house. I was prepared to supervise the building of a research centre for the Rockefeller Foundation, but I would prefer the Master Himself to create the house I would live in.

'Why we can't live here?' Anji asked.

'With the Creature from the Black Lagoon?'

'I does get along good with your mother,' she replied.

I gestured in the direction of my sisters. 'With the Hordes of Satan feeling they could walk in whenever they like and make your life miserable?'

'They can't make my life miserable,' Anji said. 'How they could make my life miserable?'

I sighed. 'You realise you just make two sworn enemies over there?' I asked.

'What I do?' She looked at me in alarm. 'I didn't do anything.'

I smiled, shook my head and stroked the hair away from her face. 'That's just what you do, darling,' I replied. 'Nothing. You didn't ask Indra where she bought her lipstick. You didn't bow down to Queen and shut up when she put you in your place. You didn't even notice when she put you in your place. You talk a pack of crap when you were supposed to be shivering in your shoes. And, worse yet, you drive their mother Jaguar. You know what they would give to drive about Trinidad in that car? They would sell their husbands to the devil.'

'But they have nice cars,' Anji said, genuinely puzzled. 'They have nicer cars than you.'

I laughed. 'They have nice cars,' I told her. 'They don't have the most expensive car in Trinidad after the President's Rolls-Royce. You going about knocking down pundit with the Jaguar. With my mother's approval. You know what it would cost to replace a fender on that Jaguar? More than it costs to replace Queen's whole car. Your ass is grass, if my sisters catch up with you.'

She sucked her teeth. 'Ved, you talking stupidness! Your mother tell me I could have that room next to yours as my study. We going and order furniture for it next week from the factory.'

'Anji,' I warned, 'what is stupidness to you is deadly serious business to other people. You living in a world populated by Durkheim and other dead people. I living among this bunch of creatures my entire life. My sisters are an Open Book to me. And my mother. My mother manipulated you into this decision. She feel she outmanouvre me, because I was making plans of my own. But this battle is not won or lost yet. You are not to go and order one stick of furniture until I say so.'

She regarded me out of the corners of her eyes. 'Who you feel you is?' she asked, imitating my mother. 'You feel you is man?'

I had to laugh. 'Yes,' I said. 'I feel I is man. You want me to show you, in front of my whole family?'

'Stop it!' she yelped.

The minute dinner was over, I announced I was taking her home. Then I swung west on the Eastern Main Road instead of east towards Tacarigua. Anji liked surprises – she didn't even ask where we were going. I headed for the club in Chaguaramas where I had once pleaded with her not to dump me. I was going to plead with her now not to marry me – at least not yet.

'Anji,' I said, taking her hand after we had settled down on one of the semicircular benches overlooking the quiet water, 'you do not know what you are dealing with. My mother is Hitler. They say Hitler died in a bunker. I think he fooled them. He came over here, shaved his moustache and turned himself into my mother.'

She laughed. 'You could talk stupidness, yes, Ved,' she said. 'That's why I'll marry you.'

'You don't believe me?' I said. 'Look at my teeth. You ever see teeth like these?'

She stared at my bared teeth. 'OK, so you have nice teeth,' she said. 'I have nice elbows.'

'I don't have nice teeth, Anji. I have perfect teeth. I don't have a filling in my mouth.'

I told her about being sent to the dentist every six months for a check-up as a kid. After a while, I just used to spend the money Ma gave me for the dentist's bill and come back and say No Cavities. She knew what I was up to, I was sure. But by that time she probably thought I was old enough to be responsible for my own teeth.

'So?' Anji asked.

'So, my mother was trying to create the master race. You see the swastika the Nazis used to have as their symbol? You notice it does be in every Hindu puja? That's an Aryan symbol. And I told you already, the Aryans came from India, not Europe. Anji, I have always said scientists should investigate me to find the cure for the common cold. I have never sneezed in my life. Not naturally. I've inhaled flour and stuff to feel how it is to sneeze. I have never had a fever, a cough. My cuts heal within two days.'

'What you saying?' Anji asked. 'Your mother practises black magic?'

I shook my head. 'Not black magic. Nutrition. My mother knows vitamins they haven't invented yet.'

I told her about the unyielding regimen my mother imposed on us as children. No sweets. Constant consumption of fruit. You don't eat your porridge in the morning? She will stuff it up your nose. Same with the Kepler's malt and cod-liver oil. I explained to her that my mother had sold all her wedding jewellery so she could afford to feed and clothe us well.

'You think Sylvia is a good cook.' I shook my head. 'It's just the quality of the ingredients. A pod of pigeon peas does not dare enter our house unless there is dew on it. And my mother knows the difference between dew and water. No vegetable crosses my mother's doorstep if it is a couple hours off the stem. Sylvia goes to the market every morning. No food goes into our fridge; my mother will not allow us to eat food that has entered a fridge. The man from Carapichaima drops off shrimp every Tuesday at six o'clock in the morning. We do not eat shrimp caught in Las Cuevas or Manzanilla.'

'Las Cuevas dirty?'

I shook my head. Shrimp caught in Carapichaima fed off plankton from the Orinoco river in Venezuela. That was the way the Gulf Stream worked, and why scarlet ibis only nested in that particular swamp in Trinidad and acquired their brilliant colour. That plankton was so rich in nutrients there had never been a shark attack in Trinidad. Sharks didn't eat people in Trinidad, people ate shark.

'How my mother works out these things is a mystery to me,' I said.

'She only went to school till the age of nine. But that's why my brother turns into a glutton every time he comes back to Trinidad. His body is desperately calling for the nutrients it got used to. What I'm trying to tell you, Anji, is that my mother is not to be underestimated. She's incredibly ruthless and far-sighted. Have you noticed that when we have salmon for lunch, she serves you a portion herself?'

She nodded.

'My mother is thinking about her grandchildren's bones,' I said. 'I notice that she gives you the soft bones of the salmon. Anji, you want a monster like that interfering in your life? You want her anywhere near your children? When we were growing up, nobody in our house dared come anything lower than first in test, you know. You didn't get under one hundred per cent in arithmetic. Ninety-nine per cent didn't exist. Same with every other subject. My mother can correct the punctuation in Durkheim, even though you might never guess it from the way she speaks. She knows English grammar to a T. She can't speak French, but she knows how to conjugate French verbs – she learnt from practising my sisters in their homework. That's why she lets you drive the Jaguar when she never let anyone else do so. You must write the best dissertation in the world. If the Jaguar has to be written off in the process, so be it. She's a total perfectionist. You see the first thing she offered you is a study? You think that's an accident? That woman is very weird, Anji. And too powerful for you. Too ruthless.'

Anji was looking at me peculiarly. 'You say your mother is weird, but your mother says you are the one who is weird.'

I sucked my teeth. 'Everybody is weird for my mother. Because they're not like her. Because I am like my father. I like bush and sea and dirt and sand. I could have chosen to be like her, but instead I chose to be like my father, whom she describes as a fool. She never says I'm stupid, just that I'm a fool. She's very deliberate in what she says. She says you are a fool because you let emotions sway you. She doesn't let emotions get in the way of her brain, Anji. You want to live with somebody like that? That woman is completely self-directed. She thinks she knows what's best for everybody and everything.'

Anji laughed. 'Maybe it will be good for me,' she said. 'I too careless.'

I shook my head. 'It won't be good for you,' I said. 'Anji, you never wondered how I ended up taking over this business and running it with half of my mind? A dreamer like me?'

'Yeah,' she said.

'I was trained to do it,' I told her. 'Trained from a little boy. I thought it was an accident that my father had a heart attack.' I shook my head. 'It wasn't really an accident. It was some kind of collusion of circumstances. It was time for me to take over that business from my father. He was running it into the ground. And that was my mother's business. Anji,' my voice was urgent now, 'do you know when I was twelve years old I was buying fire insurance for our house? Reading all the fine print in the insurance contract? She used to tell me, go and renew the insurance policy, and when I came home, she would ask me if I had increased the level of coverage to match the increase in value of the house. Just like that. She would ask me if I knew what it would cost to replace one of the windows if the house burnt down. When I was twelve years old.'

Anji was with me now.

'I thought it was a game,' I told her. 'I felt I was bright, so I tried to master the game. I used to prepare my estimates. Then she would ask me why I didn't insure for hurricane. I knew the answer to that question off the bat. A hurricane had never hit the Croissee in living memory. I insured for earthquake damage.'

'You never told me that,' she said. 'You always say it's Charlo and Nerissa responsible for the business' success.'

I took a swallow of my drink, my eyes on hers. 'That's also true,' I said. 'I actually forgot about those aspects of my own childhood. It was so normal to me. If somebody asks me to tell them the story of my life, I wouldn't think of telling them about doing the banking for my father's store at the age of nine. Taking a taxi to the bank in town in my short pants, with two thousand-odd dollars neatly counted and stacked, plus deposit slip filled out by me, in a brown paper bag. I really never thought about these things. Maybe you unconsciously construct the account of your experience to match what people expect. Only now, in trying to persuade you that it's no ordinary thing to live with my mother, am I pulling out these details from my memory. Look where her upbringing has landed me.'

'A millionaire at the age of twenty-seven?' Anji raised her eyebrows.

I shook my head. 'I have no money. Not a penny. The shareholders in Saran's are my father and mother. But that's my choice. That's the assertion of my independence. I can pay myself any salary I like, but I haven't done it till now. She can't ever tell me I'm an employee of hers and I have to do what she says. She gets management free, and she will take what management she gets. I have zilch to lose if I walk out on my mother tomorrow. But she is holding my father hostage. He might die if I leave.'

'That's why we have to stay,' Anji said. 'I know that.'

I shook my head firmly. 'Honey, I can make other arrangements.'

I told her my plan. A look of pain came over her face. 'That might take about a year!'

'We can wait, Anji.'

I had stumbled upon the remedy for lust: music. Put Ravi Shankar or Steve Coleman or some European classics on the stereo while lying in the hammock. You can calm yourself down with music.

Anji looked miserable. 'Ved,' she said, looking up with troubled eyes. 'You know the pressure I am under? My mother is very upset that I come to your house. She says what will your family say? She cannot believe that your mother doesn't care. She says they will talk about me. And maybe your sisters will. When I told her I was going to drive your mother's car today, she hit the roof. You have to look at it from her perspective. Everybody will think I am marrying you to take advantage of your family's Jaguar and swimming pool and God knows what else.'

'All right,' I said. 'I'll drive you to the weddings.'

She shook her head again. 'That wouldn't solve it,' she said. 'You know what a pressure it is for me to be engaged to somebody like you? From the time people hear your name, all they does think about is money. Saran store, Saran furniture, Saran house in Dorado.' She sucked her teeth. 'It's like I don't have any identity any more.'

I suddenly got scared of losing her again. I understood what she was experiencing. I had experienced it for years till I had developed an exterior to fend it off. Nobody talked crap to me any more because I didn't give them an opportunity. I shut myself off in my hammock, and in Dorado with Charlo and Ashok and the jellyfish. Let them think I was snobbish and arrogant. I didn't care. But I fantasised sometimes about walking away from my own self, away from the illusion of glamour, going somewhere where nobody knew me, where I could quietly start again. Trinidad is such a small place: everybody knows everybody. How could I blame Anji if she walked away from the trap she saw in other people's eyes? I knew how real that trap was, how it could constrain your behaviour, make you act like a robot because you saw everybody

interpreting the slightest gesture of yours in ways that were far from
reality.

I put my arms around her and held her close. I knew she was right.
The solution to her problem was marriage. Then we could both withdraw
into the hammock, and know there was at least one person who saw us
as we really were. I realised why she preferred to live with my mother
than her own now. My mother treated her like the slipshod crazy she was,
not like some princess-to-be.

'You'll get over that, Anj,' I said. 'That's just one more rite of passage,
as Charlo would say. You learn to deal with it. And I want to point out
something to you.' I looked down at her head on my chest and raised her
chin. 'Money does have its benefits. If I didn't have money, I couldn't
bring you here to talk to you. A drink in this place costs a criminal amount
of money. We would be sitting in the car in some side-street, with me
worrying about safety. You just have to learn to use the freedom money
brings for your own purposes.'

She put her arms around my neck and clung to me.

'All right,' I said, after a while, 'I'll agree to go along with the date my
mother chose. She probably chose it for her own convenience and made
the Patra say what she wanted it to say. We can live with them for the
time being.'

Anji looked up at my face.

'But there's one condition,' I said, touching her nose. 'You have to
agree to do anything I say in my mother's house. If I tell you move that
glass from there, you move it first and argue afterwards.'

'I must let you boss me around?' She squinted at me.

'Correct,' I said. 'I know the terrain. I know the enemy. I am the
commander of the troops. Absolute obedience.'

She shook her head. 'I can't let you be the boss of everything,' she
said.

'I'm not asking you to let me be boss of everything,' I said. 'Just of
the battleground. You can be boss everywhere else.' I lifted the hair at the
side of her head and whispered into her ear. 'Especially in bed.'

For someone accustomed to exercising his will over others, the lure of
handing over control was great. In the erotic realm, it was a safe indul-
gence, like dreaming. That was the desire I experienced with Anji, to let
her do what she would with me, to let this sometimes silly girl play with
me as with a toy. I longed to be her toy, to hand over myself, body and

soul, to her, reserving for myself only control over business, which included the management of family relations.

There was a brief flash of dimples. Anji's mischief was expanding its terrain now. She was beginning to discover the mischief of Eve, to shed the virgin shroud her mother had imposed on her. She shook her head. 'I don't want to be boss only in bed,' she said. She touched my arm. 'I want to be boss in chair,' her fingers started climbing up my biceps, 'swing, hammock . . .' the fingers reached my shoulder . . . 'and on semicircular benches overlooking the Gulf of Paria.'

You know what irresistible is? The smile on her face was irresistible.

'You've got a deal,' I said.

And that's when I let one thing lead to another.

Having made the fatal decision, I swung into immediate action. I informed Nerissa first: clear two weeks from the company calendar so I could have a honeymoon. The handover of OAG installations that year was going to be dictated by the Hindu Patra. The following Friday evening, I had a talk with my Construction and Landscape Designer, a.k.a. Charlo. Venue: the Dorado Rumshop, home to broken-down bar-stools and vomit-spattered watermelon farmers.

'I'm going to help you fulfil your wildest dream,' I started.

Charlo raised his non-existent eyebrows. 'We going to build the bio-engineering-guided anti-jellyfish laser-gun?' he asked.

'The scientists ain't arrive in Balandra yet, Charles. At our current level of technology we might blow up the American submarine.'

A US Navy submarine was damaging fishermen's nets off the coast of Dorado. The US government was not taking chances with the world's second-largest natural-gas deposits. Major construction was taking place on the drilling platform, and CIA agents were turning up in Dorado, allegedly in the form of embassy chancery officers. We kept a close watch on the US Marines that were repairing the Dorado bridge as a 'goodwill gesture' to Trinidad and Tobago. We ourselves had repaired that bridge the year before to ensure our heavy equipment didn't fall into the river, and we didn't want the Yanks doing anything too dumb. We knew they were just reconnoitring, getting acquainted with all land routes leading to the gas deposits.

But we were docile third-worlders. We knew our place. When the CIA goons recommended we fence our compound, we did it without a beep. Our peacocks had arrived. Charlo had named them Winnie and Nelson, after the Mandelas, and he said he didn't want them wandering all over Dorado Village and mating with the villagers' ducks. It wasn't his historic mission to be godfather to weird wildfowl species, he said, only to repair the errors of Christopher Columbus, who had decided this was India without taking account of the total absence of peacocks.

'Think second-wildest dream then,' I suggested that Friday night, taking a pull of my coconut water.

'Putting Hugh Hefner in his place?'

I nodded.

During our Dorado mental meanderings, we had designed a Castle in the Sand, a.k.a. our Pleasure Palace. It involved a Japanese bath-house for geisha massage competitions, an internal courtyard for external fucking, and various other conveniences. 'But I still didn't work out how we going to get the make-up mirrors to resist sea-blast,' Charlo objected.

Cunning placement of magnifying mirrors, such as the one my sister Indra used to inspect her blackheads, was a key feature of our mythical Pleasure Palace. Once a Bunny had caught sight of Ashok's prick in one of those mirrors, he fantasised, she would be lost to Hugh Hefner for ever.

'We will have to skip the mirrors for now,' I said.

I explained about the marriage date, and my wish for a place to whisk my girl away from the Mob on weekends. My sisters occupied the Saran house down the beach. The keys for the new house would be held by Uncle Charlo, as their children referred to my Construction Designer – in total defiance of their mummies' sensibilities. Terrorists loved Charlo. What he was doing at any given point in time was always a mystery. If Queen had known her daughter's favourite perch would end up being Charlo's shoulders, she would have had a hysterectomy early in life. Thus, a beach-house whose key would have to be dug out of The Negro's dirty khaki shorts was a sure Safe Haven.

'How much bedrooms?' Charlo asked.

'Six.'

He raised his non-existent eyebrows again. 'Six bedrooms? What you going and have? Orgy? You sure that girl could stomach orgy?'

'One for me and Anji, one for you, one for my father . . .'

'Your father?' Charlo's eyes opened wide. 'Suppose he bounce up with Uncle Sam? You want to kill the man?'

Uncle Sam was our mythical hands-free masturbation machine. Ashok had originally designed it for OAG's bachelor accommodation. Charlo said making wind-chimes was his form of meditation and Uncle Sam would enable him to carry out both activities simultaneously: masturbate, meditate, masturbate, meditate – who knew what great wind-chimes or spiritual journeys would result? But Uncle Sam had got stuck in design phase. It was a hand from a clothes-store mannequin driven by the motor of an electric razor, but Ashok hadn't worked out how to integrate gears from a ten-speed mountain bike.

'. . . and a couple rooms for guests and in-laws,' I concluded.

'In-laws? What you building? Pleasure palace or geriatric home?'

Actually, he said, the best thing was to begin immediately. The heliport didn't involve him; it was purely functional. The recreation centre was almost complete: guys were installing fruit machines, video equipment, billiard tables, the rest. Jeremy Jameson-Jones was drawing plans for the offices. Charlo could lay foundations for the Pleasure Palace by paying some workers overtime, and then start with plumbers and carpenters. The building plans would just be two of our normal houses stuck together around the internal courtyard. Our plans only paid brief visits to Town and Country nowadays; by the time you drank a cup of tea they were approved. The Trinidad government had sold out lock, stock and barrel of oil to OAG.

I moved on to the next task on my marriage preparations agenda: completing the research station in Balandra in record time; installing laboratory equipment in the little lab (a joy!); testing it out (a greater joy!); installing bookshelves in the little library (flipping through the books and discovering species that could blow Charlo's mind!); supplying kitchen equipment, furniture, the rest; negotiating the maintenance contract with the Rockefeller Foundation (piece of cake) and creating a crew from the villages around (sending Balandra's tamarind-ball vendor on a course in catering at the John Donaldson Institute and then letting her practise to be Chef). All fun stuff.

The tough part was the crash-course in sociology I was engaged in at the same time. I had adopted the role of research assistant during Anji's preparations for her final exams. Man, the boring journal articles I read to provide her with synopses in the hammock! Maybe it was a subconscious desire for revenge that caused me to drive her to tears with my criticisms of her dissertation draft. I drove her to the brink of insanity when I began using my encyclopaedic knowledge of calypso lyrics to challenge scholars' assertions about the local proletariat.

'You think I capitalist?' I asked. 'You should meet some of the lumpen round here.' I illustrated with a song from my calypso hero, the Mighty Sparrow cellad 'No Money No Love' in which the woman abandoned her lover for money.

'The problem with you,' I told Anji, 'is that you didn't grow up in the Croissee. Allyou intellectuals sitting down in St Augustine surrounded by samaan tree. Ask the real sociologist over there.'

I gestured to where my mother was picking rice at the dining-table. Ma had intensified rice-picking operations since they now had an end-point: wedding guests' bellies.

'Allyou studying sociology to make theory,' I said. 'Ma does study it to make money.'

My mother was a founding member of the Trinidad stock market. She was the only woman who attended its general meetings, complete with Jaguar and veil. Occasionally she let out a snort to indicate that she knew the board of management was manipulating its operations. But she wasn't ready for them yet, she said. She was too busy making a fortune buying and selling shares. Her own source of insider information was the Croissee. Ma had always wanted a two-storied house in the Croissee so she could observe the passing parade, just as she had been one of the first people in Trinidad to buy a television set so she could follow the antics of The Jackasses who appeared on the news.

By the time Anji's exams finally took place, the first-class honours were practically in the bag. Her dissertation had got rave reviews. It was chosen to be the first undergraduate research study UWI would publish and she was asked to spend the summer rewriting it for print. I reminded her that the summer would be devoted to honeymoon activities, but she claimed she could do both. What did that girl know about honeymoon activities? She would need to rest during the day. UWI also offered her a research assistantship for the following academic year – a true research assistantship, with money attached. Not much, but it could keep her in tamarind balls. She could skip straight from her bachelor's degree to starting her PhD. Well, not straight, straightish. She would have to spend her first year fulfilling the coursework on the Masters' programme.

The end of the idyll coincided with OAG's Grand Opening of its recreation centre on our Dorado compound. They worded it slightly differently: It was a 'Handing-Over Ceremony'. I was to hand over the key of the centre to the President of OAG (Trinidad Operations). The centre was to be a place where OAG staff from various parts of the island could bring their families for a little R&R. OAG's PR department just didn't know what to do with all the money in its budget. Their mandate was to fix the company in Trinidad's consciousness as a Good Corporate Citizen, so they were holding public events left, right and centre, wining and dining the Press like there was no tomorrow. Our recreation centre was to be the scene of the latest pappy-show, as Charlo called these events.

Charlo himself had already planned one of his Grand Openings, and he was not going to be deterred by the PR department. He was going to switch on his windmill-driven light-and-sound show that evening, complete with a Thai sacred-lights ceremony. That involved floating little leaf-boats containing lights down his waterways towards the recreation centre.

Anji decided this was also going to be a Closing Ceremony for her exams. She wanted to see Charlo's leaf-boats. Only problem was, she didn't have anything to wear that would fit in with the OAG folks. Worry not, I said. I had the ideal dress for a Thai sacred-lights ceremony.

'You turn transvestite now?' she asked.

'Might as well,' I muttered meaningfully.

It was the ankle-length Chinese dress I had bought for Nerissa years before in Bangkok, the cheongsam: Ma had taken one look at the dress and confirmed Mikey's observation, so I had never given it to Nerissa. But I figured it would fit Anji perfectly. She didn't have breasts worth talking about, but of course I never told her so – I talked about them constantly. When I took the cheongsam over to the Gopaul home, I also took a box of silk samples. If the cheongsam didn't fit properly, Anji could get something made out of one of those.

But the cheongsam worked. It looked very eleegant, with its long slits at the sides that provided a view of Anji's slim legs as she walked. Her mother returned the box of samples to me when I went to pick her up to take her to Dorado. The Sarans didn't need to clothe her daughter, thank you very much.

The handing-over ceremony was the usual affair. No, that's not quite true. PR had gone overboard, helicoptering in massive quantities of food and drink, the President of OAG (Trinidad) and wife, the US ambassador and wife, and Press without wife. The government had contributed the shrimp of a Minister of Energy plus wife. Dignitaries abounded. Security men swarmed. I had to Show my Face to an obscene degree. E. Duncan Rutherford, Charlo's poker mate, was host of the event, but I was officially host until the key was handed over.

Anji declined to have anything to do with this face-showing. She remained at the other end of the waterways helping string-vested Charlo prepare his Thai surprise. My sisters were in the old Saran beach-house, furious that their careless brother hadn't thought of getting invitations for them to act as Saran dignitaries, but their terrorist offspring were hovering around. Anji wrapped the female terrorists in curtain samples, stuck flowers in their hair and strung garlands around the terrorist males to give them cover for lighting the leaf-boats.

The pappy-show started at four in the afternoon. OAG's steel band played some sickly songs, the usual boring speeches were speeched, the key was handed over, the Press took photos and asked me how to spell my name a thousand times. Three letters, that's all it takes to spell my first name, five for last name. It was still a challenge to the Trinidad Press. One dumpy Indian girl even dogged me to clarify that I hadn't got my first and last names mixed up. Champagne was broken out. Guests mingled, trying out fruit machines, billiard tables and so forth.

Charlo's big moment arrived.

First, he let loose his peacocks. Now, Winnie and Nelson had been having awkward marital problems. Nelson was horny as hell and Winnie wasn't having any. That meant Nelson was constantly strutting around with an erection which, in the case of peacocks, happens in the tail. It blew the guests' minds, this gorgeous creature fluttering from place to place trying to get his girl interested. I knew exactly how Nelson felt. If I had had a tail like that, I would have been showing it to Anji as well.

Then Charlo started his windmills, and lights started fading on and off in varying colours in the swimming pool and along the waterways, in time with Mikey's music on the loudspeakers. Guests started oohing and aahing. So far so good.

Time for Phase Two. Something like a miniature Carnival band of Thai terrorists, led by cheongsamed Anji and string-vested Charlo, appeared under the fairy lights over the ornamental pond at the far end of the waterways, bearing lighted leaf-boats. They set these in the water and Charlo turned on another windmill to start them drifting towards the dignitaries. Oohs and aahs increased in volume and frequency. It was really magical, with the wind swaying the coconut palms and altering the shadows and colours in the water as the flickering boats floated towards us.

'That girl is on fire!' someone said.

That girl was my girl. The bottom of Anji's cheongsam, loose because of the slits at the side, had got blown by the draft from the windmill into a lighted leaf-boat. I bolted towards the ornamental pond. But I needn't have worried. The minute the cheongsam caught fire, the terrorists recognised an opportunity and shoved Anji into the ornamental pond. I hauled her out, sopping wet.

'Did you get burnt?'

She shook her head. 'No, but I was so frightened! I was thinking one of the lobsters might bite my big toe.'

I hustled her over to the Pleasure Palace, which was at the far end of the curve of OAG houses. The Palace was practically ready now, and OAG's PR personnel had attached it to the other houses with the fairy lights that abounded in the compound that evening. I wasn't too pleased about that: this was a private place. But I had done my docile third-worlder act. It was E. Duncan's pappy-show, after all, and he was my friend. His tip about buying OAG shares had sent a lot of money spinning into the Saran coffers.

Anji grabbed a couple of pieces of Thai silk and went into the bathroom. She came back with one, a kind of royal green with gold embossed on it, wrapped around her, sarong-style.

'Can you tie the knot for me?' she asked. 'If I do it, it will probably drop off, and I'll embarrass you even worse.'

I laughed. 'Nothing you do embarrasses me, sweetheart. You forget who is my mother – I am embarrass-proof.'

Now, you have to imagine this scene. Smell: new teak. Sound: waves lashing on tropical beach. Background: coconut palms waving in the fairy lights outside vast open windows. Foreground: tropical beauty approaching, loosely wrapped in green and gold Thai silk complete with orchid in hair.

I knew just how Nelson felt. I took the ends of the sarong from Anji's hands, bent my knees and put my arms around her neck to tie them. But my mouth was on her upper breasts. I wasn't tying that curtain sample until I had fulfilled a couple of heart's desires.

'I think I'm going to swop jobs with you,' I heard somebody say behind me. 'You guys are living like princes here while I'm sweating in Port of Spain.'

American accent. Texan.

I kept my composure. I was blocking Anji from whoever was behind me. I tied the silk securely around her neck, then, with all the dignity I could muster, I turned around.

President of OAG (Trinidad) and wife, US ambassador and wife, Minister of Energy and wife, and red-faced E. Duncan. Apparently E. had taken his dignitaries on a tour of the compound and they had ended up here. And where that mob goes, Press and security follow. Flashbulbs! Caught In the Act! Key-hander-Over and Half-Clothed Tropical Beauty with Orchid in Hair. How could a camera resist that?

With my arm around Anji, I took a step forward. 'Your Excellency,' I said, 'may I present my fiancée, Anjani Gopaul?'

Fiancée? They didn't believe it for a second. Who did this young whipper-snapper think he was fooling? They continued not believing it while they looked around the Pleasure Palace. Japanese bathhouse, external jacuzzi, hot-tub in bathroom attached to master bedroom, cunning mirror wall in that bathroom made of a sheet of glimmering stainless steel. Plexiglass skylight over hot-tub for looking at the stars, gigantic windshield wipers attached to skylight for ensuring clear view of stars. Hugh Hefner move over, make way for V. P. Saran, bachelor entrepreneur of Trinidad.

I think Anji enjoyed it, frankly. I kept my arm firmly around her as I mingled with the unwanted guests. I didn't like them poking their noses into my private house, but the damage had already been done. I told the Press firmly that this was out of bounds to them, calling over the security men to ensure the photographers didn't photograph.

The President of OAG (Trinidad) inspected the place like it was a drilling platform, even trying out the expensive stereo equipment we had cunningly installed so we could have music wherever we wanted. Mr President and I had a curious relationship. Strictly speaking, he was not supposed to deal with me; that was Trisha Almandoz's job. But we were grown men. We knew Trisha couldn't really handle my hard-headed backtracking. Every now and then, the president's secretary called me up and he and I had a highly satisfying negotio-fest over Nerissa's cost-estimates. We shadow-boxed the same way I did with Jacob. He respected me for trying to squeeze every penny I could out of him.

'How much?' he asked, coming up to me as I was assisting the US ambassador in admiring the view of the drilling-platform lights from the front verandah.

'I beg your pardon, sir?' I said.

'Saran,' he muttered. 'Cut the bullshit. How much do you want to lease this place?'

'Sorry, Mr Granderson-Powell,' I replied. 'This building is for private use.'

'I can see that,' he replied. 'My private use. Weekends in Port of Spain can be very dull, you know. Those country-club do's don't cut it for me.'

I had to smile. 'You just want to lease it for weekends?' I said. 'I can't do that. But I'll make you a counter-offer.' That was the sort of talk he liked. 'A swap,' I suggested. 'You get the benefit of this house on weekends, if you give me the benefit of that in exchange.'

I pointed to the drilling platform out at sea. Granderson-Powell burst into laughter. 'I can just see another contract with Saran's coming up,' he said, sticking a fat cigar into his mouth. 'You sure you don't want to try one of these? Best Cuban.'

I shook my head. 'I know about you guys and your exploding cigars,' I said.

Having revealed the existence of a quasi-spouse to the dignitaries, I was forced to integrate her into the face-showing exercises, otherwise their first suspicions would be confirmed. We trailed along with the rest of them as they returned to the champagne. Anji had lost her sandals when she took her duck in the pond. I shrugged; barefootedness could be regarded as part of the Polynesian look. She was game for that. If she had to show her face, she might as well show her feet.

We walked straight into an ambush. 'Miss Seepaul!' The dumpy girl-reporter accosted us halfway to the recreation centre. 'Can I ask you a question?'

'Gopaul,' I said. 'And her answer is the same as mine. No comment.'

'Ved!' Anji stared up at me. 'Nobody spoke to you. Yes, miss?'

'How does it feel to catch one of Trinidad's most eligible bachelors?' the girl asked.

That was only the precursor to what was ahead of us. By the time we arrived at the recreation centre, the buzz had gone around the American wives that a great mystery was about to be solved: who was Ved going out with? A couple of them had seen Anji on her visits to Dorado, a wet, bedraggled creature they hadn't taken any notice of. But this was Barefooted Babe, looking knock-out glamorous and daring in green and gold silk with orchid in hair. You know what American women are. Romance obsessed. And they aren't shy about it. When did I propose? they asked Anji. How did I propose? Was it in a romantic setting?

Anji looked like a rabbit caught in the headlights. 'Propose?' she asked, wrinkling her face and looking up at me. 'You ever propose?'

When was the wedding? So soon? Please describe your dress. Please. Where are you going for your honeymoon? Or is it a secret?

Sure it was a secret. From us as well. I had declared that no talk of wedding arrangements was to take place around my girl till after her exams. The honeymoon destination could be easily chosen: take a map of the Caribbean, close your eyes and stick a pin anywhere. The American wives suggested Hawaii, Cancun . . . Wedding dress? Anji didn't want to know. Her mother would go out and buy the prescribed red sari. Then somebody asked the inevitable. Was it love at first sight? Anji shook her head.

'It was hate at first sight. I hated him and he hated me.'

Now the wives looked like rabbits caught in headlights. You don't make jokes about sacred things like Romance.

I had noticed the dumpy journalist on the edge of the group, but it was difficult to control things at that point. And I was distracted by the US ambassador. He had read in *Harvard Alumni* magazine that I was building a natural-history research facility in Trinidad. Harvard Alumni Association was paying part of the costs. 'I hope he isn't giving them the headaches he gives me,' President of OAG (Trinidad) mumbled around his cigar. 'Most hard-headed man I've met in this part of the world.'

'Well, you know how we call Mr Saran,' Minister of Energy mumbled back. 'The man with the wood.'

Uproarious laughter from Trinis in that group, calls for explanations by Yanks, subsequently offered by two coy journalists. I had seen them at OAG functions before. They styled themselves 'serious journalists'. One was white, with greasy black hair that fell in a lank slant over his brow. The other was black, and always wore a tie.

'Harvard?' the black one asked. 'Harvard is building a research facility in Trinidad?'

'Best person to talk to is that guy over there,' I said, pointing to where Jeremy Jameson-Jones was leaning lecherously over a young waiter. 'He's the architect for the project.'

The white journalist asked boring questions about the research facility building. He specialised in boring information, such as how many barrels of oil were coming out of Trinidad each month.

'Why don't you talk to our coastal engineer?' I sent him off to disturb Ashok's attempts to lure one of the PR girls into a jellyfish hunt down the beach.

By the next day, Sunday, we were all over the newspapers. I was on the front page (again) handing over the key. An inside page was devoted to the Thai lighting ceremony and pictures of dignitaries, including half-clothed Anji and randy-tailed Nelson, as well as the two geniuses of the Harvard research facility – complete with their favourite assistant. Excellent publicity for Saran's Enterprises, which had hitherto been known mainly for its furniture. But. Have you ever seen your private life converted to a Hallmark card and splashed all over a newspaper features page? Believe me, it's not a pretty sight. The dumpy reporter wrote a piece that claimed to be based on an exclusive interview with 'Anjani Seepaul'.

Anji was depressed when I went over to Tacarigua. She was frozen and withdrawn when I put my arm around her and assured her it would all blow over. I had never encountered her like this; I preferred her quarrelling with me, she looked so miserable. I guess she had to face her university comrades, all those nouveaux Marxists and feminist furies.

'I'm sorry, love,' I said, pulling her down to sit with me on the verandah banister. 'I'm really sorry.'

'For what?' she murmured.

'For dragging you into all this shit.'

'Ved!' she exclaimed. 'It's not your fault. It's my fault for opening up my big mouth.'

'No,' I said, rubbing my hand over my eyes and forehead. 'You shouldn't have to shut your big mouth. It's just that you have to be careful when the Press is around.'

'You tried to warn me,' she murmured.

She reached up and put her fingers into my hair. I always liked when she did that. I bent my neck so she could reach my hair more easily. She turned towards me so both her hands could go into my hair, her arms around my shoulders.

'Ved, I'm so sorry,' she said, kissing me on the mouth. 'I'm so, so sorry.'

That was the nicest kiss I had ever got from Anji. It was worth the shit from the Press. She just kept kissing me and kissing me, her hands in my hair. She complained that there wasn't much space on my face to kiss – my beard took up most of it. I offered to shave the beard. She said don't dare, she liked my beard.

My sisters were not impressed with Anji's public performance. 'What does she think it is?' Queen asked the next time she came over. 'Claiming she didn't want to marry you?'

'Oh, shut up,' I said, and went into my room and put on a record.

And that was not the end of prenuptial horrors. 'Ma, don't you want me to see Mr Chitani for you?' Queen asked later that day.

Mr Chitani was some Indian from Bombay who made fourteen-carat gold jewellery in Chaguanas. Queen had been responsible for buying jewellery from him on the occasion of Robin's wedding. An essential part of the Hindu wedding ceremony was when the groom's family handed over some clothing and a jewel box to the mother of the bride. Anji and Ma had solved the clothing issue very quickly, ignoring my suggestion of curtain samples. Ma had produced about two thousand dress-lengths she had stored up for herself and Anji had oohed and aahed. Apparently, Ma had an inside line on Liberty cotton from the top fabric store in Port of Spain, extremely fine stuff that cost a fortune.

But Ma had bought no jewellery. It was all symbolic in my opinion. Both the bride's family and the groom's gave the poor girl horrendous-looking stuff that I figured was a hangover from when jewellery was a kind of insurance policy: in case her husband died, she would have some valuables to sell and keep body and soul together – if she didn't do the honourable thing and jump on the funeral pyre, that is.

'What I giving that girl jewels for?' Ma asked. 'You ever see her in a jewel? She will only lose it.'

'But you have to put gold in the jewel box,' Queen insisted.

Queen's vast army of in-laws were invited to the wedding, mainly, I think, so they could observe the splendour of the Saran swimming pool and suchlike, and be suitably abashed at having acquired a Saran in their midst. The contents of the bride's jewel box would also be an indication of Saran splendour. Gold was prescribed in the scriptures for a family with wealth.

'Well, I will put gold,' Ma said.

'A gold brick,' I suggested. 'Even Anji can't lose a gold brick.'

'You think I stupid like you?' Ma said. 'I know what I doing. I will put a gold credit card.'

'A gold credit card?' Queen's jowls quivered.

'Anji can't draw on no company account, you know,' I warned my mother.

'Yes, I know,' Ma returned. 'Only Nerissa could get credit card from you! But I could give people credit card if I want. I just have to open an account for her.'

'You need a certain balance in the account to get a gold card,' Queen's husband pointed out.

Ma shrugged. 'A million dollars should get a gold card.'

Anji and I were just longing for this whole pappy-show to be over. She didn't care where we went on honeymoon, she said. I chose Martinique. Trinis didn't go there because they spoke French in Martinique, so it would be a true escape. I booked a hotel that had never bought a stick of Saran furniture. I had had enough of it for the present.

Meanwhile, Ms Nerissa Hosein had abandoned me for a month. She had cashed in on my offer of an airline ticket anywhere in the known universe to abscond to Canada. 'Cana-what?' My mouth had dropped open. 'You could go Tahiti and you will go Canada? I thought you hate Canada?'

She had sighed. 'Ved, if I marry this man in truth, one day he might catch some madness in his head and decide he want to go back Canada and die,' she explained. 'He say I don't know Canada, I only know Toronto. I say I see Niagara Fall and it falling very nice without my help, thank you very much.' She sighed again. 'He say I should give Nova Scotia a chance.' She shrugged. 'That is where his bank come from.'

Well, I was the last one who should stand in the way of romance polar-bear style, I thought. Nerissa's reasoning was, as usual, impeccable. We were negotiating yet another contract with OAG by now – for a weekend pleasure palace for Mr Granderson-Powell. The best time for Nerissa to abscond was before I absconded. She would return the weekend of my wedding and take over the reins in my absence.

On the Friday, Robin arrived, complete with wife and baby. Wife was sallower and plumper than ever. Robin was hungry. 'Lead me to the curried chataigne,' he said, slapping me on the back once the luggage was squeezed into the car trunk.

I had to disappoint him. Hindu weddings normally started three days before the ceremony, with on-site food preparation, tent-building and general hullabaloo. Ma had put paid to that. She had arranged catering and rented white canvas tents. She wasn't having anybody dig holes in her garden to cook huge pots of curried this and that. Not a drum was to be heard.

'This is not a wedding,' Robin said. 'It's a funeral. You sure it's not dead you dead, boy?'

Before his sojourn in London, Robin had disliked weddings as much as any sane person. But living abroad turns any third-world nonsense into a source of nostalgia.

'Uncle Robin,' a terrorist asked. 'How your baby resemble a tadpole so?'

Robin's child was almost transparent. He was one big head with gigantic eyes. Ma claimed he looked like I did when I was born.

'You ain't see the mother?' Robin asked. 'What frog does produce? Not tadpole?'

It had turned out that Robin's wife couldn't cook. He was subsisting on fishfingers. 'Fish does have fingers?' Ashok asked. 'As far as I know, only jellyfish does have fingers.'

'I now understand this Indian penchant for bride-burning, yes,' Robin grunted.

Madhuri, as she was called, managed to achieve something I had never thought possible. She united the Saran tribes within four hours.

'We don't do it like that at home,' was Madhuri's motto.

'Home?' asked Indra sweetly. 'Do you mean Bamboo Village?'

The baby's body was not to be unswaddled on pain of mosquito bites, sandflies, sunburn, suntan, excema and other assorted third-world afflictions.

'You think she hiding something under them blankets?' the terrorists asked. 'Maybe he deformed or something.'

'Maybe he have three pricks,' Narvin suggested.

They offered Madhuri money to let them see the baby's body.

'Wait till she go in the toilet,' Ma muttered. 'That blanket coming off so fast, before any one of allyou blink.'

The terrorists plied their new aunt with drinks. Tea was all she would drink. Tea was a diuretic, I informed the terrorists gleefully. The minute Madhuri succumbed, a kidnapping occurred. Baby Anant was transported to the middle of the swimming pool by Doting Uncle Number One, a.k.a me.

'Come and get him,' Shreshtha sang, as Madhuri fulminated on the side of the swimming pool.

'That pool must be full of pee!' she whined.

'Do you think we are as dirty as the English?' Queen snapped.

The terrorists demanded ransom money.

That night, Madhuri's husband was also kidnapped. The Duchess of Peale's legal counsel was incarcerated in Ashok's favourite rumshop and force-fed rum. Money entered jukebox.

'"Drunk and disorderly!"' From all the way down the street, Robin could be heard chanting one of Sparrow's most louche calypsos. '"Always in custody! My friends and my family, all them fed up with me. Cause I'm drunk and disorderly. Every weekend I in the jail . . ."' Robin's shirt was completely unbuttoned and his hairy belly jutted out. It was turning into a joyous wedding after all, thanks to Madhuri.

But Saturday morning brought a turn of the tide. When I rose to my last day of bachelorhood, Queen had already stuffed Robin full of family news while Sylvia stuffed him with tomato chokha.

'But Ma, you didn't give my wife no gold credit card,' Robin was saying when I arrived at the dining-table.

'Your wife?' Indra's perfectly plucked eyebrows did a leap. 'What about her daughters?'

Ma had enough on her mind with relatives turning up at her house expecting premarital hullabaloo. She was in no mood for questions. 'What I have to do with daughters?' she snapped.

Indra's eyebrows remained perfectly poised. 'Indian people only think of their sons, never of their daughters,' she said, executing a delicate dip of a high-heeled slipper.

'I wish I never had to think about none of allyou!' Ma returned. 'This next jackass wouldn't even wear the jurajama I buy for him.'

I had taken one look at the pink satin get-up she expected me to wear at the wedding and informed her that it wasn't Carnival. The furthest I would go to indulge her was to wear a plain white cotton kurta shirt.

'Not sons in this case,' Robin said. 'Son. Ma only thinks about one of her sons.'

'Why I should think about you?' Ma retorted. 'You ever, in your born days, think about me? You pull your arse and gone England to think about the Duchess of Peale. What I thinking about you for?'

'So, Ma,' Indra asked, 'everything you have is for Ved?'

There was silence.

'Why you asking me my business for?' Ma shrilled. 'Why you don't ask he he business.' She gestured with her head towards my father. 'He make will.'

I hadn't known she knew about Pa's will. But it wasn't really surprising. Ma would know if Pa missed a manicou in his sleep.

'You made a will?' Queen asked Pa.

Pa took refuge in blather. 'Well, you know I don't know when I will have to leave this world . . .'

'And leave everything to Ved,' Robin finished with a faint smile.

Pa didn't answer.

Robin helped himself to a sapodilla, still smiling. Ma could always challenge that will, he explained to the rest of us. A surviving spouse's claim would always be considered by the court.

Ma laughed. 'You think I will survive he?' she asked. 'Well, then, you is a bigger fool than I think. That man sure to outlast me. The amount of sleep he does be sleeping all now, he thiefing from death already.'

'So what about you, then?' Robin put on his best lawyer-voice. 'If you think Pa will outlast you, have you made a will?'

Indra examined her manicure carefully. 'She will leave everything to her oldest son,' she observed in a bored voice. 'That's what Indian people do. And there's no Indian like your mother. She follows those scriptures to the letter of the law.'

Ma leaned towards Indra. 'You know what in those scriptures?' she asked. 'You ever try to find out? No. You too great for that, you with your OAG club in Pointe-a-Pierre.' She turned to face us all. 'I will tell allyou what in those scriptures. According to the Hindu scriptures, by tomorrow I do everything I have to do for all of allyou. I born allyou, grow allyou and married allyou.' She faced my sisters. 'I give allyou what I have to give allyou. If allyou in-laws didn't give allyou credit card for allyou wedding, that is allyou business.'

Indra had long sold her wedding jewellery to buy a sports car. Queen wore hers and looked horrible in it.

Ma pointed at Robin and me. 'And I give allyou and allyou wife what I supposed to give allyou,' she declared.

Robin had sold his wife's jewellery to pay the down-payment on a house in London. 'You didn't give my wife no million dollars,' he pointed out.

Ma put her hand on her hip again. 'My dear Mr Jackass Lawyer, I give you and your wife more than I supposed to give you. Who you think pay for you to study law in England? You think it was your father? No, it was my mortgage.' She gestured at me. 'Ask him. He used to send the money for you. And when I get my bank statements, he always send more than I could afford. You think pounds sterling easy? You should have to buy them with Trinidad dollars from a bank loan. When you pull your arse and married hurry-hurry, OAG didn't have that gas out there to pay me to build building for them to reach it. According to the Puranas, I have to give your wife according to what I have.'

She then pointed at me. 'Now, this jackass marrieding a worse jackass,' she went on. 'Who will married a man without one cent in his pocket? If one of he building fall down on he head tomorrow and he dead, the jackass wife don't even have a bed to lie down in.' She pointed at herself. 'I know what it is to married a damn fool of a Saran with everything he own mix up with his brother.' She tapped the dining-table with her forefinger. 'I know what is my dharma, my duty.'

She turned back to Robin again. 'Now you, Mr Lawyer, you asking me all kind of question. I want to ask you one simple question. You know your dharma? You know your duty? You know what the Hindu scriptures say about what you supposed to do for me?'

We all could guess the answer to that. Look after Ma for the rest of her life. Live with her. Have his wife act as her slave, his children as her minions. That's what oldest sons did. That's why they usually inherited the family property.

'I do everything correct, as the Puranas say to do it!' Ma warned, tapping the table again. 'If anybody want to challenge me, they have to read the scriptures first. Now, I could leave what I want to who I want. I thinking about leaving it to the Arouca Orphan Home. That is where I should have leave all of allyou in the first place.'

She swished off to squelch some Hindu hullabaloo that was threatening to erupt somewhere in the garden.

'All wills can be challenged,' Robin said airily. 'It is a detective-story myth that a will is sacrosanct. If you have a good enough lawyer to prepare your plea, the judge can set aside the will in the interests of natural justice.'

Now, this was an interesting subject for hammocking. What was natural justice? Would a judge determine that the prodigal son and two extremely prodigal daughters had equal claim to the one who had laboured in the vineyard?

But, for me, the more important question was the one Ma always raised, the question of duty. Interestingly enough, the Hindu scriptures dealt with this very thoroughly. The *Bhagavadgita*'s *raison d'être* was the question of inheritance. Who should rule the kingdom? God in the form of chariot-driver Krishna had seemed to argue that it was your duty to fight for the kingdom if you believed you would provide the best stewardship of it. That was why that book was Gandhi's Bible in the struggle for Indian independence.

Was that my duty? Not my duty in relation to the bloody Sarans – Indra's husband could keep her in nail polish. My duty was towards Charlo and the other people who worked in Saran Enterprises. Ma felt that Robin had abandoned his duty towards her. But I had no intention of abandoning my duty towards the man who had practically raised me. It was Charlo who, at every turn in my life and business, had driven my chariot into battle. Whenever I had cast down my weapons in despair, it was Charlo who had said, to use Krishna's words, 'Arise like a mighty fire and burn all those before you.'

I often had doubts about right and wrong, duty and purpose in life. I knew only one thing: when somebody had given to you wholeheartedly all they had to give, without asking what you would give in return, you owed them. I owed Charlo, I owed Nerissa and I owed the Antoines. The Saran name was built on the devotion to craftsmanship Mr Antoine had brought with his genes from Europe. Tony could have started that furniture factory without me, but he had chosen to hoist his sail under the protection of the Saran galleon. And, for that protection to endure, I had to hold the wheel. I had let my eye stray once or twice, and one of my deckhands had slipped overboard. I could never forget that if I had only taken a look at a liana, Jason would still be here with us. I still thought of him sometimes as I lay in my hammock.

But I was no longer boss of my hammock. This was to be my last day of solitary hammocking. I made the most of it.

On my wedding day, I grew increasingly uneasy. Hullabaloo was in full swing and Nerissa hadn't showed. Guests were eating in the garden, preliminary to shifting the hullabaloo to Anji's garden, where the ceremony was to be performed. Suppose Nerissa had got stuck in Canada? Airplane failure, weather failure, polar bear attack. I couldn't leave Trinidad if Nerissa wasn't in the country.

'I told you he's having an affair with his general manager,' Indra said, when I had asked if anyone had seen Nerissa for the umpteenth time.

I gave her the umpteenth eloquent glare. My sisters and aunts had been on my back all morning. They had come up with the bright idea that I should shave. 'You know what under this beard?' I asked them. 'Because I don't know. And Anji don't know.'

'I know,' a terrorist said. 'Lice.'

'Shaving could cause this whole wedding to get cancelled,' I told the assorted females.

I called Nerissa's house. 'She's not feeling well?' I asked her mother when it turned out Nerissa was at home. 'Try to get her to come to the phone, just for a minute. I have to talk to her.'

Nerissa sounded sick indeed. Her nose was clogged up.

'I told you not to go to that place,' I said.

No answer.

'What's wrong?' I asked.

She sniffled.

'What's the matter?'

I heard what I thought was a sob. I began to suspect things hadn't gone well in Canada. Maybe she had broken her engagement.

'The engagement off?' I asked softly.

She sobbed harder. I felt bad that maybe I had been tactless.

'I'm sorry,' I said.

She kept crying.

'Oh, gosh, please don't cry . . . I'm so sorry, sweetheart.'

She eventually collected herself. 'I'm just tired from the trip,' Nerissa said. 'I'll be OK by Monday morning.'

I turned around to find myself the centre of a ring of interested female relatives. Every eye was opened wide. They thought I was talking to Anji.

'That was Nerissa,' I said shortly. 'She has a personal problem right now.'

It turned out to be a day for crying women. Anji's mother cried right through the ceremony. She caused Beena to start crying too. At the end, when we were leaving their home for ours, Anji burst into a flood of tears and the three of them clung to each other as though this was really a funeral. Anji had to be torn away from her mother by the thickset aunt and pushed into the car with me. She arrived at the Croissee still sobbing. What to do? How do you extricate a sobbing bride from a car to face the Saran masses? People would think she really was being forced to marry me. I felt utterly helpless.

Ma came to the rescue. 'You good, you know, girl,' she said, leaning into the car. 'What about if they did married you to a Saran all the way in Dorado? Then you would know what crying is!'

Anji raised her head slightly from my chest. 'You cry?' she asked.

'If I cry?' Ma replied. 'And the jackass keep telling me not to cry. You don't see that was a good reason to kick him?'

Book Three

FOR GITA

'Hell is a city much like Port of Spain.'
The Spoiler's Return, Derek Walcott, 1980

Chapter Eleven

You don't know anything about sex until you get married. That's what I have to say about that. Until you've got a partner there, twenty-four hours a day, available, well, you don't really know what it's all about.

Our honeymoon was standard-issue, generic stuff. You don't leave your room. You intend to leave your room, you make plans to leave your room, you take a shower, you might even dress. But then . . .

We didn't even talk. You ever knew Anjani Gopaul not to talk? The girl seemed to forget even Durkheim. I had been nervous about this defloration business; I'd thought it would take time. But before I even knew what had happened, a rite of passage had come and gone and I was being urged to do it again. Not with words, eh. My girl seemed to have forgotten her voice back at her mother's house. That inarticulate stuff doesn't count; that's just sound effects. Maybe she was afflicted with some kind of psychic laryngitis?

'Anj, honey, you're OK?'

'Mmm.'

'Want something to drink?'

'Mmm.'

'Was that a yes or a no?'

'Mmm.'

I guess 'yes'. I go over to the mini-bar and get her some Coke and she sits up to drink it and then her tiny breasts are in a different position and . . .

'Sweetheart, it's almost time for lunch.'

'Mmm.'

'You go and shower. I won't come into the bathroom and bother you. We can go and see what the dining-room looks like.'

Obedience. Total, unquestioning obedience. Then she returns to look for something to wear and she's naked, and room service comes into play once again.

'I'm not touching you again for the day. This is ridiculous. Martinique

267

is supposed to be one of the most beautiful places in the world. We are going to go and get a taxi and go out.'

She stretches out her hand and starts touching my chest with the tip of her finger. Martinique can wait an hour. I wake up and realise I'd drifted off to sleep. The sun is low and the view outside the balcony is of a wide, wide bay with lights beginning to glimmer on boats in the marina. But the view next to me is also beautiful. I just move her hair away from her face.

'Mmm.'

That sounds like an invitation to kiss her. 'Are you awake?'

'Mmm.'

'Are you sure you're awake?'

She proves it. She puts her arm round my neck and her hand is in my hair. My scalp must be the most erogenous zone I've got. Previously I'd thought otherwise, but it looks like I was wrong.

Week one ends and the spell breaks. Midnight, to be precise about time.

'Ved?'

'Mmm?' Two can play at that game.

Nothing more.

I decide to initiate Conversation. I've heard Conversation is good for married people. 'Anj, you like being married?'

I thought it was a good opening line. I myself had a lot to say on this subject. I loved being married. Hey, what's not to love about being married? Skin, boobs, the whole works is there, trapped in a hotel room in one of the most beautiful places in the world that you've never seen. Marriage was It for me. I gave it five Michelin stars.

'Mmm.'

No opinion? Is this really Anjani Gopaul? Anjani Saran, sorry. Or did I fuck this girl into idiocy? They say these intellectual types are like that, flip-flop personalities. Dr Jekyll and Mrs Saran.

I haul her out of the room. I haul her to the dining-room and fill her up with a Michelin-star breakfast. Her eyes dance as she takes it all in, the hibiscus-strewn dining-tables, the fruit-strewn buffet, the ice-sculpture of a butter dish. Then, after the last slice of baguette, the Look comes over her face again. The eyes grow velvet, like Nerissa's.

I assume husbandly authority. 'Don't look at me like that,' I say.

'Like what?'

'Like this.' I touch her under the flower-bedecked tablecloth.

'Oh, like that! I wasn't looking at you like that. I was looking at you like this.' She touches me under the tablecloth.

Well, at least she hasn't lost her entire vocabulary, even if she still retains the capacity to imprison me in a hotel room.

The problem with me is that I am a bit silent myself. I need other people to switch me on; then I'm a talking toy. Without that, I just think thoughts. Thoughts like, what was this beautiful thing they called fucking? High-flown stuff like that. Why did it feel kind of holy to be on top of this frail-looking girl, looking down at her face, moving as slowly as possible so that the responses on her face changed slowly as well, like Charlo's light-and-sound show fading from one colour to another, now the violet of a tropical horizon, now the fecund green of a tropical lagoon?

I know you idiots out there will answer 'biology'. But this wasn't biology. I knew biology. I knew bloody Anji herself would give me the biology guff if I asked her – that girl didn't get first-class honours in sociology for nothing. That's why I didn't ask her. I felt I was in a cathedral, to tell you the truth. A big vaulted cathedral with a big fucking organ playing the 'Ave Maria'. (Scratch that. That's disgusting. It's not what I meant at all.)

Listen, there's nothing like fucking your wife, knowing she's your wife. Even if she doesn't look or act like anybody's wife, either in her Dr Jekyll or Mrs Saran roles. It's the next best thing to fucking yourself, which is a subject I have discussed in one of my hammock seminars. With myself, of course.

Nah, actually it's nothing like fucking yourself. You know you're gross. Anji isn't gross. Anji is like a little periwinkle that can cure cancer. (You know that a periwinkle can cure cancer? Yep. Don't know in what doses).

Actually, I was right before. Making love to your wife is like making love to yourself. You've had this body of yours for twenty-seven years and you've conducted every experiment possible on it in that time. Now here's another body to experiment on, but by now you're experienced in experimentation and can come up with some reasonable hypotheses. This arm here next to you, for instance, would surely like to be kissed all over. And if it doesn't, it would be interesting to find out why not. The crease inside the elbow is so soft and retiring. It doesn't see all that much of human society, so it probably needs special treatment, like being tickled with the tip of your tongue. Same thing with vulvas. Why would evolution make vulvas if not for kissing? It's not like women use them for anything else. But vulvas can react with something resembling panic, so you have to reassure them that they need not tense up and contract – nobody is going to hurt them and they can relax and let themselves be seen. Vulvas need a lot of reassurance, and one thing inevitably leads to another.

Actually, coming to think of it, making love to your wife is a lot like oiling your cricket bat. I often talked to my cricket bat when I was a kid. My cricket bat was my best pal then. When I oiled it, I made sure the first layer of oil soaked all the way in, so that the lovely blonde wood grew light and springy and alive. With the second layer of oil, the bat would start glowing, and I would know this bat and I could do something really exciting on the pitch. I would start looking forward to getting to the crease. But there was still all the polishing and special attention to particular spots on the bat to take care of. By that time, I was lost in the joy of anticipation. That's when I often murmured a few words, so the bat would know I didn't think of it as a mere instrument for my own glory, but as a secret sharer in any victory we incurred, my companion for life, my most beloved companion. And when my bat and I went out to Aranguez Savannah together, we knew we were together, we had a secret communication, we were as one.

But, come to think about it, a wife is really nothing like a cricket bat. A cricket bat doesn't touch you, or say your name invitingly, or hold you as hard as it can hold you. In fact, what the hell am I talking about? A cricket bat is just a long solid thing. It doesn't have places your mouth can fit over and around and into. It doesn't have little creases that can expand if they feel like expanding and make you feel you can see into the vast reaches of space, into the garden of Eden and beyond. Man, I talk a lot of crap sometimes about cricket bats. Too many idle brain cells. That's why I sometimes think a lobotomy or two mightn't be a bad idea.

'Anj, what are you thinking, baby?'

Smile. A Nerissa smile, where you think you know what's happening behind the eyes but you're not really sure. 'I was thinking, how come you're so nice?'

All I could do was smile back at her. 'And did you come to any conclusions?'

Shake of head.

Shake of head plus Nerissa smile means only one thing. Kiss me, make love to me. I was getting the hang of marriage-speak.

I pursued my vice of thinking in a giant wicker chair on the balcony. That was my refuge when Anji went to take a shower. Otherwise I might be tempted to go watch her, and, as a seasoned married person, I now knew where that led: not to a Michelin-star dinner. She would come and sit in the giant wicker chair with me, fully clothed, in my arms. If I studiously avoided looking at her face, we could make it down to dinner. I concentrated on the view, the graceful curve of the bay, the white triangles of boats' sails in the distance, the blue-green Caribbean Sea. She dug me in the ribs.

'Ved.'

'Yes, honey.'

'Where are you?'

'Right here.' I kiss her head. 'You think I'm an oxymoron? You think I'd be anywhere else?'

'I know why those newspapers wrote all that crap, you know.' She reaches up to kiss me above my beard. 'You're an enigma. You always stay quiet and act polite, but nobody knows what you're thinking.'

I lean down so she can reach my face more easily. 'I'm thinking crap most of the time. But don't tell the newspapers that.'

'So what crap are you thinking now?'

I kiss her shoulder. 'I'm thinking, why don't we go and eat, and then come back here and I'll show you some of the crap I think about?'

I kiss her shoulder again. Shoulders lead to backs. It's a known biological fact. And where do backs lead? To a curve that, if you kiss it gently enough and long enough, can cause the curve's owner to squirm about with a delicious movement. I'd sampled that experience the day before. I was getting experienced in this marriage business. Not since the long-distant past with Janet had I had prolonged access to curves like that.

But this was better than with Janet. This was waking up in the morning to curves lying invitingly beside me. This was falling asleep with curves against me. This was having curves snuggle up into me in the wee hours as though they wanted to merge with me. This was having a curve-owner take my arm and place it across her curves before she drifted off to sleep as though she was the owner of that arm.

I really liked that. I wanted my arm to be owned by Anji. I wanted everything I possessed to be owned by Anji. The obvious thing, of course, but the rest as well: the arms, the legs, the beard, the hair, the eyes, the torso, the sex appeal, the things that people always commented on. Those comments had always made me uncomfortable. Let people comment to Anji if they wanted to comment. Preferably, let them shut up. I wanted to be safe from people's probing eyes, from their wondering minds. That simple gold ring on Anji's hand promised me that safety. I was just Anji's husband, plain and simple. My private life was determined by her needs and wishes. My body was a mechanism for her pleasure. I wanted Anji to take me, in every sense of the word: in the vulgar sense Trinis mean when they talk about a woman taking a man, but in some other sense as well. I belonged to Anji now, not to my mother, or my father, not to Nerissa, not to my family, not to Symphonia, or Ashok and his jellyfish, or OAG or the Rockefeller Foundation.

I had a place in the world.

When we returned to Trinidad all was quiet on the home front. Robin and family decamped back to London, sisters safe and sound in terrorist camps, no sign of wedding guests, no sign of wedding activities. It might never have happened. Except that I had my treasure with me. Anji had her gold ring on her finger, I had her.

We seemed to just merge in. Anji started re-working her dissertation in between what she called dreaming off. She said she dreamed off a lot these days when she was supposed to be working. I didn't tell her I thought maybe dreaming off was a contagious disease she might have caught from me. You don't tell your wife everything, I had heard.

I guess this is also standard-issue stuff, that first year of marriage, when half your life is a dream-like state. You get back to work, you deal with the necessities of life, like eating and arguing with OAG, but that's just in the gaps. You might go out for roast corn at the savannah, you might take a swim together, you might even be stupid enough to try and teach your wife to play tennis when she has no hand-eye coordination. But essentially it's all just foreplay.

I myself seemed to have lost the art of dreaming off. One of my major dreaming-off subjects was always waiting for me in the hammock, and I had a hell of a lot to do in between. The avalanche of natural-gas money that had descended on Trinidad had raised demand for consumer goods. Tony Antoine's kitchen and bedroom cabinets had become a hot item since his visit to Milan and the subsequent improvements he had made. He proposed to reorganise his entire production system. I proposed to include the lumber-yard in his sphere of influence and shift my cousin, Vijay, to Dorado. Now that we had round-the-clock security there, we could keep some cash on the compound, maintain a small office there, and eliminate the need for me to rush up in time to pay the workers every Friday afternoon. We expanded Tony's factory again and built a furniture showroom in part of the space destined for our mall. Our office in the Croissee had become overcrowded, so we shifted it to the space above the warehouse. Jeremy and I designed luxury offices with luxury office furniture, to impress any clients who came to bug us when we really wanted to get on with shit-talking.

That only caused Tony to discover a new line in office furniture, with some kind of Swedish orthopaedic angle to it. Soon, every bank in the island was lining up to buy orthopaedic furniture for their senior staff. And there were lots of banks in the island these days, what with all this new money to turn around.

Then, almost out of the blue, I also had to plan a Michelin-star restaurant for OAG, who wanted their leisure facilities to become some kind of flagship fringe benefit for senior staff. They were really aiming to become the cultural leaders of the Trinidadian elite. Enough of this post-colonial order based on the remnants of European dominion – the Americans had arrived to convert this godforsaken island into an outpost of empire. The President of the Republic of Trinidad and Tobago must long for invitations to OAG's five-star dining-room in Dorado.

How I got dragged into these ambitions was a bit of a mystery to me. I had signed a contract to deliver a beautiful restaurant building designed, at great cost, by Jeremy Jameson-Jones. A restaurant building that would tell eaters what eating was all about. But I had one Ms Nerissa Hosein working for me.

It all started the first Saturday my wife and I spent at our weekend Pleasure Palace in Dorado. I had always intended that outpost of the Saran empire to be a fringe benefit for our senior staff. My nearest and dearest employees could borrow it, or join us on weekends there. Hence, one T. Nathaniel Charles held a Grand Opening of the Outpost. Nerissa, Suzanne and Mr and Mrs Antoine were guests of honour. Jeremy Jameson-Jones and Suzanne's husband were the guests of dishonour. Assorted Other Antoines were ordinary guests. Mikey was musician-in-residence.

This Opening was going to be Mouth-Opening, Charlo said. He was going to unveil to Nerissa's mother, who did catering for office parties, the truth about curry. He brought along Cassandra Reyes, Dorado's librarian and his partner in Thai curry, to assist. I was going to make stewed crayfish à la my mother-in-law. Ashok, meanwhile, was going to unveil to Nerissa his sterling qualities as a potential husband. Now that the polar bear was out of the way, he was going to cook her his inimitable Found on Land in his best, oldest, cooking-oil tin. 'That should show her how potent-ial I am,' he said, jiggling his eyebrows. 'Watch how that girl going to get Lost at Sea this evening.'

We had ordered Dorado delicacies a-plenty from the villagers. Every kind of fruit, black pudding from the lady with elephantiasis, oysters and chip-chip in their special sauce, soused conch and soused chicken feet. Ashok had even procured a bottle of the fishermen's alleged aphrodisiac for Mr Antoine, aged sixty-eight, to try out.

When the guests turned up that Saturday, however, we discovered that Nerissa's mother didn't trust men any more than Nerissa herself did. She had got up at the crack of dawn and prepared a huge quantity of her dalphouri and curried chicken. Mrs Antoine was no better. She had filled their car trunk with home-baked bread and cassava pone, home-baked ham, home-made piccalilli and black fruitcake drenched in Madeira wine. Tony and Bernard's wives were not to be outdone. Spanish pastelles steamed in banana leaves, corn bread . . .

Mr Antoine, our Dignitary of the Day, cut the ribbon with a pair of pliers. It was suspended between two jugs of Dorado lime punch. Ashok was planning to knock out Nerissa that evening and had hand-picked the limes. Guests, honourable and dishonourable, imbibed, had lunch, comprised of the Dorado specialities, and then dispersed to look over the compound while the kids ensconced themselves in the jacuzzi. Cooks and cooks' consorts (or would-be consorts in the case of Nerissa) remained behind, wielding pliers and hacksaws as they started preparing the ingredients for dinner.

Charlo had built a gigantic wooden verandah at the front of the Pleasure Palace. It was raised a little way above the beach so we could get a good view and a lot of breeze. At the right side, the kitchen jutted into it, so cooking and verandahing could be carried out simultaneously. As the sun began to cool, we slid back the trademark cocoa-house roof.

'Howdy, neighbour,' came a voice from below our verandah.

It was a Texan voice, the President of OAG (Trinidad) to be exact. He had come to inspect progress on his own pleasure palace, which was being built a little way down the beach. He was accompanied by E. Duncan and wife, ensconced in the wheelchair with the mountain-bike tyres Ashok had attached so she could whizz through sand.

Of course we had to invite them up for lime punch. Of course they had to partake of the home-baked ham. Of course they had to sample other delicacies. Of course Mrs Antoine had to give them her lecture on Pastelle-Making From a Historical Perspective. Of course E. Duncan and Charlo had to have an argument about their last poker game.

'Poker?' Mr Granderson-Powell, President (Trinidad), asked with a gleam in his eye. He was at a loose end. His wife was in New York, purchasing Art for their pleasure palace.

E. Duncan got a deck of cards. They needed a fourth. Ms Nerissa Hosein proposed herself. I squinted at her. 'You could play poker?'

'Why you think I couldn't marry the polar bear?' she said. 'I used to bust his ass in poker. How I could marry a man who can't beat me in poker?'

Mr GP looked her up and down as he lit a cigar. 'Let's see if you can marry me,' he suggested.

That question was still unresolved by the time dinner was served. The moon was rising, a near full moon in the clear Dorado sky. The peacocks were hanging around. Charlo's Japanese lanterns were being lit.

Mr GP was a big guy, about six foot three, one of those Yanks who jogged seven miles before breakfast and then ate sixteen eggs and a crate of bacon. He made a serious contribution to demolishing the mountain of food and drink we had unwittingly stockpiled.

'Ved,' he asked, 'why are you handing me an empty restaurant?'

I was busy cracking Anji's crab shells for her. That girl really had two left hands – she had already injured her thumb with the pliers.

'Because that's what's in the contract we signed,' I said, glancing up.

'Since I got here last year,' GP replied, 'I have never been not negotiating a new contract with you. Why are we stopping now? You are managing maintenance of this facility on our behalf. Why not the restaurant too?'

'Ask the government that question.' I grinned at him. 'Saran is the man with the wood. I deal in lumber, furniture and buildings, and have stretched my capacities to maintain my own property here. I don't deal in food.'

'So I deal in food?' GP retorted, re-lighting his cigar. 'I deal in money.

That's another name for oil and natural gas. I don't deal in food any more than you do.'

'Mr GP . . .' I picked up Anji's hand and licked the crab sauce from one of her fingers. 'I have better things to do than run a restaurant for you.'

'Ved just lazy,' Nerissa put in. 'Talk to me. I deal in money. That's another name for food.' She looked at me. 'Don't forget Tunapuna Market.'

GP placed his cigar in an ashtray, tilted his head and stared at Nerissa. 'You deal in money?' he asked. 'Then how come you haven't won a penny in this game so far?'

Nerissa gave him one of her smiles, all inscrutable velvet eyes. 'You just said it. So far . . .'

The poker game was still going on when all other overnight visitors went to bed. I left Saran Enterprises' General Manager and OAG President (Trinidad) to it. I had a wife with me and she had extremely scrutable eyes.

By the next week, Ms Hosein and Mr GP were having business lunches together. Food, she informed me, made a minimum of forty per cent clear profit. Michelin-star food would make a hundred per cent profit. Michelin-star food that was subsidised by OAG? The sky was the limit. We made dining-room furniture. We imported dishes and cutlery. What was the problem with running a restaurant?

Management, I informed Nerissa. My cousin Vijay was management, Nerissa informed me. He was so neurotic he would make an excellent restaurant manager. Chef was the next problem, I told Nerissa. Chefs are for stealing, Nerissa replied. You just find one at a luxury hotel in one of the islands and make him an offer he can't refuse. Roger had told her so.

I stared at her. 'Roger? But I thought you dump Roger?'

'Not that Roger!' she said testily. 'Roger Granderson-Powell.'

Nerissa was on first-name terms with the President of OAG (Trinidad).

'How you have such a Roger-studded life?' I asked, fishing for information as to what was going on at those business lunches.

She shrugged. 'Must be my karma, as your mother would say.'

She and Roger II were cooking up a restaurant-management proposal to put to the board of Saran Enterprises. Of course they came up with an offer I couldn't refuse. Ashok had to get busy building apartments for our chef and office manager in Dorado, while Charlo finished OAG's complex and accommodation for staff. Mr Antoine started designing the ultimate in dining-room furniture.

We all met up on weekends at the Pleasure Palace. Jellyfish was no longer our staple subject of conversation; Trinidad was getting more weird than jellyfish. 'Trinidad skip over development altogether,' Cassandra Reyes said. 'We gone from underdevelopment to decadence in one fell swoop.'

Tony claimed that the wash of new business was also fuelling drug-trafficking. He spent a lot of his time at the port, receiving deliveries of lumber and dispatching furniture to other Caribbean islands. Trinidad was slam-bam on the route between Latin America and the United States. While US customs officials in Miami scrutinised imports originating in Colombia, they ignored those from Trinidad. Our ports were now so busy, customs officials in Port of Spain didn't examine containers of shoes from Venezuela to see whether they contained cocaine. They were just stamping papers left, right and centre, without looking at anything except the bribes the importers handed them.

Roger Granderson-Powell took to joining us on our verandah. He was often riding solo at his pleasure palace down the beach. Or jogging solo. He would jog ten miles down the beach at dawn, help the fishermen pull in their nets, which is damned hard work, and come back with his New York Marathon T-shirt full of fish to dump on our doorstep. We always had cooks around. Mrs Gopaul, Mrs Antoine, Ashok. Roger II, of course, had to be invited to eat some of his fish. That was my mother-in-law's dharma, not to leave the hungry unfed, especially ten miles of solid, hungry muscle such as Roger was. She was scandalised that his wife didn't think of feeding him. 'How come that white man wife don't ever come Dorado?' she asked with a wrinkle in her brow.

'His wife in the US, settling down his son at college,' I replied.

'But last month she was in the US, checking on their house there,' Tony's wife pointed out.

'She say Dorado boring,' Ashok said. 'I tell her, take up collecting jelly-fish, but I don't think she liked that suggestion.'

'She say her husband does spend all his time in Dorado playing poker with Charlo and E. Duncan and Nerissa,' Anji put in. 'Allyou corrupt a good, good business executive.'

'She say her husband does spend all his time in Dorado playing tennis with your husband,' Charlo pointed out.

'He say he only waiting for the golf course to finish, then he going to bust my ass in golf,' I added.

The golf course was on the other side of the road to Guayaguayare. We had to build a little pavilion there so golfers could get drinks, so staff and maintenance were involved again. Things kept growing bigger and bigger in Dorado. When Charlo and Ashok went off for two weeks to examine golf courses all over the Caribbean, I had to take their place at our Outpost of Empire. No problem: I had my consort to keep me company, and Pierre Bergerac, our new French chef, to make things unpredictable.

Pierre had been found for me by the French embassy. He was the scrawniest human being I had ever seen. Ashok said he looked like an albino coconut tree, swaying with the Dorado breeze in his tall chef's hat. It's guys like Pierre who make me feel that I always encounter caricatures. When that man wasn't sulking in a peculiarly French style, he was in ecstasy over some new dish he had invented, such as breadfruit soufflé. Breadfruit soufflé was just Ashok's 'Found on Land' in a baking dish, but I enjoyed Pierre's drama. Being laboratory rats during the Creation of Cuisine was a fine occupation for my wife and myself.

'Dorado Délicieux' was the name Pierre had chosen for the restaurant. I had a lot of fun helping him write the menu – oysters with Dorado sauce was called 'Go Brave'. We ordered pliers a-plenty for cracking crab shells, and Mikey designed a beautiful logo to stamp on them, the two D's of Dorado Délicieux echoing the S's of Saran's Symphonia. Mrs Antoine got linen napkins embossed with the logo, and Thai silk tablecloths. After Mr Antoine had designed the Ultimate in Exclusive Dining Chairs, Tony designed the Ultimate in Advertising Leaflets to peddle them to resorts in the rest of the region. Charlo reinvented origami to hang from the ceiling. Silk origami, believe it or not. The central one was based on Ashok's myth about a beautiful woman who lured men to their deaths in the forest; another portrayed an ugly woman who turned into a ball of fire. There were, of course, silk origami jellyfish in droves.

The dining-room's Grand Opening went without a hitch. It was President of OAG (Trinidad) and wife entertaining President of the Republique de Trinidad-Tobago (as Pierre referred to our homeland) and wife. Ashok and I predicted that a strong breeze would cause Pierre's Ultimate Chef's Hat to lift off and he would get stuck in one of the helicopters, but we weren't in control, so no accidents occurred. Mrs Granderson-Powell was in control, in a black dress whose back dipped

all the way to that curve towards the end of the spine of which I may
have written earlier in this book. On Mrs GP, however, there wasn't any
curve, just more ribs. How could somebody have ribs there? Don't ask
me. That woman had worn out several gyms in the course of her lifetime, I had been reliably informed by her husband.

I had done the decent thing with this Grand Opening. I had invited
my sisters and their husbands. Terrorists were strictly banned, on pain of
being forced to eat a silk origami jellyfish. I had also brought them a
Nintendo game from the shop to keep them busy in their beach-house.
Unfortunately for my sisters, however, the Press was totally uninterested
in the Sarans this time. They had every ambassador known to the Trinidad
elite, complete with glitter and greasepaint, to photograph. And I was
practically unrecognisable anyway. I had been forced into a suit for the
occasion by my wife, who hated my father's white shirt-jacs.

'You look so handsome, Ved,' Anji said comfortingly at the round table
where we sat with my sisters. I had changed Mrs GP's placement so I
could sit next to her.

'As handsome as the President de la Republique?' I asked. Trinidad's
president was a spectacularly ugly man. Think toad.

'Handsomer!' Anji said, then raised her eyebrows. 'But not as sexy. He
exudes an invitation to kiss him and see if he will turn into a prince.'

Her dimples were in evidence. While I continued griping that my tie
was choking me, my left hand gravitated to her thigh. Everything here
was completely under control and, if it wasn't, Mrs GP would bring it
under control, if she had to crack three ribs at the bottom of her spine
to do so.

'This thing really boring,' Anji began saying.

Indra didn't agree.

'You could always make it interesting the way you did last time,' I said
to Anji, my hand moving up her thigh under the silk tablecloth.

'Ved, please behave with some dignity,' Queen pleaded.

I ignored her. 'Want to see a grand Opening?' I asked Anji, moving
my right hand to my tie. 'It's either here or back at the house.'

Yes, marriage was about the best thing that had happened to me. A
lot was going on around me, but there was this quiet space in the
centre that Anji and I occupied.

Not that there weren't problems, of course. My sisters were seriously bothered about being excluded from the Pleasure Palace. I told them it was a business facility. Tony entertained clients from the rest of the Caribbean there, and I got Roger GP to fly them from the airport with one of their helicopters. It was a great PR stunt, what with Pierre and his Michelin-star act. But my sisters saw through that excuse. Anji was the doyenne of the Pleasure Palace, which was not, in their view, an appropriate role for a Nouveau-Saran. With a family like mine, though, I always expected problems. I was used to solving them. And having Anji there drew a line in the sand, so to speak. The Saran bad blood was not going to affect her happiness. That was my aim, objective, and the rest.

Similarly with the business. We had big problems sometimes. Most, however, could be dealt with by my managers. I encouraged Suzanne to talk to me if she had any staff difficulties before she took radical action. For the rest, Tony and Charlo could deal with them. Tony was somewhat like me, easy-going but ultimately as rigid as the knot in his tie, and no one dared cross Charlo. You just had to look at Charlo, Ashok said, and you knew where jellyfish grew – in your backbone. Ashok himself could be problematic. He could disappear into drinking and womanising for three days on end. But when he returned, he would make work happen with such magic you soon forgave him. On rare occasions, his temper would get aroused and then he was unstoppable. Except by Charlo. Charlo could stop a speeding bullet. He once sat on Ashok when he tried to go for Pierre over some silly piece of restaurant equipment. Ashok ended up laughing because Charlo threatened to fart on him.

An increasing problem, though, was that of security. Trinidad had a serious edge of violence, and it was getting worse all the time. To start with, I figured it was time we found a solution to Jacob's presence in the lumber-yard, so Nerissa offered him a big raise to go work on the Dorado plant. For a couple of weeks before, I had primed him with talk about all the nice, fish-fed girls with gigantic bottoms who lived in the villages around Dorado. Spending the week with those girls, and weekends with his wife in town, was like a fairy-tale come true for Jacob. The rest was history. But Jacob eventually did something Charlo didn't like, Charlo treated him with the scorn he was capable of sometimes, Jacob pushed things to a fight, Charlo told him to 'bring it come' and Jacob backed down. Easy as pie and sweet as a mango in July. Jacob slunk back home. I didn't know anything about it till a week later. I had nothing to do with it; Saran couldn't be blamed. It was this big, black man without a nose-bridge who raised peacocks on an isolated beach who had humiliated Jacob. End of story.

But the shop in the Croissee remained a security risk. All that glass could easily be broken. I hated the iron bars that were appearing around all homes and businesses, so just installed an electronic security system and hoped that our location on the well-lit Eastern Main Road was another form of security. We had a break-in, though, around 3 a.m. one morning, and that caused Charlo to get inspiration. He reminded me of the metal doors we had seen in shops in Rome. You slid them down at night and bolted them shut with huge steel padlocks. Expensive. Extremely expensive. Implemented.

It broke my heart to install burglar bars upstairs in our living quarters. Our house was our house because of those louvred french doors leading to the wide verandah. Again, Charlo came up with an idea. He designed burglar-proofing based on a Portuguese model, all black metal curlicues. It looked nice and took a weight off my mind. Now, I didn't worry any more that some bad guys would get in through the french doors furthest away from my bedroom.

But our house was big, those doors were far away, and I didn't hear when some guys cut through the burglar-proofing of the kitchen doors one Sunday night about two-thirty.

Anji and I had stayed late at the Pleasure Palace that evening, doing something or other that may or may not have involved the curve at the base of her spine. By the time we got back to the Croissee it was ten in the evening, and we went straight to sleep. When noises in our bedroom woke me up and I found a guy pointing a gun inches away from my head, my first thought was: Thank God for that overactivity in Dorado, otherwise we would have been naked in bed now. Instead, Anji was wearing a nightdress and I was in shorts.

That's the way with crisis, I find. You think about the most mundane things at the beginning before the reality really hits you.

We were hustled out of our room by two guys, the one with the gun, a big black guy with sweat streaming down his face, and a brown-skinned guy with a mean-looking moustache and a long cutlass pointed at Anji. We found my parents in the dark living-room being guarded by a short, wiry fella wielding another cutlass.

'Listen, fellas,' I said. 'There is nothing valuable in this house. Everything is in the bank.'

Whap! One of the guys hit me in the face.

'Shut your focking mouth!' the one with the gun growled.

Here I have to put in a linguistic note. Every noun and verb the robbers uttered was prefixed by obscenities. Henceforth, I'll leave them out. Too boring.

They told us to lie down on the ground, face downwards. I tried to go and help Pa and was hit a couple of times again. Somehow I didn't feel the blows. The guys shoved my mother and Anji roughly, swearing at them to hurry up. When Ma didn't move fast enough, one of them slapped her. I wasn't sure who I should worry about.

'Listen,' I said, after I was forced onto the floor. 'That man over there have a bad heart. If allyou cause him to get a heart attack, allyou could end up with a murder charge, eh.'

The guy who had had the cutlass pointed at Anji kicked me twice, and I heard Pa grunt. But they didn't touch him after that. Ma and Anji were totally silent. I tried to stretch out my hand to hold Anji's and got a couple of kicks and a few obscenities from the robbers. They tied my wrists together with some electrical wire. Then, while the one with the gun kept watch over us, the other two started searching the house.

You know how robbers search houses, I suppose. They pull every drawer out and dump its contents on the floor. They smash things. They rush from room to room making lots of noise and uttering lots of obscenities.

They started with my bedroom. I heard my precious old LPs smashing to the floor. I heard my stereo equipment get broken. I didn't care. All I could think about was getting these guys out of the house before they hurt a member of my family. I wished I could give them some money to induce them to go. But every time I moved slightly, the guy with the gun kicked me. 'Keep your focking backside quiet!'

I still didn't feel the kicks. I just lay there, hoping Anji and Pa weren't too frightened, trying to figure out what to do.

The robbers' language grew more foul. There were a lot of cupboards to search, a lot of furniture to destroy before they found what they wanted.

'I tell allyou it don't have nothing valuable in this house,' I said. 'Allyou wasting allyou time.'

Kick. 'Nothing valuable?' The guy was heaving now as he kicked me. 'That woman lying down next to you not valuable? Well you will see how valuable she is to me and my partners. I always like a nice Indian cunt.'

My heart suddenly slowed. If this son of a bitch touched Anji, I thought,

I wasn't going to just lie there, gun or no gun, cutlass or no cutlass.

You think a lot of things lying on the floor like that. If you leap to your feet suddenly and knock the guy over, what could be the consequences? If Pa started to groan, what would you do? If they really attacked Anji?

'Where the money?' they kept demanding.

'It ain't have no money in this house,' I kept saying.

'You see this woman here,' one said, his voice coming from directly over Anji's prone figure. 'If we ain't find no money, we taking her with us. You will have to pay money then to get her back.'

'The money in that room over there,' I said, waving with my bound hands at the other side of the house, in the direction of Pa's room. 'In the safe.'

Kick! 'You lying mother-cunt!' I felt the point of a cutlass against my own back. 'If you lying to me, you know what going to happen to this woman here?'

I just hoped there was enough money in Ma's safe to satisfy them. I had no clue what she had besides papers in there. 'Look,' I said. 'Any money it have in this house in the safe in that room over there. The key in the freezer in the kitchen, in a chicken at the back.'

One of them rushed to the kitchen, then to Pa's room. I heard cursing coming from the room. He couldn't get the key to work. I heard the other guy join him. More cursing.

'That lock kind of weird,' I said to the guy holding the gun above me. 'I will have to open it for you. I am the only one who can open it.'

No response. More curses and hysteria coming from Pa's room.

'Get up!' the guy with the gun barked. I looked up and met his eyes. He kicked me. 'What happen? You deaf? I say get up.'

I rose, my hands still tied behind my back. One of the other guys had come back into the room. The one with the gun looked me in the eye. 'If you lying to me . . .' He described what he would do to my mother and Anji.

The third guy handed the key over to the one with the gun, then pointed his cutlass at Ma's back.

'Move!' the robber bawled, jabbing me with the gun.

'I can't open the safe with my hands tied,' I pointed out.

Swearing and threatening even worse, they untied my hands. I led the guy with the gun to the corridor and into Pa's room.

The safe was one of those heavy old-fashioned things, set on blocks on the floor next to Pa's old-fashioned cast-iron bed. Mounted on the wall above was a series of cricket bats signed by famous cricketers that Pa had acquired since we had started supplying equipment to the West Indies Cricket Board.

The robber handed me the heavy iron key. It was cold from the freezer. I warmed it in both hands, then bent and opened the safe. I looked around at the robber. He motioned me to take out what was inside. I began pulling out envelopes full of documents, tins and jewellery boxes.

'Open them box,' he said.

I did so, emptying the contents onto Pa's bed.

'Where the focking money?' he demanded.

'This is what it have,' I replied, spilling an envelope full of money on the bed.

'You focking lying!' He bent at the door of the safe to check I had left nothing inside.

I had already planned what I would do if I got a chance. As the robber poked his head towards the safe, I grabbed the nearest cricket bat from the wall and brought it down against the back of his head. He grunted. I swung the bat again and hit him harder. He fell forward against the edge of the safe. The gun slid under the bed. The robber remained still, sprawled with his head rested on the edge of the safe. I watched him for a few seconds, the bat poised over my head. He didn't move.

I heard footsteps coming along the corridor. I looked around for Pa's shotgun. It was standing in the corner near the door. I grabbed it and dropped the bat. I moved to the door and saw the guy with the moustache coming through the corridor towards me. He stopped when he saw me with the shotgun in my hand, then started reversing. I moved towards him along the corridor. I was going to beat that cutlass out of his hand. He turned and started running. I rushed after him and grabbed his shoulder at the door of the living-room.

'Where you think you going?' I heard myself asking him.

I dropped the shotgun, put both hands around the guy's neck and squeezed. He gasped and thrashed about, dropped the cutlass, and tried to prise my hands from around his neck. He started to choke. I let his neck go and he lurched. I smashed my fist against the side of his face. He stumbled. I hit him full in the face. He fell to the floor. As he tried to get up, I kicked him in the ribs and then bent and hit him in the face again.

I heard myself breathing heavily as I looked around the living-room for the other guy. There was no sign of him. Pa, Anji and Ma were looking up from where they lay.

The guy on the floor started begging me. 'We wasn't really going to do anybody anything, boss,' he said, holding his stomach. 'We was only trying to frighten allyou.'

Blood rushed up to my head. 'Hush your focking arse!' I shouted.

My shout didn't dispel my anger. It just seemed to make it expand. I kicked the robber.

I heard Ma knock over some china ornaments as she began to haul herself up with the aid of a nearby table. I went over to Pa and helped him up.

'You all right?'

He nodded.

I looked around at Anji. She was sitting up.

'I sorry, boss . . .' the robber began again.

Those words seemed to enrage me. I went over to where he lay, his nose and mouth bleeding into his little razor moustache. His face was wet with sweat.

'You wanted to frighten us?' I asked. I grabbed him by the shoulder and smashed my fist into his face again, then let him fall to the floor. He remained there, squirming and saying he was sorry.

'You OK?' I asked Anji.

She nodded, her eyes big and scared. I felt my heart thumping hard as though it was going to come up and block my throat. I rushed back to Pa's room. The robber there was still immobile, bleeding into the safe. I figured it was better not to touch him. Let the police find him exactly as he was. I went back to the living-room.

'Pa? How you feeling?'

He nodded. 'All right,' he said. 'I sorry the gun wasn't loaded.'

I looked from Anji to Ma. Ma sighed, looking at me and shaking her head. Anji just stared at me. She was in shock. I went and put my arms around her. Somehow it surprised me how small she was. I hugged her hard. 'It's OK, darling,' I said. 'Everything is OK. I just have to call the police. Everything will be all right now.'

I went to the kitchen and phoned the San Juan police station. A constable answered in a sleepy voice. When I explained what had happened, he was silent. I asked if they would come right away. They had no vehicle available, he said. They would send a police car as soon as one returned to the station. I repeated what I had said before, that one of the robbers was unconscious and bleeding from the head. I had hit him with a cricket bat. 'Good!' the constable said. 'Then he not going nowhere. We could take our time.'

He put down the phone.

The guy I had beaten was groaning on the floor. 'Shut your arse!' I barked.

He went silent. I returned to Pa's room. The guy there was really still. Completely passed out. He had slipped from the safe to the floor and a puddle of blood was growing on the carpet. Pa appeared in the doorway, then came in and examined the guy as well. I felt the guy's wrist for a pulse. I thought I felt one. I went back to the living-room and called the nearest hospital, St Joseph. They had no ambulance, they said. Only the Port of Spain General had ambulances. I called Port of Spain. They had no ambulance available. They would send one as soon as possible. I went back to the living-room and held Anji to me. She started to shiver.

'Ma?' I looked over Anji's head. 'You OK?'

She nodded silently. Anji started to sob.

We waited half an hour, expecting every car that approached to be the police. But no police appeared. I checked the robber's pulse again. It was still there. I called the police station again. They told me to have patience. I called the hospital. Still no ambulance available. Ma started fuming and swearing. After nearly an hour, I, too, was swearing.

'Let me show you how we will get police here,' Pa said. He picked up his shotgun and went to his room. He came back with his box of cartridges and headed towards the verandah. I followed him. He loaded the gun and pointed it into the sky.

Pow!

The shot echoed loudly in the quiet of the night. Sounds began to emanate from the houses nearby, like birds waking up, a kind of rustling. Pa lowered the gun and reloaded it. He shot and reloaded, shot and reloaded until all his cartridges were finished.

We heard a police siren start in the distance. People began coming out of their houses to find out what was going on.

'Good thing I save them cartridges,' Pa said.

I rested my hand on his shoulder. 'You must be kill every corbeau for miles,' I said lightly, but I was very pleased at his action.

It was nearly five in the morning when the police arrived. An ambulance only came for the robbers at about six. At about eight-thirty, after we had made tea and drank it, and Anji's sobs had finally diminished to sniffling, the police returned.

They had come to arrest me on charges of manslaughter, they said. The guy I had hit with the cricket bat had died in hospital.

'Good!' was my mother's response to the policemen bearing the news. 'I wish he did hit the other one with the cricket bat too.'

'Arrest?' Anji broke into sobs again.

'It's just a formality, sweetheart,' I said, putting my arms around her. I looked up at the police sergeant for confirmation. He assumed police impassivity. 'I could call my lawyer, right?'

He did a brief nod. I arranged for my lawyer to meet me at San Juan police station. Then, without asking the policeman again, I called Tony Antoine and asked him to get his ass over here pronto. Emergency. Then I accompanied the policemen to the station.

I spent a long time writing my statement. I had learnt this from my lawyer. Throw in every detail. Bore them. We had to wait for the courts to open so I could go before a magistrate and my lawyer could apply for bail. It was nearly eleven-thirty when my case was called and almost one when I left the courthouse. By that time, Ashok and Charlo were at my side, and the Press were waiting outside the court. I believe they have arrangements with the police to let them know when anything exciting occurs. Flashbulbs flashed. I left it to my lawyer to say 'no comment'. I wasn't even opening my mouth.

The same cannot be said for my mother. She was surrounded by reporters when we got to the house. There were more flashbulbs when Anji ran down the stairs as I got out of Ashok's car. She put both her arms around me as though she would never let me go. My shirt got wet with her tears.

I went upstairs to the verandah, ignoring the reporters who were swarming around me, asking questions. I went straight into the kitchen into Sylvia's arms. She garbled something about having faith in the Lord, and wet my shirt again with her tears. I was finally able to detach myself from her, found some bread and fried plantain, and made Anji eat some with me while leaning against the kitchen counter. I could hear Ma through the open door giving the reporters her account of what had happened.

'Imagine the fastness of the police!' she said to them. 'Arresting my son for manslaughter when it's the government who kill the man. If they did send a ambulance when we call, he might be alive allnow, going to rob somebody else house.'

I took Anji's hand and led her through the interior of the house to the bathroom attached to our room. After we had both showered and changed, we returned to the verandah. We found Ma giving her story to a television crew. Pa was butting in to make sure they were aware that it was a cricket bat with the signature of the former head of the West Indies team, Sir Garfield Sobers, that had knocked the man for six.

The reporters, photographers and radio crews swarmed around me, asking questions that I ignored. It was turning into a pappy-show, with Ma informing the television camera that she was going to sue the Ministry of Health for not coming on time, and recover any legal expenses she incurred on my defence. 'All police know how to do is take bribe!' she told the camera. 'You call them when you have three donkeys beating you in your house, and they have no time for that. But if you call them and say you have a roti for them, they will reach quicker than a fly smelling shit.'

I decided the Press had got more than enough. I moved through the throng to where my mother was sitting. 'Party's over,' I said. 'Time to wrap up, fellas.'

'Mr Saran,' pleaded a young female reporter, 'but you didn't tell us how you feel.'

'I feel fine,' I said, looking down at her face. 'I will feel finer when you leave my house.'

'Do you feel any remorse about killing the burglar?' she went on.

I stared at her, lost for words. Then I saw Charlo straighten up from where he was leaning on the verandah railing. He walked over to stand in front of the TV camera so it was getting a close-up of his string vest.

'You hear what the man say?' he asked the cameraman.

The cameraman stared at him.

'You didn't hear the man say time to wrap up?' Charlo asked.

The cameraman didn't move. Charlo reached round the back of the camera and detached the cord leading to the sound equipment. An over-made-up TV reporter rushed over to him.

'Who are you?' she demanded in a peremptory manner.

Charlo turned to look at her and raised his non-existent eyebrows. 'Who is me?' he asked, pointing to his string vest. 'You want to know who I is? You asking me questions, girl?' He shook his head slowly at her. 'I didn't hear you ask me for no interview.'

He continued removing cords from the back of the camera.

'Don't you dare touch that camera!' the reporter snapped.

Ashok suddenly appeared next to Charlo. 'But he done touch your camera,' Ashok pointed out. 'What you going to do? Call the San Juan police? You have money to bribe them to come and save your camera?' He smiled his engaging smile at the girl, then pointed at his own chest. 'But if you ask me my name, I will tell you,' he went on. 'It's a long time I want to talk to you. I want to tell you you shouldn't wear so much lipstick when you going on TV. It does hurt my eyes when I watching the news.'

By the time the afternoon newspapers hit the streets, I was famous. Pictures of vulnerable wife embracing hero-husband were splashed all over the front page. The radio news had been full of the story, every hour on the hour. I should have killed the other burglar with the cricket bat as well, people said on radio call-in programmes; I shouldn't have just broken his nose, ribs and collarbone and dislocated his shoulder.

The next day, this guy went to court to answer charges of attempted robbery with violence. He was heavily bandaged. He claimed all the violence was on my part – I had surprised them while they were robbing the safe. 'Why you didn't break he jaw?' Nerissa asked me later when I went to the office.

By the day after that, however, the news coverage had begun to change. I had been dubbed the Cricket Bat Killer. The *Trinidad Sentinel* had got a Scoop. Ved Saran was in the habit of dislocating shoulders, it revealed. Would you believe it? A journalist was the current resident of the St Ann's flat my former girlfriend Sharon had occupied. Her landlord had given her an exclusive. That dignified look, with beard and innocent-looking little Indian wife, was just a mask for an explosive individual. When I was involved with less innocent, non-Indian women, I was given to violence. When I was involved with Alsatian dogs, I was murderous. I had paid my way out of facing the legal consequences of my actions then. Standard practice for businessmen in Trinidad.

The *Trinidad Times* outscooped the *Sentinel*. Saran was not just a danger to dogs and girlfriends; his employees were at risk as well. One had even died at the company's Christmas party. They had interviewed the head nurse at Port of Spain General Hospital Casualty Department. She knew

Mr Saran well. He was always practising his hooliganism in her department; the police had once had to intervene and throw him out.

When the newspapers ran out of scoops they began to editorialise. The *Sentinel*'s leader-writer pointed out that Trinidad was not a Muslim country. Tooth-for-tooth and eye-for-eye didn't belong here. We were Civilised. We lived by the Rule of Law. Rich businessmen couldn't just take the law into their hands and kill people who broke into their houses to steal. Neither should they hire goons to protect them from the legitimate enquiries of the Press. Freedom of the Press was a sacred cornerstone of our democracy, enshrined in our constitution.

Controversy began to rage, with yours truly at its centre. I sucked my teeth. I had no time for this bullshit: I had trauma on my hands – a wife who kept waking up at all hours of the night and going into the living-room to encounter my father, who was re-living his last great kill, a.k.a. Empty Sky. I had my process of Extreme Avoidance to carry out: avoiding journalists, avoiding curious people who came into the store hoping to catch a glimpse of Cricket Bat Killer, avoiding questions from acquaintances who could then relay my remarks to the newspapers. I stopped going to the tennis club, to the store, to anywhere that I could be gaped at.

The *Sentinel* went for Expert Commentary next, asking notable jurists what they thought of the case. The *Times* asked the Minister of Justice his opinion. He replied in a highly dignified way, saying it would be improper for him to comment while the matter was in the hands of the court. But the bastard smiled and added that, no matter who you were, you had to face the due process of the law. The *Times* editorial was headed: 'NO MAFIA HERE, PLEASE'.

And then, somehow, both newspapers had the same scoop on the same day. Both had acquired hot documents relating to 'Hooligan Businessman, V. P. Saran'. Not only was I in the habit of attacking armed robbers, non-Indian girlfriends and unarmed Alsatian dogs, but I was a danger to inanimate objects as well. I had been charged by the police in the past with damaging standpipes, libraries and a huge bridge in Dorado. The charges had been later dropped, but no doubt there were easy explanations for that. Anybody with eyes could read between the lines, where words like 'bribery' and 'Mafia intimidation' dangled. A photo of the vast Saran estate in Untamed Dorado was published.

One editorialist waxed ironic, pointing out that standpipes didn't come into your house trying to rob you. The other editorial was analytical. Trinidad was turning into some kind of Wild West where everyone thought they could take the law into their hands. It was a gold-rush environment, with all that natural gas flowing on the Dorado frontier. During gold-rushes, survival of the fittest was the rule. It was up to the Trinidadian courts to ensure that civilised values continued to prevail.

Nerissa shook her head. 'There's more in the mortar than the pestle,' she said. 'I could smell some rotten fish somewhere.'

'You don't have to have attended the University of Tunapuna Market to smell that,' observed Roger GP. 'The newspapers are out for Ved's blood.'

It was the backlash for stealing the most lucrative contracts in the country from under the noses of the guys who owned the newspapers. I was grabbing gas money at its source, the filthy rich oil company, while they were stuck with the peanuts the government dispensed from its royalties on the gas. Now they would show me where jellyfish grew.

The public fought back with letters to the editor defending my action. Only a jellyfish wouldn't have done what I had done, one letter opined; no man worth the name would have done differently. My employees were members of the public, as I had argued years before to my mother. It was easy to recognise Ashok's rhetorical style.

This kind of macho talk roused Liberal Opinion.

Now, Liberal Opinion in Trinidad was White Wimp Opinion, the arty-farty sons and daughters of French Creoles who wanted to distance themselves from their families' links with slavery and European brutishness. Liberal opinionists Understood criminals, they didn't Condemn them. They spoke in sentences that lacked proper structure so they didn't have to come to Logical Conclusions, just Express the Ineffable. To this group, Criminal Behaviour should, of course, be Deplored. But Deploring and Doing-Anything-About were two different things. These folks didn't believe in doing anything about anything. They were not accustomed to doing anything about anything – they didn't have to scrabble in the dirt of Trinidad to get enough money to build a house or compete for a job. They benefited from being members of the elite, but didn't want to be associated with it. They disassociated themselves by issuing Opinions.

In this instance, Liberal Opinion knew its position right from the start. Against a rich Indian businessman owning a shotgun; for a poor, unemployed black sucker who was only stealing to support his children. One Catholic priest on a television discussion programme so evoked Ma's ire that she broke my rule and phoned them up. Once she had announced who she was, they connected her with the studio.

'That priest there,' Ma's nasal voice came over the telephone line into the studio. 'He don't have a wife. Why he don't go and get a wife so he will know how it feel to lie down on the ground while people saying they going to do nasty things to her? He only hiding behind that white dress he wearing.'

There was silence. Ma only grew more angry. 'Eh?' she demanded on the phone. 'I ain't hear allyou saying nothing now. Why the hell all of allyou don't go and do some work instead of talking rubbish on my TV? I rather watch Mickey Mouse. This is the government TV, so it's my taxes paying all of allyou. If anybody had any sense in this country, all of allyou would get fired.'

With Ma defending me, I was in sure trouble. She swore she would spend every penny she possessed to sue the government, which allowed criminals to walk the land, free to steal and harass and rape decent people. The newspapers tried to lecture her on Civilised Values. 'Civilised!' she snorted on a radio show. 'What Trinidad know about civilised? Set of thief and robber running this country. All they know how to do is wine their waist at Carnival.'

The editorialists pointed out that such remarks had a whiff of racism about them.

The gutter press focused on the dark side of the Saran Empire. It had grown so fast because the Sarans practised some obscure form of Hindu witchcraft, one weekly alleged. Sources couldn't be named because Fear stalked Saran employees. In the ghettos of East Trinidad, it was believed that the Sarans were in the habit of killing one of their black employees every year to placate some Hindu goddess or the other. A certain young man named Jason Grant had been one of our victims. His mother had almost gone mad with grief, and had been spirited out of the country by the Sarans. A certain Jacob from Santa Cruz had got out of Saran employment before he became another victim.

The whole thing began to disturb me deeply. The media campaign against me was succeeding. From being on my side, Ordinary People began to say they saw the other point of view. Then they began to espouse the other point of view. They suggested that I should get a light sentence, just a few years among the criminals and rapists who over-populated the jail cells in Carerra. The jury who would decide my fate would be made up of such Ordinary People and I realised you couldn't trust Ordinary People. They all wanted to be Civilised. And the newspapers told them what Civilised People thought.

My brother, Robin, flew to the rescue like Batman's sidekick.

It was time for Robin to come on vacation anyway, and my lawyer was a solicitor, not a barrister, so didn't practise in the courts. Robin couldn't practise in the Trinidad courts either; he had never been called to the Bar here. So he hired some top legal gun from Guyana, a great fat Queen's Counsel with gigantic lips who reminded me of the fictional character Rumpole, but had a sizzling reputation both in London and in other parts of the Caribbean.

Robin appointed Nerissa his legal assistant. She had kept a detailed file of every newspaper clipping. The team got down to work.

Robin first sent a letter to every media agency in the country, reminding them that this case was *sub judice*. Newspapers knew what *sub judice* implied, Robin informed me: straight to jail on contempt of court charges. Do not stop at Go. Do not collect two hundred dollars. No newspaper editor could countenance the company in Carerra. The case vanished from the Press immediately.

But it simmered in the public consciousness. The Cricket Bat Killer made his appearance in the lyrics of a couple of calypsos that year. I went to Dorado with Anji, and let Robin, Nerissa and Rumpole get on with preparations for defence. I only returned for the opening of the trial at the end of Janaury.

Then, I was forced into a suit again and hustled to the Hall of Justice, to a courtroom full of people sitting on benches made in my furniture factory. Press, idlers, my family, Anji's family, friends and well-wishers were there. I glimpsed many familiar faces. I just shut them out of my mind and concentrated on the business.

First, Robin and Rumpole squabbled with the prosecution over the jury. They didn't want anybody with any shred of education, I realised – nobody who could read a big word like Civilised, nobody who aspired to live under the Rule of Law. They were going for Natural Justice. They wanted women on the jury, housewives who were scared of robbers breaking into their houses and raping them. They wanted lower-middle-class homeowners. They wanted black and brown people, nobody of a lighter shade of pale. They got what they wanted. The government prosecutor was no match for them.

The prosecution case was very short. I had hit the man with the cricket bat and he had died as a result. That amounted to manslaughter. The government lawyer offered the jury some guff taken straight out of newspaper editorials. Rumpole and Robin stretched their legs under the benches and pointedly twiddled their thumbs. The judge took a mini-nap.

Then Rumpole called me to the witness stand. I gave my account of what had happened clearly and concisely. When the prosecutor asked what I was thinking of when I hit the man, I said, 'Nothing.' I wasn't thinking, I explained, I was escaping from a dangerous situation. So why did I beat the other guy to a frazzle, he asked, listing in detail the injuries I had caused. I had got angry, I said. The guy had terrified my family for more than an hour. So I was motivated by revenge? I nodded. He said he hadn't heard my reply. '*You* could say I was motivated by revenge,' I said clearly. 'I think I was motivated by adrenalin.'

I don't think I did a good job on that witness stand. The housewives and lower-middle-class homeowners squinted at me suspiciously.

With my mother taking the stand next, the courtroom sat up. People had heard my mother on the radio and television. She did a slightly different act this time. When Rumpole asked her questions, she turned to the judge to answer. She didn't deal with lower-downs. In her account of events, she concentrated first on how the robbers smelled and how they comported themselves in her precious living-room.

'I change every carpet the next week!' she said. 'You know where those shoes must have been before they come in my house? The rubbish dump. Those men smelled like corbeaux. I call Rentokil to fumigate my house. The language they used needed fumigating out of my house.'

There was a ripple of laughter in the public benches. Ma looked at the judge. 'They laughing,' she said, gesturing at the public gallery. 'They don't know what it is to have three big nasty man coming cussing in your house and talking nastiness about what they going to do with your daughter-in-law. And kicking your son. Whole time, whole time, kicking your son with their corbeau boots!'

The courtroom grew quiet. Ma raised a finger at the judge. 'I don't know if you have a son and know what it is to grow a son big,' she went on. 'But it's plenty work. Boy-children does wear out clothes fast. Every time you look around, their shoes too tight for them. They does give you worries and headache. And then, when they finally get big and you married them and think the headache over, man coming to kick up your son in your own living-room.'

She sat back in the witness box and tucked in her veil. 'Man,' she went on, 'I wanted to get up and give them a few kick myself. But I know that would have caused more trouble for Ved. He would have get up too, and they might have shoot him or something. And his father might have had a next heart attack. So I keep my tail quiet.'

The prosecutor decided not to cross-examine my mother.

My father was next, after lunch. He concentrated on the fact that he had used his last remaining cartridges to call the police when we couldn't get an ambulance to come and take the robber away. It was an act of pure desperation. He knew while he was doing it that no more cartridges existed in the world that would fit his antique gun. But he didn't want the guy to keep bleeding on his will and gun licence, both stashed in the safe.

In cross-examination, Pa was asked why he kept a cricket bat in his bedroom. Was it meant for smashing the heads of breakers-in?

Pa stared at the prosecutor in disbelief. 'You look at that bat?' he asked. 'Read the signature on it. Sir Garfield Sobers! The greatest cricketer the world ever produce. How could I not keep that bat in my bedroom? I didn't want it to get thief! If it could have fit in the safe, I would have put it inside.'

There was another ripple of laughter in the public benches. The judge banged his gavel for order, but he was smiling too. That encouraged Pa. 'That signature says: "To a loyal supporter and friend, Ganesh Biswais Saran."' Pa pointed at his chest. 'That's me. Sir Gary know that I travelled to Barbados and Guyana to watch him bat at all his last test matches. Me with my bad heart! He does buy bats in my store and get the family discount. The whole West Indies team does get family discount by Saran. I promise them that the night they lose to Australia and come crying in my swimming pool. I tell them I will supply them with better bat.'

The prosecutor tried to win back the advantage. If Pa had such a bad heart, how come he hadn't got sick the night of the robbery? How come he was able to discharge his last remaining cartridges at the sky?

'Boy!' Pa leaned over the railing of the witness stand. 'That is a good question! I ask myself that many times. I figure I jump over heart attack stage. Like it had a little something extra in the tank that I was keeping in reserve for emergency. It's like,' he turned towards the judge again, 'you know when you already sure you losing a match, and you start batting with all you have in you, just not to look so bad? Like in 1958, when Kanhai make a century after we had already given up against England? And we come and win the test in the end, against all odds?'

The judge nodded. He was of the generation that would remember victories like that. Pa waved his finger.

'That is what happen! When they kick Ved the first few times, my heart start to beat hard. I say, it's curtains for me now, my heart not allowed to beat hard. And, once I say that, it's like I get a new determination. I say to myself, let me try and see how I could prevent my son from getting killed here tonight too. If I could only find a way to get to my gun, I could frighten them fellas away. If somebody had only created a diversion, that was my plan.'

The prosecutor gave up.

Then Anji took the witness stand. I was tense. She answered the questions concisely, as I had told her to do, her eyes big and solemn. You could hear a pin drop in the courtroom.

'Were you frightened?' Rumpole asked.

She nodded. 'Yes, very frightened,' she said softly.

'How frightened?'

Her eyes grew even rounder. 'Terrified,' she said. 'I still can't sleep at night. I wake up every time the wind blows against one of the doors.'

'What were you afraid of at the time of the robbery?' Rumpole asked.

Anji stared at him like she was afraid to bring the answer out. She got a helpless look on her face. The whole courtroom leaned forward to watch this vulnerable-looking girl say the word rape.

'What were you frightened for, Mrs Saran?' Rumpole asked again. Anji's eyes grew opaque. She opened her mouth, closed it again.

'I was frightened for Ved,' she said.

There was a bit of a stir in the courtroom. Rumpole tilted his head to one side. 'You were frightened for your husband, not for yourself?' he asked.

Anji swallowed. She nodded, then shook her head confusedly. 'I was frightened for myself,' she said, as though begging for understanding, 'but they were just kicking Ved and kicking Ved, and I couldn't see.' Her voice trembled. 'I could just hear them kicking him, and I didn't know if he was getting hurt . . . And he kept talking to them in a nice way, telling them he would find the money for them, telling them where the key for the safe was . . .' She put her hand over her mouth and looked at Rumpole. 'But no matter what he said, they only kept kicking him. And then,' her voice started trembling again and she rubbed her forehead, 'they started threatening me. And I knew Ved would end up getting killed or shot, or I don't know what.'

She wiped her nose with her finger, and then wiped her eyes.

'So you were primarily afraid for your husband's safety?'

Her head was bent. 'I just knew that if they tried to hurt me,' she said, 'Ved would try to do something. And I didn't know what could happen. They had a gun, and cutlasses . . .' She looked up at Rumpole appealingly. 'I didn't know what would happen to Ved.' It came out as a bit of a wail.

She rested her head on the railing of the witness stand. Of course Anji had no handkerchief with her. She wiped her face with her hand in a most inelegant way.

The prosecutor declined cross-examination.

The next day, Rumpole called character witnesses. He made a heavy speech about how the newspapers had already convicted me in the Court of Public Opinion. He gave the newspapers a dose of big words that were sometimes bigger than their own. Words like reprehensible and irresponsible and dangerous to the cause of justice. He could have given Jeremy Jameson-Jones a lesson in talking. He talked about the spirit of the law versus the letter of the law, the basis of law, and the right to protect your family. A couple of jurors developed stars in their eyes.

Character Witness Number One was Cassandra Reyes, Dorado's librarian. She explained how I had 'damaged' her library, referring to a file of correspondence Nerissa had given her. Cassandra stressed the dates on the letters, which made it clear how much time and effort had been lost before the library was finally 'damaged'. She caused intakes of breath among the Press with her stresses and emphases. She sounded exactly what she was: a dedicated but frustrated public servant. Jurors, members of the public, even the Press, nodded in unison as she spoke. Her testimony brought everybody together in sympathy and anger against the Ministry of Education. They began to look at me as somebody who had managed to confound the government's determination to neglect their children's education.

The prosecutor again declined to cross-examine.

Character Witness Number Two was the parish priest of Dorado. He was an elderly Irishman who had been in Trinidad so long he had developed a dialect of his own. He said if anybody should be charged for damage to the Dorado standpipe and for water-theft, it was he. He had personally commissioned the installation of a water tank and pump, assuring Mr Saran that the villagers would pay for it.

The prosecutor decided he had been silent for too long. He had a question for this witness.

'How much did the accused charge the villagers for this installation?'

'The accused didn't charge anything,' Father McVeigh answered. 'The accused didn't know anything about it. I was dealing with one of the accused's goons, Mr Ashok Saran, specialist coastal engineer to Harvard University, sitting down right over there.'

Everybody craned their necks to look at the goon. Ashok had worn a white cotton shirt to come to court. It was of a thick, heavy cotton and starched to a T. Ashok tended to wear expensive clothes. He always bought the best quality. He said it gave him access to the best quality girls. With his heavy build and shiny black skin, you could perhaps discern some potential goondom, but really he just looked like what he was when he wasn't playing the fool, a handsome young man and respectable professional engineer.

'So how much money did you collect from the villagers to pay for the installation?' the prosecutor persisted.

Father's face assumed a look of surprise. 'Money?' he asked. 'My parishioners don't have money. This is Dorado we're talking about, not Goodwood Park!'

'How did your Dorado parishioners pay the Sarans for that expensive installation then?'

Father shrugged. 'Well, with what they have to pay with. With prayers! We said a mass for Ashok's soul. Ashok's soul can always use some prayers.'

The courtroom went up in laughter.

I had to hand it to my brother and Rumpole. They had chosen their witnesses well. What prosecutor could interrupt a frocked Catholic priest when he starts giving a lecture on the economics of Dorado? Father McVeigh had his own agenda. He spoke directly at the Press.

'People in Port of Spain don't care what goes on in Dorado,' he said. 'It's another planet. Until they are ready to prosecute a Dorado lad for something or another. In Dorado, we don't have government. We have me. I'm the closest thing Dorado has to any form of authority. Sometimes, that is, when the alcohol is not running too high at the rumshop. For the rest, the tides rule our lives.'

He held up a finger at the entire courtroom. 'Now,' he went on, 'God sent me a couple of agencies in the form of the Saran lads. They grew up in Dorado. Do you think Mr Ashok Saran, Specialist Coastal Engineer, dares refuse me anything I ask? I caned that boy in elementary school so many times, he knows that I don't wait for God's wrath.'

Laughter in the courtroom again. The public was agog, the judge was agog, the jury was ready to make the sign of the cross and say Amen. Father McVeigh leaned back. He had made his points about the neglect of Dorado, and could relax and shit-talk, as he sometimes did at the rumshop when the tide there was running high.

'I've been reading in the newspapers about damage Ved Saran has done in Dorado,' he said, looking at the press. 'You fellas doesn't know the extent of the damage. You should come up to Dorado and inspect the damage. Interview the electricity poles. They could give you good stories.' He leaned forward and let a glimpse of his anger come through. 'When an electricity pole rots and starts falling, do you think I wait for the Electricity Commission to come and prevent cows and children from getting electrocuted?' he asked. 'They haven't visited Dorado in decades. As a result, we have the best electricity poles in this country. Mahogany poles. Good, solid mahogany poles from the Saran building site. Those poles will outlast every building in Port of Spain. I am looking forward to a hurricane, to show it what mahogany can do.'

He reeled off a list of 'damages' he had instigated. The girls' school toilet, the boys' school roof, the generator in the fish-storage depot, Miss Maisie's chicken coop . . .

The courtroom erupted in laughter again.

Father McVeigh backtracked to clarify that Miss Maisie's chicken coop was not actually accountable to himself. A Saran truck had run over one of Miss Maisie's chickens. Miss Maisie had claimed it was her favourite chicken: that chicken listened to her when she talked. She charged Charlo one hundred dollars for it. Charlo had sent a couple of workers to 'damage' every chicken coop for miles around. No duck, turkey or goose ever strayed onto a road after that.

Dorado was still at the stage of simple barter economics, the priest explained. Where did Ashok get limes to make his punch? Miss Maisie's yard, next to the chicken coop. How did we get breadfruit and sapodillas? We paid with 'damage' to public and private property. It was often our employees' property anyway; or it was their children who got wet when it rained and the school roof was leaking. They just borrowed some tools from Charlo and went on the rampage, damaging property left, right and centre.

The prosecutor closed his cross-examination as soon as he got a chance.

It was late in the afternoon when Rumpole's final character witness was called. She was a surprise to me, a slim, elegant lady with a familiar face. It took me a minute to recognise Jason's mother, Miss Grant, now domiciled in the States. She described the sad event of her son's death, and the help I had given her to get resettled in New York.

The prosecutor got up to cross-examine. He first asked Miss Grant whether the Sarans had flown her to Trinidad to testify. She shook her head. No, she had come on her own. Why? The prosecutor asked.

'Somebody sent me a newspaper a few weeks ago, saying Mr Saran practised black magic, and calling my son's name,' she said.

'Yes?' the prosecutor asked.

'And I know where that rumour start,' Miss Grant said. 'From me. It's I who used to tell people Mr Saran have some kind of powers. And people living around my house agree. Ved Saran do something to my son.'

The courtroom went into hubbub. After repeated calls for order, the judge gave up and declared the session adjourned till the following morning.

Robin told me not to worry and disappeared for a conference with Rumpole. He didn't come home till late. When I accosted him on the way to his room, he kept assuring me that all this talk of black magic would be demolished under cross-examination. Who would believe in black magic once Rumpole had done his wrap-up speech?

Those housewives on the jury, that's who, I thought. Scratch a Trinidadian and you find a believer in necromancy. Never mind that they had worn their church hats to court and gone into paroxysms of Christianity when Father McVeigh was around. That was only part of their belief systems. I lay awake thinking how easily ordinary people could be led to imagine things and change their perspectives. Miss Grant had always expressed so much gratitude to me. Somehow, time and distance had altered her perception of what had occurred back then.

I made a vow that if I got through this trial without going to prison, I would leave Trinidad. I made plans for if I did end up going to prison. I would ask Anji to go live at her parents' house till I came out. Then we would leave Trinidad. I tried to imagine what life was like among those creeps who populated the prisons. I would have to get through somehow.

You can imagine the headlines next day. Gigantic: 'BLACK MAGIC!! MOTHER OF DEAD BOY ACCUSES CRICKET BAT KILLER.' I didn't pay attention. I was a bit groggy from lack of sleep. Anji was tearful. Robin got up late and kept telling me not to worry as he wolfed some breakfast before heading off to pick up Rumpole and meet us in court.

The courtroom was overflowing.

'You said yesterday you believed Mr Saran practised magic on your young son,' the prosecutor asked Miss Grant with the utmost gentleness when she took the witness-stand again. He looked like he had slept well all night and had had a fine breakfast that morning.

I slouched in my chair and watched Miss Grant, searching for the signs that she had changed. She certainly looked different. Nerissa had told me she had married a hard-working Trinidadian guy in Brooklyn. But, obviously, underneath that sleek exterior, her grief over Jason's death had never been erased.

'Objection, your Honour!' Rumpole rose to his feet lazily, as though he was immensely bored by this nonsense. 'Whatever supernatural beliefs the witness might hold are not relevant to this robbery and manslaughter charge,' he drawled.

'Your Honour . . .' The prosecutor's manner matched Rumpole's. He was obviously expecting this. 'This witness has been introduced into these proceedings as a character witness. Beyond that, we have already listened to a lot of testimony about barter systems in Dorado.'

He argued that my intentions when hitting the robber were crucial to determining the charge of manslaughter. I had beaten the other robber nearly senseless, although it hadn't been necessary. That suggested a streak of violence and ruthlessness.

The judge decided to let Miss Grant go on. Rumpole subsided into his chair calmly. This was only his first blow. You could read that in his body language. He had lots more in store for this magic-peddling witness. The prosecutor repeated his question.

'Yes,' Jason's mother replied. 'I used to tell people that Mr Saran knew some kind of magic.'

'What did he do to your son?' the prosecutor asked.

'Bawl at him,' Miss Grant replied. 'Cuss him up. Tap him up. Threaten to beat him. That's what Jason told me, anyway.'

Hubbub in the courtroom.

I closed my eyes and shook my head. I used to treat Jason roughly because that's what he needed. He was a young guy when he started working for me, just fifteen. But he was big and clumsy and liked to think of himself as macho. So I used to treat him macho. It had been our culture in the store, you could say. Jason and I were the guys; the other employees were girls. I treated the girls gently, but deliberately adopted a rough manner with Jason. I thought he liked it. I treated him like a man, not a girl. I was sure he had liked it. Jason had been utterly devoted to me, running every silly errand I gave him eagerly. He had liked to show off his strength to me, picking up heavy things and acting like nothing was too difficult for him. That would cause him to break things sometimes, or endanger his back, or endanger himself or other people. Customers, sometimes. When he overreached himself, or made some remark to the girls that went over the boundaries of good taste, I gave him a tap behind the head. A friendly tap, like I would give one of my nephews. He used to say I was disturbing his hairstyle to get the girls to like me, not him. It wasn't the way Miss Grant was depicting it now. Somehow, in her years of mourning over her son, she had distorted things in her mind.

'So your son was afraid of Mr Saran?' the prosecutor asked.

'If he was afraid of Mr Saran!' Miss Grant opened her eyes wide. 'He was afraid of Mr Saran more than he was afraid of God. If Mr Saran told him jump, that boy would start jumping so high he would damage himself.'

'What was he afraid Mr Saran would do if he didn't jump?' the prosecutor asked gently. Rumpole sat up, poised to counter-attack.

'Fire him,' Miss Grant replied promptly. 'Jason was terrified Mr Ved would fire him. He would have given his liver-string not to get fired.'

I was surprised at her words. I had never considered firing Jason. I wasn't even sure when I had hired Jason. He had just turned up at the store one day, tracking Suzanne, who was older than him. He had pretended he was shopping, but I could recognise his moves, being only a couple of years older myself. I told him that if he was going to hang around my store without buying anything, he had better make himself useful. I needed to move some furniture from one part of the store to the other, and asked him to pick up the other end of a couch. He had moved every other piece of furniture voluntarily. I had given him ten dollars, and he had turned up the next day and asked if I wanted anything else moved around. The rest was history.

'Why was your son so terrified of getting fired?' the prosecutor asked.

'Why he was terrified of getting fired?' Jason's mother repeated. 'Because Jason get fired from everything else! From school, from church, from Boy Scouts, from his grandmother's house. I myself used to get fired because of Jason. I get put out of my mother's house because Jason destroyed her toilet. Then we had to real scrunt for a living. Rent a little place in Tunapuna, get a job washing for people, catch hell. And Jason knew that. He knew he used to make my life hell half the time, with police coming to ask me questions about him jumping over people wall and stealing their mangoes.'

She shook her head and paused. Her voice went soft when she started speaking again.

'Jason didn't mean anything,' she said, as though appealing for the courtroom's sympathy. 'He was just a boy without a father. And he was too big for his size, like his father. If he got into a fight, he would bust some other boy's head and then I would have big trouble, with parents coming to quarrel with me.'

The courtroom was still. Everyone recognised Jason now, those many fatherless boys growing up in Trinidad, getting into trouble because there was no source of male authority in their homes.

'You know how many people used to say my son would end up in jail?' Miss Grant went on, her voice shaking a little. 'I used to pray and pray for Jason. I used to get down on my knees by my bed every night and pray for God to put his hand on Jason, and make him stop doing stupidness, and save my child from ending up like his father.'

She sniffed and wiped her eyes.

'And God put his hand,' she continued. 'That's why I believe in God.'

I saw a juror wipe her own eyes. Another made the sign of the cross. Miss Grant swallowed.

'Somehow Jason find himself in that store in the Croissee,' she continued. 'And the next thing I know is he come home and put ten dollars in my hand.' She paused. 'My heart stopped when he did that. I say, he thiefing now! Jason swear and swear on the Bible that the man in the store give him that money for helping him. And the next day he come home with twenty dollars! He say a girl who was working in the store was living near us in Tunapuna. I could go and ask her if he lying. I make Jason march with me to that girl house, a thin little Indian girl named Nerissa, to ask her.'

She wiped the tears from her cheeks.

'And God knows, God knows,' Miss Grant went on, 'that child change. From that day, Jason getting up early every morning, and polishing his shoes, and going to see what they will give him to do in the store.' She wiped her eyes again, and I heard a sniffle somewhere behind me in the courtroom. 'He used to say Mr Ved used to send him to buy things and never count the change when he come back, just tell him to push the change in his shirt pocket because his hands tied up. And Mr Ved used to send him to the bank to cash check for him. Three hundred dollars . . . six hundred dollars. The girls in the bank on the Eastern Main Road get to know Jason well.' She laughed through her tears. 'I remember him saying one of the girls in the bank like him, but he wasn't taking her on because Mr Ved say that girl too stupid.'

She laughed again, shaking her head with her memories.

'You know the fright I get the day my son come home and tell me Mr Ved let him drive his car? Move it from one place on the pavement to the other. The boy didn't have no driver's licence! I start one set of quarrelling with him. He say Mr Ved say that he was moving car since his foot could reach the gas pedal, and how else you does learn to drive car? I say, that is all right for Mr Ved, he come from a rich family. I send my son to get his driving permit one time! I didn't want no police coming by my house.'

You don't really know, do you, how the tiniest act of kindness you perform can affect another person. I hadn't even intended to be kind to Jason. That great lug of a boy had just been useful. There were so many things in the store that required more strength than the girls had: lifting heavy boxes, unloading goods from a van, all kinds of stuff. If Jason hadn't been in the store, I would have been hampered with all these tedious jobs. And, for that, I had been in Miss Grant's prayers for over ten years. She had decided I had done magic when all I had done was the same thing Charlo did when I showed up in his mas' camp as a little boy wanting to be a part of things. We were a bunch of young people in that store then, having laughs when we weren't busting our asses trying to keep bankruptcy from the door. As long as Jason paid his dues, he could be a part of the ass-busting and laughs. If he was willing to bust his ass for twenty dollars a day, who was I to stop him? I had bust my ass making Carnival costumes for free in Charlo's mas' camp.

Somehow this magic talk had got twisted in repetition, or perhaps as a result of malice on someone else's part. I guess that's what happens when you exaggerate. I've been trying hard not to exaggerate in this book, and yet I know people won't believe that everything I have written is the simple truth. They won't believe that I saw magic happen every day in Trinidad, the magic that human beings are capable of if they are open to each other. Because, ultimately, having thought about it for many years, I think Miss Grant was right: there was some magic around. It didn't start with me or end with me. It flowed through me, from Charlo and Nerissa and Mr Antoine and Ashok and the priest in Dorado and the jellyfish and the natural-gas deposits and Ordinary People.

The Ordinary People on the jury didn't take any time to consider their verdict. I was Not Fucking Guilty of manslaughter. And I wasn't leaving Trinidad.

Chapter Twelve

My relief was short-lived. The next day, when I picked up the newspapers, there was no sign of my case. Suddenly, something else had taken over the front pages. The only mention was a little item on page three: 'CRICKET BAT KILLER FOUND NOT GUILTY'. There was a hushed, appalled atmosphere around our dining-table, like after a death in the family. Even Ma wasn't her usual rambunctious self. Only Robin, who could laugh his way through a hurricane, had his usual hearty tone. The success of his team was inscribed in the law books.

For the rest of us, the case had been lost. I would forever be inscribed in the public mind as a killer, a violent individual who had evaded conviction because of . . . Who knows? A technicality? Bribery? The newspapers hadn't explained what led the jury to come to their verdict. On Anji's face, I saw the same furrowed expression I had often observed on her mother's, that bemused, hurt look of someone who doesn't understand why others are cruel. I felt forced to react, but I didn't know how to.

'Focking sons of bitches!' I scraped back my chair and went down the stairs to the garden, not knowing where I was going. I headed over to the bench under the pommecythere tree, where I could see no one else's face, just the reflection of the sky in the water of the swimming pool. There were fluffy white clouds in the blue of the water. The plants in the garden were as green and glorious as ever. A couple of birds fooled around in a hibiscus bush nearby. I sat there feeling numb. So this was it, then. Those fuckers in the newspapers didn't see fit to clear my name, to let the public know that the court had truly vindicated me, that all the talk of witchcraft and 'damage' to public property had in fact proved that I was a serious contributor to society, not a volatile hooligan. My chest felt full. What to do? I bent my head and looked at my feet. My head seemed empty. Not a suggestion arose. I ran my hands through my hair and left them at the back of my head. I studied the dirt around my feet, the long bumps where the roots of the pommecythere tree raised the surface of the earth.

I felt a hand on mine. 'Ved?'

I looked up at Anji's face. She looked so miserable. I pulled her down beside me, put my arm around her and drew her face against my chest. She remained there, still.

'Don't worry,' I heard myself murmuring. 'It doesn't matter.'

She looked up at my face. Hers was really worried.

'At least,' I said, smiling at her, 'you don't have to bring food for me in Carerra jail.'

She stared at me as though she didn't know whether to relax and stop worrying or not.

'C'mon,' I said. 'Smile. I ain't going to jail and catch AIDS from the other prisoners.'

Her face grew more shadowed.

'At least I still have my sex life.' I kissed her cheek. 'If my wife ever recover, that is.' I kissed her jaw. 'C'mon, Anji. You know the one thing I can't do without is my sex life, so you better try and recover.'

I started kissing her neck. I slipped my hand under her blouse and concentrated on the feel of the skin on her back. I made myself concentrate. I let my hand slip around her body to the soft skin under her breast, stroking it with the tip of my finger. I shifted my mouth all the way up her neck to the side of her face and then her mouth. I buried myself in the feel of her mouth, kissing her harder and harder, forcing myself to banish thought with sensation.

'Ved!' She shook my mouth off hers. 'Everybody upstairs can see us.'

'That's their problem,' I muttered. 'If they don't want to see, they can not watch.'

I captured her mouth with my own again and ran my hands all over her body, wherever I could feel the skin. 'Let's go back to bed,' I said.

She broke away and looked in my face. 'OK,' she whispered.

That whisper inflamed me. I didn't care who was watching. I started kissing her on her neck again, moving my mouth downwards to get as close to her breasts as I could. I tried to kiss her breasts through her blouse.

'No!' she wriggled away from me.

'Yes,' I said, pulling her back into my arms. 'Yes, Anji, yes, yes, yes . . .' I kissed her wildly.

'Ved, your father could be watching! Your mother –'

'Let them watch if they want to watch. Maybe they will learn something useful.'

I got her upstairs and into our room and buried myself in Anji, in the feel of her slim body, in the need to evoke response from her, in the need to feel myself wanted. I knew how to make Anji want me, make her forget everything else in her desire for my body. I made myself forget everything else in the task of making this girl cry out for me.

And so a new phase began in my life. A phase of hunkering down, getting serious about what I was doing, becoming, in some ways, a harder man than I had been before. What became clear to me as I stood in the shower that day was that I couldn't afford to show vulnerability. Anji was too vulnerable. She needed me to be strong, and so did my parents.

Ashok was soon on our verandah, full of outrage against the newspapers. I let him express the disgust and hurt I felt. I let Nerissa do so when she joined us, and Suzanne, Tony and Bernard Antoine. I listened to everybody who called to offer their indignation, and responded quietly and calmly. I was the leader of this pack. It was my role to be calm, to take whatever decisions needed to be taken. The others could fulminate. The verandah filled up with people – Father McVeigh, Cassandra Reyes, Rumpole, other sympathisers. It turned into a party. Once the anger over the newspapers' treatment of the case had been expressed, jokes started to flow.

I noticed that Ma was totally silent. I think it was the first time she had experienced defeat and she didn't know what to do with this feeling. I felt like telling her that sex was the answer, but of course I didn't. Charlo was also quiet, but that was to be expected. Charlo was always quiet in a crisis. He only talked and laughed when we were relaxed and had nothing better to do.

'How can we strengthen the security around this place?' I asked him quietly.

He stared at the wall at the back of our property. 'You think anybody will try coming in here again?' he asked with a little laugh. 'I don't think so.'

I shrugged and nodded towards Anji and my parents. 'Right now it's a psychological problem,' I said.

Charlo nodded. 'We put barbed wire at the top of the back wall.'

I hated the sight of barbed wire but I nodded.

'I tired telling you we have to get guns,' Ashok put in.

The babble on the verandah quietened. Arguments started about the efficacy of owning guns, about the violence in Trinidad, about the contract killers that had come with the drug dealing, about the fact that people now hired them to settle personal scores such as love triangles and the like . . . I retreated into silence. I did want to own a gun, I realised. I didn't ever want to feel the helplessness I had experienced the night the robbers had broken in. Or the helplessness I felt now.

By the end of that day, I had made the decision to learn to use one. Ashok signed us both up for firearms training at the Trinidad Rifle Club. That was a place full of white people, I realised when we went there. Ashok did all the talking. I saw the officials glancing at my face. I could imagine what they were thinking. I acted like I didn't care.

That was the mask I now habitually wore. My face had become recognisable from newspaper photos. Strangers tried to talk to me about the burglar I had killed, but they were usually pretty gross people who had gory ideas about what should be done to burglars. I didn't want to hear, so I brushed them off. Other people looked at me speculatively. I ignored them as well. Ignoring people became my *modus vivendi*. I concentrated on my own affairs: on the business and on making my wife happy. It had suddenly become easy to do both. I really only needed to deal with my managers nowadays; they were the ones who dealt with the public at large. For the rest, I only dealt with top managers of the businesses we dealt with – OAG, the hotels, the embassies – and they needed the services we offered too much to dare say anything to offend me. The issues surrounding my trial became buried in silence; the questions raised about my character remained a matter for private speculation by others. I felt a sort of space surrounding me, a buffer zone between what people thought of me and what I felt was the reality.

Anji, on the other hand, clung to me. I think there was a kind of defiance in it. She wanted the world to see that she believed in her husband, no matter what others might think of him. She was always touching me in public, which I liked and appreciated very much. I loved the closeness with her, the feeling of shutting out the entire world, the sense of being two, young beautiful people with perfect bodies who could make each other happy and let the rest go to hell. Looking back now, I can see the arrogance in it. But, at the time, I really didn't care. I was going to be happy in spite of anything, I determined. So I would do anything for

Anji, indulge her in any way I could to preserve our happiness, give in to her slightest whim. But now, she always wanted me to choose what we did. 'If you want' became her motto.

'Want to go for a drive?' I would ask after dinner.

'If you want,' she'd reply absently.

'Or you want to take a swim?'

'Whatever you want.'

'What do you prefer to do?'

'Whatever you prefer to do.'

'Sweetheart, I'll do whatever you want to do.'

'I don't care. I'll do whatever you want to do.'

'Anji, you choose.'

'You choose.'

'OK then,' I'd say, 'let's go for ice cream round the savannah.'

We would bump into people she knew from the university or people I knew from the business world or the world of steel-band or Carnival or somewhere. Anji would stroke my arm as I talked to them, act the part of the utterly besotted lover, behave quiet and devoted – not the old argumentative Anji at all.

'What's up with you?' I tickled her waist. 'Why you so quiet?'

'No reason,' she murmured, smiling up at me.

I loved those smiles. I felt I was drowning in happiness when she smiled at me like that. I had never known anyone to love me like that, and it was the greatest feeling in the world. Nothing else mattered.

But I think Charlo felt there was more in the mortar than the pestle.

'Why you don't take a holiday?' he suggested one evening in Dorado. 'Get a break from Trinidad.'

It sounded like a very good idea, so Anji and I went to Paris and Amsterdam for three weeks that August to celebrate our first wedding anniversary. We found Europe was full of young people like ourselves, friendly people who would strike up a conversation in a train. Germans, Scandanavians, Australians, kids from all over, travelling around with backpacks, heading from one youth hostel to another. I started to wish I was one of them, a university student with nothing to think of except making the best of the glorious summer months. There was this air of gaiety in Europe, this feeling of easy leisure, this security in which you could serenely wander around and look at places and people. Anji and I sat at pavement cafés observing coffee drinkers. We found ourselves sitting on a bench in a park in Amsterdam – Vondelpark, I think it was called. The atmosphere there was magic. A group of boys and girls were practising acrobatics on the grass. Another boy was trying to juggle. Couples were making love on little rugs they had spread on the grass, clearing away other people with the attitudes of their bodies, establishing an intimate world in the midst of other people.

I wanted to be all of the young people I saw: the juggler, one of the acrobats, one of the lovemakers. I wanted a backpack and a university course I would return to at the end of the summer.

Instead, I returned to find barbed wire installed at the top of our high fence. This was what my life was now, barbed wire and wealth and distances from people. This was what I had to accept, and put a smile on my face. It felt like I was putting on armour.

Ashok had gone to Miami in the meantime. He came back with two revolvers, Smith & Wesson .38s, small, squat, dark-grey things, like miniature bulldogs. I hefted one in the palm of my hand.

'Beauties, eh?' Ashok said.

I couldn't really see the beauty he was talking about, but he kept exclaiming at the engineering involved, at the balance, at the way the guns fit in your hand. Pa also grew excited. He kept playing with the mechanism, marvelling at the improvements in technology since he had last examined a new gun. Anji just stared, her eyes big and round and scared. Ma was silent. We then discussed where I would keep my gun. Pa, Ashok and I went to my bedroom and examined the bed. Anji trailed behind us. We decided to build a little shelf under the frame of the bed, at the edge of the sideboard. The gun could remain on that shelf, loaded, just where my hand could reach it in a crisis.

This eventually caused an ugly scene with my sisters.

'Out!' I shouted at my nephew Ravi one Sunday when I found him in my bedroom. The kids were not allowed in my room, and I usually kicked them out if I found them there, but in a more friendly manner.

'Oh gosh, Uncs,' Ravi pleaded, 'I was only looking to see if you have any *Playboy*. You don't have to put on that murderous look.'

'Get out!' I snapped, pointing at the door.

Ravi slowly retreated. All the other children ran up to see what was happening.

'If I see one of allyou cross that doorstep,' I said seriously, pointing towards my room, 'I going to give allyou a cut-arse allyou wouldn't forget.'

Fifteen-year-old Shreshtha tilted her head to one side and studied my face. 'The girls too?' she asked.

Shreshtha was wearing jeans and a cropped T-shirt that showed off her stomach and emphasised her growing breasts. She smiled and moved a foot in the direction of the doorway. I grabbed her arm. She twisted it, trying to break my grip. 'Uncle Ved!' she squeaked, 'You hurting me.'

'You think this hurting?' I asked. 'You don't know what hurting is. The day I find you in my room, you will understand what hurting is.'

She twisted and turned. I kept holding her arm. I looked around at all the children. 'All of allyou understand me?' I asked. 'Nobody is to enter my bedroom.'

Shreshtha's face contorted and she started to cry. 'Let me go!'

'Do you understand me, Shreshtha?' I asked.

Indra's high-heeled slippers beat a measured tattoo on the floor as she approached. 'Let Shreshtha go, Ved,' she said.

I ignored her. 'Do you understand what I said to you, Shreshtha?' I asked again.

'Ved!' Indra shrieked. 'Let go of the child!' She yanked Shreshtha away.

I left them all on the verandah and went downstairs, got the lawnmower out of the tool shed and mowed the lawn. Then I came back upstairs and went into the shower, ignoring everyone. Anji came into the bathroom while I was drying myself off.

'The children very upset,' she said. 'Indra very upset. Everybody very upset. They say the stress from the case driving you crazy.'

'Good,' I said, leaving the bathroom and going to find clean clothes in the bedroom. 'Let them think I crazy.'

If my nephews knew there was a gun in my bedroom, they were sure to get curious and go looking for it. It was better for no one to know it was there.

'Well,' I heard Ma's whiplash voice saying to Shreshtha when I went back to the verandah, 'when your Uncle Ved tell you not to do something, you shouldn't do it.'

'Ved has no right to touch my children, Ma!' Indra ejaculated.

'Your children have to learn to listen when big people talk,' Ma snapped. 'They too damned disobedient.'

I went over to the dining-table, picked up the newspaper, and sat on a chair nearby.

'Come, Shresh,' Pa said, getting up. 'Uncle Ved buy nice coconut ice cream for allyou. Let us go and eat some.'

'I don't want any coconut ice cream,' Shreshtha sniffled.

'Good coconut ice cream,' Pa pleaded. 'From Willy's.'

I looked over the top of my newspaper. 'You didn't hear the girl say she don't want any ice cream?' I asked my father. 'Don't beg her to eat ice cream if she doesn't want.'

I went into the kitchen and started dishing out ice cream. That dissolved the matter as far as the other children were concerned. We got busy arguing over who was entitled to how much ice cream. Then we went down to the garden to play swimming-pool cricket, a game we had invented long before. Shreshtha remained upstairs with the grown-ups.

'I don't understand why Ved is the only one who can use the bigger house in Dorado,' Queen was saying when the kids and I returned to the verandah for dinner. 'Why should we be confined to that small, poky place while he is living in glory down the beach, with his in-laws and his friends . . .'

'What's the problem with your beach-house?' I asked casually. 'You want me to add a couple more bedrooms for you?'

'That's not the point!' Queen returned. 'I feel like a second-class citizen down there. You make rules about who stays where, who does what, where the children can go —'

'Queen,' I said as I helped myself to some food, 'you have to recognise that most of the buildings in Dorado are leased to OAG. Your children can't just go annoying Pierre, annoying Charlo, playing the fool with OAG's top management.'

'Their grandfather owns the place, but they are not allowed to go in the swimming pool,' Indra put in. 'But Anji's sister can go in the swimming pool, in the restaurant, everywhere . . .'

'Anji's sister behaves herself,' I said.

'Yes,' Indra snapped, 'Anji's family is better than us . . .'

I glanced at Anji. Her head was bent over her plate. There was a long silence. Pa looked like he had a sudden and painful bout of constipation. Things were strained on the verandah for the rest of the evening.

'What's the matter?' I asked Anji that evening after my sisters had left.

'I just feel so uncomfortable about these arguments with your sisters,' she said eventually.

'Don't worry about it, sweetheart,' I murmured, stroking her hair. 'My sisters have always been like that. You just have to ignore them.'

'That's easy for you to say,' she answered. 'They are your sisters. But I feel like an interloper in all this Saran business. When they talk about my family . . .'

'Let them talk anything they want to talk,' I said, cuddling her. 'Just don't listen.'

'Maybe my family shouldn't come to your house in Dorado,' she murmured. 'It just causes more complications.'

'Maybe you shouldn't wear a bra,' I murmured back. 'It just causes more complications.'

'Ved!' She pushed away my hands. 'I'm talking to you.'

'OK,' I said, letting her go and leaning back against the other side of the hammock. 'What you want me to do? Let my sisters use our beach-house and then have them talking shit to us there too? The reason I built that beach-house was to escape them. I'm not giving in to them. The next thing I know is I will have no peace –'

'You think I have peace when they always making all kinds of remarks about us?' she asked.

I lapsed into silence. She started picking at the edge of the hammock. Eventually she looked up at me. 'I don't know what to do,' she murmured.

I pulled her into my arms. 'I know what to do. Stop worrying.'

But of course Anji didn't stop worrying. And my sisters didn't stop their jibes. They referred to her as Princess Anji when she wasn't around. Princess Anji went to Europe on holiday and came back with new clothes. Princess Anji didn't have to run a household, bother herself with arranging meals, even give orders to servants. Everything was done for Princess Anji, and Princess Anji's husband worshipped the ground she walked on, acted like she was better than everyone else on earth. My response was to turn their jibes against them.

'Come here, little princess,' I would say, pulling Anji onto my lap when my sisters were around.

'Uncle Ved,' fifteen-year-old Narvin asked one Sunday afternoon, 'what about if the boys go for oysters round the savannah?'

'Depends if my wife say I could go,' I would reply. 'I married now, you know. I can't just run off with the boys just so. I have to ask permission.' I would look down at Anji. 'What you say, boss? Can I go and hang out with the boys?'

'Uncle Ved!' Narvin would go into paroxysms, 'you can't let a woman rule you so!'

'Why not?' I would ask, just to increase Narvin's shock.

Perhaps I was wrong to provoke my sisters this way. Frankly, to this day, I don't know what else I could have done. It didn't help the situation, but what would have helped the situation? My sisters' resentment of Anji became a fixed aspect of our family relations, something I just accepted and tried to ignore.

And then, a year after I had faced the manslaughter charge, my brother Robin decided to return to Trinidad for good. He had enjoyed fighting my case in the courts so much he wanted more of the black magic, the bacteria, the sheer fun of Trinidadian life. As he explained, it would take time to develop a local law practice. He therefore planned to take it easy in the meanwhile, live in my parents' house and consume as much of Sylvia's food as he could to make up for the lost years in London.

Robin arrived with his entire family, which now included two children, and his hearty lawyer-manner. He proceeded to attack Trinidadian life like a jaguar, devouring it in gigantic bites. 'What about if we go and eat some oysters round the savannah?' he would suggest in the evenings.

'Again?' I'd ask. 'Last night you make me stay out till after midnight. I not accustomed liming every night of the week, you know. I have to work in the morning.'

He would suck his teeth. 'What work you does do?' he would ask. 'Nerissa does do all the work in that office. You does just hang around and talk shit.'

'Talking shit is my work,' I would say.

I had offered him office space in our building behind the store. He couldn't actually begin work in the first three months; he was preparing to be called to the Trinidadian Bar. That left him a lot of time to drift into our offices and chat.

'Come on, nah, man,' he would nudge me in the evenings. 'What you want to do around here? Sit down and watch them flowers grow?'

Actually, watching flowers grow as I exchanged the day's news with Anji was one of my major evening entertainments. I myself was amazed that I could sit on the bench in the garden for hours watching flowers grow and touching Anji idly. Apart from that, there was reading a book in the hammock and touching Anji idly. She had spent the last year studying research methodology, a subject that was too finicky and full of mathematical reasoning for her taste. I had taken to reading her books and explaining them to her. I actually liked the challenge of understanding the research methodologies, and, frankly, I liked even more the look of admiration on Anji's face when I was able to immediately grasp their logic and explain them to her in a jokey fashion, using all kinds of silly examples. Now she was involved in a literature review, but I kept on reading bits of the books she brought home and talking to her about them. 'Let's do some research,' I would say, picking up one of her books and drawing her over to the hammock.

But now the house was full of other people and 'research' had to be limited to our bedroom.

'Why this room smelling so?' I asked one evening as I entered Anji's study, which had evolved into a private living-room for the two of us. After the robbery, I had moved my music system there.

'Vintra pee on the carpet yesterday,' Anji informed me.

Vintra was Robin's baby. I sucked my teeth irritably as I looked at the stain. 'Get another carpet,' I said.

'Ved!' Anji's eyes opened wide. 'That's a new carpet! You can't just throw it away because a child pee on it.'

'Well, what you intend to do?' I asked. 'You expect me to sit around in a room smelling like this?'

She went silent. I sucked my teeth in irritation again.

'Don't be so grumpy, nuh,' Anji put on a begging tone.

'I not being grumpy,' I returned sharply. 'But I can't deal with this smell. Come and sit with me in the hammock.'

She followed me into the hammock, but my bad temper wasn't so easy to disperse. I was often irritated now, and had no way of expressing it. Living in a house with Robin's wife meant being constantly irritated. With this new baby, Madhuri had adopted a whole new approach to child-rearing. Now, it seemed, children were not supposed to be restrained in any way. The baby was not to wear any clothes at all. Her skin was supposed to breathe. That meant she peed everywhere. Every time you sat on a cushion, it would turn out to be wet. I wasn't used to this. I was used to a very neat, very tidy, very organised house. The only disorganised factor was Anji, but she didn't pee everywhere; she just lost things, forgot things, spilled things. We could cope with that, my parents and I. But now we were drowning in disorganisation. With one toddler running around, and a baby peeing everywhere, you didn't know what to expect from one minute to another.

But the worst was Madhuri's voice. 'Where is the tin of milk?' I would hear her whining in the kitchen. 'It was right here on the counter. Sylvia, did you move the baby's milk?'

I would imitate her whine in the hammock. Anji would shut me up. Madhuri would come out of the kitchen and stand on the verandah, her brow wrinkled, an expression on her face like she wanted to pee. 'Anybody knows where the baby's milk is?' she would ask.

'I think I put it in the cupboard,' Anji would say.

Madhuri had a way of hovering on the verandah after she got an answer like that. She was like a pale, fleshy ghost that had experienced some tremendous injustice during its lifetime so it couldn't rest in the grave.

'You put it in the cupboard?' Madhuri would repeat, her whole face getting wrinkled.

'Yes.' Anji's voice would take on a flurried note. 'In one of the top cupboards where we does keep the other things . . .'

Madhuri would look like the urge to pee had got urgent. 'Which cupboard?'

Anji would scratch her head. 'I think the one on the right-hand side, where the coffee and sugar is.'

'Where the coffee and sugar is?'

Madhuri's mouth would remain slightly open. Anji would get out of the hammock to go and find the milk. She'd return and we'd try to settle down again. Madhuri would come out to the verandah again to feed the crying baby.

'You get wind waiting for your bottle?' she would ask the baby, letting us know it was all Anji's fault for causing the child to have to wait.

Somebody else might come along. 'She had to wait too long for her feed so she got tetchy,' Madhuri would explain, though no one had asked for an explanation. 'I couldn't find the tin of milk to make her feed. I was looking everywhere. Anjani put it in the cupboard, but I didn't know that . . .'

She would go on and on about this minor incident. I would feel like bashing her over the head to shut her up.

Perhaps it was the total absence of a sense of humour that caused me to dislike Madhuri so much. She didn't seem to notice that there was anything to laugh at in the world. She didn't seem to need to laugh. My mother was one of the most difficult, obstreperous, demanding human beings ever created by the process of evolution, but in the midst of her unreasonable behaviour there was always a kernel of irony. You could enjoy her, even when she was annoying the living daylights out of you. The same applied to my sisters. But with Madhuri, there was no enjoyment. Life was pain. Life was meant to be pain. Life was annoyance. Anji's shifting the tin of baby's milk seemed to be a reason for anguish, not just a momentary inconvenience. If a mango wasn't ripe enough, it was something to be irritated about, a cause for small but heart-felt complaint. Madhuri focused on the most mundane things as though they were the centre of the universe, and found in them a reason to be unhappy about the universe. She seemed to live her life in a constant atmosphere of strain, and I felt strain if I was around her. I understood why Robin exploded at her sometimes.

'Madhuri!' he would suddenly boom. 'Just shut up!

There would be a heavy silence. Anji would look deeply pained. I would feel sorry for Madhuri, but I would completely empathise with Robin – I longed for Madhuri to just shut up. But then Madhuri's silences were pretty bad as well. I wished she would just vanish. She brought this heavy dreariness into everything.

I think Madhuri confused me. She got me mixed up in all my emotions. On the one hand, I felt sorry for her; on the other, I felt guilty at disliking her so much. I was used to thinking of myself as a nice guy, an easy going guy, kind to other people, understanding, a good employer, a socially conscious human being. And now, suddenly, there was this person making me have negative thoughts for no reason at all. I retreated into my usual silence. Let Ma deal with Madhuri, let her snap at her and tell her she was stupid a million times a day. Let my sisters be condescending and bitchy. I would have nothing to do with anything.

But that was actually impossible because of the children. Those were two of the weirdest children in the world. The little boy, Anant, just stared at you out of his great big black eyes. He was completely asocial. He didn't blink when you spoke to him. If you picked him up and spun him around your head, he didn't react. And, to make matters worse, Ma kept claiming that he was like I had been as a child.

'You used to just watch people out of your big-eye too,' she said.

'Like that, Ma?' I asked. 'Like you plotting to zap them with a laser beam out of your eye?'

I refused to believe her. I found Anant too creepy for words. I swore there was something wrong with him, that he was Silas Marner reincarnated, that he was possessed by an evil spirit. I swore all kinds of things. Robin said he suspected Anant was autistic, whatever that meant. Or else he was still in shock from discovering who his mother was.

'Boy,' I asked Robin one day, 'how you does only have bad thing to say about your wife?'

'You could think of a good thing to say about my wife?' he replied.

There was no answer to that, so I didn't pursue the subject. Robin himself was deeply disturbing. His heartiness was too much. I don't know how to express it differently, but he treated Ma and Pa like things. It wasn't that he treated them like objects – they walked and talked so they weren't inanimate objects – but to Robin it was as if they were things, not people with emotions to consider. I don't know if Robin ever thought of anyone's emotions. He seemed to have drawn a line between himself and emotions. He was funny and smart and good company, but he had a way of walking onto the verandah with his heavy tread as though he was saying, 'Emotions begone! I banish ye, henceforth!'

Naturally, this all brought out Ma's quarrelsomeness. I think, in a way, she welcomed the new chaos in our home. It had been too peaceful before, with Anji and I just getting on with our activities and being lovey-dovey in our corner of the verandah. Now, here was a bunch she could condemn to hell. Here was Robin, who would give her back as good as he got, and Madhuri, whose utter stupidity could be a focus of her wonder.

'Madhuri!' Ma would shriek.

Madhuri would approach, her blank, immune-to-the-rest-of-the-world expression on her face.

'Why the arse you put those diapers in the dustbin?' Ma would demand.

Madhuri would gaze at her serenely.

'You don't know they will stink up my kitchen?' Ma would scream.

No answer. Ma would be reduced to intense bitchiness.

'I don't know where the hell you come from! Why that next jackass didn't leave you in England I don't know!'

Sylvia would tremble at the harshness. Anji would retreat into her study.

'Madhuri does just do things to get a clout,' Robin would say calmly. 'Where she come from in Bamboo Village, woman does get clout. She feeling left out.'

A lot of Anji and my conversation began to focus on Robin and

Madhuri. And their children. And my mother's reactions. 'Why he don't divorce her if he dislike her so much?' Anji asked me as we lay in bed.

'I don't know,' I said. 'I don't really know why he married her in the first place.'

'Ved,' she held me tight, 'how come the two of allyou so different?'

'I don't know,' I replied.

'I find he is a monster,' she said.

I didn't reply.

'You don't like me saying that, eh?' she asked.

I stroked her hair. 'You could say anything you like, sweetheart.'

'But you don't like when I criticise your brother.'

I was silent. 'Nah,' I said eventually. 'I could see why you say that. I don't blame you.'

She clung tighter still to me. 'I does just think,' she said, 'suppose I was married to a man like your brother? What I would do? That's like a nightmare.'

I chuckled. 'I does think,' I returned, 'suppose I was married to a woman like Madhuri, what would I do?' I replied.

'I think I would kill him, Ved,' she whispered.

'I think I would kill her,' I said.

'You love me, Ved?'

'Yes, of course.'

At the time, I only wondered slightly why Anji asked me if I loved her. Looking back on it, I think she was scared. The ugliness of Robin's relationship with his wife was really unsettling. It was like a tree that shed a shadow over parts of the house, a shadow that sometimes extended over the whole house, depending on the position of the sun. In some way, that shadow was familiar to the rest of us, but for Anji it was a new element, and one we couldn't ever quite escape. Robin came to Dorado with us on weekends – he, the wife, the two children, the baby's milk and Madhuri's voice. We no longer had a refuge.

One evening, I came home to find Anji sulking in our bedroom. She was lying on her stomach across the bed, her hair a bit untidy. There was no book around. She just seemed to be lying there.

'What you doing?' I asked.

'Nothing.'

I sat on the bed and bent down to kiss her. She didn't respond. It was late. I had been in the city at a meeting and was delayed by traffic. The room was dim. I switched on a lamp and brushed her hair away from her face.

'What happening?' I asked. 'Guthrie giving you horrors again?' Guthrie was a sociologist whose turgid prose made Anji dizzy.

She didn't answer.

'What's up?' I asked again.

She sighed. 'I just fed up,' she murmured, picking at the sheet.

'Fed up of what?'

'Everything. This house. Your mother . . .'

I stroked her back. 'What my mother do this time?'

'Nothing. She just getting so quarrelsome.'

'Come.' I took her into my arms. 'Let's go out for dinner.' I really didn't relish the prospect of going back into the traffic but I figured she needed to get out of the house. She shook her head.

'I'm not hungry.'

'I'm hungry, honey. I'll just take a shower and then we'll go down to the Bite, OK?' The Bite was a new restaurant that had opened in Chaguaramas. It was a very pleasant place that jutted out into the sea, so all your normal troubles got swept away by the breeze.

Anji didn't reply. I decided to take her silence for assent.

As we passed through the verandah on our way out of the house, I sensed the tension between Anji and the rest of the family. She didn't look at anyone. When I said we were going out to dinner, neither my father or mother made any comment.

'Going out for dinner?' Robin asked, raising his eyebrows. 'When Sylvia cook curry crab?'

I grinned at him. 'Curry crab does taste better the day after. Scientific fact.'

Anji was quiet all the way to the restaurant. When we had settled down and ordered a drink, I took her hand. 'So, what my mother do today?'

She hung her head. 'Nothing,' she muttered. 'It was my fault.'

I squeezed her hand. 'So what you do, then?' I squeezed again. She glanced up at me.

'I drop a big bowl of dhal on the floor.' A brief twinkle of her dimples accompanied the admission.

'Well, what's the use crying over spilt dhal?' I asked.

She looked up at me. 'It was a glass bowl,' she said ruefully.

I couldn't help laughing. 'And what Ma say?' I asked.

'What you expect?' Anji took a gulp of her rum punch. 'She say I shouldn't ever touch anything in her kitchen. She say I too dotish to live. She say she know why they make book out of paper, not glass. It's so that people like me wouldn't break them.' She was smiling back at me now. 'Oh gosh, Ved!' she sighed, 'sometimes the tension in that house does get unbearable, you know.' She pushed back her hair with a soiled finger. 'I was dodging Vintra's pee on the floor, which is why I break the bowl full of dhal. The floor was covered with dhal mixed up with pee, and Anant slip and fall. When the bowl shattered on the floor, Vintra started screaming like a fire engine. Madhuri started getting on hysterical, saying she think a piece of glass get in Vintra eye. Ma tell her to shut her backside, that child does scream for no reason at all. Then Ma started shouting at me.'

'I felt as though I should just run away and find a river and jump in it and drown myself,' she said, then chuckled. 'Except it ain't have no river deep enough near the Croissee to drown in. And I was so nervous by that time, I would have surely had a accident if I did take the car to find a river to drown in. And then I'd have been in more trouble . . .'

We were soon laughing over the incident.

But obviously the same tale had been repeated at home. Robin was lurking on the verandah when we returned.

'So you done cry?' he asked Anji as she came up the stairs. She didn't reply.

I felt myself to be in a quandary. Obviously Robin wanted a little chat on the verandah before going to bed. But Anji wasn't in a mood for chatting, and I felt I should be with her. 'How was the curry crab?' I asked Robin, just to offer him a token conversation.

'You miss one of the best curry crab in the history of world cuisine,' he said. 'Let me see if I could think of some adjectives to describe it. Delectable, divine, divinely inspired . . .'

Anji continued walking towards our room. I lingered behind a little.

'Boy!' He shook his head as he watched Anji's retreating back. 'Woman is a curse, you know! When it's not one getting on stupid for no reason, it's another.'

I didn't know what to say. Robin shook his head again. 'You does spoil that girl like she is some little child,' he said.

I was still lost for words. Then I said, 'I'm tired, gotta hit the sack,' and went to join Anji in our room.

Similar incidents followed. Robin adopted the attitude that Anji was just as much trouble as his wife and children. Ma followed suit. My sisters, of course, were delighted. Anji became a butt of their humour when they got together. I kept my patience, hoping that Robin's law practice would soon build up and he would buy a house and leave. But that didn't happen. The cases Robin got were small, trifling affairs. They only annoyed him. 'A next drunk driving!' he would groan, strolling into my office. 'Why somebody don't kill somebody else, instead of just hitting down lamppost?'

He began to discover that the legal business in Trinidad was sewn up by a few big firms in the city. Old legal firms, white firms. It was a sort of cartel. He went out to lunch with other Indian lawyers who explained to him how the system worked. It would take years for Robin to develop enough of a reputation to compete fairly in this system. He became disgruntled, more short-tempered with Madhuri than ever, more dismissive of Anji, more irritable with my parents. I felt sorry for him, and, when he asked me to go out with him in the evening, I gave in to his entreaties, knowing that he had had a frustrating day.

'You smelling of rum,' Anji murmured sleepily the first time I came home late at night and got into bed.

'I just had two drinks,' I replied, as she shifted to get close to me.

She kissed my mouth.

'How come you not sleeping?' I asked.

'I am sleeping,' she replied.

'Sure?' I asked, kissing her again.

'Sure,' she said, pressing herself against me. 'I'm fast asleep.'

I think the smell of alcohol was somehow exciting to her. The idea of waking up to a man with the atmosphere of the rumshop gave her some kind of thrill.

'What allyou does be doing in them rumshop?' she asked, when I continued going with Robin about once a week.

'Nothing.' I shrugged. 'Talking shit with other drunk man.'

I didn't tell Anji that Robin was also flirting with women in the rumshops. I didn't tell her when I began to suspect he was having an affair. I didn't tell her when he made it clear to me that he was having an affair, and when he had the second affair. She only found out about these things when Madhuri began to suspect.

'You think I don't know what you and Ved do when you go out at night?' Madhuri whined at Robin one day.

'Ved,' Anji asked me later, 'what was Madhuri talking about?'

I shrugged. 'How I will know what Madhuri was talking about?'

Anji narrowed her eyes and frowned at me. We were in the garden at the time, sitting on the bench under the pommecythere tree. 'What allyou does be doing when allyou go rumshop?' she demanded, holding my hand fiercely.

I shrugged again. 'Drinking. Chatting.'

She stared at me hard.

'Anji, honey,' I said. 'If I was doing anything else, why would I want to make love with you when I come home?'

She continued staring at me suspiciously.

'Come on,' I said. 'Isn't it logical?'

But the matter didn't end there. Madhuri's suspicions increased, and Anji asked me direct questions about whether Robin was pursuing other women. I had to admit to the truth.

'And you encouraging him?' Anji asked. She began to frown at me when I said I was going out with Robin at night.

'So what happen?' Robin asked her one evening when she showed her disfavour at our departure. 'Ved supposed to stay here and hold your hand every night? The man in prison, just because he married?'

'I think I will take a rain check tonight,' I told Robin.

He grew irritated. 'What the hell wrong with you, boy?' he asked. 'One minute you say you going, next minute, just because this one swell up her face, you change your mind?'

I stared at him. 'Yes,' I said. 'That is exactly what happen. I don't want to go if Anji going to get vex about it.'

To my relief, he began developing other companions, mainly other lawyers he met in the courts. He started having an independent social life, lunch dates, dinner appointments, barbeques, the usual stuff. It cheered him up. He began to hope that developing local contacts would bring more business his way, and began inviting his friends to Dorado, where he presided in his lordly way over the Pleasure Palace, the French restaurant, the general splendours of the Saran estate.

'I had a long chat with the Minister of Justice,' he said one day, after he had been to a party the evening before. 'Nice fella. He say he know you.'

'Suratsingh?' I said casually. 'Yes, I know him a little bit.'

'I invite him to come to Dorado this weekend,' Robin said.

So the Minister of Justice, the one with whom I had had a major conflict in the distant past, became a visitor to our property in Dorado. He and Robin got on like a house on fire. Robin put on his legal-counsel-to-the-Duchess-of-Peale manner. The minister put on his slightly distant I-am-an-important-person manner. Chef Pierre put on a gourmet spread. Roger Granderson-Powell, President, OAG (Trinidad), fitted in well. The minister's wife was a reasonable person, so she and I got along. The minister and I maintained an appearance of cordiality.

Robin cheered up a lot. 'The Minister of Health walk out of the Cabinet meeting this week,' he told me gleefully one Sunday while we were returning to town. 'It was bacchanal!'

Robin was now privy to insider political gossip. He began to feel part of the elite, not a marginal dog-bite-case lawyer. 'Things ain't going good for Frog-face,' he would say, referring to the Prime Minister.

The Cabinet rebellion the Minister of Justice had long been trying to foment was gaining support. Other influential people began to frequent our beach-house. Anji and I went for long walks, ending up at Charlo's broken-down old concrete house near the village. We would linger there, sharing the usual old-talk, sending out for snacks to the village, staying till late at night. It felt delicious, like old times. The area around the house was very dark. It seemed to bring out the sound of crashing waves. You could hear crabs scuttling in the sand. We started studying the stars again, arguing in our old, vague ways, dreaming up silliness.

'Back to basics, eh,' Charlo muttered one night, giving me one of the private looks we shared.

'Back to focking basics,' I replied.

We had been patching up an old chair to ensure the combined weight of myself and Anji didn't cause it to crash to the floor again. We enjoyed the task, creating solutions to fundamental problems, exercising our carpentry skills, getting back to the makeshiftness that had always been our bond. And I enjoyed having Anji in my arms, perforce, since we didn't have sufficient furniture – we, who supplied furniture to the most luxurious settings in the entire Caribbean region. The bareness of our

NIALA MAHARAJ

surroundings underlined the feeling of intimacy among us. When voices speak in the dark, in between the swish of trees and the rustle of night animals, they feel more true and more precious.

'Where Ashok?' Charlo asked.

'Liming with the lawyers,' I replied.

Ashok loved the elite political gossip that took place at our beach-house. He relished the feeling of being in the know. Between the high-placed lawyers and Roger Granderson-Powell, the company over there was truly of a calibre. Intense discussions about the future of Trinidad took place. My father was usually there as well. He was awed.

But it wasn't only political talk that was taking place in my absence, I was to discover. 'Why you don't start work on the weekend apartments OAG want?' Robin asked me one evening when we were back in town.

'The crew busy finishing the pavilion on the golf course.'

'So you can't expand the crew? Hire more workers?'

I shrugged. 'Charlo say he ain't want no more workers to supervise,' I said. 'When he watching what one set do, the other set will be doing shit —'

'Hear, nuh,' Robin asked abruptly, 'who running this business? You or Charlo?'

I glanced at him.

'Me *and* Charlo.'

He laughed his supercilious laugh.

'Charlo could run business?' Ma snorted. 'A man who never have a cent in his back pocket?'

'All the cents he make in your bank account!' I retorted.

'Actually,' Anji said quietly, 'Charlo supporting his sister's three children in university. And he pay for Cassandra's mother to have a major operation . . .'

Everybody stared at her.

'How you know that?' I asked.

She shrugged. 'He tell me. I ask him.'

Robin stretched out his legs in front of him. 'So we have a man who does give away all his money running our business . . .' He was sitting in a lounge-chair a little way from me. I stretched out my own legs till they almost touched his.

'Any time you ready to run it,' I said, 'I will go to England and do a law degree.'

326

That night in bed Anji stroked my face. 'You really want to go to England and do a law degree?' she asked.

I laughed. 'I don't know. I just said that. Maybe. What I will study if I get a chance to study? Law might be an interesting thing.'

'Ved,' she said.

'Mmm?'

'I love you.'

I pulled her closer and kissed her fiercely. It was what she wanted. We were under siege, although I didn't realise it then. We had to batten down the hatches, repair all the chinks in our armour, make our defenses impregnable. But they weren't, of course.

'Hear, nuh, why you don't build a couple more beach-house for rent?' Robin asked on another evening. It turned out that his high-faluting friends who were visiting our beach-house would like to rent it, or something like it. I brushed him off, but the question came up again and again.

'Ved, we have land from Guaya to Dorado Village doing nothing except making coconut,' Robin urged. 'If you put down a few beach-houses, we could make a nice little income from renting them out.'

Then Pa piped up. 'What Robin saying making plenty sense, Ved,' he observed.

I tried to explain to Pa that to build beach-houses and maintain them you needed workers. Workers needed supervision. You needed to manage the supply of materials. My team, specifically Charlo and Nerissa, had their hands full. But no one in my family bought the arguments. 'It's a holiday camp Ved running in Dorado,' Queen put in. 'Charlo spends half his time making decorations with peacock feathers.'

'But seriously, Ved,' Robin asked, 'if Charlo doesn't want to supervise a wider production system, why not make Ashok site manager?'

'Ashok!' I snorted.

'Why not?' Robin asked. 'Ashok has a financial interest in exploiting the Dorado property.'

I refused to discuss it. The business had grown the way it had grown. What was the need to expand it further? To give myself more headaches? My family just saw land, demand for buildings, and more money rolling in.

Then Robin came up with a new suggestion. I should tender for a government contract to repair two rural court-houses. I sucked my teeth and informed him that I never got government contracts when I tendered for them. It was a waste of time.

'You will get this one,' Robin said. 'The Minister of Justice is in charge of that contract.'

I caught sight of Pa's face. It looked worn-out with these arguments.

'Look,' I said to Robin irritably, 'if you want to tender for that contract, why don't you come into the business and do the tendering? Why don't you supervise that building work?'

He laughed. 'I don't know nothing about building. I's a lawyer.'

But a week later, Pa came back to the subject. 'Why you don't come into the business?' he asked Robin. 'We could pay you more than you making with that law-stupidness.'

Soon, Robin had agreed to the suggestion. With his slow law practice, he had ample time to do some work in the business, he said. I gave him the title of 'Manager – Special Projects', and he got busy organising to rebuild the court-houses. Ashok was put in charge of technical operations and the two of them got a building crew together.

The court-house project was immensely profitable. I hired a book-keeper to manage the finances and stayed out of the whole operation. But Nerissa had to handle the supplies.

'Ved,' she said to me one day, 'you realise that they pay a kickback to the minister?'

I shrugged. 'I figured that would be involved,' I said.

The court-house project led to a second, to repair three other court-houses. Ashok was in his glee. He was no longer stuck in Dorado; instead, he lived a free-wheeling life, rushing from one site to another, then into the office to confuse Nerissa, then to the lumber-yard. He rented an apartment in the Tunapuna area and took to eating his meals at our house, where he and Robin were at one on both projects and politics.

But things in our office became really dishevelled. Tony's supplies of lumber had come under siege and at some stage, we ran out of wood for one of the buildings on the OAG compound. 'Look!' Nerissa snapped at me one day, 'you telling me to do one thing, and your brother telling me to do another and Ashok dashing in here throwing all arrangements to the winds! I only have two hands, two eye and one brain, you know!'

'We have production schedules!' I snapped back. 'You can't arrange things to cater for them?'

'That blasted court-house schedule get moved up,' she protested.

It turned out the minister had scheduled a Grand Opening of one of the court-houses for a date prior to delivery. 'We have to cooperate,' Robin said. 'This court-house opening is important to Suratsingh.'

Suratsingh was looking to increase his political base in the south of Trinidad, where mainly Indians lived. That was why he was anxious to repair court-houses in small towns down there. He wanted to open the new court-house in time for Eid ul Fitr celebrations, make a big speech, have masses cheer him, and let Frog-face, the Prime Minister, know how much he was needed for the party to maintain its electoral majority.

'Robin,' I said, 'we can't get sufficient hinges in time to complete our contracts! We are running out of toilet seats, nails, tools –'

'That's Nerissa's fault,' Ashok said. 'She should have put in the order before . . .'

I decided to make a quick trip to Miami to order some emergency supplies.

'Come to Miami with me,' I suggested to Anji.

'Ved!' she snapped.

I stared at her, surprised. It had just been a suggestion for us to get away from the others and have a few days together. She looked at me and heaved a long sigh.

'I have to finish the introduction to my thesis so my supervisor can see it before he go on holiday. What about if we go next week?'

'In a week, I will have a building crew standing idle in Dorado. You can't round off the introduction earlier? You working on that for the last year.'

She suddenly dissolved into tears. 'You always interrupting my work,' she sniffled. 'I run away to Dorado with you last Thursday to get away from the mob here, then you decide you want to stay in Dorado for the weekend. You didn't think about how that would delay my work . . .'

'But you could have done some work in Dorado . . .' I protested.

'With all those people there?' she demanded. 'If I leave the dishes in the sink to do my work, Madhuri does act like I commit a crime . . .'

Everywhere I turned there was stress. But Robin seemed to thrive on stress. His hearty manner kept increasing. He was talking now about another government contract, to rebuild the headquarters of the Ministry of Agriculture. Suratsingh had got so much political kudos from sprucing up the court-houses, other politicians were seeing opportunities to bolster their political support with building projects. Robin was Their Boy, their agency for making that happen. He had found a place for himself in the Trinidad elite. He was a Somebody.

'You know,' he observed, sitting on the verandah after dinner, his increasing belly pointing at the sky, 'most of the business executives in big firms abroad does be lawyers.'

He was attending more and more government events these days, lobbying officialdom for other government contracts. Sometimes, if I bumped into officials elsewhere, they referred to discussions they had had with my brother. I began to sense that, to many, I was the junior Saran, the unimportant one. 'I really don't know what going on around here any more,' Nerissa sighed repeatedly. I began to feel I was failing her. She and I were constantly trying to catch up with new demands on our supplies. As soon as we had catered for one project, another would suddenly appear to shift all the parameters of our planning. We ended up working till late some days.

'Let's go out for dinner,' Anji suggested one evening.

'I'm tired,' I replied. 'What about tomorrow evening?'

But the following day we had some minor emergency. I forgot I was supposed to go out to dinner and came back to the house late. When I got home, Anji was in our bedroom sulking. I prised her out and coaxed her into going for ice cream. But I didn't really feel like it; my mind was still on some invoices we had to prepare for the next day. I was just going through the motions, sitting in a little open-air mall, listening to Anji with half a mind when I wanted to be in bed.

Then one of Robin's children threw some toys into the swimming pool. They blocked the filter and the pool turned filthy. We would have to drain the pool before it could be used again, but I didn't have time to make the arrangements for a couple of weeks. The pool turned a mossy green, still, stagnant. Ma complained endlessly.

'Oh shut up, Ma!' I heard myself snap one evening.

Ma stared at me.

'I tired hearing you about the pool,' I said. 'You don't know I have a million things to do when the day come? I have to find some workers to drain the pool. And everybody busy.'

She turned on her heel and walked silently back into the kitchen. Robin hummed a tune. Anji stared at me, her eyes big and round like Nerissa's.

I think, now, that my bad temper had to do with the fact that I wasn't able to swim for a while. Give me a week without exercise and my body starts to feel like an alien object to me. I start to feel uncomfortable deep inside myself.

That night, when we went to bed, I kept shifting from side to side, unable to get comfortable. Anji started stroking my back, but even her hand felt uncomfortable. I ignored it. Eventually, I dropped off to sleep, but I woke at about 3 a.m. I started feeling bad about my temper that evening. I started stroking Anji's arm, then her back. Eventually she stirred, moving to a position that opened her body to me. 'I want to sleep,' she murmured.

'Sleep,' I replied. 'I just want to touch you.'

Eventually, she seemed to want me. But when I rolled on top of her, she winced. 'You're hurting my arm.'

I shifted to free her arm.

It was unsatisfactory sex.

Anji was fraying at the edges too. I know this sounds strange, but it's the best way I can describe it. She was constantly losing things, forgetting things, breaking things. And I had no time or patience to help her as I had before, finding the books she had misplaced, cheerfully starting a search for papers she lost. Her hair started looking untidy, it lost its shine. She developed a pimple on her face, then another, then a boil on her bottom. She got a cold, and it left her pale, her complexion a bit blotchy. By now, I know those symptoms. PhD syndrome. I've seen enough PhD students to know that after a couple of years immersed in issues that have nothing to do with anyone else, people become a bit stale, lose control of their bodies and begin to degenerate. But at that point I wasn't noticing anything. There was a constant state of emergency in our central organisation. Tony's factory got overcrowded with court-house benches, and furniture for the shops we supplied began to run out.

'Just raise the prices on the furniture,' Robin suggested. 'When demand goes up, prices can go up.'

That wasn't as simple as he thought. You had to change catalogues, you got complaints, you had to deal with these as diplomatically as possible.

'Shit, Ved, I hungry!' Nerissa said one evening. I looked at my watch. It was seven o'clock. But I wanted to finish off the work we were doing. Nerissa went out to the parking lot and bought a roti from the vendor there. She brought one back for me. When I got home, I was too full to eat, but Anji had been waiting for me to eat dinner. I sat with her as she ate, but I was really anxious to go have a shower. I didn't have the energy to give her attention.

'We have to reorganise,' Robin announced one evening. 'I going and tender on a contract to rebuild the Agricultural Research Station in Mausica.'

By that time I was fed up of the constant stream of office work. Robin was happy to attend all Grand Openings, so I left the PR work to him. But it left me office-bound. So I was open to Robin's suggestion that we appoint Ashok head of overall production, so he himself could take over some of the work in the office. Since Robin liked dealing with our big clients, I shifted those functions to him. But he was impractical, promising delivery in shorter times than we could manage.

'How you could tell the Hilton we could deliver teak panelling in three weeks?' Nerissa asked Robin.

'Tony must have some teak panelling in stock,' he said, waving her objections away.

'That is for the Caricou Hotel in Tobago!'

'Who more important?' Robin demanded. 'A little piss-in-tail hotel in Tobago, or the Hilton?'

Nerissa came to me. She had promised the Caricou people that wood. Their Grand Opening had already been scheduled.

'Nerissa just making a fuss about nothing,' Robin shrugged. 'We could tell the Caricou people the wood get held up because of this big national strike in Guyana.'

Sometimes I didn't feel I could solve the problems Robin created. He was anxious to grasp any order and figure out how to fulfil it later. 'Details!' he said. 'Allyou does get in a twist over details.'

'Details' was often breaking our promises to clients.

Then Robin began to lobby my parents to place him on the Board of Directors of the company. 'Look at all the new contracts I bringing in,' he said. 'The business expand by a third since I involved.'

Pa agreed immediately.

'Why we should change the Board?' Ma snapped. 'Things going good as they going.'

'You know,' Robin said heavily a couple of weeks later, 'With all this work I doing in the business, I don't have time to take on more legal clients. I have to make a choice whether to continue in the business or concentrate on law. Right now, Suratsingh offering me a case to defend the government against the National Union of Teachers. That is a big case, an important case. If I win that, more government work will come my way.'

I saw Pa glance at Ma. The Saran empire was expanding fast with all this profitable government work. We needed Robin to help manage it. Eventually, he was placed on the Board of Directors. But his management style contradicted mine. I didn't notice when Nerissa and I slipped into the habit of 'bad-talking' Robin, making ironic remarks behind his back. But at some point we had somehow become underlings, complaining about our unreasonable boss when he was not around.

My sisters were in their glee. When they were around, Robin waxed expansive, sharing political gossip, talking about big deals he was working on. 'Suratsingh holding talks with that fella Sudesh Maharaj,' he informed us. 'By the time the next elections come around, he and the other Indians in the Cabinet going to break off, join with Maharaj, and start a new political party. Then Frog-face going to be in shit. He will only have the niggers behind him.'

'What kind of fella is this Maharaj?' I asked.

'Nice fella,' Robin said. 'Bright fella. Financial genius. I was talking to him the other day and he say what Trinidad need is more Indian firms like ours. Then things could get moving in this country.'

'Indian firms will cause things to start moving?' Anji asked.

Ashok stared at her. 'Anji, you see how quick them court-house repair?' he asked. 'You ever know any construction project in this country get done under schedule before?'

'That's because you is Indian?' she pressed.

'Of course! Them other firms does fart around when they doing government work. They know they could get away with anything. Them Africans in the government don't be serious about getting anything done.'

My sisters would join in eagerly, talking about a bridge that had been under repair for five years, about the government workers who idled on the job, about the ministers who were only concerned about the pomp and ceremony involved in initiating the project and then didn't bother about implementation.

'You want a job done well?' Ashok said. 'Give it to an Indian.'

Anji's face grew tight. She was outnumbered in this company and didn't bother to argue. The others hooted when she accused them of racism. 'Anji, it's just a fact,' Robin said. 'Black people can't do nothing. Look at Charlo up in Dorado. He does take a year and a day to complete a building.

You give that same building to Ashok to build, and by the time you turn around the work done and painters painting.'

I always grew irritated when they started criticising Charlo, but I tried to keep my patience. I was keeping too much patience these days, and sometimes I grew annoyed at little things. 'Anji, where are the documents I put on the dressing table?' I would ask.

She would look at me with a blank face. 'I don't know . . .'

But of course Anji had moved my documents.

'Well, what your papers was doing on the dressing table?' she would argue. 'That is a place for papers?'

'Where I will put them then?' I would ask. 'Every space in the other room full of your papers.'

'You does get vex for nothing at all!' she would accuse.

'Nothing at all? Anji, these are contracts!'

'Yes, all that is important to you and you family is contracts! Contracts with the government to make money –'

'Anji, stop talking stupidness!'

'Yes,' she would reply, 'I does talk stupidness! That's what you and your family think . . .'

I was hurt that she included me in the term 'you and your family', and sometimes I just didn't have the energy or time to try and make up these silly arguments with her.

'That girl face swell up again,' Robin commented wryly when Anji's face looked closed and she moved around in a distant manner. And in fact Anji's sulks sometimes annoyed me. I couldn't defend her, defend Charlo, defend the way I had been running the company, all at the same time. When she grew annoyed at something any member of my family said, she shut herself off from us all. It was a relief to indulge in bitter laughter with Nerissa at the office.

'His Highness say we have to draw up the estimates for this tender before Friday,' Nerissa told me one evening.

'His Highness way of drawing up a estimate is to pull a figure out of thin air,' I replied. 'It's six o'clock. You go home. I will finish it.'

Her eyes went big and round. 'Ved, you think I will leave you here with all this work?'

I went out and bought Chinese food for us both. I was hungry. I bought beers as well, to drink with the food, and called Anji at home to see if she wanted to join us. But she said she had already eaten.

After that, when we were in a jam to get something completed in time, I would ask our bookkeeper, Gobin, to stay late as well. I would go out and get Chinese food for us all for dinner. Occasionally, Anji would come over and join us for a while, but she only got in the way of the work and didn't stay long. Then the end of the financial year began to approach, and we had to start putting all our records in order in time to submit them to the auditors. Staying late became a regular practice. We drafted our secretary and clerk into the late-night crew. With Robin out of the office in the evenings, a party atmosphere developed, a chaotic mess of papers and barbequed chicken and beer, and finally, bottles of rum punch Gobin brought from home. The secretary put on a radio and we sang along to the music in between work.

One evening, Anji came in. 'So that is how allyou does work late, eh,' she commented.

I didn't like letting the female office staff go home by public transport after dark. Our clerk lived south of St Augustine, in a place called Kelly Village. That was across the Churchill Roosevelt highway, where rural Trinidad abruptly began with a swath of canefields. I took to dropping her home after we had completed our work. Gobin would come with me and I'd drop him off in Curepe afterwards. One evening, he suggested we stop off at a country rumshop he knew that produced special spicy snacks for rum-drinkers. I didn't like to refuse. Though this extra work the office employees did would be reflected in their bonuses at the end of the year, it was still voluntary.

The snacks were indeed special: bits of curried duck so heavily spiced they could penetrate the numbness the rum caused in your tastebuds. After eating one piece, you had to drink more liquid to cool your mouth. Gobin had ordered a nip of rum and some soda. I poured a small quantity of the rum into my soda. Gobin got into conversation with a couple of guys he knew there, funny characters, argumentative loud-mouths. It was a relief to listen to their banter after the heavy, responsible work of getting our accounts in order. I didn't realise when an hour slipped by.

It became a habit, stopping off at the rumshop after work. When I got home, Anji was often in bed. I would get into bed quietly so as not to disturb her. But Anji slept heavily anyhow, so she rarely woke up. We hardly had time together in the morning; I was always rushing off to work. When she protested that I was always late in the evenings, I reassured her that it was only temporary. As soon as the accounts had been handed over to the auditors, things would slow down and we could go on holiday together.

'Holiday?' She looked at me like I was mad. 'I have to finish my paper for the conference!'

'What conference?' I asked.

She stared at me. 'Ved, how many times have I told you that I have to prepare a paper for the first conference on East Indians in the Caribbean?'

I remembered that it was a big honour for her to be asked to present a paper at that conference. It was an international meeting. Bigwigs in the field from all over the world would be there.

Anji said nothing more. When I talked about going to Dorado that weekend, she brushed me off, saying she had to work. I was willing to stay in town with her, but I needed to discuss something with Charlo, so I went alone on the Saturday. I intended to return that evening, but it was such a long drive back to town, I ended up staying the night. I figured Anji would be glad for the extra time to work. Charlo and I went down to the village rumshop and hung out with the fishermen.

It was a relief to be there with them. Wherever you were in Dorado, there was this breeze from the sea that washed away other realities. In the broken-down rumshop, with the hearty man-talk, I was able to forget the power struggle I was waging with my brother in town. Here I was just Ved, a young guy the fishermen knew since childhood, a rich guy but a regular guy. The conversation grew louder and more hearty and I drowned myself in it. One glass of soda water with a drop of rum in it grew into another. In a rumshop, guys pour drinks for you. Some of the drinks became standard portions. I found myself pleasantly drunk, what they call 'sweet' in Trinidad, where your cares blur into the background of your mind. I was cheerful when I went back to the beach-house, where Robin and his gang of politicos were drinking whiskey and coconut water on the verandah. I joined them.

'Boy, you was drunk last night!' Robin commented the next morning.

I felt a bit hung-over. Sprawling on the verandah seemed like the best thing I could do with my time. One of Robin's cohorts had brought along his servant with him and she had prepared a tasty breakfast of hot-bake and saltfish buljol, with tomatoes and ochro. When I felt well enough to eat, I began to enjoy it. I sat back on the verandah, satiated, not wishing to move.

That afternoon, when I returned home, Anji glanced at me. 'So you get a lot of work done?' I asked.

She shook her head. 'Sylvia gone to some Jehovah Witness convention and I had to help Ma with the cooking.'

My sisters were there with their children.

'It's impossible to work around here,' Anji said, without looking at me. 'I going down to the library.'

I was alone with my family in the house. I went to bed and took a long nap. It was refreshing. When I woke it was almost dark. Actually, it was Anji moving around the bedroom that woke me.

'Anj?' I called, stretching out my arm to her from the bed in invitation. She came and sat on the edge of the bed. 'You got a lot of work done?' I asked.

She hung her head.

I stroked her hand and then her arm. Then her shoulder. Then I pulled her down onto the bed.

'Allyou coming to eat?'

It was my mother's voice at the french doors leading from the verandah to my bedroom.

Chapter Thirteen

Board meetings of Sarans never took place. The Board met every evening at dinner on the verandah. That's when decisions were taken.

'I have a proposal to put to the Board,' Robin announced one evening. I looked up. He shovelled some food into his mouth.

'I think we should get a management consultant to examine the company.'

'Why?' I raised my eyebrows. 'This company doing excellent.'

'Our systems are not adequate to the scale of our operations,' he said, picking up a bottle of pickles and looking around for a spoon. 'A proper management consultant can analyse what we are doing wrong and make recommendations.'

It turned out that Sudesh Maharaj, the politico from the south of Trinidad, had a son who was a management consultant.

My mother sucked her teeth. 'Management consultant, my backside!' she said. 'What I paying the two of allyou for if I have to hire management consultant? Robin, you always full of shit, you know.'

Robin said nothing further. But he invited Maharaj and Son over for dinner. Son turned out to be a tall, lively guy who had a way of kicking his legs about like a restless horse in a paddock and a long face with big, popping eyes. He talked in the dialect, in a very friendly way, but he had big-time credentials. He had done his MBA at Cornell University and was now back in Trinidad, consulting for the banks. His name was Shiva.

Pa took an instant liking to this Shiva. He was a highly personable guy. He even knew how to talk to Ma. His grandfather had been one of Ma's father's pundit-cohorts, and he talked with great verve about the inbuilt managerial skills of that generation of Indians. Sudesh, the father, also had a nice manner. He was quiet, with greying hair at the temples and alert eyes. He talked with Pa about cricket. It was a surprisingly pleasant dinner party. Even Anji and Shiva got along. They talked intellectual talk. Madhuri was the only fly in the ointment; she whined occasionally, but we all ignored her.

Eventually, we agreed to hire Shiva to do an analysis of the company. As Robin argued, it would come out of our costs of operations and so wouldn't really be any expense to us.

I was surprised at the report Shiva presented. It was a thick, paper-bound booklet of about sixty pages full of graphs and diagrams. Shiva had looked at the business in an entirely different way from how we had always done. Cost-benefit analysis, he called it. He identified high-profit sectors and low-profit sectors, demonstrating that the projects Robin was bringing in were actually the money-spinners, since they involved fewer steps from inception to execution. Supplying furniture to shops in Trinidad actually should have the lowest priority. The business should be switched to carrying out building projects for government, with the rest as extras. He drew up proposed organisational charts and diagrams of flow-processes. 'What you now call "Special Projects" should be your core business,' he said.

We all knew what this meant. It was Robin who should be the head of the company, not me. We didn't make any changes to our organisational structure as a result of the report, but it hung in our minds, like a skeleton in the Saran closet.

One day, Nerissa said she wanted to talk to me privately. She proposed we stay behind after the others had left. I agreed and she came into my office that evening at about five-thirty and perched on the edge of a chair. She cleared her throat. Then there was a long silence. 'I think I want to leave Saran's,' she said eventually.

I stared at her in shock. 'Why?'

She shrugged. 'I'm just not comfortable here any more.'

My mind was numb. I knew she wasn't happy with Robin around but I hadn't guessed it had got so bad. I fished around my mind for a response. 'Where you will go, Nerissa?' I asked.

She shrugged. I looked at her closely.

'Somebody offer you another job?' I was thinking of Roger Granderson-Powell, President of OAG (Trinidad). Nerissa often had lunch dates with him. They had become friends. Perhaps she had confessed her unhappiness to him and he had seized on the chance to get her on his side in the constant struggle between OAG and Saran's.

She shook her head.

'Well, what you will do?' I asked.

She didn't reply. She just looked down at the papers on my desk. 'I just can't handle it any more, Ved,' she said eventually, her head bowed.

'I know Robin is a pain in the ass, Ner,' I said. 'But give me some time. I will try to get things under control. I'll have a talk with him.'

She shook her head vehemently and looked down at her desk again. 'It wouldn't help.'

'Give me a chance, Nerissa,' I pleaded. 'Let me try . . .'

She kept shaking her head. 'It's not just the business things,' she muttered. 'It's just the way your brother does deal with me . . . Always touching me.'

I felt something squeeze inside me and go still. Was she saying what I thought she was saying? 'What you mean, touching you, Nerissa?' My voice came out sharper than I had intended. She looked up at me.

'Always putting his hand on my shoulder, trying to hold my hand, making little remarks about how a nice woman like me not married . . . Looking at me in a kind-of way . . .'

'He don't mean nothing . . .' I said.

Her large eyes regarded me solemnly, like they were trying to bore into me, like she was trying to say something without saying it. 'He mean something,' she said emphatically.

'You can't just ignore him, or cuss him out?' I asked. 'Nerissa, you's the expert in putting man in their place.'

She scratched at the desk with her fingernail. 'I've been ignoring him for more than a year, Ved. And I try putting him in his place. But you know what he tell me the other day? He say the consultant's report show that I shouldn't be holding the position I holding. I am only the general manager in this business because of my relationship with you. He ask me –' she bent her head again and her voice was very soft when she continued '– why I like one brother so much and not the other one.'

I could feel my chest moving up and down as I breathed. It's something to do with when you tense up the rest of your body so you don't just explode. I rested my left elbow on the desk and rubbed my forehead. I covered my eyes with my hand and eventually closed them. Nerissa remained silent. Then I opened my eyes and looked at her again.

'Nerissa,' I said eventually, and noticed to my surprise that my voice was hoarse, 'I will deal with this.'

She stared at me dubiously.

'You go home now,' I said. 'I will have a talk with my brother. I will sort it all out. Don't even think about leaving Saran's. You help build this business. You can't leave it.'

I was bluffing, of course. I had no clue what I was going to do. But my whole life had been based on bluffing, not knowing what to do, but doing something to solve whatever problems came up.

Nerissa held my eyes for a little while and then got up and went to her own room. She came back with her handbag and looked in. I watched her, a beautiful woman of thirty-one, with soft, wavy hair around her neck and shoulders, a perfectly proportioned body, and a worried look on her face. 'I'm sorry, Ved,' she said. 'I didn't want to tell you for a long time. I thought I could just ignore him and he would stop. But he only getting worse.'

I shook my head. She stood in the doorway for about a minute.

'You will be all right?' she asked.

I nodded.

'OK, goodnight,' she said.

I nodded again. I heard her steps go out the door and then the door close. Then I relaxed in my chair and stared at the ceiling.

Time passed. I don't know how long. But somehow I didn't want to leave that chair. Everything that had happened since Robin came into the business passed across my mind. How had I been so foolish as to let this happen? Giving Robin the opportunity to insult Nerissa. I grew angrier and angrier. As I have said before, I am not very used to the emotion of anger. I just recognise it when something seems to fill all the empty spaces in my body – spaces I don't even know exist – and makes me feel tight all over. I kept imagining things, Robin touching Nerissa's shoulder, brushing against her, making silly remarks and grinning. I kept imagining Nerissa's confusion, her discomfort, the thoughts that must have gone around in her head before she came to the decision to quit her job. I felt so bad at what she must have gone through before coming to this decision.

The phone rang. 'Ved?' It was Anji. 'Allyou working late?'

I heard myself heave a sigh. 'No,' I replied.

'Well what you doing then?' she asked.

'Just thinking.'

'Just thinking?' Her voice went up an octave. 'Ved, I waiting for you to come and eat for more than an hour.'

'You eat without me.'

'Why?' she demanded.

'Just do it, Anji,' I snapped. 'I just want to stay here for a little while.'

There was a silence on the other end of the line.

'Anji, just do what I say,' I repeated, even more firmly. 'Eat your dinner. I'm not hungry right now.'

She kept the line open for a while. Then she put down the phone.

When I got home, no one was on the verandah. I guessed that Anji was in her study reading. I went and looked into the living-room. Robin was there, watching television with my parents. I stood at the door and fixed my eyes on him.

'I could talk to you?' I asked.

'Sure,' he said. He followed me out to the verandah.

'What you been doing with Nerissa?' I asked.

He shrugged. 'What I been doing with Nerissa?' he repeated. 'Nothing.'

I could feel something rising in my stomach at his innocent manner. 'She want to quit her job,' I said.

He shrugged. 'Well let her. Nerissa does get herself confuse with the work and get in a tizzy –'

'She say you always touching her and making suggestive remarks.'

'Nerissa just like to make a fuss about nothing,' he replied. 'What suggestive remarks I does make with her? Just the usual Trini old-talk.'

'Just stop it, eh, Robin,' I said. 'Stop the old-talk. She don't like it.'

Suddenly his tone changed. 'Who the arse you think you talking to, Ved?' he demanded in a louder tone. 'Stop what? Stop behaving normal? Nerissa just getting on like a big baby to get your attention because she inefficient. She don't get nothing right, and you does just indulge her. For what reason, I don't know. But I does wonder what hold Nerissa have over you.'

He let the words hang in the air. My head grew cloudy. I couldn't think. 'You does wonder what?' I snapped. My voice had risen louder than Robin's. Over his shoulder I saw Anji come out of our room and stand a little distance away on the verandah.

'I does wonder what the relationship really is between you and Nerissa,' he replied. Then he laughed. 'She sure don't deserve the position she holding in this company.'

Suddenly, I couldn't bear the joking and laughing and banter. 'Robin, what the fock you know about this company?' I asked. 'You was in England when this company start! What the arse you talking about my relationship with Nerissa? You don't have any kiss-me-arse respect for nobody?' I heard that I was shouting, but just wanted to continue. 'You just come here and throwing your weight around, with your blasted big-time-lawyer behaviour. You know how this company build?'

I was bellowing by now, trying to rock Robin out of his smug, dismissive manner. Pa had come to stand at the doorway leading to the kitchen. Ma was close behind.

'I mightn't know how it build,' Robin rejoined, 'but I know it ain't running good now. Allyou ain't have a kiss-me-arse organisation! It's just catch-as-catch-can.'

'If you don't focking like it,' I shouted, 'you know what you could do! Leave us! Go back to your piss-in-tail law, defending people who get bite by their neighbour dog! We was doing very well without you!'

He took a step towards me. 'You was doing well?' he replied. 'That's what you think! That's not what anybody else think.' He waved an arm in the direction of Santa Cruz. 'Ask Tony. Ask Ashok. Ask Roger Granderson-Powell . . . Everybody else glad I get into this business. Leave? If anybody should leave it's you. Nerissa threatening to leave? Good riddance! She is just a pain in the ass. Always whinging and complaining. But you like woman like that.'

There was a silence.

'I glad if that woman leave,' Robin muttered. 'Too full of sheself. Don't know how to take orders. Always want to argue. Let she leave! Always getting on like she so innocent!' He stared at me. 'You want to know about your precious Nerissa? Ask Roger Granderson-Powell. He will give you the full dope on Nerissa.'

Something filled my head. 'Shut your arse, Robin,' I said quietly.

His voice rose again. 'Why I should shut my arse?' he demanded. 'Because I telling the truth? Because I don't just sit down and stare into Nerissa's eyes and get on like the moon shining out of her arsehole?'

'Shut up, Robin!' I said, moving towards him. I grabbed his shoulder. Pa was suddenly between us.

'Ved, Ved!'

Ma was at my back, pulling at my arm. 'Ved, stop that!' she shrieked in my ear.

I let go of Robin. I stood and stared at him while Pa held on to me. 'Let me hear one more word about Nerissa from you,' I said, 'and I will bust your focking mouth, you hear me? And you give her any more pressure and you will have me to deal with.'

I shook Pa off. What to do now? I glanced around the verandah, from

343

Anji, who was standing on one side, to Madhuri, who had come out the kitchen door, to Ma and Pa and Robin in a cluster near the dining-table. I moved blindly to the stairs and descended them, not having a clue what I was doing. I strode across to where my car was parked in the curve of the driveway. I was moving mindlessly, just trying to get away. I drove to the gate, scrambled around the dashboard for the switch to open it, and then drove out. I turned right, to the corner, and then to the Eastern Main Road. I was just driving, taking the route I took on evenings when I went to drop the secretary home. I drove to Curepe and then took the Southern Main Road. Where was I going? I had no idea. I glimpsed an empty rumshop. It was dim and quiet and the parking area in front of it was empty. I pulled into the parking lot and sat in the car for a couple of minutes. Someone, the owner perhaps, came and stood at the door, looking at me, probably wondering what I was up to. I got out of the car and went in.

I ordered a Coke at the bar and stood drinking it. Some guys came in and stood around me at the bar, and, to get away from them, I went to the furthest table and sat down. My Coke was soon gone. The owner's wife, a thickset woman who had served me from behind the bar, came to collect the bottle. 'You want something else?' she asked.

I looked at her. It would seem strange to sit here without drinking anything. But I didn't want another Coke. Too much sweetness.

'Ammm . . . Give me a soda water.'

'Just a soda water?' She looked surprised. People didn't drink plain soda unless they had stomach ache. She was a lumpy woman in a worn-out dress, the most ordinary rumshop owner's wife in the world.

'Well . . . A little bit of rum to go with it,' I said vaguely.

She brought what is called a petit-quart of rum, two drinks in the smallest-size bottles. I tipped a little rum into the empty glass and then poured half the soda into it. I took a sip and then stretched out my legs under the clumsy little table. It was a rough table, nothing like what we at Saran's made. It comforted me to be here, away from everything that resembled Saran's. Nothing here was elegant. The floor was gritty concrete, painted red, with places where the paint had rubbed off, and more places where dirt had been rubbed in. The bar was raw wood that had been smoothed with ingrained dirt and spilled drinks. Heavy PVC wire had been set above it to protect the owners from hooligans and robbers. This was just an honest rumshop, a place where fellas came to get drunk and talk nonsense away from the effort to make something of their lives, away from the curtains their wives hung at windows and the schoolbooks of their children.

Another guy came in, ordered a petit-quart of rum, was given a bottle of water to chase it with, and settled at another table. He was a thin guy, a quiet guy, a guy whose manner and face spoke of years of petit-quarts. He was a typical rumshop habitué, the kind of guy who couldn't really afford more than a petit-quart, and came here to drink what he could afford in solitude, not looking for company or joviality, just the blur of rum in his bloodstream. He could have been one of the labourers in my business, just a guy who was doing what he could with his life, and came here to drown out any dreams that threatened to disturb him. I felt good in this company. I felt good with the rumshop owner's wife. She wasn't trying to be beautiful, like my sisters, or snooty, like my mother. She was just a woman serving drinks at night to men because she had to. And I was sitting here because I had to.

'Ay, that's you, man?' a young guy called to me from the bar.

I had no clue who he was. Just someone I must have met in the course of my life, someone who didn't really know me very well. 'How you doing?' I replied.

'Can't complain,' he said, then turned to order a drink.

I poured more rum and water into my glass, and took another sip.

I liked this rumshop anonymity. You didn't have to say anything that made sense here. In fact, it was better not to. It was better not to enquire too deeply into anyone's life. Keep things on the surface. How you doing? Can't complain. We knew the codes. After a few drinks we could have more conversation, but then it would be drunken conversation. Passionate conversation maybe, argumentative conversation probably. But conversation that didn't matter the next day. Conversation without consequence. Here was where we took time away from life. I rubbed the rounded edge of the rough table. I liked the feeling of the grooves in it, the grooves of broken-hearted lives, where dreams didn't flourish, where ambitions that had insisted on being born were quickly squelched.

The rumshop owner's wife appeared at my table again. 'Another one?' she asked.

I looked at my glass and the bottles that had held the rum and soda. They were empty. I hesitated. I really didn't want to drink any more. Anji would be waiting up at home for me. But I didn't want to go home yet.

I didn't want to talk about what had happened. I didn't want to have to explain what Nerissa had told me. I didn't want to hear Anji's judgements. I knew what she would say about Robin. I didn't want to face her bitter words about my brother. I didn't want to deal with pressure to do more than I could do.

'Yeah,' I said to the rumshop owner's wife.

I stared at the wall plastered with posters advertising alcoholic drinks. 'GUINNESS IS A MAN'S BEST FRIEND,' one read. 'OLD OAK – THE DRINK OF TRINIDAD,' read another. They were old and dingy and torn.

Did Tony really think I wasn't doing well in the business? Did Ashok think so? Did they say that to Robin? I couldn't quite digest that. Fucking arseholes if they did. I had given them jobs, let them do as they liked, let them grow with the business, and this was how they repaid me? Fucking arseholes! And I had thought they were my friends! Did they all criticise me behind my back? Charlo's face popped into my head. He wouldn't criticise me to Robin, I was sure of that. Charlo criticised me to my face when he disagreed with me.

A couple of guys came into the rumshop and started putting money into the jukebox. UB40's 'Red Red Wine' came on. I found myself listening. It was so familiar, so comforting, the sentimental jukebox tunes. I could lose myself in them.

I should go home. Anji will be waiting for me. But at home it will be still. The verandah will be still. There will be this air of waiting in that house, waiting to see what I would do next. Anji will be waiting, to hear from me what I thought about what had happened that evening. She will be waiting to talk to me. I didn't know what to say to her. Did Ashok and Tony and Roger really say things about me behind my back? Did they say I was a bad manager? I propped my elbow on the rough wood of the table and rested my face in it. I looked down at the grooves in the table. Was I a bad manager really? I didn't choose to be a manager. I only did what had come along. I felt sorry for myself. I hadn't intended to get myself in this jam where the business had grown above my head. Suddenly an image of Charlo's gardens in Dorado popped into my head. Those were beautiful gardens. Those were all I had wanted, the beauty of those gardens. How could I have turned my back on the possibility to have those gardens created, with their little lush pools and still spaces and the occasional heady scent of rare tropical flowers? Oh, God, how had I got myself into this mess? Tears were suddenly in my eyes, but I brushed them away. I looked up. There was a fresh bottle with rum in it in front of me, and a fresh soda. The rumshop owner's wife must have come and gone while I had my face in my hand. I poured and drank. The soda was refreshing. The slight taste of rum was delicious.

Bob Marley began at the jukebox. 'Coming In From the Cold.' The guys at the jukebox were singing along. I hummed with them.

I haven't eaten, I thought. I will get drunk if I don't eat something. But I didn't feel like going out and finding anything to eat. Somebody put on an Indian film tune and I began drumming on the table in time with the music.

A couple of women came into the rumshop. Bawdy laughter began as guys offered them drinks. Conversation grew louder. 'Play a tune for me, nuh,' one of them said to the guys at the jukebox.

'What tune you want to hear?'

The woman went over to the jukebox and studied the selection available. She had rusty red-dyed hair. She made her choice and then stepped back. The rumble of steel-band emerged from the jukebox. It was Symphonia, my steel band, Saran's Symphonia. I found myself smiling as I watched people begin to dance.

It took all my concentration to drive back home. I stared at the road carefully, keeping close watch on the ditches at the side so I didn't veer towards them. When I got to the house, it was totally still. I drove through the gates, parked carefully and then went up the stairs. There was a sound at the kitchen door.

'Ved?' I heard my mother's voice.

'Yes, Ma?'

'You reach home?'

'Yes.'

She said nothing more. I stood and looked towards the door for a minute, but I couldn't really see her very clearly. She was standing against the light. I felt myself threatening to sway, and kept a tight hold on my body. Then I drifted off towards my bedroom.

Anji sat up in bed. 'Ved?' Her voice sounded full of liquid, like she had been crying.

'Mmm . . .' I replied.

'Where were you?'

'Curepe.'

'With who?'

'With nobody.'

I got out of my clothes and got into bed. She wrapped her arms around me. 'I was so worried . . .'

'What you worried for?' I murmured. 'I just went for a drive.'

'You was drinking.'

'I took a couple drinks to cool my head.' I stroked her hair. 'Go to sleep,' I murmured. 'Everything will be all right.'

Her arms tightened around me and I dropped off to sleep.

And it was all right the next morning. I got up, had a shower and went out to the verandah to eat. Nobody referred to the events of the evening before, and I did not. I went to the office and proceeded with the work as usual, as though nothing had happened. And the work, the routines I was accustomed to, the normality of calls from clients, made me feel as though I was in control. I didn't say anything to Nerissa, just tried to convey to her, by my calm manner, that everything would be all right. Robin watched me uncertainly when he spoke to me and I acted unruffled. Let him wonder what was going on in my head. I now knew what he was thinking. I now knew that others in the company were being disloyal towards me. They didn't know what I was thinking, what I was planning. Actually, though, I wasn't planning anything. I was just watching and waiting, that's what I told myself. But I was really just stalling, hoping the problems would go away, for I had no solutions.

And so I went on, day after day. I kept more control of the business, kept a watch on Robin and tried to anticipate him. When I spoke with him, I adopted a crisp clear manner that cut through his bullshit. I didn't laugh along with him any more. And I waited to see what would happen next.

Nothing happened for weeks. The business went on as usual, but I was tense, waiting for the next problem to crop up, the next conflict with Robin, the next one of his suggestions for improving our operations. He continued with his hearty manner but it irritated me more and more.

'Don't make promises to people we can't keep!' I snapped at him one day. 'Check with me first.'

'How the hell I could check with you in the middle of a cocktail party?'

he asked. 'You not there. I have to indicate interest in a project to start deliberations.'

'You don't know how to stall?' I asked.

'Not like you,' he responded. 'You have a reputation for stalling. You sure it's not a paddock we running here, all the stalling you does do?'

Score one to Robin. I grew more irritable.

Anji had started her field research for her PhD thesis. She was going deep into the countryside every week to interview old Indian people about their lives during the colonial period. She used the Citroen, the car we called Santa Claus's sleigh, which was not a comfortable vehicle for those long journeys on pothole-strewn roads. She returned home exhausted, laden with notes and tape-recordings. Transcribing recorded interviews was a long, frustrating process. She sat in her study with the tape recorder for days, rewinding back and forth, getting confused, sighing and grumbling. 'I press the wrong button again and went backwards rather than forwards,' she would say.

'Just take your time, Anji,' I replied. 'Watch what you doing.'

'I feel this tape recorder is my enemy! It does always do what I don't want it to do! I can't find half of the interview I had.'

'You must have pressed the wrong button and it didn't record.'

She grew close to tears.

I knew she wanted me to help her, involve myself in her work as I had done in the past. But transcribing interviews was really a tedious job and I found it a pain in the ass to come home from my own tedious work and then spend my evenings fiddling with a tape recorder.

'Anji, how other researchers does do this?' I asked one night. 'Why you can't manage a simple tape recorder?'

She glared at me. 'Leave me alone!' she snapped. 'If you have nothing better to say than that, just leave me alone. Go out and drink in a rumshop or something. Don't stay here and make me feel worse.'

I would retreat from her, go read a book or take a swim. But that only kept me within hearing range of Madhuri's whining and my mother's snapping. I would go down to the tennis club and look for a game, but I hadn't been comfortable there since my trial. I felt that the other members whispered about me behind my back. I would stop off in a rumshop on the way home and have a drink or two.

Then the paper Anji had delivered at the conference on East Indians was chosen for publication in a prestigious journal of social sciences. She was elated. Her smiles returned, her cheeky manner, her old Anji-self.

'Ved,' she said as we travelled to Dorado that Saturday morning, 'I was thinking.'

'What you was thinking?' I asked, giving her a sly look. 'If we reach Dorado early we could take a nap after lunch?'

The sex the night before had been great. I was in a good mood. Robin had to go to a wedding the next day, so we would have the Dorado place to ourselves.

'No,' she said, tickling the back of my hand, 'I was thinking maybe you should get out of your parents' business.'

I glanced at her. 'Get out of the business and do what?'

She shrugged. We were driving along the stretch of coast that led to Dorado and the wind was whipping her hair around her face. Her shrug was in keeping with that breezy landscape where nothing seemed to matter.

'I don't know,' she said. 'Do whatever. Anything you want to do.'

'Like what?' I asked.

She looked at my face. 'Get a job somewhere else?' she suggested.

'What kind of job, baby?' I asked. 'What I could do?'

She shrugged again. 'You could do plenty things . . .'

'Plenty things is not a job description,' I said. 'It's not a profession.'

She looked at me in a quizzical way. 'Managing something?' she said. 'That's what you does do now. You could do it for another company.'

I laughed. 'You could see me going to McLaughlin's and asking them to hire me as a manager?'

We continued in silence.

'So you don't think you could get a job,' she asked a little while later.

'Anji,' I glanced at her, 'I don't have any qualifications to do anything. What happen? You think I am a failure in this business like everybody else?'

'No!' she said quickly. 'But it have so much conflict now. And you don't look happy any more. You does sound like you hate your work.'

I didn't reply.

After a while she added in a softer tone, 'And you does drink too much nowadays.'

We got to Dorado and busied ourselves opening up the place and settling in. It was lunch-time by then, so we ate and then sat on the verandah watching the noon-time sun turn the beach to a blinding white and the sea to a thin strip of glitter. The unaccustomed quiet of the beach-house was strange. I had wished for it for many weeks, but now it was here I didn't know what to do with it. It was like the ghosts of discomfort were still hanging around, evident in many small and big things: furniture that Robin and his companions had shifted around to suit themselves; children's toys and books; dishes that had been chipped or broken; items we couldn't find. This was no longer our beach-house, our refuge from my family.

And Anji's words hung in my mind as well, her dissatisfaction with me. Several times I thought of getting her into the bedroom and having our afternoon 'nap', but something about her movements prevented me. She had shrunk a little from me and it would take some psychic effort on my part to bring her back. I didn't feel like making that effort. I couldn't face another effort to make someone see things from my point of view, to see I was trying my best in the face of developments I had never anticipated. I was slightly irritated by her suggestion that I should leave the business. It was as though she thought the problems were my fault.

Eventually Charlo turned up and we got into the usual conversation, went to see something he was doing on the building site, then returned to find Anji reading a book. We made dinner, sat around and chatted in our usual desultory way, but it was not as before. The spaces in our conversation were not the usual ones. Ashok showed up and asked for Robin; there was something he wanted to discuss with him. That irritated me slightly. There was a time when there was no Robin; it was just me that Ashok and Charlo needed to consult. I suppressed my annoyance. Ashok lingered and the usual drinking started. At first I drank plain soda, but gradually I began pouring more and more rum in my drink. As the moon rose over the sea, the rum eased away the nuances of the situation and I began to feel more and more comfortable. It was like old times again.

At some point, Anji said she was going to bed. I stretched out my hand to her. She came and took it. 'I'll come soon,' I said, looking into her eyes.

There was something in her eyes as she nodded, some kind of shade or shadow or impediment. I would remove it later, I thought. I would bring Anji back to being fully with me.

But by the time I went to bed, Anji was fast asleep and I myself had no enthusiasm for anything else myself.

The next morning I woke late. It was ten-thirty when I looked at the bedside clock in the bedroom. I stumbled out of bed and went outside.

Anji was sitting on the verandah with her book. She followed me with her eyes as I made coffee, drank it, and then approached her.

'You stayed up late,' she said.

'It's a long time since Charlo and Ashok and I had the chance to talk about things,' I replied. I leaned on the banister and studied the sea and the coconut trees, felt the cool Dorado breeze that was so relaxing. It was wonderful to wake up in Dorado. But I felt Anji's eyes studying me in a critical way. Maybe I looked unappealing. Maybe I should have a shower. I didn't feel I could touch her till I had done so.

'Ved?' she said.

'Yes, honey?'

'Why we don't move from your parents' house?'

I stretched my arms to exercise my muscles. 'Move and go where?' I asked.

She shrugged. 'Anywhere. Buy a house. Rent a house. Just leave!'

I looked at her. Anji looked lonely, uncomfortable, sitting with her legs folded under her on the chair in this vast beach-house. I nodded. 'OK,' I said.

Her face lit up suddenly. 'OK?' she asked.

I nodded again. 'OK, if that's what you want.'

A smile broke out on her face. I came closer to her and kissed her lips. She put her slim arms around my neck. 'Watch out,' I said. 'My face is scratchy. I need to shave.'

'We could really move?' she whispered.

'Mm-hm, if you want to.'

She tightened her arms around my neck. But I wasn't comfortable. I needed to shower and shave before I could let things go any further.

'Give me ten minutes in the bathroom,' I murmured.

But in ten minutes Roger Granderson-Powell was on our verandah talking about something on the site, then Charlo turned up, then Ashok, and the day began to take its usual course.

Over the next weeks, I thought about Anji's proposal that we should move. I would have to buy land and build a house. I began looking around for land in an appropriate place.

Then, one night, Robin raised the question of implementing the recommendations Shiva Maharaj had made in his management report.

That implied setting up a clear hierarchy, in which both Charlo and Nerissa would report to Ashok. I knew Charlo wouldn't accept that. He had always reported only to me, and it was a casual sort of reporting, more consultation than taking orders. It also implied a demotion for Nerissa.

I refused to consider making those changes. An argument broke out. Why were our labour costs higher per head than every other firm in the construction industry? Robin demanded. Why was I paying our draftsman, Mikey, a retainer, when he was out of work for weeks? I had no answers to these questions except to say that that was why Saran's was such a successful company – because we had loyal employees.

'That's a myth.' Robin laughed. 'Saran's is a successful company because of the land we happen to own in Dorado. And you not even making the best use of that land. Charlo don't have one blasted thing to do up there nowadays except maintain that property. All the major OAG buildings completed. We could be building a string of beach-houses and coining money. But you prefer to have that lazy nigger sitting down minding peacock up there. You prefer to coddle the workers, so they will like you. You just glad if they smile with you and drink with you and slap you on your back, and say Ved is a great fella. You think everybody happy about that? Ask Ashok what he think. His family could be making more money out of that Dorado land if you wasn't so pig-headed. You think they happy about your foot-dragging?'

'I don't have to ask Ashok what he think!' I snapped. 'If Ashok not happy, he could haul he arse from this company, set up his own and build beach-house. That son of a bitch making a hell of a salary from me without taking on no risk himself. So I don't need to consult him on nothing.'

Ma and Pa were silent during the argument. I saw Robin glance at them occasionally as though for support. This had been discussed before, I realised, outside of my presence. I flew into a temper and left the house.

When I returned home at about midnight, Anji was in her study. 'Ved,' she asked, 'what happen this evening?'

I shook my head. 'I'll tell you in the morning. I don't feel like talking now –'

'You mean you too drunk to talk!'

'Whatever,' I said, and turned and went into the bedroom.

'Ved!' she cried, following me and grabbing my shoulder, 'why you wouldn't tell me what happen?'

I turned to face her. 'Nothing ain't happen, Anji!' I snapped. 'It's just the usual shit. Stop bothering me. I want to get some sleep.'

I stripped off my clothes and got into bed. She turned and walked through the door and back into her study. I was really tired. I soon fell asleep.

She didn't talk to me for two days after that. When we finally made up the quarrel, she wept and wept in my arms. 'That's why I tell you we should move,' she sobbed. 'The atmosphere in this house is terrible. Ved, when you going to get a place for us to move to?'

I was silent. I had realised that if I moved, I would lose whatever control I still had over the company. With Robin living in the house with my parents, any amount of plotting could take place behind my back. I had decided that it was a bad idea to move.

Later, I tried to explain my reasons to her.

'Ved!' She stared at me as though she had seen a ghost. 'You mean we will never move from here?'

'I'm not saying we will never move from here,' I replied. 'I'm saying it's not a good idea to move now.'

'Well, when will be a good time to move?'

I shrugged. 'I don't know, Anji! Can't you see there are big things hanging over me now? You want me to lose this company to Robin?'

'I don't care about your bloody company!' she snapped. 'This whole company can go to hell as far as I am concerned. All this fighting over money and power! Look what it doing to you. Every night you coming home drunk —'

'Anji, I don't come home drunk every night. That is a lie!'

'Well, nearly every night, then!'

'Nearly every night, my backside! What you want me to do? Stay here and transcribe tapes for you? You feel nothing is important except your bloody thesis. The whole world should drop for that! You ain't bothered about people losing their jobs. You ain't care that a man and a woman who work their liver-string out for me will get demoted if I give Robin the chance. You was the one who wanted to hurry up and get married and live here. Now you want to hurry up and move! Everything have to happen the minute you want it. You really spoilt, yes, girl! Well, this time you not going to dictate the pace at which I do things. You will wait till I good and ready.'

She stared at me silently. When I couldn't take it any longer, I turned and left the house.

And so began that terrible period, with Anji angry at me, Anji angry at my family, my family hostile to Anji, my family frustrated with me, and me angry at myself. I felt my own weakness deep inside. I wasn't really doing anything to resolve the situation; I was waiting for something to happen. But what could I do? I racked my brains but had no ideas.

Anji's anger became a firm, hard thing. Every now and again it overflowed into a quarrel in our bedroom. Those often ended in tears. At the beginning, that gave me the chance to comfort her, pet her, make love to her. But after a while she just turned her back to me in bed or went to the study. Sometimes I was the one who went to the study to escape the confrontation with her.

'All you thinking about is Nerissa!' she snapped one day. 'You don't think about me, how miserable it is to live with these people who hate me, hate you, hate everybody in the world.'

'Anji, who will think about Nerissa except me?' I asked. 'You have any idea how much Nerissa do for me? You don't have a clue.'

'Sometimes I myself does wonder what it is between you and Nerissa,' she spat.

The higher the tension rose between Anji and me, the more cheerful Robin seemed. When Anji stalked past the group on the verandah in the evenings with a tight face, he exchanged amused glances with the others. 'That girl worse than Madhuri!' he would say, in Madhuri's presence.

He seemed to expand. All around him there were developments to entertain him. Sudesh Maharaj's political base in the south of Trinidad was growing fast, and Robin was one of his confidants. Sudesh dropped by our house regularly, chatting with the family, discussing politics, eating Sylvia's food and generally merging in.

'That's the next Prime Minister of this country,' Robin crowed. 'Sudesh have more brains in he back pocket than Frog-face have in he head.'

I had to admit that Sudesh was an impressive character. He had lots of ideas how to use the wealth from Trinidad's natural resources to improve welfare in the country.

'I say Saran's should take a big share in the sponsorship of this mela Sudesh holding in south,' Robin urged.

The mela was some kind of Indian fair, with huge displays and demonstrations of Indian culture. Companies could support the event by setting up booths there to advertise their goods. But Saran's didn't need to advertise, I pointed out to Robin.

'Then why you have a advertising manager?' he retorted. 'One Charlo.'

'How much advertising Charlo does do?' I asked lazily. 'A few radio spots and some shop window.'

'And a pack of money to the steel band!' Ma put in.

'That's not advertising,' I said. 'That's sponsorship. That's just about goodwill.'

'So why we want goodwill from the blacks and not the Indians?' Pa asked. 'Indians is not people too?'

'Indians is not our customers,' I pointed out to him. 'Our store selling to the people around here.'

'Small-time thinking!' Robin waved his hand. 'This whole country is our local community. Ved, if Sudesh and them form the next government, you know how much building contract they will control?'

My father's eyes gleamed. He liked the idea of Saran's becoming a powerful business empire. So we ended up sponsoring part of the mela, with Robin sitting on the podium among the bigwigs at some of its events. My sister Indra was one of the judges at a beauty contest they held. She dangled her slipper authoritatively. Ma was scornful of the whole thing. 'Stupid Indians doing dotishness!' she snapped. But it was just normal habit for her to despise things. The rest of Indian Trinidad was enthralled with this mela. It went on for two weeks, with singing competitions every night, dancing and music. It was a huge success, and Sudesh's party got a big boost. The political conversations on our verandah intensified, with much joking and laughter and a lot of whiskey and coconut water.

Anji was disgusted. 'Race politics!' she snorted. 'When this country will stop voting based on race?'

'Never!' replied Ashok. 'What base you think the niggers does vote on?'

Anji just glared at him out of the corners of her eyes. Ashok's language offended her, but there was no point in upbraiding him about it. She would only get laughed at.

And, strangely, she herself got some political mileage out of the mela. Reporters who were writing feature articles about Indians came to the university seeking authorities in local Indian culture. They were directed to Anjani Gopaul, the hottest young researcher into the subject, who proceeded to attack the Hindu Maha Sabha. The Maha Sabha defended itself in statements to the Press. Anji counter-attacked with a long letter that was published as an article. Other people started quoting her.

Sudesh and Robin were all smiles. They wanted to seize the Maha Sabha's political base and Anji had launched the first blow for them. Sudesh made careful, judicious interventions in the debate between Anji and the Maha Sabha. Anji was furious at having played into his hands. 'He too smart!' she fulminated.

'You sounding like Robin,' I teased. 'That's what he does say. Sudesh smart.'

She stared at me. 'Ved,' she asked, 'you will vote for Sudesh?'

I shrugged. 'Why not? As you say, he smart. He smarter than them jackasses that in government now.'

'But he playing race politics!'

'Politics is politics, yes!' I shrugged again.

She glared at me. 'You don't care about nothing, eh!'

I shrugged again. 'I does just mind my own business,' I said lightly.

'You don't even mind your own business!' she snapped. 'You don't even notice that I desperately unhappy living with your family. You don't know when I have a paper to deliver at a conference . . .'

I tried to switch off, ignore her. Anji was becoming what I'd heard about, a nagging wife. Being around her was no fun at all. It was always tense. Sometimes, when I walked away from her and went to sit on my own near the swimming pool, I reflected that this was the reality of marriage. What I had experienced before was just the honeymoon period, the intoxication of sex. I often sat there, under the pommecythere tree, just to be on my own, away from Robin's heartiness, his children's noisiness, the banter and constant movement on the verandah. Ma would sometimes drift over to the bench under the pommecythere tree as well. She liked being away from the chaos on the verandah in the evening. She would spend over two hours in the garden, watering plants and complaining about Charlo's neglect of them. 'That damn exora growing all over the place like it's a joke. And the damn fool ain't even know. He haul he tail to Dorado and leave me here with this set of unruly bush that he plant.'

I found it pleasant to be with her. Sometimes I defended her plants, just to give her an excuse to complain some more. It soothed me.

I really was drinking too much, I knew. I made a resolve to stop going to the rumshop entirely. But a week later I accepted one drink with Robin and Sudesh Maharaj on the verandah, and one drink led to another, and I ended up sitting late with them in the cool evening breeze. Ashok turned up at some point and I found it pleasant to let the hearty talk swirl around me. Anji was sour with me the next day. I tried to ignore her, but her bad temper lingered. 'You turning into a typical rich-Indian,' she sneered.

By the end of the week, I had given in to the desire for the peace of the noisy rumshop. If my mind wasn't muffled by rum, I found myself going round and round in circles. Ashok was clearly in agreement with Robin as to how the company should be run. He was enthusiastic about all the government work we were now doing and was constantly in and out of the office, discussing projects he and Robin were working on. They were also putting together cost projections to feed into Sudesh Maharaj's political programme, providing figures to cover the construction projects his party would undertake if it came into power. They now ignored Nerissa, and related directly to the bookkeeper and secretary. That caused confusions, misunderstandings, the typical problems that arose out of lack of communication. Nerissa was looking more and more miserable.

Things only seemed to get worse as the time began to approach for Anji's thesis to be submitted. She was in a bad mood most of the time and she flashed out at me for the slightest thing. She was working late most nights, so if I went to bed early, I went to bed alone. Sometimes I ended up in the rumshop in the evening, and when I returned she glared at me in a hostile manner. I went to bed alone then too. Occasionally, we ended up touching one another, having intercourse, but it was mechanical, restrained emotionally. I tried to communicate some feeling by being as gentle and caring as I had been before, but we were both sexually deprived and our actions quickly turned fast and furious. It was exciting in a way, this abrupt rise in passion, but afterwards there was an emptiness as thoughts rose in our heads again, thoughts we dared not express for fear of rousing a quarrel.

I was actually glad when a new project arose to turn my life topsy-turvy again. The research station we had built in Balandra needed a large extension. Jeremy Jameson-Jones proposed to build a small outpost of the extension on our land in Dorado, so scientists could collect samples of wildlife there to compare with species in Balandra. It all had to be done rapidly, since the Rockefeller Foundation wanted to use up the money in a particular budget before closing that account. Nerissa and I got busy with the planning and ordering of supplies. We ended up working late in the evenings sometimes, and, occasionally, it was like old times, the old times of furiously trying to get everything done in the cosy atmosphere of colleagues who understood each other perfectly.

One evening, I went into Nerissa's room to discuss something with her and found her hunched over the phone. I waited for her to complete her call.

'I have to go now,' she said into the receiver. 'I'll talk to you later.'

Her voice sounded clogged up. I looked at her closely. Was she unwell? Had she got a cold under the pressure of the increase in work? She didn't meet my eyes. 'Is something wrong?' I asked.

She shook her head.

'Your mother sick?' I asked.

She shook her head again without looking at me.

'Why we don't go out and get something to eat?' I suggested after a while. I thought perhaps some fresh air, away from the office, would cheer her up. I called Anji and said I'd be late.

We went to a new restaurant Nerissa knew on top of one of the hills overlooking Port of Spain. The air was really fresh there, and the food was served at little tables outside. You could look at the stars, smell the vegetation, hear crickets and frogs. The place was trying to carve out an identity by serving cocktails instead of the usual Trini drinks. Nerissa chose a pineapple daiquiri. She said it was delicious and ordered another. I tried one too.

'Thanks for bringing me out, Ved,' she said, gazing at me, her big eyes more peaceful than before. I smiled at her. It was nothing. It was the least I could do after all we'd been through together.

She took a deep breath, inhaling the fresh air of the mountains. It was more of a sigh than a breath, something in between that caused her whole upper body to raise and lower in a long, relaxed movement. She was wearing a thin white blouse, and in the dim light you could just glimpse the shape of the bra she wore under it. When she sighed, the blouse remained in place, but her body shifted. Hell, what's the use being coy? Her breasts shifted up and down, firm breasts, big breasts in comparison with her slim torso.

I shifted my eyes into the nearby undergrowth.

'Why all men can't be like you, Ved?' she asked when we began to eat.

'Like me?' I laughed. 'I am a waste of time. You should hear my wife talk about my bad ways.'

It was her turn to look at me in surprise. 'Your bad ways?' she asked. 'What bad ways?'

'Drinking, idling, not being able to make decisions . . .'

Nerissa sighed again. Her breasts moved up and down slightly. 'Your wife don't know what is bad ways,' she murmured. 'She should have another man to deal with.'

I smiled sadly. 'I does really drink too much, Nerissa . . .'

Her eyes were full of sympathy. 'You know,' she said, 'I does sometimes take a drink when I go home in the evenings, too. A whiskey and soda, to smooth over the rough edges of the day, as they say.'

'I does take more than one,' I muttered.

'I does take two sometimes,' she replied. 'I don't need more than that. I don't live with Robin and your mother and the whole shebang. It does be quiet home by me. Just my mother and the TV. I does go out in the porch and drink a drink and cool myself. I can't imagine how you does put up with all them people in your house after the kind of days we does have in the office.'

I smiled ruefully. 'I does run away,' I said. 'But then I does end up in rumshop . . .'

After dinner, she looked more relaxed. We sat sipping final drinks and gazing out over the dark shadows and shapes of the hillside.

'So,' I asked, 'Robin getting you down again?

She shook her head in a definitive way. 'Nah,' she said. 'I decide just to wait till Robin leave.'

'What make you feel he going to leave?'

She glanced at me quizzically. 'You don't know he going to get a big job with the government if Sudesh Maharaj come into power?'

'Where you hear that?' I asked.

She shrugged. 'From Roger. Roger in on all their schemes. OAG is not really happy with the way this government running things. Too inefficient. They will prefer if Sudesh and company come into power. Roger supporting those guys. But that's highly confidential. Only I know that. So don't blurt it out.'

I nodded. I was wondering how it was that Nerissa got such confidential information from Roger. I had always suspected that the gossip about a private relationship between them was true. But I had never liked to pry.

When I looked into her eyes again, I knew she had read my mind.

'Roger like to talk to me,' she said. 'You know how much secrets I know from sitting down right in this chair and listening to him?' She laughed bitterly. 'It look like this is the restaurant for big shots with problems in their marriage.'

I stared into the bushes and considered my next question. 'So it's true about you and Roger then?'

She shrugged. 'You know what they say,' she said lightly. 'When better can't be done, let the worst continue.' She looked down at the checked tablecloth. 'He always saying he going to separate from his wife. But I feel the situation suit him.'

I stared at the soft waves of her hair gleaming in the dim light.

'How I get myself in this shit?' she murmured, then looked at me suddenly. 'You know how many fellas liked me, Ved?'

I nodded.

'Not only shit-pot fellas like Ashok, you know,' she said, and then heaved a deep sigh. 'All kinda fellas . . . Why I always have to fall for married men, I don't know.'

I chuckled. 'What you mean *always*, Nerissa. The first Roger wasn't married.'

'The first Roger was a polar bear,' she said. 'He don't count. He was like a stuffed toy you carry in your bed to comfort you when you don't have a real person . . . I feel real bad about that Roger. I use him . . . Just because you was getting married.'

There was a silence.

'I couldn't handle it,' she murmured. 'You engaged to Anji, going crazy over her, and having to see and hear everything. I tried to force myself to fall in love with Roger.'

I remained very, very still, my habit when confronted with something I didn't know how to respond to. In some way, Nerissa's admission wasn't much of a surprise. But I began to feel even more irresponsible. I should have paid attention to Nerissa's feelings. I should not have made her feel bad.

'God will have to forgive me for what I do to that poor Roger,' she said, shaking her head again. 'Maybe this Roger is a punishment.'

We both shifted our eyes into the surrounding darkness. There was a clatter near the kitchen. One of the waiters had dropped a tray. Most of the diners were leaving. Those who remained were couples, leaning close to each other, getting into the second stage of the evening. I called for the bill and paid it. Nerissa got up and adjusted her skirt. Then we started making our way back to the car. The path to the parking lot was uneven, and Nerissa had to pick her way carefully in her high-heeled shoes. At one point, I took her elbow to steady her. We reached the passenger door of my car. I opened the door for her, and she stood in the crook of the door and gazed at me with her big, soft, honest eyes. I put my arm around her and gathered her to my chest, then stroked the soft waves of her hair with my hand.

'Everything will be OK,' I said.

I felt her nod against my chest. She raised her face and looked at me. I noticed that Nerissa had full lips that seemed to balance her large eyes. Smooth, dusky skin on her cheeks. I had an urge to kiss her. God, how I wanted to kiss her! But I didn't. She made a slight movement and I released her from my embrace. She got into the car and I went around to my side, started the engine, and drove back towards the Croissee.

When I got home, Anji was waiting up for me in our bedroom. She was wearing a thin white nightgown and sitting up in bed with a book. She gazed at me, waiting for my explanation as to why I was so late.

'I went out for dinner with Nerissa,' I said. 'She was upset about something.'

'Something Robin did?'

I looked at her and shook my head. 'Something personal,' I replied.

I had a shower and then joined her in bed.

'So what was Nerissa's problem?' she asked.

I shrugged. 'It's very personal,' I said. 'I don't feel I should tell anybody else about it.'

She glared at me. 'I am anybody else?' she demanded.

'I really don't think I should talk about it, Anji.'

She stared at me in a hostile fashion. I put my arm around her and drew her towards me. She resisted. 'You don't want to talk to me, just . . .' She pushed my hands away.

'OK,' I said. 'I'll tell you something Nerissa told me this evening.'

I told her about Robin's expectations of getting a senior position with the government if Sudesh Maharaj's party got into power.

'So you just going to wait for him to get another job and solve your problems?' she sneered.

I was surprised at her reaction. I had been happy at the thought that my problems with the company would be solved. I had thought she would be happy too.

'Ved,' she said, drawing away from me, 'I want to move from this house. I want to stop being surrounded by Sarans. I want my own life, my own environment.'

'Anji,' I said, 'you just have to wait a little and you will get those things.' My voice was a little sharp.

'Not if you have to move a finger to get me those things!' she retorted. 'Those normal things that everybody else has. You wouldn't make a move to give me what I want. But let Nerissa have a little problem and you forget everything else and run off to dinner with her.'

The argument turned bitter. I got out of bed, went to the kitchen, and poured myself a whiskey and soda. I sat on the verandah with my drink and tried to get calm. Anji appeared in her white nightgown. She seemed to me like a ghost, haunting me, refusing to leave me in peace. 'Anji,' I snapped. 'Leave me alone! I came out here to get some quiet.'

'You came out here to get a drink!' she snapped back. 'To escape into alcohol in your usual way.'

Madhuri emerged at the door leading from the kitchen 'Allyou could be a little more quiet?' she whined. 'Allyou waking up the children.'

The politics heated up and Robin grew more and more involved. 'Sudesh giving them a run for their money,' he crowed. 'Even black people in North Trinidad getting involved. The day Suratsingh abandon Frog-face party and join with them, you will see trouble. All the Indians in the country will be on one side, and some Africans too.'

'So they are Africans now,' Anji commented. 'They ain't niggers again, once they in your party.'

'Correct!' Ashok said, holding up a finger. 'Once a nigger see the light, he turns into an African.'

Anji glanced at me. I kept my face straight. I didn't want to be drawn into the argument. I was tired from a long trip to Balandra that day. I was supervising the extension of the research station, while Charlo was starting work on the field office in Dorado. He had come up to Balandra to consult with me, and had given me some disturbing news.

He had said that Roger Granderson-Powell was complaining about our building the field office so close to the OAG compound. Roger had plans for buying the compound from Saran's once a new government was in power. He expected that the new government would change the law to allow foreigners to acquire land in Trinidad. That's what he had been told by Robin and his political friends.

That night, when Anji went into her study to continue work, I lay on the verandah and contemplated the news Charlo had given me. The sale of the OAG compound would catapult cash into the Saran coffers. It would finance the heavy equipment we would need to fulfil the contracts Robin expected to get from the new government. It made sense from a business point of view – we would be relieved of the maintenance of the Dorado site – but Charlo would also lose the work he now liked and become a site supervisor on one of Ashok's projects. I didn't think he would like that, going back to ordinary building. Charlo was now over forty. Possibly he could adapt to new circumstances, but I couldn't see him taking orders from Ashok and Robin.

Anji appeared in the doorway between her study and the verandah. 'What you doing?' she asked.

'Just lying here.'

She came over to the hammock and tried to get in beside me. 'Careful!' I warned, as the hammock lurched. 'You going to spill my drink.'

She stopped in mid-move. 'I was going to tell you something,' she said in a cold voice.

'What?'

'Dr Brown's sabbatical got approved.'

I waited to hear more.

'Ved!' She looked at me sideways. 'You don't remember that Brown asked me to take over his teaching if his sabbatical got approved?'

'Oh, yes!' It meant she would have an assistant lecturer's post, teaching basic social sciences. 'That's great!' I said, trying to sound enthusiastic.

She turned and went back into her study.

Anji didn't understand, I thought often as I drove back and forth from Balandra in the weeks that followed. Those hours in the car, sweeping round the breezy curves of the north coast, became a kind of meditation for me. I loved that drive, the smell of earth and damp vegetation that seemed to emanate from the roots of the big trees that clung to the hills on one side of the road. The road was shaded by those old trees, their patched, mottled barks festering with parasitic orchids, whose roots dangled like tough hair for feet below their anchorage. Occasionally, the earth of the hills was broken by a patch of bright, spiky green from ferns that nestled in little forest springs. The scent of mountain water suddenly touched your nostrils and was away again.

Anji didn't understand my feelings for this place, for this work, for the business I had created that occasionally gave me opportunities to do what I was now doing, building a building that would mean something to people who meant something. My mind couldn't really bend around the potential value of the research taking place in Balandra, but from the little I heard from the scientists, it could have long-term value to the human race. I clung to that dim vision in my mind, that sense that I was participating in some- thing worthwhile beyond the chaotic, mundane struggles taking place down in the plains. There was a kind of order here, in their minds, in their methods. It was part of a long process of advancing human knowledge. In those weeks, I had many occasions to interact with the scientists, those oddly dressed eccentrics who gave up normality for the smell of this earth as they traced the small developments of plants and butterflies in this outpost of the known world. They were overjoyed that we were extending their labora- tory facilities, expanding the scope of the studies they were able to do here. Being among them refreshed me, made me feel like a person of value again.

But once I got back to the Croissee, the talk of money and politics and sociology assaulted me, and the feeling that I was in the way of everyone's desires – of Robin's desire for a massive business empire, of Anji's desire for a simple home of her own, of my father's desire to be somebody in the world. I would retreat into silence, trying to hold on to the scents of the mountains and the sights of green vegetation.

Anji was in a fever of papers and books. She was working hard on her thesis, but now had to prepare for the courses she would teach in the following academic year. She developed an antipathy to Robin's children, who came into her study and disturbed her papers if she left the door open. 'Why these children can't leave my things alone?' she grumbled.

'They are just children,' Madhuri whined.

'Children?' Anji muttered. 'Leprechauns, you mean! They does turn over everything . . .'

'Anji,' Madhuri said in her long-suffering tone, 'you keep your own things in a mess. No wonder you can't ever find anything.'

I avoided any comment. Madhuri was right.

Anji took to whining as well. She had left her watch under some papers, couldn't find it, and was losing track of appointments. When she got into a tizzy, she expected me to sympathise and leave what I was doing to help her. But I was very busy. After returning from the building site in Balandra, I had to check on things in the office. Nerissa was often there late in the evenings, waiting for me with issues that needed my attention.

One evening I noticed that Nerissa was unusually silent and distracted. 'What happen to you?' I asked in the usual jokey tone.

She just avoided my eyes.

The work took longer to complete because of her mood. She kept losing track of what we were talking about, hesitating over simple decisions. She seemed to have little energy.

'Why you don't go home?' I asked. 'Just leave the papers and I will see what has to be done.'

She refused, of course. Nerissa never left the office before me. We ended up staying till after nine. When the work was finally completed, I waited while she tidied her desk and got her personal stuff together, then we went into the reception area. Nerissa moved slowly. She looked forlorn now that the day's work was completed and it was time to go, like a balloon whose string had been untied and had begun to sag. I opened the outer door of the office and waited for her to move ahead of me towards the stairs. As she did so, on an impulse, I put an arm lightly round her shoulder. 'Things bad?' I asked quietly.

She paused, looked up at me and nodded. 'It's over,' she said.

I squeezed her shoulder. 'Never mind,' I said. 'Somebody better will come along.'

She looked up at me and shook her head again. There were tears in her eyes.

'Oh Nerissa,' I said, and pulled her close to me.

She sobbed against my chest as I stroked her back. Then she broke away and started fumbling in her bag for a tissue. I stood looking at her, feeling helpless.

'I've been so stupid,' she said. 'Waiting for him all this time. Waiting. Waiting.'

'Don't mind, Nerissa,' I said. 'He isn't worth it. You are a beautiful woman. There'll be lots of guys who want you.'

She sobbed even more. When she spoke again, her voice had a wild quality, a note of desperation. 'Ved, I feel like I've been waiting my whole life. First,' her voice broke, 'I was waiting for you. But you never wanted me. And then, I started waiting for Roger –'

'Nerissa,' I said, pulling her into my arms again. 'It's not that I didn't want you.'

She kept shaking her head against my chest. 'You never saw me as somebody to take seriously,' she said brokenly. 'You was only interested in the white girls and Anji, and the sexy girls . . .'

'I took you too seriously, Nerissa,' I murmured. 'I couldn't just fool around with you.' I kissed the back of her neck. She went very still in my arms. Then she shifted and looked up at me with those big eyes that drew the truth out of you, and I dared not say more. Instead, I drew her close against me again.

'Ved, you don't know how much you break my heart, you know . . .'

'Oh gosh, Nerissa,' I muttered against her hair, 'don't say that. Please don't say that.'

'It's true . . . To see you so crazy about Anji, getting married, going on honeymoon . . .'

I stroked her hair, those thick waves that I had wanted to touch for so many years.

'You never thought about me,' she said. 'You never, ever thought about me.'

'That's not true,' I replied. 'I thought about you all the time. You know how many times I almost called Anji by your name? You were always in my thoughts, Nerissa.'

I heard a movement behind me and looked around to find Anji standing in the doorway.

Chapter Fourteen

Anji left me. Left me with that memory of her face staring at me as I stood there with Nerissa in my arms. She had looked like a ghost in the harsh light of the landing. Or maybe it was just the shock of her pale skin compared to Nerissa's.

She had turned and blundered down the stairs. She was wearing a red peasant blouse and a long, wide skirt, dark blue Liberty cotton with little red and green flowers on it, and I was afraid she would trip. But she didn't. When I got to her and put my hand on her shoulder, she shook it off the bunched cotton on her shoulder, then looked up at me with tears streaming down her face. 'All this time, I believed you,' she sobbed. 'I believed you when you said there was nothing between you and Nerissa.'

'There is nothing between me and Nerissa, Anji.'

'Ved!' she screamed. 'Stop your lies! I just saw you!'

'It's a mistake, Anji,' I pleaded. 'You don't understand what you saw.'

She screamed my name again. 'Ved! When you will stop lying to me? I heard what you were saying!'

She rushed across the street to our house. I followed her. 'Anji! Anji!'

'Leave me alone!'

She flew up the stairs, past my father and Robin, who were sitting on the verandah, and returned downstairs with her handbag. I remember being worried all the time that she would trip and fall. I wished I could help her. She ran to her car, the little Citroen.

'Where you going?' I asked.

'Leave me alone!'

'Let me drive you.'

'Leave me alone!'

I stood and watched her reverse clumsily, then drive towards the gateway, then fumble with the electronic device. The gate opened and she lurched clumsily out.

I was more worried for her safety at that point than anything else. Anji was a bad driver at the best of times. I assumed she was going to her parents' home. I took the stairs three at a time, and called them. Her father answered the phone. I explained that we had had a quarrel and she had left the house in her car. I asked Mr Gopaul to let me know when she had arrived. Then I went to my hammock to await his call. I saw my father and brother looking at me, but ignored them.

Finally, Mr Gopaul called me back. 'She reach,' he said. 'What you do the girl, boy?'

'It's a misunderstanding, Pa,' I replied. 'Please believe me. It's a misunderstanding.'

I went back to my hammock. Pa came and hovered above it. 'Ved?' he asked. 'What happen?'

I shook my head. 'Nothing. Don't worry.'

I heard one of Robin's children begin to howl, Madhuri's whine in response, my mother's bark. But it was all far away to me.

What had happened back there in the office? What had I done? Would Anji ever forgive me? My brain felt like a donkey that wouldn't budge no matter how I pushed and pulled it. I couldn't seem to get a grip on the events of the last hour. I couldn't get the sight of Anji's face out of my vision.

How long did I lie in that hammock? I don't know. At some point, my mother came and told me to make sure and lock up when I went to bed. That amounted to 'Good night' in Ma's personal dialect. I must have murmured something in response because she went away again. I needed to take a piss, and when I got up to do that, I went to the kitchen to find myself a drink. I decided to take the bottle of whiskey to the hammock with me to save myself another trip. The next thing I knew was that birds were chirping. I had drifted off to sleep.

I woke into the dim morning light, with the shadows of the hills behind the Croissee, and the first thing I remembered was the feel of Nerissa in my arms. It was a comforting feeling. Nerissa's body was soft, cushiony. In that dimness between sleep and waking, I could allow myself to wallow in my desires. I clung to the memory of Nerissa in my arms, pushing away the thought of Anji's face as long as I could.

But as the sun became brighter, guilt assaulted me. I recalled the awkward angle of Anji's body as she stared at me, her long skirt somehow pathetic in contrast to Nerissa's compact form. Nerissa always wore these narrow business skirts and light cotton blouses, something like my own dark trousers and light shirts. Anji's peasant blouse and skirt strayed all over the place, as though her being didn't know where to end, as though her body was too slight for reality and her clothing had to substitute. I felt pity for Anji, for the trauma she had suffered and was now suffering. But I had always pitied Anji. I had always felt she wasn't capable. She needed me.

I heard my mother opening the doors leading from the verandah to the kitchen and got out of the hammock before she completed the action. I went into my room, our room, Anji and my bedroom, and caught sight of the unused bed. Then it was that the whole mess I was in swept over me. My wife had left me after having found me in the arms of another woman. I slumped onto the bed and stayed there while the rest of the family woke up, had breakfast, went off to their normal activities. Then I had a shower, dressed, muttered something to my parents and went off to Anji's house.

She wouldn't see me. She barricaded herself in her old bedroom.

Her mother's face was creased and red. Her father's face was still.

'It's a misunderstanding, Ma,' I kept repeating.

'She only crying,' she said.

'Nerissa was upset and crying,' I told Anji's parents. 'I was just trying to comfort her.'

Mr Gopaul looked like he believed me. Mrs Gopaul just looked worried. After a while, there was nothing else to do but leave.

I went to Balandra and called my secretary to tell her where I was. I became consumed in the work, but part of my mind was on Anji and the incident of the day before. I stayed late at the building site, then dropped by the Gopauls' house again on my way home. But Anji still wouldn't see me. Arun was at home, and we drank a beer together on their front porch. We were both quiet and restrained.

When I got back to our office, it was after nine in the evening. Nerissa's car wasn't there, thank God. I went into the office, which felt haunted now with the scene of the day before. I signed some papers that were lying on my desk and went home.

I found a gathering on our verandah – Robin's political comrades, including Ashok. They offered me breezy greetings and I went to my room. My mother appeared at the door. 'I leave some dhal and bhaji for you,' she said in her flat voice. 'You want me heat it up now?'

I didn't look at her. I hadn't eaten since the day before but I wasn't hungry. 'Don't bother,' I said. 'I will heat it up later.'

'Don't bother?' Her voice took on its querulous tone. 'You leave the food to waste yesterday! Good-good shrimps and peas. I don't want to see food wasting in my house every day, you know –'

'I going to take a shower,' I said, moving in the direction of the bath-room.

'Well, I going to heat up the food,' she returned.

I ate quietly at the dining-table while the political talk swirled around me. At some point, Ashok poured me a drink. I took a sip. Then I sat back in my chair and took another, longer draught. Ashok poured me another drink.

Anji refused to talk to me for two weeks. I dropped by her house every day. Nerissa and I never referred to what had happened; she just looked at me in a worried manner. I didn't know what to say, so I said nothing. I tried to get on with the work. Building projects don't stop because your wife has left you. You have to keep on doing what you do.

When Anji at last agreed to talk with me, she looked at me as though she were frightened of me.

'I'm sorry, Anj,' I said.

Tears welled up in her eyes. I moved towards her.

'Anji, I'm so sorry . . .'

I tried to put my arms around her, but she shrugged me off. She sat in a chair and sobbed. Then she dried her eyes.

'Please come back home, Anji,' I said.

'I don't have a home,' she replied.

I drew a breath. 'Anji,' I said, 'I will build a house for us as soon as I can.'

Her voice took on a scornful note. 'As soon as you can?' she asked. 'I know when as soon as you can is.'

I had no answer. I was busy with the building in Balandra, but I intended to get started finding land to build a house for us as soon as that project was completed. I told Anji that.

'And you and Nerissa going to continue to keep on with allyou affair!' she accused.

'We have no affair,' I pleaded. 'What you saw was just an incident.'

'What I saw?' Her voice rose. 'I heard you tell Nerissa you were always thinking about her. That you nearly called me by her name!'

I had no answer to that, so I kept silent.

Anji filled in the silence with sobs. 'Why did you marry me?' she asked brokenly. 'Why did you marry me?'

We had several conversations like this over the following weeks, going over the same ground via different routes of varying directness. We never seemed to come to any resolution. It was like a series of negotiations.

'Why did you marry me?' she would sob in the early stages.

'I loved you, Anji,' I replied.

'Loved,' she said. 'Past tense.'

'I love you, Anji,' I said.

She looked at me sceptically, but my words were true. I missed Anji terribly. I lay on my bed in the evenings and summoned up the memories of the early days with her, how happy we had been with all the jokes and laughter and love-making. I swore to myself that when she came back to me, I would do everything possible to recapture the old times. I felt that, now that she was talking to me, it was only a matter of time before she came back. I just had to keep visiting and trying to persuade her.

'And Nerissa?' she asked one day.

'What about Nerissa?'

'Do you love Nerissa?' she responded.

I stared at her. 'Anji, if I wanted to marry Nerissa, I could have married Nerissa. She was always there.'

'You didn't answer my question. Do you love Nerissa?'

No answer. She broke into tears again.

The question was raised again a few days later. 'Do you love Nerissa, Ved?'

'I love Nerissa as a sister.'

'As a sister!' She sneered. 'You will pardon me if I don't believe that.'

I had no answer, just said firmly, 'Anji, I promise you there is nothing between myself and Nerissa. If you come back, I will never, ever touch Nerissa, ever again.'

'Do you love Nerissa, Ved?'

Her eyes were blazing. Suddenly, anger rose in me. 'Anji!' My voice rose. 'I have told you I love you. What else you want me to say?'

We parted in a strained atmosphere.

The next time we met she seemed to have made a decision. 'I will only come back to you if you leave the business or if Nerissa leaves the business,' she said.

'Leave the business and do what, Anji?' I pleaded.

'Figure that one out yourself,' she replied. 'You want me to come back to a house where I don't feel comfortable, to the same situation as before . . .'

We had arrived at a stalemate. I didn't have a scheme for leaving the business, so I just kept on visiting Anji and the stalemate dragged on.

Eventually, after four months I got somehow used to the situation. I was working very hard and had a lot to do. I went to visit Anji in the evenings, let her berate me, sometimes ate dinner at her parents' house, and contented myself with that *modus vivendi* for the time being. Gradually, everyone had come to know that my wife had left me, and that became the status quo. It was almost as if I was single again, with a girlfriend I visited in the evenings. Except that the visits were tense, full of quarrels and denunciations of my behaviour. And visiting Anji took away from the time I had left to go to the office and carry out my functions there. Nerissa filled in for me as best she could, but I took to rising early and going to the office before going to Balandra. I saw Nerissa only in that first work hour of the morning, when I was busy getting everything done in time to go to the building site. The other employees were around and there was none of the intimate camaraderie of late-night work. I was grateful for that. I didn't enquire about the status of Nerissa's private life, and she didn't offer any information. We dealt with each other strictly as colleagues. When she cut her hair somewhat shorter and it bobbed around her face I noticed that it looked nice and wondered if I liked it better this way. But I made absolutely no comment.

Then Anji cut her hair as well: short, absolutely short, shaped around her head in what must be called a pixie hairstyle, with little spiky strands around her face. It made her look like a different person – cute, naughty. It brought out her mischievous expression, her youth and freshness. It confused me. It was as if she really was a different person, like she had cut off her past with her hair. I studied her closely when I went to visit her. She moved differently now that her long hair was gone. She moved her head more swiftly, with a kind of febrile movement.

I realised it all had to do with her taking up her teaching assignment in September. She was preparing for a new role at the university. 'UWI is providing me with a house,' she said. 'I'm moving.'

'What?' I asked.

She nodded, her dimples showing. 'A furnished apartment on St John's Road.'

Her mother's face grew even more creased and worried. 'I tell Anji she can't live alone!' she snapped.

'You tell me I have to marry Ved,' Anji returned. 'Well I do that to please you, and look where it leave me.'

My heart sank.

'Can I come there and live with you?' I asked Anji later.

She shook her head. 'Either you have to leave the business, or Nerissa has to leave.'

At the end of August, I had to go to Miami for a few days. I begged Anji to come with me. I hoped that being away would be a new start. I would have made it as nice for her as I could. She adamantly refused, shaking her head hard in the new way she had. 'I'm moving that week,' she said.

I returned home late on a Tuesday night, knowing that Anji had moved. I called her mother the following day to get the address and, once I had got things in order at the office, I went to Tunapuna to find the apartment where she was living.

St John's was a steep road that started at the Eastern Main Road and curved all the way to the top of a large hill. As I drove higher, the houses became more sparse and the landscape suddenly turned rural. This was an old settlement interspersed with newer houses. Anji's apartment turned out to be one floor of a fairly large house that was built into the hillside. To get to her door, you had to park your car outside the house and walk down about a dozen steps surrounded by flowering plants. The door itself was of cedarwood with glass panels built into it.

I rapped at one of the panels and Anji came to the door wearing shorts. I was surprised at her appearance. She never wore shorts usually, except at the beach. With her pixie hairstyle and the shorts, she looked very young and gay.

'Isn't it nice?' she asked, waving her hand around the living-room.

The house faced the valley so it had a lovely view of big old trees on sloping hills. But I felt that front door was too flimsy. So were the doors leading to the balcony. They were all of cedar and glass. Nice, but not strong enough to keep out intruders. I opened the balcony door, went out and bent over the concrete balustrade to see what the climb was like. It was fairly steep but a determined intruder could get to that balcony. I looked around the rest of the house. There was a small kitchen at the back of the living-room and then three steps that led, presumably, to the bedrooms.

'This place isn't safe,' I said.

Anji's face fell. 'You just want to frighten me into coming back and living in the Croissee.'

'I will move in here as well,' I said. 'I can't leave you here on your own.'

'No!' she yelled. She narrowed her eyes. 'Ved, if you think you going to get your way on the sly, without doing anything to change things, you lie! You are not moving in here. This is my place! I did something to get it. I worked and studied and I am entitled to university staff accommodation. You did nothing to improve your own life. You are satisfied to live with your mother for the rest of your days! With your disgusting brother and his disgusting wife and disgusting children. And work in their business, and take orders from everybody, and drink so you don't have to face the consequences of your laziness . . .'

I stared at her for a long time.

'You are not coming here to live!' she snapped. 'Our marriage is over. You killed it.'

I kept on staring at her.

'Don't look at me like that!' she shouted. 'That's all you can do? Stare at me? Like I am killing you? Why don't you do something for yourself?'

'So I shouldn't even look at you now, Anji?' I asked quietly.

'No!' she shrieked. 'You don't deserve to look at me. You should get out of here! Get out of my eyesight! Go! I don't ever want to see you again. You are just trying to make me feel bad because I proved I could make it on my own and do what you can't do. Live my own life without the Sarans and their bloody money and bloody furniture.'

Suddenly I was furious. 'Anji!' I said, and heard that my voice was loud. 'I am not leaving you here. That's final. It is not safe. I don't care if you don't want to see me. But you cannot live here alone.'

'Get out, Ved!' she shrieked. 'I said get out of my house! I don't want you here!' She came up to me and began pushing at my chest. I tried to embrace her. 'Let me go!' she screamed, beating at my chest with her fists. 'Go back to Nerissa!' She started sobbing hysterically. I tried to calm her, but she wouldn't let me touch her.

'All right, Anji, you want me to go?' I said. 'I'll go.' I walked towards the door. Behind me, her sobs suddenly ceased. I opened the door, went outside, shut the door behind me, walked two steps, then turned. I looked at the lock on the door and aimed the hardest kick I could at it. I heard the wood crack. I kicked again, and the door opened a couple of inches.

'Ved!' I heard Anji shriek from inside.

I stood in front of the door and waited. She pulled it open and stared at me.

'You son of a bitch!' she screamed.

'I'm going to get somebody to replace that door this morning,' I said.

'I don't want your bloody help!' she screamed. 'I never want to see you again.'

'You don't have to see me again,' I said. 'I'll send some workmen.' Then I turned and started up the stairs to my car.

A young Chinese woman was standing at the top of the stairs peering at us. When I got to the top she stood aside to let me pass. I ignored her, assuming that she was the upstairs neighbour. I could feel her eyes on my back as I went to where my car was parked at the side of the road. I got in and headed towards Santa Cruz.

All the way to the lumber-yard, my head was in a daze. The things Anji had shouted at me hurt. I tried to push them away as I did a mental inventory of the security measures I wanted taken in her apartment. I wanted discreet burglar-proofing at the balcony doors, but I hadn't seen what the bedroom windows were like. I needed to send somebody to the apartment who would assess the situation and do whatever was necessary. I wished with all my heart that Charlo was around. He would be able to do it for me.

When I got to the lumber-yard, the first car I spotted was Ashok's. I breathed a sigh of relief. Ashok could take charge of the changes to Anji's place. I could rely on him to do a complete job.

He was supervising the loading of a truck. A number of labourers were around. 'I want you to do something for me,' I said.

'Boy,' he replied, glancing round at me, 'I in a real rush. This lumber have to reach Rio Claro this morning.' Two workers started approaching him to ask something. He directed his attention to them.

'This is more urgent,' I said.

'What?' Ashok asked, turning to me while the labourers waited.

I took a deep breath. 'I want you to go and fix a door for me,' I said.

He stared at me, his big eyes opening wide. 'Fix a door?' he asked loudly. 'You want me to leave what I doing to fix a door?'

'Yes,' I said quietly, trying to communicate with my eyes that I didn't want to discuss it in front of the labourers.

'You mad or what?' Ashok asked. 'I have a government project held up in Rio Claro and you talking bout fixing door? What I look like to you? A locksmith?' He turned towards the labourers and started giving them orders. Another worker joined them.

'Ashok,' I said, 'I want you to leave what you doing and go and fix this door for me.'

He turned towards me irritably. 'Ved, what the arse wrong with you?' he bawled.

I opened my mouth and enunciated slowly and firmly. 'I said, Ashok, I want you to go and fix this door for me, before you finish what you doing here.'

He glared at me. 'And I tell you,' he said, even more loudly, 'that I doing something important here. What the mother-cunt you think it is? A joke I involved in? I must drop what I doing because you have some focking door to fix? What happen? You drunk or what?'

The workers were all still. I felt my face go red. 'Ashok,' I said clearly, but without raising my voice, 'either you do what I tell you here today, or you leave this lumber-yard for good.'

Ashok's head remained still for a minute as he stared at me. 'You threatening to fire me?' he eventually asked in a cracking voice. He moved closer to me.

'Yes!' I snapped, heat spreading throughout my body. 'If you don't do what I say, you're fired!'

He stood close to me, glaring into my eyes. 'What the focking mother-cunt wrong with you?' he hissed.

I didn't respond. Didn't speak. Didn't budge.

'You come here with some kiss-me-arse little errand to do, and now you threatening to fire me? Getting on like a focking arsehole because your wife leave you and you have problems? Look, man, get the hell out of here before I pick up one of these planks and lick your arse down, eh!'

My whole body grew tense. My head felt tight, like it was filled with something that was pressing against the inside of my skull. Other workers had come up to the group that now surrounded us. I remained as still as possible and when I spoke my voice was very soft.

'Try it,' I said. 'Pick up a focking plank and lick my arse down! You have mouth? You feel you could cuss me out in front all these workers? Well, either you focking do what I say, or you out of this business today.'

Ashok turned furiously. 'Who the arse you think you is, coming here and getting on like a jackass . . .' He moved towards one of the piles of wood that was standing nearby, shouting and swearing. The workers grabbed him and he shook them off.

'Leave him,' I said to the workers. 'Let me see him lick me down.'

I spotted Tony Antoine running towards us, his white shirt stark against the hard blue sky, his dark tie flapping. 'What the hell you doing, Ashok?' he shouted.

Ashok turned towards him with a large door-jamb in his hand. 'This mother-cunt tell me I fired!' he bawled hoarsely. 'You ever see any kiss-me-arse thing so in you born days? This son of a bitch come here, getting on like a cunt and –'

Tony grabbed Ashok round the shoulder. 'Take it easy, boy, take it easy . . .'

I turned and went over to the furniture factory. From there, I called Tony and gave him the address where I wanted Ashok to go. Then I drove to my office. I was shaking inside and wished there was somewhere else I could be. I had an image of Lopinot river with its spreading trees in the days before Jason had died there. I had never been back since. Suddenly, I longed to be in Lopinot again, sitting on a rock at the edge of the cool, shady river.

There was a lot of work waiting for me at the office. I tried to concentrate on it, but something inside me just wanted to let go. I wished I could just rest my head on my desk and cry.

'Ved?'

Nerissa was standing in the doorway. She needed some documents that I had. My mind was so dazed it took me some time to find them.

'You OK?' she asked.

I tried to smile. I knew it wasn't much of a smile, but it was all I could do. 'I will be OK tomorrow,' I said.

She stared at me with those big pools of eyes, those eyes that seemed to contain the immensity of the universe, that seemed to know everything there was to know about hurt and loss. I turned my own eyes away to stare through the big glass window of my office. I heard her go out and then return. 'Here,' she said.

I looked down at the package she was holding out to me. It was a piece of transparent plastic containing a slice of cake. Yellow cake with a sliver of pink icing on top. Nerissa's mother's cake, one of her specialties.

'It's my birthday today,' she said.

I took the cake from her hand. I realised that I should say happy birthday and apologise for having forgotten. But somehow the words couldn't come out. She had also brought poncha crème into the office and she poured me a glass. I took a sip and looked down at the birthday cake on my desk. I opened it slowly and took a small bite. After a moment, the flavours in the cake exploded onto my tastebuds. Nutmeg and clove and vanilla and egg and butter. Nerissa smiled at me. I ate the last bit of cake.

By the time she left my room, I was a bit better. Perhaps it was the sugar in the cake and poncha crème. I continued trying to get the work in the office done, to check documents and take phone calls, pushing past the numbness that seemed to be spreading in my brain, the prickling memory of Anji shrieking at me in that apartment at the top of the hill. My phone rang and it was Ashok.

'When you kicking down door,' he said, his voice full of laughter, 'why you don't check first that we have other door the right size to replace it with?'

I kept my tone light. 'We don't have a door that size?'

'Well, I could get one made, but it will take a couple hours,' he replied. 'But why you didn't kick down them door in front the apartment too? Them thing real useless. A ten-year-old child could kick them down.'

'I figured just some burglar-proofing would be enough. You had a look at the bedroom windows?'

He had. He was measuring and trying to contact our burglar-proofing specialists. He seemed to have immediately understood why it was neces-sary for him to have dropped what he was doing to undertake this task, and had lost his resentment completely. By the time I put down the phone, I felt much better. Everything was OK between myself and Ashok; the securing of Anji's apartment was in hand. I continued to work, pushing away the thoughts of the scene with Anji from my mind. The whole office went out to lunch to celebrate Nerissa's birthday, and the necessity to be cheerful in the midst of my staff made the incident begin to fade.

Late in the afternoon, Ashok appeared at the office in his usual jovial mood. 'Here,' he said, dropping a set of keys on my desk. 'That's dupli-cates for the apartment locks.'

379

'She told you to give them to me?' I raised my eyebrows in surprise.

He laughed. 'You think that girl even realise a lock does come with a duplicate key?' he said. 'I figure if I give her the two keys she will lose both of them, so I just tell her to call your secretary if she lose her key and we'll send a locksmith to replace the lock.'

'Good thinking,' I said, slipping the key into the top drawer of my desk. 'Everything secure up there?'

'Safer than Fort Knox,' he said, spreading his arms open wide. 'You know when you want a job done properly, the man to call is Ashok.'

I had cause to remember those words later, and to think about them over and over. But, for the moment, it was enough to settle down with my wounds. They really were wounds inside my head. I felt, in the beginning, like there was a patch of raw, bruised flesh inside my skull. Lying in my hammock at night, I went over and over everything that had happened with Anji. She had said she never wanted to see me again, and I didn't know what to do about it. I could not face another scene such as we had had that day. I felt that she had been right in what she had said about me. I was useless, lazy, passive. I had only let things happen to me, never taken any positive steps in my own life. I didn't deserve her, or the life she wanted, the life of a happy, brave, independent young couple charting their own destiny. I was just the guardian of the Saran kingdom.

To my family, I became Morose Uncle Ved, the quiet guy with the beard who lay in the hammock while chaos ensued around him. One of my nieces used the adjective to describe me and it echoed and echoed till it stuck. Ved was the failure of the family, the one who remained sad and silent while everyone else was jolly and lively.

Our house had become one of the meeting places for the new political party that was gaining ground every day. There was a lot of excitement surrounding this, and there were many visitors and a lot of discussions on that verandah. My father was in his element and my brother in his glee. Ashok was full of quips and wisecracks, and my sisters felt themselves moving up a further notch in Trinidad society. I was in the background, looking after the business. Robin took more and more time off the duties he was paid for, but I never complained. Nerissa and I just took up the slack, and, since we understood each other without discussing things, it turned out to be easy to take over his responsibilities.

On weekends, I went to Dorado and spent time with Charlo. He never asked what had happened with Anji. We were both just quieter, suddenly older. One evening, when the moon was full, he moved to pour another drink in my glass and I held out my hand to cover it, preventing him from filling it. He glanced at me.

'You stop drinking again, or what?'

I looked at him, puzzled.

'That was only the second drink I was going to pour,' he said.

I shrugged. 'I ain't feeling to drink,' I said.

Then I began to think about it. I realised that I had gradually stopped going to the rumshop in the nine months since Anji had left me. I had just subsided into my hammock with my feeling of loss like a spent balloon. I was really inert. It was too much trouble even to drink. When I consumed alcohol, the thoughts became really painful.

That night, Charlo mentioned that the Ministry of Education had offered Cassandra a promotion to library supervisor. She would soon have to travel all over North Trinidad to inspect libraries. Maybe they would have to move from Dorado, to make the distances shorter.

On the drive back to town I felt more of a failure than ever. Now that my relationship seemed to have ended, now that my wife had ceased living with me, Charlo's quiet, unassuming relationship with Cassandra seemed to have grown more secure. On a sudden impulse, as I was passing Tunapuna, I swung up the hill to St John's Road. I had no idea what I was going there for. I had no idea if I would ring Anji's bell, even. I felt like there was a desert inside me, a vast area of rasping sand, and I was just moving blindly, hoping to find an oasis somewhere.

The road was dark. It was just after eleven in the evening. I had to concentrate on the twists and bumps. I began to wonder why I was doing this. I thought maybe when I got to Anji's house, I would just turn around again and go home. But when I got there, several cars were parked in front of the house. It seemed like some kind of party was taking place in the upper-floor apartment. No parking spaces were available, so I turned my car a little higher up the hill. I stopped lower on the hill where the road curved, parked, and thought whether I should try to go and see Anji, and what I would say to her. I could see lights on in her living-room, so I knew she was awake.

Finally, I got out of the car and started walking up the hill towards the house. The smell of barbeque floated down from the upstairs verandah,

and the sound of cheerful voices that heightened my own feeling of isolation and loss. As I went down the stairs to Anji's apartment, I realised
that my heart was pounding. I could retreat still. But my legs kept going
on. I stood still in front of the door for a long while, then forced myself
to ring the bell. Eventually, I heard the sound of her voice on the other
side asking who was there.

'Ved,' I said in a low voice.

There was a silence. Then, 'What you want?'

'Just to talk to you.'

Silence again.

'Anji, please . . .'

I saw a head appear at the balustrade to the upstairs verandah, then
another head, then hushed voices. I swallowed my shame and just stood
in front of Anji's door. After a while, I heard the key turn in the lock,
and the door opened. Anji was standing there in a red silky dress with
buttons all the way down.

'Ved, why don't you leave me alone?'

'I just want to talk to you, Anji.'

'What about?'

'Anything. I don't know.'

'Well, I don't want to talk to you.'

It was only then that I realised Anji wasn't alone. There was someone
sitting on the couch at the far end of the living-room, a big guy of mixed
race, with thick, curly hair.

My heart seemed to squeeze. 'All right,' I said, and turned and went
away again, feeling numb, just concentrating on putting one foot before
the other on the dark road, knowing faces were watching me from the
upstairs verandah, watching this fool, who had been supplanted but was
still begging for another chance, being shooed away. I started my car and
drove in a blur to the Eastern Main Road, then through the cheerful night
lights of the main road to my house, then into the driveway. I parked the
car behind my mother's and my brother's, but didn't feel like getting out
of it. I remained behind the steering wheel for a while. Then I hauled
myself out, went upstairs, past the little group sitting on the verandah,
and went to my bed.

About a month later, I got a shock. I opened the newspaper one Sunday
morning to find Anji's face staring at me from an inside page. She was
smiling, looking young and happy and gay. It turned out she had been

asked to become a regular columnist with the newspaper. Robin was chuffed. It meant that the Indian political party was getting sufficiently important for the paper to hire a columnist to write about Indian history and culture. I read Anji's column and was deeply impressed. The girl wrote elegantly, with quips and turns of phrase that were fresh and original. I felt both proud and disturbed. I felt I had really lost something valuable in my life, something I was not worthy of. I hadn't given Anji the support she had needed to be the person she could be.

The column caused reactions in the letters pages. In the weeks that followed, Anji's name was constantly in the paper – Anjani Gopaul. She really began taking on a life of her own. It hurt me to know that she was moving on, making her own life, while I was stuck with the same-old, same-old. I saw a picture of her taken at some university function, laughing, with a glass in her hand. I decided I should try and forget her, forget she had ever belonged to me.

A few months later, my own picture appeared in the newspaper. It was taken at the Grand Opening of the field office of the research station in Dorado. I had asked Nerissa to do the handover of the keys, and she wore a beautiful silk dress that day, ruched around her body in many folds and creases that subtly enhanced her curves. The photo was spectacular, Nerissa's dark good looks contrasting with the pale, washed-out appearance of the senior scientist to whom she was handing over the key. I was in the background, sitting on the podium on a chair, looking up at the two of them.

A week later, I received a petition for divorce from Anji. It cited adultery as the cause. Nerissa was named co-respondent. 'We better not let this get into the Press, you know,' Robin said. 'They will make mincemeat of you.'

I was somewhat stunned. I let him identify a good lawyer for me and he began preparing a response.

That Saturday, I went to Dorado. Charlo wasn't there; Cassandra's mother was in hospital so he had gone to town. As evening turned into night, I remained sitting on the verandah listening to the waves crash on the invisible beach. Gradually, the regular rise and fall of the surf lulled my senses and I began to feel as though my spirit had expanded till it was being embraced by the dim bowl of sky. I noticed the scent of the tuberoses Charlo had planted close to the verandah. God, I'm lucky, I suddenly thought. All this was mine, this beautiful world of sea and sand and flowers and beautiful houses. To one side of me was the string of beach-houses we had created, their warm lights creating a halo of contentment around them. In the distance were the gay coloured lights that surrounded the restaurant. I suddenly began to imagine the scene there, people eating delicious food that I had helped design with Pierre. God, I thought again, we've created something wonderful here, me and Charlo, Pierre and Tony and Ashok and my bunch.

I started recalling all the steps we had gone through. I began to be grateful to be alone with this house, with the breeze and sea, and with the book I had brought to read, which I hadn't even picked up. I had an image of my mother, suddenly, and thought about how she had grown quieter in the last months, how she had seemed to shrink. I started wondering what was going on with her. I had been too involved in my own miseries to pay attention. Was Ma growing old? Had she lost her old fire? Was she worried about me? I had begun to recognise that she worried about me despite her iron exterior. Nerissa had said it a couple of times. Then I thought about Nerissa in her fuchsia ruched-silk dress. She had smiled so brilliantly that night, I had thought then that I could hand over more of these public events to her. We had kept a little distance between us since the night Anji had left me, but now, sitting in the darkness of Dorado, I let my mind's eye travel over the silk dress again, following the curves of her body. I felt that old, familiar stiffening in my crotch. I had an impulse to slap my thoughts down, but then I thought what the hell? I was private here, private in these beautiful surroundings, with the scent of tuberoses rising from under the verandah. I could be allowed to have the mental company of a beautiful woman, why not?

The next morning I took a long walk on the beach. I bumped into Roger Granderson-Powell, who was jogging, and jogged a mile back with him. Then we played a game of tennis. He beat me solidly. I was out of condition, but I felt great, with the sweat pouring out of me and my muscles aching in the old way, the way that had given me so much pleasure in the past. We sat together on the terrace of the restaurant having drinks. Members of Roger's staff came up to say hello in a deferential way. I realised that members of my own staff also came up to say hello to me in a deferential way. The breeze was drying the salty sweat on my skin and I wanted to go back to the house and have a shower, but I felt lazily content and I lingered, chatting with Roger. I began to realise that we had a lot in common. We were both men without women, both attached to this Dorado landscape, to the solitary pleasure offered by the bright blue sky, glittering sea and salty breeze that seemed to blow everything else away and dry up other concerns. We both preferred the stark reality of a dangerous nature to the thin joys of everyday human intercourse.

I had lunch with Roger and then he left. I wandered over to the pile of rocks at which the bay ended, the edge of the Saran property. I climbed to a high point on the rocks and sat there watching crabs scuttle between them. The water gurgled in and out of those stones as they had for centuries; pools formed in their indentations, then slowly drained, then filled up with the next wave. I looked at my watch and realised that I had been sitting there for an hour and a half without noticing the passage of time. This was something I had always loved to do since childhood, just sit on a pile of rock at the beach, disturbing snails and watching their reactions, digging at barnacles, scraping at bits of moss for no reason that made sense at all. It was as satisfying to me now as it had ever been. I watched some of the American women from the OAG site in their bathing suits and gave critical remarks on their bodies inside my head. I noticed a pair of pretty young girls among them and wondered who they were. I thought briefly about going and making contact. But I was too lazy. Women were always available, always there for me. They would probably be disappointing anyway. Probably stupid and impressed by the fact that I had money. Nerissa's image came into my head again. She always acted like she was totally unimpressed with me, but she had said she had always been waiting for me. What would happen if I took her up on those words? Would it work between me and Nerissa? Or would I just ruin a good thing? Was I hopeless with women? Too lazy and careless to give them what they wanted? Then I remembered Janet. That had been wonderful. Perfect. But that had been a long time before. I had been just a boy then, not burdened by the responsibilities I now had. Maybe it had only worked because it had been short-lived. But it was good to remember those wonderful times. Nowadays, when I recalled the good times with Anji, bad thoughts inevitably followed. I let myself fall into a daydream about the good times with Janet, the drives through mountainous green landscapes, their beauty heightened by the sexual tension between us. God, how I would enjoy having those times again, now that I knew more about life! I even started thinking about the good times with Sharon. It had been so much fun. Would I ever have fun again? Or would I remain the guy with the business to think about, with decisions that always hung on my mind even when I was supposed to be relaxing?

When I returned home that evening, I felt in some way better. It was as though the sea air had worked some magic on me, dried up some open wounds, made me feel fitter to take up the inevitable burdens of my life. And, in the week that followed, I kept thinking about going back to Dorado the following weekend. I kept that as a reserve weapon in my pocket, like a love letter you keep and touch sometimes for magic.

The following weekend, however, Robin and his cohorts were in Dorado, so I didn't go there. Instead, I went to Lopinot on the Saturday afternoon and sat on a rock by myself, recalling the good old times we had had there before Jason had died, the times with Nerissa and Suzanne and Charlo and Jason himself. Lopinot had changed somewhat. It had become popular with picnickers who did the same as we had done – cook ducks on stones on the bank. It was no longer our special place. Somehow, that was good. It didn't feel haunted; it was just a beautiful, cheerful place. Some guys called out to me and gave me food out of what they were cooking, and I had a couple of drinks with them. These were simple guys, with big bellies and big wives, talking a coarse form of the dialect. I enjoyed their hospitality for a while.

The following week, I had a meeting with Mr Hosein the lawyer who was handling my divorce suit. Robin went with me and we both got a shock. Anji's lawyer one Mr Garcia was demanding financial compensation for the mental damages she had suffered as a result of my 'adultery'.

'Ved can't pay much.' Robin laughed. 'Show Garcia his bank statements.'

There was outrage on our verandah. 'But Anji get a million dollars when she got married!' Madhuri ejaculated. 'She still wants more money from this family? And she never did a thing while she was here. Only sit around like a queen!'

Anji's 'greed' became a talking point in my family. I said nothing. I figured it was divorce-lawyer tactics. Three weeks later, Garcia wrote to Mr Hosein saying it was absurd to claim that my personal financial resources were limited to my bank accounts. Obviously, being the managing director of my family's business implied that I owned property, which property should be divided with Anji. I figured Anji had nothing to do with this letter. She knew I owned no property. I sent copies of the property deeds relating to Saran Enterprises to Hosein to be forwarded to Garcia.

This sort of correspondence dragged on. The next letter Garcia wrote suggested that the ownership arrangements relating to the Saran properties constituted something of a scam aimed at evading taxes. Elderly people paid less tax than young income earners, so it was profitable for the ownership of the company to remain in my parents' hands. This would all have to be fully explored during the divorce proceedings. Robin and Hosein prepared a response, but that only raised the demands Garcia began to make. I had never provided a home for my wife, his following letter stated, which had imposed mental stress on her. That had to be compensated. She had never shared in my income during the period we lived together. I had never supported her, although my financial resources far surpassed hers.

'Mental stress?' Ma commented. 'Anji want some mental stress in truth!'

Anji's name became a constant focus of agitated conversation on our verandah. I kept up my policy of silence. I knew that legal matters involved making threats and demands that would be reduced during negotiations.

Ultimately, Garcia proposed that all the Saran holdings be assessed, my own share determined, and half of this amount be handed over as Anji's divorce settlement.

'Anji really gone mad,' Robin said at home. 'She wants a share of everything – the business, the Dorado property –'

'The Dorado property?' Pa went grey. 'What Anji have to do with my property?'

'According to Garcia, the value of that property is a result of the work her husband put in.'

Pa looked at me as though I had betrayed him. 'But that is the land my father left –'

'What you talking bout?' Ashok asked. 'That is my father land too! What the arse wrong with this woman? She want something she never worked for, she never inherit, she never do nothing to deserve? Anji want a good lash!'

'It's all Ved's fault,' my sister Queen put in. 'He's the one who made Anjani feel she was better than everybody else. He put her up on a pedestal. Now she really thinks she's a Saran.'

'Ved's fault?' Indra interjected languidly. 'You should blame Ma. Who was handing over her precious Jaguar the minute Anji arrived on the scene?'

'And a million dollars!' Madhuri muttered.

The fulminations went on week after week, while the lawyers played cat-and-mouse with their correspondence. Hosein argued that I had supported Anji through university. Garcia demanded documentary evidence of this. No such documentary evidence existed.

'So what support did you provide?' Hosein asked, his brow wrinkled.

'Emotional support,' I said.

He looked at me as though he wanted to laugh.

'It was a lot of emotional support,' I argued. 'I helped her with writing her thesis.'

It was there, I think, that I made a huge mistake with Anji. I believe her pride must have been stung when she saw the dry letter Hosein wrote, claiming that I had contributed intellectual input into her work and career. But I didn't know this until the day of the terrible public showdown I had with her.

This happened at the wedding of Shiva Maharaj, the management-consultant son of Robin's political leader, Sudesh Maharaj. Robin had to take his wife and family, so I went as chauffeur to my parents.

This wedding was a tremendous affair. Everyone who was anyone in the Indian community was there. My sisters doffed their usual snobbish attitude to Indian weddings to be present. I wasn't aware of it, but the bride was Anji's cousin. I had heard this from my sisters at the beginning of the event, but did not pay much attention. It was only when the party of the bride appeared and I began to notice members of Anji's family in the group, that the true dimensions of the situation I was in became apparent to me.

I was hanging out at the edge of the crowd with a group of men near the gate of Sudesh's home, when the bride's party arrived in a large queue of cars. The situation became strained as members of Anji's family greeted me in various shades of warmth or coldness, or simply pretended not to see me. A while later, I noticed Anji's immediate family approaching in a group. Anji was wearing a sari, looking thin and bothered in the garment, as she always did. It looked even more awkward on her now that she had cut her hair so short. I was unsure what to do. Had they seen me? I kept looking at them, waiting for them to make the first move. I saw Beena tug at Anji's sari and say something to her and then Anji looked at me. Then her mother looked in my direction, and the expression on her face was heartrending. She looked scared and desperately unhappy. I tried to summon up a smile and moved forward a bit to greet her.

'Hello, Ma,' I said.

'Ved . . .' She got this desperate, vacant look on her face.

'How you doing, Ved?' Arun asked, holding out his hand to shake mine.

Anji continued walking while the rest of the group paused to talk to me. Beena looked at Anji's retreating back, then up at me, then at Anji's back again.

'How you going, Beens?' I asked. 'That's a nice dress you wearing.'

'I OK,' she said, looking down at her feet.

'How school going?'

'Good.'

Anji had stopped a little way off, waiting for her family to catch up with her.

'We better go and get seats,' her mother said. She looked at me once or twice as though she wanted to say something else, then left to go towards the large bamboo tent where the ceremony was taking place. I remained in the entrance area with my father-in-law and brother-in-law. We made some forced conversation, trying to get back to our old jovial ways together, but it was difficult. Other male relatives joined our group and that made things somewhat easier.

Suddenly I saw Anji storming towards where we were, her mother and Beena trailing in her wake. Arun moved towards her and his father followed. I hovered a little way behind. From the conversation, I gathered that Anji had bumped into my sisters and they had said something offensive to her. She trailed off her story and glared at me.

'Anji, I'm sorry . . .'

'You're sorry?' Her voice was sharp. 'That's always your story. You're sorry. You're always sorry, but you can't do anything.'

'Anji, leave Ved alone,' her mother pleaded. 'He didn't do you anything. He is not his sister.'

Anji turned to glare at her mother. 'He didn't do me anything?' Her face was furious. 'Ved didn't do me anything, Ma? That's what you always feel. Ved is innocent. Ved is an angel just because he have money. Ved is God's gift to your daughter. Ved is God's gift to all women. That's what he feel.'

'Anji, hush,' her mother implored. 'Everybody hearing you.'

'Everybody hearing me?' Anji pointed at her chest. 'Everybody didn't hear his sister inside that tent?' She gesticulated wildly. 'Everybody didn't hear her say that I'm trying to get my hands on Saran money?'

'Shh, Anji,' I said. 'You're making it worse.'

'I making it worse? I making it worse? Your sisters never make it worse? Always making remarks at me the whole time I live in allyou house. Always laughing at me. You think that was nice to put up with? For five years. And me begging you to leave, and you never want to leave from under your mother dress-tail?'

I didn't reply. A crowd was listening, so I decided to say nothing more.

'And now,' Anji moved towards me, 'you have the gall to claim that you were responsible for my academic success?' Her voice took on a note of contempt. 'You don't have no shame! You want to take the credit for work I did? You?' She pointed a finger at my chest. 'Who never even finish high school? Who only know how to count money?' Her lip curled. 'Ved, you will pay for everything you did to me! And everything your family did to me! You will pay with the only thing that means anything to you! Money!'

Her father and brother ushered her towards the street, their car, their home.

I remained among the group of men, stunned by what had happened. Then I caught sight of my cousin Ashok. I told him to let my parents know that I had left and that they should get a ride home from whoever they could.

The next time I saw my lawyer, Robin wasn't with me. I instructed Mr Hosein to give in to all Anji's demands, then went home and informed my parents of what I had done.

'You say you will give her anything she want?'

My father's normal rumble became a screech, like the sound of your car braking when you encounter a dead dog on the highway. I nodded.

'Ved, you gone mad?' he asked. 'What Anji do to get so much of my money?'

'What you going to do with money?' I asked. 'You don't have all the money you could possibly spend?'

'But that is our money! Why she should get it?'

'Because she's entitled to half of anything that is mine.'

That evening, the storm broke on the verandah. 'Ved, you mad in your arse?' Ashok bawled. 'I work in this business night and day, without taking holidays, stick up in Dorado for years, just to hand over money to that blasted skinny little girl without a backside to call her own?'

He ranted and raved. My father joined in. Madhuri started putting in her two bits.

'Madhuri!' My mother screeched suddenly. 'Hush your backside!'

Everyone stared at her.

'And you, Ashok!' Ma shrilled. 'What the arse you always talking about, that land is your father own? What the hell your father was doing with that land before my son went and build house on it?' She paused. 'Eh? Your father was breathing it into he nose-hole, that's what he was doing! Just breathing sand in and out, every God day in that hammock in Dorado. He never get off his kiss-me-arse backside and do a thing for heself! I pay for repairs to his house when hurricane did blow off the roof.' She pointed at her chest. 'I! Me! I, who not working nowhere!'

She glared around at everyone.

'I fed up hear everybody talking shit on my head!' she snapped. 'Allyou giving me a blasted headache. Saran money and Saran property! Where Saran could have ever get money if me and my son didn't make the money for them? Eh?'

And so it was decided that Anji would get whatever the judge ruled she was entitled to. There was deep resentment, but it was no longer expressed on the verandah in open conversation. 'Well,' Robin would just say airily in the office when a cheque came in as payment for one of the projects he had been working on, 'more money for Anji.'

'That woman better hope she never meet me anywhere,' Ashok muttered. 'The kind of cuss I will put on she . . .'

'Cuss?' Robin rejoined. 'It's not cuss Anji want. It's a good cut-arse! If Ved used to put his hand on she, she would have had some respect for the Sarans, instead of taking us for suckers.'

'She could take me for a sucker?' said Ashok. 'You know I mad to send some of the workers to put a good cut-arse on she.'

I was surprised at how much this financial settlement rankled with Ashok. It was Charlo who came up with an explanation. 'What Ashok need is a woman,' he said to me. 'You ain't notice how he getting fat?'

I laughed. 'But you was the one who always say man shouldn't depend on woman,' I pointed out.

'Well . . .' He thought. 'I ain't say Ashok should depend on a woman. Just that he need a woman. I feel he getting old.'

'All of us getting old,' I returned. 'I going back to your original wisdom. Woman is too much trouble.'

Anji's behaviour at the wedding had left me feeling that women were too unstable, too easily given to breakdown. Now, in the evenings after leaving the office, I swam fifty laps in the pool before dinner. Sometimes I went to the savannah in the mornings and jogged three miles. It was nearly two years since Anji had left and I felt I was coming back to my old self again, that the relationship with her was fading into the past. I felt a wrench when I thought about it sometimes, and pushed those thoughts away. There was nothing I could do to revive the past. Let it lie. Let it die. It reminded me of Sharon and the abortion she had had. Occasionally I thought about that, about the age the child would be by now. There was no way to know if I had made the right decision then. That child would have changed my life for ever. But I had made a decision and had to live with it. I realised that, in some way, I had made a decision about Anji and had to accept that my life had to continue without her.

But it became evident that she didn't feel the same. Her columns in the newspaper began to focus on the new Indian party with which my family was now linked. It was a racist party, she alleged. Its leadership had nothing but contempt for the black masses. The party's leader, Sudesh Maharaj, was forced to defend himself publicly, to point to the political programme which contained measures for increased training for unemployed black youth. 'Window dressing,' Anji retorted in her next column. That political party was going to shift funds into the coffers of the Indian business firms that were backing it, she alleged.

'I tell Ved he was doing shit when he give in to her about the money!' Ashok bawled on our verandah. 'Now, she ent satisfied with that. She want to destroy Saran completely.'

'Anji can't destroy Saran,' I replied quietly.

'Anji can't destroy Saran?' Ashok's voice went into a squeak. 'Anji saying Saran's get contracts because of political connections. Our reputation going down the drain!'

'But we do get contracts because of political connections,' I pointed out.

He began to sputter. 'She only know those things because of sitting on this verandah listening to the talk here. That isn't fair. All government contracts are awarded based on political connections. You know how many workers we employ for those new contracts? If we stop getting them, we have to lay off people.'

I shrugged. I was trying to ride out this hysteria about Saran wealth.

But it only increased. In calculating what Anji was entitled to, the lawyers worked out what my share would be worth when my parents died – after inheritance taxes were paid.

Ma hit the roof. 'Forty per cent?' she sputtered, her hands on her hips. 'I have to give the government forty per cent of what I have just because I dead?'

Robin shrugged. 'Well, that's why Indian people shift ownership of their property to their sons while they are alive – so they don't have to pay inheritance taxes when they dead.'

Ma stood stock still and gazed at him. Then she pointed a finger at her chest.

'*I* must put my property in your name so you could put me out of *my* house and turn me into a pauper in my old age? You think *I* is a damn jackass? You think *I* want to land up like de la Guillame?'

I smiled. Mr D's liver had recently collapsed and he had been forced to move to a geriatric home where he could get nursing care. I had informed Ma that Saran's would pick up the bill for the home. She had just nodded. Not a murmur of protest. She seemed to be more concerned about her own fate at the moment.

'Forty per cent!' she muttered. '*I* have to give them thief forty per cent, or end up with de la Guillame? If it wasn't for we, that man would be begging on the street.'

Was Ma softening in her old age, I wondered, or did she just recognise that Mr D was an obstacle to our current progress? He would have been a pain in the ass if he had stayed in that house in Santa Cruz, for we were involved in a massive new adventure there.

Tony Antoine had just landed a huge contract to supply furniture to a US marketing firm and we were extending the furniture factory once again. Tony and I were flying to Ohio to hammer out details of the agreements. The drama between Anji and the new political party only inhabited the background of my consciousness. Then, one day, I had a call from Sudesh Maharaj asking if we could have a private talk. We met at his legal chambers, a crumbling old building in the centre of San Fernando. His office was modest, but there was an air of quiet dignity about the secretary. And Sudesh himself, sitting behind his big old desk in a dark suit, looked as distinguished as usual.

'Ved,' he started, leaning back in his chair, 'we're getting kind of nervous about the talk your wife is stirring up.'

I opened my hands in a gesture of helplessness.

'Is there anything you can do to stop her?' he asked.

I shook my head. 'Anji doesn't approve of your party,' I said. 'She feels it's an Indian party.'

He sighed and rocked on the springs of his chair. 'It's only an Indian party because Indians support it at present,' he replied. 'But our aim is to provide a better future for all Trinidadians.'

He started going into details of his political programme.

'Look, Sudesh,' I broke in. 'That's something you have to persuade the public of. I have nothing to do with it.'

He stared at me in silence for a moment. Then he stroked his curly greying hair. 'I don't think so,' he said finally. 'Your wife is stirring up animosity against us because of our links with your family.'

I shook my head. 'She heard a lot of racist talk among your supporters on our verandah.'

He sighed again. 'Ved, what do you want me to do?' he asked. 'I can't stop them from talking this way. There's a lot of grievance against the black politicians.'

I shrugged. He leaned forward in his chair.

'Don't you realise what a change of government could mean for this country, Ved?' he asked.

I didn't reply.

'And,' he added, 'for your company as well? We will be undertaking a lot of new construction once we get elected.'

'Look, Sudesh,' I said clearly, 'Saran's never depended on the government for work.'

'I can't believe your nonchalance is real.' He laughed. 'You guys put a lot of effort into costing our construction programme.'

It was my turn to laugh. 'You really think any effort went into those costings?' I asked. 'Robin and Ashok just dreamed up those figures in their sleep. They never consulted our general manager, Miss Hosein, who is the real expert in costings. When you come to commission that work, you'll find that the costs will be much higher.'

He thought. Then he said, 'I had my son go over those figures, and he confirmed that they were realistic – if Saran's reduced its wages to the national average.'

'That's a big if,' I said. 'We have no plans in that direction.' I made a move to get out of my chair. 'I can't help you, Sudesh.'

'Maybe not now,' he replied in a mild tone. 'But perhaps later.'

I wrinkled my brow.

'What I've heard from Robin is that you are not really a businessman,' he said. 'He says you think your business is the government, mainly aimed at the welfare of its employees. Perhaps where you really belong is in government.' He tilted his head and studied me. I shook my own head.

'I have never got along with government.'

'That could change.' He leaned forward in his chair. 'Ved, have you ever thought that Robin could be right? That you are more suited to a public function than to private enterprise? That he is the one suited to business?'

Something caused me to pause, to put on my guarded manner, the silence I adopted when I wanted to know more.

'My analysis,' Sudesh went on, 'is that if we take over the government, the area where we will need real expertise is construction. That's where this current government has failed. Look at the roads, look at the infra-structure of this country. Somebody like yourself could be very useful.'

His manner had become a bit fatherly. 'You might be right,' I murmured.

'I know I'm right.' He leaned forward in his chair again. 'Look, your brother wants the business, he wants the money. You don't. Why not give it to him? He and Ashok could take it places it has never been. Your future could be elsewhere.'

I left his office feeling thoroughly confused, and in the weeks that followed, I thought a lot about what he had said. It actually made sense.

Eventually I decided, for the first time in my life, at the ripe old age of thirty-five, to consult my mother about my future. I did so on a weekend when Pa, Robin and his family were in Dorado. Ma and I were alone on the verandah that Sunday evening, so I mentioned what Suresh had said to me. I didn't ask for advice directly, I just waited to hear what she would say.

She said nothing at all. No response whatever. I had expected her to screech that Suresh was trying to manipulate me, that he was talking shit. I had expected her to blow his logic out of the water with a few well-chosen expletives. She just went into the kitchen, got a bowl of rice, came back to the verandah and started picking the rice. I repeated some of the things Suresh had said, emphasising their wisdom. Ma looked at me thoughtfully and pursed her lips. I gave up. I was alone with my decision.

In the meantime, I focused on the business at hand, organising the construction of the new wing of our furniture factory. Prototypes for the new furniture were underway, and we had started a process of testing them among our staff and the American residents in Dorado. That was immense fun, asking people how they felt when they sat in our chairs, what the flaws were in our tables. I offered our office staff free beds so they could test them and we enjoyed a couple of weeks of bawdy jokes. Gobin claimed Nerissa had only tested her bed for sleeping, which was only one of its uses. Nerissa turned purple.

That evening, as I was relaxing in my hammock at home, the image of Nerissa's purple face came back to my mind. I started wondering what her personal situation was at present. She had said on that fateful evening that it was over with Roger Granderson-Powell. Was it? Was there anyone new in her life? We had never talked about private things since that evening. I had become wrapped up in my own misery after that. Nerissa had said she had spent years waiting for me, but she had found the two Rogers to comfort her in the meantime. Had she found a new source of comfort?

Then a new explosion of anger against Anji took place on our verandah. In one of her columns she hinted that the Minister of Justice was planning to abandon the government and join Sudesh's new party. She also argued that US interests in the island would be served if the new party came to power. Hatred of her seemed to harden on our verandah like the concrete foundations of our new factory wing.

I only laughed. 'I don't have time to think about those things, nuh,' I said. 'Me and Tony working night and day on the new factory.'

'I thought that factory was Tony's responsibility?' Robin said.

'That factory going to open up a whole new line of production for our company,' I replied.

'For Tony's company!' Robin snapped. 'Tony is the one going to make the money from that deal. And Saran's financing it.'

'Tony only makes fifteen per cent of the profits,' I returned. 'We make eighty-five per cent.'

Robin laughed. 'Ved, admit it. That was a stupid deal you made with Tony. Saran's takes all the risk involved in that furniture factory, and Tony makes profit. You see how Tony lives? Big house in Santa Cruz, swimming pool, everything. Tony playing golf these days.'

Suddenly my blood boiled over. 'Why the arse you don't stop talking shit?' I growled. 'This company was built on the Antoine talent for making furniture! If it wasn't for Mr Antoine, we would be nowhere now!'

Ashok sucked his teeth loudly. 'Before Mr Antoine get involved with Saran, he was catching his arse to sell two bed and three dining set a year. The man hardly had a pair of khaki pants to his name! Tony was working for a little measly salary! How come Tony gets a share of Saran profits when I don't get a share, Ved? I does be running from project to project, from Sangre Grande to Moruga. How come Robin don't get profit-sharing? He bring in all the new work into the company.'

'Every employee gets a share of the profits,' I said lamely.

'Every employee?' Ashok was hoarse now, shouting at the top of his voice. 'We get the same as the loaders in the lumber-yard.'

'Look,' I said, 'you and Robin accepted jobs with this company, just like I did. You agreed to work for salaries.'

'That was when it was a small company!' Ashok gesticulated wildly. 'I help build this company, but I have no say in the organisation. You control that.'

'Well, actually,' Robin's voice was, as usual, reasonable, and tinged with a kind of humour, 'the Board controls the organisation. It's the Board that should examine whether the current organisation is suitable.'

'The Board?' Ashok's voice became a squeak. 'The Board does rubber stamp anything Ved do. Everybody know Ved is the dictator in Saran's. He appoint Nerissa general manager without the Board knowing anything about it. How Nerissa could be general manager of a construction company when she don't know a fart about engineering is beyond me.'

Suddenly I really lost my temper. 'Ashok, you could kiss my arse, you hear!' I snapped. 'If you don't like the organisation of the company you working for, you could leave! I could always find an engineer to replace you.'

I stormed off, only glancing at Ma as I passed her. I wondered if she realised that I knew what she had done the week before. I had only stumbled across her actions by accident in some papers sent to her by our lawyers. Ma had transferred all her property to my name.

We had built the new factory on a slope on the Santa Cruz hillside next to our old one. At its front, we constructed a large plate-glass showroom to display pieces for international clients who came to place big orders. We called in Charlo to landscape the area. This turned out to be a large job: we needed to shift the gate and the driveway so that the new showroom would be the entrance to our whole compound. All our buildings in Dorado were completed and Charlo merely had to oversee maintenance there, so he went to town on designing the grounds at Santa Cruz, planting lawns and palms and flowering shrubs and installing a fountain. He got carried away and began sprucing up the other buildings, the storage sheds and offices.

One day, he asked me to go with him to Mr de la Guillame's abandoned house. I had imagined that we would demolish it, but Charlo pointed out that it had been built of tropical hardwood and the basic structure was good. We only needed to refurbish it and it would be spectacularly beautiful, sitting on its rise in the valley surrounded by giant immortelles with their waxy red flowers. But what would we do with it? Create another showroom? A clubhouse for the employees? It was too fragile for that kind of use, Charlo said.

Suddenly I thought that I would like to live there. Tony and Bernard lived nearby in big concrete houses with huge lawns and gardens; the Santa Cruz Valley was a wonderful environment for bringing up children, with its fresh-water streams and wooded hillsides. As Tony said, it was the safest place in Trinidad, locked in at two ends by narrow mountain roads that made it difficult for bandits to escape the scene of their crime. If my mother would ever agree to leave the Croissee, I thought, this house would be perfect for us. But I knew better than to bring up that suggestion at present. I wondered if I could move there alone, get away from the arguments on the verandah. But I realised I would turn into Mr de la Guillame. I would have to get a few dogs and my father's old shotgun to keep me company, and develop some eccentricities.

I put off the decision as to what we would do with the house. Maybe I could talk my mother into moving there at some later stage. In the meantime, the extension of the compound became so impressive that Tony decided to hold a grand opening, a reception to unveil the new furniture we had designed for the US market. He asked Nerissa to handle the arrangements and the next thing I knew was that our Dorado chef, Pierre, had been drafted in to prepare hors d'oeuvres. I started to hear of plans for flying in all kinds of French-sounding stuff on one of OAG's helicopters. The reception began to snowball into a major PR pappy-show.

Tony had invited the Minister of Trade and Development to speak, but Nerissa had also invited officials of the US embassy. The next thing we knew was that the First Secretary of the Embassy was calling Nerissa to say the US ambassador wanted to say a few words at our reception. He invited her to a meeting to discuss protocol.

'Maybe he wants Washington to see that he's making something of his posting in this little backwater,' I surmised.

Nerissa shook her head. 'The Yanks want to get more involved in Trinidad. Anji embarrass them by saying they on the Opposition side, so they trying to do things sneaky.'

The issue came up again the following weekend when I played tennis with Roger Granderson-Powell in Dorado.

'I had a very sticky meeting with Frog-face this week,' he said, referring to the current Prime Minister. 'He wanted to know if there was truth in the Press reports that US interests in the island were backing the Opposition. I told him we were strictly neutral.' Roger laughed in an ironical way.

Once again, I felt, I was getting mixed up in larger politics, in everybody else's ambitions. 'I feel like a pawn,' I said to Charlo.

'A prawn?' he replied. 'Boy, you know how long you's a prawn? Mind you ain't find yourself covered with cocktail sauce, yes! Them fellas will eat you up so fast and then start looking for something for their main course. I realise, from working up in Dorado with these Yankees, that we is nothing more than hors d'oeuvres to them.'

It was such a joy to be talking nonsense with Charlo again, to be planning some major silliness like a Grand Opening, that I myself went overboard and invited all of Saran's employees. I even agreed to buy new uniforms for Symphonia's members, who were going to play all night and turn the event into a major fete. Robin shook his head sadly at the waste of money.

'Allyou don't know if any furniture going to sell,' he pointed out one evening on the verandah. 'Allyou only supplying a few pieces on consignment.'

'Americans don't have no taste!' Ma snapped. 'Next thing you know they will really want to buy all that shit Ved and Tony does make in that factory.'

Charlo and I smiled at each other.

'And imagine the boldface-ness of Miss Nerissa Hosein!' Ma said. 'She send me Invitation to this stupidness! Read this! Saran's Enterprises would be honoured to have the company of Mrs Chandrawattee Saran at the presentation of its new export product-line!'

'So you not coming, Ma?' Charlo asked.

Ma placed her fists on her hips. 'Mr Charlo . . .' She paused meaning-fully. 'Have I ever, in all my born days, ever attended any of the stupidness you and Ved does hold? I don't want to be there when some of your furniture break off and fall down on all them people head. You think I don't remember them Carnival costume you used to build who head used to break off in the savannah?'

The two of them started arguing. I was surprised at how animated Ma was. I realised that Ma, too, had missed the old times quarrelling with us all – with Charlo, with me, and, when she got an opportunity, with Nerissa. She piled Charlo's plate with food, flakes of paratha roti and stewed chicken. He protested at the quantity, but Ma insisted on adding curried chataigne to the heap, brushing aside his objections with the same scorn she had brushed away every idea we had ever had. Charlo's presence in town had brought with it a party atmosphere that added to our anticipation of Tony's Grand Opening.

I saw Robin glance at Ashok a couple of times. No one could enjoy this nonsense unless they had been part of our early adventures. It was a parody of old times. We were playing ourselves, the selves we had been in the early days of the business, when our Grand Openings had accompanied major investments. Now, we had become our own Carnival figures, drawing from the legends and myths we ourselves had created. Robin finally got up heavily, said something about going to a meeting with his politicos, and he and Ashok left.

They returned later that night. Robin looked worried. Ashok was expostulating, as he was often doing these days. I gathered from their conversation that the politicos were worried about the effect of Anji's latest revelations. The Minister of Justice was now afraid that Frog-face would pre-empt his resignation, find an excuse to fire him instead on grounds of corruption, and so destroy his reputation.

'So it's the corrupt firing the corrupt for being corrupt,' I remarked.

'Ved, what you think?' Robin asked. 'Politics is a tea party? You think it's one of them Carnival band you and Charlo does be organising in the name of business?'

'It really sound like a Carnival band,' I returned. 'Robbers and imps and king and queen.'

*

On the day of our Grand Opening I was, of course, in a fury of activity. We worked all morning at the factory putting the finishing touches to the arrangements, and I went to the office in the afternoon to see to any urgent business that had cropped up before returning to Santa Cruz for the evening reception.

'Anji called for you this morning,' my secretary said while briefing me. 'Twice. She wants you to call her back.'

This was the one day I had little time. And I couldn't afford to get upset from a conversation with Anji. I needed to present a good figure at the reception that evening.

'Did she leave a number?' I asked.

My secretary shook her head. 'She asked you to come to her house. She said it's urgent. She sounded very upset.'

I looked at my watch and sighed. I could run up to Anji's house before going home to shower and change for the reception, but I was very sweaty. I had been helping Charlo and the others to mount some big decorations all morning. I didn't really feel up to another showdown with Anji.

When I rang her bell and she came to the door, I was surprised at her appearance. She looked worse than I felt. Her face was thin, somewhat haggard. She was wearing a loose dress in plaid cotton that hung around her body. I vaguely recalled the first occasion when we had met, when she had wished to discourage any interest on my part.

'What's the matter?' I asked.

She stared at me as though she was seeing a ghost. I was both mystified and slightly alarmed. She moved back into the house and I followed her.

'Is something wrong?' I asked.

She went over to the sofa and sat down, her dress dangling between her thin knees, her hands twisting over each other nervously. I perched on a big chair nearby.

'Ashok came here last night,' she said.

'What did he want?'

She looked down at her lap. 'Ved,' she said, 'he abused me in the worst of ways.'

I went still, waiting for details. Anji looked really distressed, very nervous.

'He accused me of using confidential information to build up my own career,' she murmured.

After a short silence, I collected myself and leaned towards her. 'Don't worry about Ashok, Anji,' I said. 'He is only vexed because you are getting in the way of their political party.'

She looked up at me appealingly. 'I only write what I think is right,' she said in a small voice.

I nodded. 'Don't bother with Ashok. If you write in the Press, you must expect to get people vexed.'

She looked down at her lap again and then up at me. 'So you don't think the same way Ashok does?' she asked in her small voice.

I laughed. 'You ever know me to think the same way as Ashok?'

'He said I'm trying to destroy Saran's after I bleed them of money,' she said.

I smiled at her. 'And you didn't answer him back?' I asked. 'I never know you not to have an answer for anybody.'

She broke into a weak smile then. 'Of course I answer him back!' she said. 'I put him in his place. That's why he got so vex. He started shouting at me and I put him out. I tell him get out of my place.'

Somewhere back in my mind I recalled her doing the same with me. But I pushed the thought away and concentrated on the business of the moment.

'I could see him getting vexed about that,' I said.

She smiled at me some more. 'He was furious!' she said. 'He said he sorry you ever make him fix the doors to this place. It would have been better if somebody come in here one night and teach me to keep my arse quiet.'

I laughed. 'And what did you say?'

She looked down at her lap again and was silent for a long time. 'I told him it's a good thing I have a decent husband who care about me and not a hooligan like him to think things like that.'

There was a long silence.

'I abused him back, good and proper,' she murmured. 'He said you was a blasted fool who let me walk all over you. I told him he was a jackass without a grain of sense in his body, who always trail after you, taking advantage of your ideas. I told him he always talking about Saran's, but it's you who build Saran's up and he just trying to get the benefit of your work . . .'

She looked up at me.

'It went on and on, Ved. He got madder and madder. He looked like he wanted to pick up something and hit me. He was shouting and I shouted back. I think all the neighbours heard us. He say something about Robin and that really started me off. I think I went crazy. I said Robin was a pompous son of a bitch without any character, trying to steal the business from his brother. That none of them have any talent. The only one with talent was you. And that's why they did their best to break us up.' Tears formed in her eyes and started running down her face.

'Don't cry, Anji,' I said, leaning towards her. 'Don't cry.'

She turned her face into the backrest of the sofa and sobbed quietly. It broke my heart. I got up, went over to the sofa and stroked her thin shoulder. She turned towards me and buried her face in my neck. 'Why it can't be as it was before, Ved?' she mumbled. 'Why it can't be?'

I stroked her hair. It felt thin, that straight, spiky hair, the contrast reminding me of Nerissa's thick, wavy hair on that fateful evening when I had comforted her the same way.

'Ved,' Anji raised her tear-streaked face, 'you think it could ever be the way it was?'

I looked at her face, demanding sympathy, demanding comfort and understanding from the old Ved, the Ved who had taken care of her to the best of his ability, and had lost her when that ability was not enough. But part of my mind was on the Grand Opening that needed to be opened shortly.

I think Anji saw my hesitation. Something crept into her eyes, some form of understanding, some uneasiness and loss of confidence. 'Ved?' she said.

I pulled her back to my chest to avoid seeing the plea in her eyes. She wrapped both her arms round my neck. I stroked her thin hair. Then she removed her arms from round my neck and slipped them around my middle, under the T-shirt I wore.

'I missed you so much,' she murmured.

Her hands felt good on my back, those slim hands I had remembered for so many months. Her mouth was kissing my collarbone, then my neck. Then she raised her head and reached up to kiss my mouth.

'No, Anji,' I murmured.

She moved her hand down to the waistband of my trousers.

'Don't seduce me, Anji . . .'

'Why not?'

'Because I don't want it.'

'That's what you're saying,' she teased. 'That's not how you're feeling.'

Suddenly, in spite of the spark of temptation I felt, I was irritated with her lighthearted attitude. I pushed her hands away. 'I'm really busy today.'

She shifted slightly away from me and looked at my face, her own beginning to close down. 'You always busy,' she said in her accusatory tone.

'It's true,' I said. 'We are opening a new branch of Tony's factory and I should be on my way there all now.'

She stared at me, hard. 'You don't want to make back up, do you?' she asked.

'I don't know, Anji,' I muttered.

Her face slowly shrank. She began to look scared, helpless. It was a look I recognised, the look on her mother's face.

'I'll come back later on and we'll talk about it,' I said.

There was a flicker on her face, but the scared look remained. I noticed again how thin she looked. I rose and adjusted my clothing, waiting for her to see me out. When she made no move to do so, I glanced at my watch. It was getting really late. 'I have to go now,' I said. 'I'll see you later, OK?'

She kept her eyes on me without moving. There was nothing else to do but turn and leave.

Somewhere deep inside me, I knew, as I drove home to dress, that I didn't want to make up with Anji. Now I can face that. I can accept, now, that I was a person who never wanted to say 'no', who shrank from uttering harsh truths, who took refuge in silence and the superficial confusion in my mind that I expressed with 'I don't know'. But at a deeper level, I knew what I was doing. I was being propelled by my instincts towards the point later that night where I would, once again, let one thing lead to another.

As I drove down the St John's hill, I briefly tried to summon up an image of myself living with Anji at Mr D's old house in Santa Cruz. But what instantly came to mind was the twist of her mouth at the thought of living in an old slave-plantation estate house. She would sneer at the nouveau-riche aspirations of Tony and Bernard's wives. She would find it imprisoning once again to be ensconsed in a Saran compound. She wanted real freedom from it all. She had tasted that freedom in that little rented apartment in Santa Margarita, quarrelling with politicians, making trouble and feeling abused. I pushed away the decision.

I had more urgent things to deal with, anyway. 'That beard does make you look like a hooligan!' Nerissa had said that morning. 'These is Americans we dealing with. You have to wear a suit this evening.' So I hurried to shower and get dressed in the suit Anji had made me buy for the restaurant opening in Dorado. I trimmed my beard and stared at myself in the mirror. Was that the look the Americans would like, that tall, dark-suited man? I thought I looked reserved in the costume, like someone who held himself apart from his employees. But I was someone apart from my employees, I concluded. The costume just reflected the reality.

When I arrived at the factory with my father in the Jaguar, guests had started arriving and the steel band was playing inside.

'Ved! You have me making excuses for you all this time!'

I almost didn't recognise Nerissa. She was wearing a loose, flowing trouser suit in deep-blue velvet, and her hair was pinned up on the top of her head so curls cascaded forward. 'Nice outfit,' I said, reaching out to finger the velvet of her sleeve.

She looked into my face, her dark eyes dancing. 'You like it?' she asked. 'Your mother's seamstress make it for me.'

I smiled. 'It's very nice. You look wonderful.'

She stepped back and swept her eyes over me. 'You ain't looking so bad yourself. Nobody wouldn't recognise you in that suit.'

'Thank you, Miss Hosein.'

'Now get your arse inside!' she snapped. 'Any minute the ambassador and the minister will reach.'

I joined Tony and his father in the reception line. Mrs Antoine was wearing a major hat and flowered dress. Robin was chatting with some of the more distinguished guests, looking more distinguished than them all in his Savile Row suit with a red handkerchief protruding out of the breast pocket. Finally, the minister arrived and we trooped into the factory. Symphonia launched into the national anthem and I stayed absolutely still. I was on the podium and had to set an example for the employees. Then the speeches started, the inevitable hypocrisies of such an occasion.

'We are delighted to see a Trinidadian company making inroads into the American market,' the ambassador intoned, glancing at the few Press representatives there as he launched into a political speech. 'We are hoping that this will be the start of a new series of developments. We see a huge future for Trinidad as a partner of US free enterprise.'

It all went off fine. Not a hitch. We had finally conquered the art of

Grand Openings. Once the dignitaries had done their thing and left, Symphonia began playing calypsos and fete exploded. Tony's wife was wearing a long, complicated dress with so many straps Charlo wondered if it had come with an instructions manual, while I wondered how she could possibly walk on the eight-inch stilleto heels of the shoes she wore. But she suddenly let loose with a spate of wining that left the factory employees open-mouthed. Then she dragged her husband into the centre of the dancing.

'It's time for me to go home,' Pa said.

I couldn't leave, so I started looking for Robin and found him at the edge of the party talking to Ashok. Robin said he intended to leave early, so I handed Pa over to him. Then I found myself accosted by Thomas, the big man from the lumber-yard whom I had taken to the hospital years before, when he was injured. He was with his wife and son. 'You remember this boy, Ved?' Thomas asked, indicating his son, now a tall guy of about twenty-two. 'He was in short pants when I started working here. He used to come and help in the factory on Saturdays. I used to tell him he have to study hard and work hard like you.'

The boy had just graduated from university with a degree in engineering. 'You outdo me,' I laughed. 'I don't have a degree in engineering. I always wanted to do one too, but I never get the time.'

'Yes, but you didn't have to go to no university,' Thomas said. 'You could have teach them in the university! You always had brains coming out of your back pocket. Look what you turn this place into! When we started working here, all we had was a few cocoa-house and bush. Mosquito used to bite we when we working. Now it looking like heaven self!'

The words were echoed over and over as I chatted with other workers. It was the first occasion that so many of us were together, and there was a lot of self-congratulation. I drifted from one group to another, taking drinks with them all, and my mood began to blur into a general feeling of well-being. I found myself embraced by a massive arm. It belonged to our store-manager, Suzanne, who had got immensely fat over the years. While she held me fast round the middle, she started moving to the music. 'Why Nerissa don't ever take a rest?' she shouted into my ear. 'That girl don't know how to relax and have a good time.'

I looked in the direction she was indicating. Nerissa was giving instructions to the waiters. Everybody else had given up trying to control things, was eating and dancing and talking, but Nerissa was still at work. I made my way over to her.

'Why you don't ease up on yourself, girl?' I asked.

'How I could ease up?' she replied. 'All allyou gone on strike! Tony, Charlo, all of allyou drunk. I have to keep an eye to see everything go OK.'

I tilted my head and looked down at her intently. 'Well, I have to inform you that everything not going OK,' I said.

'What not OK?' she demanded.

'You ain't dance with me yet,' I said, putting my arm around her shoulder and starting to move in time with the music.

'Ved, you stupid, yes!' she exclaimed.

The blue velvet was deliciously soft and springy under my arm. I steered Nerissa into the mass of dancing people. Then I reached out with my other arm and grabbed Suzanne again. With the two of us moving to the music, Nerissa had to dance as well. I began to feel good, really good, with the two girls of my youth in my arms, moving to the music of our band, celebrating the years together. Nerissa extricated herself from my embrace and moved slightly away. I reached towards her and put both arms around her velvet-clad shoulders.

Some time later, she slipped out from the dancing mass again. I searched for her and found her outside one of the side doors of the factory, fanning herself. We were at the loading ramp, a wide stretch of concrete that ended in a little parapet. Nerissa moved towards the parapet and sat down. I perched beside her. She stretched her arms and shoulders wide.

'You're tired?' I asked.

'A little bit,' she said.

I was tempted to offer to massage her shoulders, the way we had done in the early days of the store. But I dared not.

'Everything went well, eh?' Nerissa said.

'What you expect?' I replied. 'You organise it.'

She looked at me and smiled. The coloured lights we had strung outside reflected on the roundness of her cheeks and made them gleam. Her velvet outfit took on a dark, mysterious softness, and the waves in her hair shone like the sea at Balandra.

A desire crept over me to scoop Nerissa up in my arms, really cele-brate our triumph, hold that mysterious velvet closer than I had held anything in my life, bury myself in it. I didn't care whether Nerissa had another man, whether she had other plans, whether something would change in the future. I just felt I had paid my dues and deserved to enjoy the moment. I dared not, of course. We sat for a while in silence.

'Nerissa,' I said into the cool darkness, 'you know what you want out of life?'

'How I will know that, boy?' she murmured. 'I does take one day at a time. If that day go good, I does be satisfied and hope the next day will go good too.'

I looked down at her, trying, in a half-deliberate way, to seduce her with my eyes. 'So there's nothing you really wish for?'

'Ved, what you asking me?'

'Just that. You don't have no wishes?'

Her eyes suddenly took on a pained look. 'Ved, what you trying to do?'

I reached out and brushed a curl from the side of her forehead. 'I not trying to do anything,' I said softly. 'I just asked you a question.'

'Why you don't ask your wife that question?' she replied, putting on an impatient tone. 'Ain't you went by her today?'

I held onto my poise. 'I don't ask my wife that because I don't want to know my wife's answer,' I said. 'I want to know yours.'

Her face took on a defiant look. 'Yes,' she said. 'There's something I wish for.'

I held her eyes and waited.

'A child,' she said softly.

I went still, very still, as I usually did when confronted by the unexpected. 'I thought you always said you had a child,' I replied. 'Me.'

'You kind of grow up,' she said. 'You don't behave like a little rascal again. I miss the rascal. I figure I should get a little rascal of my own.'

I studied her face for about a minute. I felt that my whole future hung, for that minute, in the balance. Then, with great deliberation, I slid an arm around her shoulder. 'Well,' I whispered in her ear, 'I only know one way to make that wish come true.' I kissed her ear.

'Ved, what you doing?'

There was pain in her voice. I became determined to erase it. I kept hold of her, pushing aside the border of soft, wavy hair with my chin to kiss the back of her neck.

'Ved, this not going to work.'

'When we ever do anything together that didn't work, Nerissa?'

Now that I was breathing in the scent of her body, I couldn't let her go, couldn't let Nerissa slip away again. It was just too delicious to have her in my arms, that velvety body which promised so much, the dissolution of questions I had asked myself for many years. It was like letting yourself go with the surf at Dorado, giving in to the tide that had hypnotised you as you sat on a safe rock in Balandra.

'Ved . . .' Her breath was sweet. The scent imprisoned me in longing. Her full lips looked melting from this distance.

'Nerissa,' I pleaded, 'you don't know me long enough to trust me?'

I tried to make everything happen in those next few minutes, to dissolve all the boundaries we had built up between us for so many years. When I looked into her eyes again, the silvery reflection of the moon in their depths was like the gates to heaven.

We were interrupted, of course. Someone came to the door, peered out and went back inside. We had to return to the party.

Chapter Fifteen

When I got home, the birds were singing. The sky had just started to clear. It was that mysterious, shadowy moment when streaks of violet-blue and grey appear and gradually grow brighter.

As I turned into the driveway to our house, my heart took a leap. There was a police car parked in my usual space. What the hell! Hurriedly, I parked and leaped up the stairs to the verandah, where the whole family was gathered with two policemen. My eyes shifted from my mother to my father.

'Where have you come from, Mr Saran?' one of the policemen asked.

I glanced round the group, trying to read from the faces what had taken place. 'From a party at our factory,' I said. 'What's happening?'

'Your wife was shot at 2 a.m. this morning,' the policeman said.

'Shot?' I repeated blankly.

'Yes, killed,' he said.

Killed? My head filled up with cotton wool.

A burglar had entered Anji's apartment during the night, the policeman said, and shot her three times in the chest. The neighbours had woken with the noise, and had glimpsed a figure running to where a car was parked further down the hill.

I had to concentrate hard to get the sense of his words. It was like there was a delay between what he was saying and what I was hearing, like when a film's soundtrack is out of sync. I reached for something to lean on and found the balustrade.

'Her parents?' I asked.

The policeman nodded. 'They know,' he said.

I rested my face in my hands, imagining Mrs Gopaul's feelings, Beena's feelings, Arun, Mr Gopaul. There was something hard in my stomach. Anji had lived through this before. She had suffered this terror before . . . I don't know when I began crying. I just felt that my face was wet. My head grew cloudy. I reached for a chair and sat down.

Later the news was announced on the radio and Charlo turned up at our house.

'You will carry me to Tacarigua?' I asked.

We drove to Anji's parents' house in silence. There, the horror and grief was terrible. Arun's face had dissolved into bits of red flesh. Mrs Gopaul was tossing and whimpering on her bed, surrounded by relatives. Beena was sitting on the floor of her mother's room, her face a picture of bewilderment. Her father was on the porch staring into space, not speaking to anyone. I stayed the whole day. In the evening, a pundit came and people began singing devotional songs in the living-room. I sat among the men on one of the sheets that had been spread on the floor. At some stage, I recognised my mother across the room, and briefly wondered who had brought her here.

The next day the newspapers were full of Anji's death. Apart from everything else, she was something of a public figure, one of their columnists. My private affairs were once again dragged before the public, the fact that Anji and I were separated and were in divorce nego-tiations. I was consumed with guilt. If I had never married Anji, her parents would never have had to go through this. She wouldn't have ended up in that apartment alone. Beena wouldn't have to go through what she was now going through. If I had behaved differently, maybe things would have worked out between us. If this, if that, if the other, if, if, if . . .

I signed documents Nerissa gave me at the office without really reading them. I looked at Nerissa, and saw the woman I had wanted so much, but whom I didn't want to touch now. I shook my head, trying to clear it, trying to think of something to say to her, but no words came.

At the funeral, I looked at Anji's body in the coffin and saw what I had seen at Jason's funeral: beauty, but dead beauty. I came back home feeling empty, absolutely empty. I had tried to make Anji happy, tried to make things work with her, but had failed. I should never have married her. If it hadn't been for my cleverness, she would never have had to go through two robberies and end like this.

For two weeks afterwards, relatives gathered at the house in Tacarigua in the evenings to listen to a pundit read from the scriptures. 'Life and death cannot touch you,' the pundit intoned, translating words from the *Bhagavadgita*, 'for the spirit is beyond life and beyond death.' His words soothed, but later, during the day, I saw Anji's slim young figure in my mind's eye and felt guilt and loss again.

'I feel like I ruined her life,' I said to Nerissa. 'It would have been different if she hadn't married me. If she had got involved with some-body else, she wouldn't have been living alone . . .'

'You can't change what happened, Ved,' Nerissa replied, her eyes taking on the look of immeasurable pain they sometimes did.

An item appeared in a newspaper saying that the police were unsure whether there had been any attempt at robbery. There was no sign of a break-in at Anji's flat: all the burglar-proofing was intact; the lock on the door was undamaged. Anji may have known her attacker, may have let him in. I remembered the guy I had seen at her flat. Maybe he had come that night and they had quarrelled over her attempts to make up with me. But the following day the newspaper reported that the police had ques-tioned a male friend she had had. He was married, it turned out, and his wife had testified that he had been in bed with her on the night of the murder. The whiff of scandal inflamed the Press. One of the newspapers broke the story that divorce negotiations between myself and Anji had been hostile, that Anji had been demanding a huge financial settlement. They interviewed Anji's neighbours, who told about the angry scenes between us. Anji had thrown me out several times, they said, the last time being the evening before she died.

I grew furious. Lies! These newspapers habitually peddled lies! Anji hadn't thrown me out. Then I remembered that Anji had told me she had thrown Ashok out of her flat that evening. The neighbours probably saw his car, an identical white station-wagon to mine, with the Saran 'S' sten-cilled on the side, and had concluded that it was me. Once again, I was under suspicion of murder by the Trinidad population, this time of my wife. The papers rehashed the old charge I had faced; they described the Saran business empire. We were the financial power behind the burgeoning new political party, they said.

When I went to my in-laws' house in the evenings now, I wondered if they shared the newspapers' suspicions. The shock was still fresh and they all looked numb. The relatives had always looked at me a bit warily, even when Anji and I were together. Then, I had accepted it as part of the price of being rich. Now, I wondered what they were saying behind my back.

'That girl dead and she still causing trouble,' Robin commented.

The police came to see me again. 'According to our records, you own a gun,' the sergeant said and asked me to produce it. He then observed that my gun used the same kind of bullets as those found in Anji's body.

'Half the guns in Trinidad use those same bullets,' Ashok said dismissively. 'The robbers does rent guns like that up in Laventille. The forensic department will show that that gun wasn't fired for a long time.'

The sergeant's face took on a guarded look. Ashok was probably right. He was usually right about things like this. He made it his business to know all that was going on at every level of society. But the police still asked me to come to the station to make a statement. That caused sensational headlines. I was confirmed as the chief suspect in the case.

'That girl can't even dead good,' Robin said when we read the newspapers the following morning. 'She was always a troublemaker.'

I couldn't bear these kinds of comments. I felt that we were a big part of the reason Anji had ended up in a flat on an isolated hillside by herself – although I had done my best to secure the flat. Mentally, I went over what Ashok had said to me when he carried out the work. Had Anji left the door unlocked somehow? A thought struck me. I had said I would return later. Could she have left the door open for me? Or thought that the person at her door that night was me? Could she have let the killer in because she was expecting me?

Later that day, Ashok called me at the office about some problem that had cropped up on one of the building sites. One of the workers had defied him, and he was spitting mad over it. 'I was mad to let the other workers put a good cut-arse on him, yes!' Ashok said.

All at once, I recalled him threatening to do the same to Anji. My skin went cold at the memory. He had said to her that he was sorry we had secured her apartment so thoroughly that no one could get in. The only person who could get in there, in fact, was me, because I had the duplicate key.

It was a good thing the police didn't know that, I thought. Perhaps I should hide that key more carefully. I opened the top drawer of my desk and searched among the miscellaneous items it contained. I couldn't find the key. I took out my passport, my driving licence, a rubber stamp, a pair of socks, a packet of tissues, a couple of little gifts people had given me, a Rubik's Cube, and piled them on the desk. The key was not at the bottom of the drawer. What had I done with it? I racked my brains, but couldn't remember taking it out.

At the end of the two weeks, there was a ceremony at my in-laws' marking the end of the first period of mourning. The men of the family were required to go to a river, have a ritual bath, and be shaved by a barber. We went to Lopinot, where Jason had died, to the dappled shade of the bamboos and the clear pools of water.

Arun was the first to be shaved. He sat on a chair we had brought for the purpose and the barber set to, shaving first his face and then his scalp. When the barber finished with him, he looked like a different person. His scalp was white, totally exposed. The barber shaved Anji's father as well, and some of her uncles and cousins, trimming their hair very, very short, down to a stubble. Gradually, all the men of the group became transformed. They looked a bit like fledgling birds. I went to the barber's chair and sat down. The barber examined my beard and assumed a wry expression. He sharpened his razor and moved close to me.

For the first time in my life, a razor touched my face. It felt cold from the water of the river. Then I felt it scrape my skin and the blade began to tug at the hair. It was painful, but I tried not to wince. I sat still and felt part of myself coming off. My face grew gradually lighter. Then the barber cut the hair on my head. I watched as curly black hair dropped all around my feet, nestling in the stones of the river. I reached up when the barber was finished and ran my hand over my head. It was prickly with stubble.

When we got back to Anji's house, people didn't recognise me. There were exclamations over the way Arun looked, but everyone had to stare at me for a while before realising it was me.

'Ved, you look so different!' Anji's mother said.

I felt different – cleaner. I sat with the other shorn men at a table in the garden and we ate a simple vegetarian meal. Suddenly, I could taste again. I asked for a second helping of curried chataigne.

But as I drove back to the Croissee, a terrible feeling of anticlimax came over me. Was this it? Would Anji's family just have to get used to the horrible thing that had happened? Would the police never find her killer? There had been suggestions in the newspapers that the murderer could have been a contract killer. Anji had been disturbing a lot of people, including even the US authorities in Trinidad.

I went to my office and shut myself in. But I couldn't work. To do something, I went through all my desk drawers again, looking for the spare key to Anji's apartment. It was nowhere. I went to the outer office and searched in a key cabinet that hung on the wall, but all the keys there were labelled neatly with the names of our building projects. I asked my secretary if she had taken out a bunch of keys from my top desk drawer.

She shook her head. 'I don't ever go into that drawer. I know you does keep your personal stuff there.'

I scratched my shaved face. 'You're sure?'

'The only time I remember going into that drawer recently was to put back your driving licence,' she said.

I squinted at her. 'To put back my driving licence?'

She nodded again. 'Yes,' she said. 'It was on the floor when I went into your office, so I put it back.'

'When was that?'

She shrugged. 'About three weeks back.'

I returned to my office, sat in my chair and propped my face in my hand. Only Ashok knew that I had put that key there. Could he have removed it? Was Ashok capable of hiring a killer, supplying him with a gun, and sending him to kill my wife? The thought was mindboggling. I thought about his knowledge of Trinidad's underworld, about his posture of being as tough as the toughest of the lowlife. I thought about the scorn he displayed towards everyday concepts of morality.

Late that afternoon, when I went over to the house, Sudesh Maharaj and his son were there. They all greeted me with jokes about my changed appearance. I felt irritated. Didn't they understand that this wasn't a subject for jokes? The usual political chatter was taking place, the usual good-humoured talk. It put me in a foul mood. They were all so happy, so totally unconcerned about what Anji's family was going through. They were probably relieved that Anji was dead, relieved that the Sarans wouldn't have to part with money in the divorce settlement, that Anji would no longer write troublesome articles about them in the Press.

I went down the stairs to the swimming pool and caught sight of my reflection in the water. It was a shock. That guy with the short hair and smooth face could be anybody – a clerk in a government office, a young accountant trying to fit in with the world, trying to look socially unthreatening. That wasn't me, that wasn't the rapscallion I was accustomed to thinking of myself as. In the neat white shirt I had worn to the ceremony that day, I was just a young businessman, a new person. I recalled Nerissa's judgement that I had grown up, I was no longer a rascal, and suddenly I really didn't want to be a rascal any more. Anji's death weighed on my shoulders. I decided to keep on shaving, to inflict that discipline on myself as some means of atonement for Anji's death. I would try to be less reckless in the future, to keep in mind that death could result from the smallest slackness.

There was an explosion of laughter on the verandah. I glanced up and saw Ashok standing in the evening shadows, gesticulating. I could understand, now, how Anji's neighbours had taken him for me on the night before the murder. We had the same curly hair and beard, though I was taller and he broader. I sat studying Ashok. He dressed the same way I did, in light-coloured cotton shirts and dark trousers. I thought I also recognised something very similar in our stance, in our way of walking and moving. Perhaps it came from growing up together. I had learnt a lot in my childhood from Ashok; perhaps I had unconsciously imitated him or he had imitated me, or both. As I watched him, it struck me that if Anji could take anyone for me, it would be Ashok. He even had a similar voice.

Then I recalled that he also had a similar gun. I shook my head. What was I thinking? Ashok had a terrible temper, but he wouldn't go up to Anji's house at that hour of the night with the express purpose of killing her. He could perhaps hit somebody in anger and kill them, but he wouldn't do it so deliberately. It was absurd to believe that Ashok would take such a risk. I had read too many detective stories.

When Maharaj and son left, I went upstairs. 'I want to ask you something,' I said to Ashok. 'Do you know where the spare key to Anji's apartment is?'

An irritated look came over his face. I was spoiling the party mood. 'How I will know that?' he asked.

'You saw where I put it and now it isn't there.'

'The amount of keys it have in that office, it must be get mixed up with them.'

I shook my head. 'No,' I insisted, 'it didn't get mixed up with any other keys. But it's missing now.'

'The amount of junk you have in your drawer,' Robin put in, 'that key must get lost.' His voice was reasonable, tinged with humour as usual. I turned towards him.

'How you know what in my drawer, Robin?'

Robin shrugged. 'I must have gone into your desk to find something . . .'

Something about his remark was unconvincing, but I couldn't put my finger on it. It irritated me still further, this dismissive attitude, this posture that Anji's death didn't matter.

'Well,' I said, 'I think I should tell the police about this missing key. Perhaps it's how the killer got into Anji's apartment.'

Ashok half-rose from his chair. 'Ved! What wrong with you, boy? You going to go and tell the police that we had a key to Anji's place? That will focus more attention on us!'

'What you mean, *us*?' I asked. 'There's already attention on me.' I shrugged. 'It would be better if the murderer is found.'

'Ved, that girl really turn you stupid!'

They started pleading with me to be reasonable, and I began to enjoy their discomfort. The more they talked at me, the more determined I was to wipe the comfort and contentment off their faces. I wanted them to feel something for once, some guilt and shame that we, with our quarrelling and arrogance and greed, had caused unimaginable grief to Anji's family. 'Ved, you gone mad?' Ashok's voice cracked. 'Why you want to create more trouble? You don't find Anji create enough trouble when she was living? The woman was a bloody pain in the ass! Who care if she dead? She always thought she was better than we. Good riddance to bad rubbish, is what I say!'

That got me angry. 'I am also going to tell the police that you own a gun just like mine,' I said. 'That you went to Anji's house and quarrelled with her the night before she was killed. That you said you were sorry we had secured her apartment so no one could get in –'

Ashok's eyes were almost all whites in shock. 'What the fock wrong with you, Ved?' he bawled. 'You take leave of your senses in truth?'

My father stared at me from the rocking-chair in which he sat. 'You will really do that?' he asked.

I became very, very calm. 'Yes,' I said. 'You think I want Ashok around me if he had anything to do with Anji's death? You think I want him working with me?'

Robin fumbled in his pocket and lit a cigarette. 'Well,' he said, 'if you have those suspicions about Ashok, maybe Ashok shouldn't continue working for the company.'

'What the arse!' Ashok turned wildly to Robin. 'You selling me out?' he croaked. 'Because Ved come up with some cock-and-bull story, you focking ready to sell me out?'

Robin opened his hands in a gesture of reasonableness. 'Ashok, you could get a good job anywhere. You are a good engineer with a lot of experience.'

Ashok got up from his chair and rushed over to Robin. 'You focking son of a bitch!' he hissed. 'You think I going to leave this company after all I put in it? Well, you lie! I will tell them who really take that key out of the drawer. If you think I going to cover up for you, you mad!'

There was a silence. Ashok remained leaning over Robin's chair, his chest heaving.

My vision went blurred. I couldn't seem to keep track of what was going on. My brain seemed suddenly to have lost power, like a gadget whose batteries are dying.

'Ashok!'

It was Madhuri's voice. Dimly I watched her move towards Robin's chair as well. Then she stopped, put her hand over her mouth and leaned against the dining-table. I noticed big tears start to roll from her eyes, but felt I had missed something, like bits of time were skipping out from my consciousness. Madhuri was propping herself up with one arm against the dining-table, her round face turned into a ball of red dough. I myself seemed to have a kind of vertigo. Had I heard right? Was I making a mistake about what Ashok had said? I felt I couldn't hold myself up straight, so I leaned against a pillar and put my hand up to my eyes.

When I removed it, Robin was a little distance away, his back turned to us, staring over the verandah rail. Ashok was in a lounge-chair, his face like thunder. Madhuri was crying at the table, her face in her hands. Pa's face had crumpled into a streak of shadows. I looked around for Ma. She was still standing at the kitchen door, suddenly looking very small. Her face had turned an odd bronze colour and had contracted till her eyes seemed to shrink into nothing.

'I have to go to the police . . .' I muttered.

A sob emerged from Pa's direction. 'Ved . . .' he muttered. 'Son . . . don't do that. Don't do that, Ved . . .' Tears were streaming from his eyes. He looked like a dingy old rag, like a helpless old beggar. I felt something inside me shudder.

'You expect me to go on just so?' I heard myself asking. 'Allyou expect me . . .' my voice broke, 'to just let these two kill my wife and get away with it? To continue working with them like nothing happen . . .'

I felt tears on my own cheeks. I reached for my handkerchief and put it to my eyes, then heard Ashok's voice mumbling something.

'Ashok, shut your arse!' I heard Ma screech. 'If Ved don't want to work with allyou he could fire allyou! Ved could do what the hell he want! So you just hush your arse right now!'

With my face in my handkerchief, all I heard was Pa and Madhuri sobbing. 'I begging you, son . . .' Pa said. 'Don't get involved with the police . . .'

My mother made an impatient sound with her mouth. 'It wouldn't help nothing,' she snapped. 'Ashok will blame Robin, and the police will say Ved was involved too.'

Somewhere, in the far reaches of my muddled brain, I realised that she was right. My mind was too cloudy to think things through, but Ma's words were like the ray of light you see in religious pictures streaming out of Jesus's body. I looked up at her. Her face was closed tight. It was like all her flesh had turned to leather. She looked like the mummy I had once seen in a museum, perfectly preserved, refusing to degenerate after hundreds of years had passed.

At the verandah railing, Robin had turned around to face us. He was quiet and serious for once, a big, handsome man with greying temples and an air of distinction. This was the man I proposed to throw into prison on charges of murder. If he was convicted, he would be sentenced to hang by the neck until dead.

'After you work so hard, Ved,' Pa mumbled, 'you going to throw it away like this? I's a old man . . . I wouldn't last long again . . . Everything is yours.'

I raised my handkerchief to my eyes and noticed that my hand was shaking. I felt that everything inside me was shaking, that I couldn't control my body. What were they saying, my mother and father?

I needed to sit down and moved towards a chair. But when I got to the chair, I couldn't sit down. I swerved to the left, but then I was at the top of the stairs. I stood there, my back turned to the others, perched like a bird over the garden, like a suicide threatening to jump from a building. I knew that sooner or later I would have to turn around and face my family on that verandah, that verandah where everything took place, that verandah I had been proud of designing with Charlo. I would have to involve myself in the discussion of what to do now, how to cover up what had happened to Anji. I couldn't bear to do that.

I put a foot down to the stair below. I moved to the next step, then to the one below it. I continued going down the stairs, those stairs I had built with Charlo so many years before. That felt better – movement, movement away from this monstrous conversation. I got to the bottom of the stairs, turned and started walking down the driveway. Moving the large muscles in my legs made me feel stronger, steadier. I picked up momentum and found myself at the gate.

The gate was locked.

I hit it with the flat of my hand. Then I balled up my hand and hit it with the heel of my fist. I hit it again, harder, then began pounding against the secure, heavy steel with both fists like a prisoner, again and again and again. I felt there was something theatrical about this, something of a child throwing a tantrum, but for once I didn't care. I could throw a tantrum if I wished. I didn't care about caution any more, about hiding my feelings from the gaze of others. I put all my weight behind the blows, all the momentum of my shoulders and upper body, like a boxer using a punching bag.

Suddenly, the gate swung open. Somebody had pressed a button upstairs to open it. I went through the archway and found myself in the cool cheerful night air of the Croissee. I was now facing our beautiful glass-enclosed furniture showroom, with our suite of offices upstairs, the offices where my brother had taken the key to Anji's apartment from my desk drawer and given it to a hired killer to eliminate her from this world. I felt hemmed in. At my back was the beautiful Saran house, at my front was the headquarters of the Saran business empire. I turned to the left and walked blindly towards the corner. Then I turned and moved towards the lights of the Eastern Main Road, towards the commonness of the rest of the Croissee.

It was a shock to me to encounter everyday life, the evening lights, normal voices and behaviour. It made me feel dazed again. There were cars going one way and the other on the main road. I leaned against one of the pillars holding up our store to try and clear my head. But suddenly I couldn't bear its touch either. I started walking, just walking, away from the Saran building.

Epilogue

That was a long time ago. Seventeen years ago, to be exact. Seventeen years since I walked away from the Saran building.

It was a sort of revolt, I suppose. But revolt is ultimately futile. To do anything serious, you need a plan. And I had never had a plan, had lived my life just letting one thing lead to another. What was I really thinking that evening when I walked away? Nothing, really. My mind was just going in circles, imagining my brother plotting Anji's murder, then veering away to Anji herself, to my familiar efforts to imagine what she felt that night when she confronted a murderer in her apartment. I had tortured myself with these imaginings every night as I lay in bed, but now something was screaming at the edges of my mind. It was I who had exposed her to this, I who had kept a key to the apartment, I who had underestimated the greed and anger of my own family. I was a careless fool, a dangerously careless fool.

I kept walking. Stopping would mean deciding what to do with my thoughts. But eventually my feet started to hurt. I looked around and realised I had got to St Joseph. If I walked another mile, I would get to the rumshop in Curepe where I had drowned my thoughts many times. But these thoughts were probably unquenchable. I might start babbling them out, just to get rid of them.

I perched on a culvert at the side of the road and became hypnotised by the lights of cars flowing to and fro in the warm tropical night. Then a group of noisy guys began to congregate around the culvert as well. I recalled that Charlo and Cassandra had rented a house at the top of St Joseph's hill. If I could make it there, I could rest. But it was dark on that road; I could get mugged. I turned and started walking up the hill. Anji had got mugged in her apartment even though I had barricaded it. Barricades don't work. As I plodded up the hill with my head laden, I almost wished I would get mugged. It would be nice to hit a mugger, again and again and again. It would also be nice to die at the hands of said mugger.

I don't know what Charlo's reaction was to my walking into his house late at night. I didn't care. I just plonked myself on a chair in the verandah. He sat in another chair muttering things, but I couldn't really concentrate on what he was saying. I could see stars in the sky, pinpricks of light beyond the shadows of trees. Could one of those stars be Anji? What if the Hindu notions of reincarnation were right and Anji were born again, on another planet, on one of those stars, perhaps? I felt like waving at the stars. Hello, Anji! Anji, I'm sorry. I'm so, so sorry. I hope you're in a better world. You are a star yourself. You should be a star.

At some point, Charlo disappeared. At some further point, my star-gazing interests waned and the couch in the living-room began to look appealing in a fuzzy sort of way. Horizontal would be a nice position to be in, I felt.

The next thing I knew was bright morning light splitting through my head. Why the hell did Charlo never want curtains? Then his voice started rumbling at me from above the couch. Nerissa had been calling in panic. No one had turned out to work that day – no one from management, that is, not Ashok, not Robin, not me.

'Nary a Saran is to be found in the Saran company,' Charlo said cheer-fully. 'Your mother say Robin and Ashok resign.'

I turned my head into the cushions on the couch. 'Go to hell,' I said.

'You better tell Nerissa that,' Charlo replied.

But, of course, when Nerissa called again, I couldn't say that. Her voice contained the puzzlement and anguish I often saw in her eyes. I muttered some suggestions about what she could do, and then took a draught from a cup of coffee Charlo had been holding out. It was scalding hot and I burnt my mouth. That kept me a bit occupied as Charlo led the way to his van, talking about arrangements to cover the gaps left by Ashok and Robin's absence. And then we were driving off into the breezy hilltop morning through the smell of giant trees. Then there was the familiar hard odour of traffic and we were on the Eastern Main Road. And soon enough, there was the familiar Saran building, looking somehow strange now, like I was just a passer-by in the Croissee. And then we rounded the corner and were parking at the side of the other Saran building and I kept my glance away from my parents' residence across the street, just followed Charlo into the building and up the stairs to the office.

And work just took over after that – stop-gap work, crisis manage-ment, Charlo and Nerissa making suggestions about how to handle all the building projects and me nodding. All the while I kept having a sick feeling in my stomach, like when you've eaten something bad that isn't bad enough for you to vomit it up, but you can't digest it.

And, in no time, it was nightfall again, and I had spent the day shoving the thoughts about my brother into the back of my mind. But I wouldn't go home. I would stay in the office and confront these thoughts head on. Make a decision about what to do. Summon the resolution to go to the police.

'Why don't you come by me and eat something,' Nerissa said. 'You didn't eat anything all day.'

Her eyes looked like tombs in her face. Tombs, I swear. Ancient tombs without any light, carved into a hillside somewhere in the Old World.

I shrugged. It was no use refusing. Nerissa wouldn't go without me.

We ended up on her verandah after dinner with a bottle of scotch. I took one drink, then another, then a third. And then her mother was showing me the spare bedroom at the back of the house, beyond the bathroom and kitchen, telling me the sheets were clean, and giving me a towel. I looked around me, dazed at where I had got to. My gaze settled on the face that was raised to mine. Mrs Hosein stretched her arm and patted my shoulder in an awkward gesture. She was short and could barely reach my shoulder, but she kept patting and tears suddenly sprang to my eyes. That hand, belonging to this square, squat woman who had once sold vegetables in Tunapuna Market to raise her six children, seemed to penetrate the cotton wool in my head. I sat on the bed and felt it sink as she sat beside me. Then I felt her arm around my shoulder pulling me to her massive bosoms, and her voice murmuring, 'Ved, oh, Ved.' She stroked my bristling scalp and then said the fatal words, 'Don't cry, son.'

And I was lost. I couldn't control myself at all. Mrs Hosein and Nerissa quietly left the room and, when I came to some kind of consciousness again, the house was quiet. They had both gone to bed. I went into the shower and tried to wash away the tears. When I returned to the spare bedroom, I felt empty and weak. My limbs felt shaky, like I had had a fever. I lay on the bed in my underpants, wondering if I could really sleep. And then there was nothing: unconsciousness, total, dreamless unconsciousness.

I woke to sunlight and warmth and the chirp of birds, and a breeze blowing the silky curtains at the window. I heard a knock on the door and Nerissa's voice. And then there was breakfast to confront: fresh roast-bake and eggplant chokha, saltfish and plantains and tea. Nerissa's mother bustled around, not saying anything about my breakdown the night before.

'This evening I cooking cascadoo,' she said, looking at me. 'You prefer paratha roti, or sada?'

I was silent.

'Paratha,' Nerissa put in.

'I asked Ved,' her mother said. She placed both fists on her hips. 'What does go better with cascadoo, Ved?'

'Sada,' I muttered.

The day was full of tumult, with all these loose ends in the company and the lump still in my stomach making me feel I was only halfway present. By evening, I was relieved to have somewhere to get away from the chaos, so I drove with Nerissa back to her modest house in Tunapuna and consumed two cascadoos with pigeon peas in curry. Then Nerissa's mother stuck a bowl of chopped fruit in front of me and nagged me to tell her if that wasn't the sweetest mamee-sepot I had ever eaten. I began to feel drugged. Between my stomach and my mind, I didn't know which felt heavier. I just collapsed on the couch afterwards, listening to Nerissa's mother talk about some quarrel that had taken place that day in the neighbourhood. I tried to follow her story, to enter into her lively life while my own remained suspended.

There was a complete void of information as to what was going on across the road from our office, and I didn't want to enquire. I was just presiding over the chaos in the business till I summoned up the clarity to go to the police.

The next day I told Nerissa's mother that I would go and sleep at Mr de la Guillame's old house after work. It was perfectly restored, and empty, and mine. Why was I imposing on other people?

'And tell me,' Mrs Hosein demanded indignantly, 'who going to eat all that crab I buy yesterday?' She turned and waved away my protestations. 'Boy, take it easy, eh!'

So I put off leaving for another day. And, after the crab, there was a giant breadfruit that demanded urgent consumption before it started to ripen. And living in Nerissa's modest house became a kind of holiday even though my workload was so heavy. It was a pause in my life, a temporary relief from care and watchfulness, a welcome interlude.

The house was the sort of two-storeyed structure normal people built in Trinidad, a house on stilts. Downstairs, Nerissa parked her car and her mother washed clothes, killed crabs and giant breadfruit, and carried out the other unsightly household chores. The real living quarters were upstairs: a small living-room full of Saran furniture, three small bedrooms dominated by silk bedcovers from Thailand, and a small kitchen decorated with expensive Italian tiles that I recognised from Tony Antoine's stock. The Saran furnishings gave the place an air of grace and comfort. It was like a cottage in a movie, like the place Doctor Zhivago found Lara in after trudging through tons of snow in a dissolving world. But here, instead of snow, there were fruit trees all around, a pomerac laden with deep fuchsia blooms, a huge chennette, a wandering plum with knobbly, speckled branches and little oval leaves in an almost liquid green. At the back, sunlight presided over a vegetable garden where plump aubergines in hues of violet dangled among red tomatoes and yellow peppers.

I enjoyed the modesty of it all, the practicality, the lack of ambition. Although, as I discovered, there was a lot of ambition involved – but small ambitions, like acquiring a dishwasher, or repairing the fence. I heard the history of the house and its contents from Nerissa's mother; how Nerissa had entered into a mortgage arrangement to purchase the land when she had been promoted to store manager, how afraid Mama was that, if Nerissa lost her job, they would be left in debt. How they got another mortgage with Nerissa's next raise and began building the house. Nerissa's mother revelled in the drama of every detail. She wasn't afraid of the past; she loved it. She was totally open, and totally proud of her daughter's climb out of poverty.

I looked at Nerissa with increased admiration. This beautiful, dark-skinned woman who moved like a girl had determinedly, inch by inch, created a life while I was creating a company – a vast, mythical thing that seemed to me now to have no real meaning in the world. I felt that Nerissa had really lived, had lived in touch with the earth, while I had merely existed in a sort of fantasy. But when I said this to her, she laughed at me.

'Most of my life take place in the Saran building,' she said. 'I does only come back here to eat and sleep. Saran's is my life.'

And I felt humbled. This company that I had always despised, had felt so humiliated to run, had been the source of life for numerous people. For Thomas, whose son had gone to university as a result, for Charlo, who had been released from the ephemera of creating Carnival characters, even for poor Jason, whose mother had ended up with joyous memories of her son. Anji had despised the company, and I had despised myself for running it. For me it was a sort of game. But for Nerissa it was dead serious. Her achievements at Saran's were the source of her self-esteem. Everyone in the neighbourhood respected Nerissa because of her position at Saran's. She drove a white car with the long snake of an 'S' on the side, indicating that she had real status. And it wasn't just the money or the status. Saran's was her identity, almost her child – although she had said on the night of the party that she wanted the real thing.

I had never touched her since that night. Things had just turned tragic in my life after that, and I had had no zeal to involve myself in romance. And now I couldn't lay a finger on her while living in her mother's home.

I didn't ever see my own mother, or the rest of my family. Nerissa kept in contact with Ma and sometimes gave me news of them. The Saran Board seemed to have dissolved that night when I walked away from them. Charlo, Nerissa, Tony and I were just left running the company. The Sarans became like absentee landlords, like those slave owners in our history who remained in England living the life of the gentry while plantation managers grew sugar cane for them on islands like Trinidad.

Gradually, I became content to let it be so. If I went to the police, who knew what would happen? I was necessary to keep things humming in the office, to keep Nerissa and the others content.

But contentment doesn't last with me. After about three weeks, my old, old devil began to awake again. Nerissa's closeness disturbed me. Seeing that beautiful figure go into the shower, observing her in various states of dress or undress . . . Well, it created the urge to touch.

'I really think it's time I move to Mr de la Guillame's place,' I said to her one night after her mother had gone to her room.

She didn't reply. I took it as acceptance, and went to bed. But I couldn't sleep. I kept imagining how the future could be if I weren't living here. I could invite Nerissa out to dinner, I could wine and dine her, I could invite her over to Mr de Vertenil's house . . .

Late that night, I got up and wandered out to the living-room, then noticed that the door to the front verandah was open. Nerissa was out there, sitting in the darkness.

'What's the matter?' I asked.

For once, she looked small and pathetic, sitting with her knees drawn up on a lounge-chair, gazing into the dimness with her big, frightened eyes. I went closer. She straightened the house-dress she was wearing, a flimsy cotton thing. The light from the streetlamps created shadows around her breasts.

'Nerissa?' I perched on a chair near to her. 'You're not feeling well or something?'

She shook her head.

After sitting in silence for a little while, I reached out and touched her hand. She didn't stir. Her hand was surprisingly small and soft. In my mind, Nerissa was like one of the electricity wires that power the whole place, but her hand felt fragile, like the hand of a child.

'Ner?'

She hung her head. I leaned forward. I could smell the soap she had showered with, mingled with a warm human odor.

'I suppose I feel sad that you want to leave us,' she murmured.

'I don't want to leave you, Nerissa,' I said.

She looked at me but I couldn't really see her eyes in the dimness.

'Ner . . .' I shrugged, figuring the only thing to do was be totally honest. 'Ner, I'm not a polar bear.' I hesitated. 'I can't live with a beautiful woman like you without having certain feelings.'

Suddenly I saw a slight glimmer in the darkness. Nerissa had opened her mouth. She was smiling. I began to feel silly.

'I does feel like you does lock me into my deep-freeze in the night,' I said.

The smile broadened.

I started stroking the palm of her hand. Then I stroked her arm, then her shoulder . . .

And with that, a spark came back into my life again. With Nerissa's mother safely in bed, I could have her in my arms again. I hadn't had a woman since Anji left me, and it was like a new discovery, like riding a bicycle again after many years. You know what to do, your instincts are sure, but you've forgotten the total softness, the sweetness of intimacy.

I pushed away the thoughts of what had happened to Anji, the sense that my whole life had amounted to nothing but calamity, the shame of my silence about the murder, my doubts about whether I was a worthwhile person after all. And soon we gave up pretending to Nerissa's mother that I was just a refugee in her house. Actually, it was she who gave up the pretence first, started referring openly to the fact that Nerissa's sleeping quarters had shifted to the spare room at the back of the house. I simply became Nerissa's man, a tall, light-skinned guy who accompanied Mama to the market on Saturdays, carrying her basket and enduring the stares of her former colleagues, the other vendors. 'I didn't tell you I got married again?' Mama would answer when people asked about me. 'It's about time,' one of them said.

Mama and I became really good friends. She taught me to cook. Nerissa wasn't interested, but I hung around the kitchen in the evenings while the Indian radio programme blared out Bollywood hits, and eventually I learned all Mama's little culinary secrets.

And somehow I found myself developing a new interest in life. I had got wedged into this modest little setting and grew fascinated with the small things that happened in the neighbourhood. People lived with such fervour in that part of Tunapuna. If the electricity company started cutting down trees to clear the wires, it was a big talking point. How would they survive without the tamarind tree at the corner? Everybody had been using those tamarinds to make pickles for as long as they knew. What would happen to the mongoloid girl down the street who had started having her period and showed signs of sexual need? Was the old lady on the other side going to die today or tomorrow? And when she did, who would inherit her house?

A few months later my own father died. I had heard a while back from Nerissa that he was sick, but I couldn't bring myself to go and see him. The habit of shutting out the people who lived across the road from our office had turned rock hard. I entered the big Saran gate for the first time on the day of the funeral. Elections had just taken place and Robin had been named Minister of Justice, so there was an element of celebration in the gathering. I stood at the back while people fawned on my brother. I went up to my mother, and we stared at each other, saying nothing. There was nothing to say. Ma had a public face on, an expression of irritation, like she wanted everyone to leave. I looked at Pa in the coffin, and quickly turned away. I could feel eyes on me, eyes feeding on the prodigal son, the one who had been banished from the big-shot Saran family, who lived in a modest neighbourhood in Tunapuna with a Muslim woman. I retreated as far back as I could. People spoke to me briefly, but Robin was really the focus of attention. He was the one who had made the Saran name, the name that implied power in Trinidad now. He and Ashok, who was head of Town and Country Planning and sat on the boards of several state companies. I was just the quiet one, the somewhat-disgraced younger brother who ran the business, who made the Saran money.

I accepted that role. With Pa's death, the entire company was mine. But, of course, a death causes you to review the life of the person who has died, and your own as well. Was this all that my life would amount to? Living in a modest house in Tunapuna with two wonderful women and running a big business?

Fortunately, at that moment my efforts of the past months bore fruit, as I put it to Nerissa. She was pregnant, and smiling a wonderful smile.

'You want to get married?' I asked.

I couldn't help smiling back at her in those days. It was like a light had been switched on in Nerissa's head, a Christmas tree light that changed the atmosphere all around her, bringing joy to the world and peace on earth.

She shrugged.

I preferred not to get married. There had been so much fuss about my marriage to Anji. But if Nerissa wanted marriage I wouldn't deny her.

The question was left unresolved. Instead, I started nagging that the three of us should move to the house I owned in Santa Cruz. The valley was safer for bringing up a child, I argued. The huge Saran compound was fenced and had security guards. After some persuading, I got my way.

The move brought tranquillity. The greens of the surrounding valley, and the blues and violets of the hills and mountains beyond, were soothing after a day in the office. The creaky wooden house felt like a link to my childhood, to the time when Trinidad and I were innocent, or as innocent as human beings ever are.

My child was born with only smiles and laughter inside her. And my world was transformed. I don't know what it was, but from the moment I glimpsed that little wrinkled shred of humanity, tears popped into my eyes and I was lost to myself. I became only Gita's father.

I preferred her to have her mother's last name. I blathered on about the security risks of having a child linked with the Saran fortune, the possibility of kidnapping and so on. But I think Nerissa understood that there was more to it than that. So she came up with the name of the Hindu book she had seen me excited about many years before, the book that was still in my office, the book that had guided Gandhi's struggle for Indian independence, the *Bhagavadgita*. We agreed that our child was to be called

Gita Hosein, a combination of the Hindu and Muslim backgrounds of her parents.

What a joke that is! Gita was always so much herself, so unblemished by any religious or cultural tradition, that the whole question was always moot. If Gita is anything, she is like a reflection of Anji. I have never said this to Nerissa, but since Gita turned six, I began to observe this resemblance. She was the sweetest child who ever lived before that; laughing, curious, immeasurably affectionate. She would climb into my lap as I sat on our wide wooden verandah in the evening, place her face against mine, and, every now and then, give me a little kiss. There is nothing sweeter than the spontaneous kisses of a little girl, I swear. Nothing like that to make you feel worth something.

But once Gita started growing out of her baby fat, different aspects of her personality started developing. Maybe this is the way girls are now: sharp, demanding, full of assurance that the world is theirs. They acquire concepts in childhood we never had, concepts they seem to breathe in from the air of this so-called information age. 'So I don't have any rights?' I remember her demanding at age seven when I imposed some rule on her in the kitchen. 'We need to talk,' she announced, turning away. 'In the living-room.'

I swore she would end up as a lawyer.

Before Gita even learnt to read, she would study books intently, trying to work out what they were saying, and then implore me to explain them to her, bursting into tears of frustration if I didn't have the time. Between that and television, she acquired a lexicon of slick come-backs. She would nag me incessantly to explain my behaviour, and, if I refused to do so, nag me again. 'You think you're my psychiatrist,' I said to her once. 'You always want to know why I do everything.'

'And how do you feel about that?' she asked, with an air of serene objectivity.

And when she hit puberty, living with her became like living with a conscience outside of you, one that opens its big mouth at awkward moments. I guess a teenager doesn't know that her parents have uncertainties, that her big, strong father, ruler of a business empire, is, inside, a quivering mass of jelly hoping only for her love. For Gita's sake, I settled into the life of a powerful businessman in this society, put aside all thoughts about running away from Trinidad, going to the US, going to England, going somewhere where I could start again, be the person I was meant to be, not a man who just makes money. I hungered for that little girl's smile, the light of delight in her face. But once Gita started getting breasts she evolved into an argument machine. Sometimes I think she is my mother all again, my mother who died quietly in her sleep eight years ago. Sometimes she is my mother and Anji rolled up in one. She has Nerissa's big eyes and shadowy skin, but I swear that child inherited my mother's brain.

And when she was fourteen, one of my secrets came out.

I had picked up Gita from school one afternoon and brought her to the office to wait till either Nerissa or I had finished our work and could take her home. We often did this after Nerissa's mother died and there was no adult at home in the afternoon. Nerissa had a visitor in her office that day, and Gita was supposed to sit at a table in the reception area and do her homework. But half an hour later, I noticed she wasn't there, and went looking for her. I found her standing next to her mother's chair posing for a Press photographer.

'What's going on?' I asked.

Nerissa introduced me to a young reporter, a girl called Niala Maharaj.

'I'm doing a profile of Miss Hosein for International Women's Day,' this Miss Maharaj said to me. 'Few women penetrate the glass ceiling in big business –'

'So why are you taking a picture of Gita?' I asked.

'Well, a mother who manages to juggle a career and bring up a child as well . . .'

This Miss Maharaj – another Anji-clone with dishevelled hair and clothing – had constructed a whole myth around 'Miss Hosein', Saran's general manager. She never even thought of asking who the child's father was.

I left them and went to my own office. The following Sunday, Gita leafed through the newspaper. But there was no article about her mother, no picture with her in it. She pondered loudly about what must have happened. I took no interest.

The storm broke the following day. I was on a building site, and when I returned, I found both Gita and the young reporter in Nerissa's office. Miss Maharaj was in a state of fury. Her article had been killed without any explanation. 'The editor said he was acting on instructions from senior management,' she stormed.

'Well, it's not important,' I said.

Her eyes flashed at me. 'Not important? A role model for women who want to make it in business?'

I shrugged. 'You can always find another model and write another story.'

She pointed her finger at her chest. 'Me?' she asked scornfully. 'Not me. I told the editor what I thought about him and walked out. Spineless ape. Can't stand up to the big businessmen who own the paper. By now, I must be fired.'

She started on a harangue about freedom of the Press and democracy and all that stuff.

'Look,' I said, 'I'll talk to your editor. I'm sure you'll get your job back –'

'To write only what they want?' she interrupted me. 'What do you think I am, a PR stooge?'

Later, when we were driving home, Gita brought up the subject of the girl's article again. All the talk about freedom of the Press had made an impression on her.

'You should really talk to the editor,' Nerissa said to me.

'The girl says she doesn't want to work there any more,' I said.

Nerissa laughed. 'Of course she wants to work there,' she said. 'The girl just confused. And it's you who caused this.'

'Why you saying Dad caused this?' Gita demanded.

Nerissa just glanced at me and shut up. But Gita wouldn't rest. She insisted on an answer to her question.

'I told the *Sentinel* I didn't want a story in the paper about your mother and you,' I said finally.

Gita bent over her mother's seat to stare at me. 'So because of that they didn't print the story?' she asked.

'Well,' I said, 'I have some influence.'

Gita's long, untidy plait hit me on my face as she retreated to the back seat. I swear Gita's hair has a life of its own. That curly hair she inherited from me seems to connect more directly with her brain cells than the rest of her.

'So what did you say to the editor?' she asked later, at dinner.

'I didn't speak to the editor.'

'So who you talked to?'

'The chairman of the Board.'

'So you just have to say that, and they wouldn't print the story?'

For days she kept coming back to the issue. 'So why you didn't want a story about Mummy in the paper?'

'I don't want people talking about us.'

'So since when you care? You always tell me I shouldn't care what people say.'

That was a reference to the fact that Nerissa and I weren't married. When Gita asked about that I always said we had forgotten to get married. We were too busy with work. She had liked that attitude; Gita loved the fact that her parents were somewhat different, that we created our own little world among the trees and flowers of our Santa Cruz Valley and ignored the customs of everyone else.

But now she was puzzled. 'So you know the managing director of the *Sentinel*?' she asked a week later.

'I know everybody in Trinidad.'

She fixed her gaze on me. 'You don't know Cheryl's father,' she challenged, mentioning a school friend.

I laughed. 'I don't want to know Cheryl's father,' I said. 'Cheryl don't want to know her father. Cheryl's mother doesn't want to know Cheryl's father. The police don't even want to know Cheryl's father . . .'

She glared. She hates not getting a straight answer.

And eventually, under all the 'So's', the truth came out. I was practically the owner of both national newspapers. In the early years of Gita's life, I had steadily bought shares in the Press until I controlled the majority, and had made it known to the newspapers' management that I wanted no mention of Ved Saran in their pages. It was just an exercise in caution, to prevent them raking up the old talk about Anji's death.

But Gita knew nothing of Anji. Gossip fades quickly if it isn't fed. I had always worried that, one day, someone would tell her that her father had been suspected of his wife's murder.

Now, however, she began to accuse me of something else. 'So you could decide what is printed in the paper, just because you have money,' she observed some weeks later, her head tilted thoughtfully so the stray hairs created a little halo in the sunbeams. 'You don't find that's a kind of corruption?'

My heart sank. I never wanted to be associated with corruption.

I began to figure that Gita's doubts about me were due to the little puzzles in our existence: why she didn't carry my last name; why her mother and I weren't married, why I had no contact with my own family.

She saw my brother's picture often in the paper. He was an important man now, deputy leader of the ruling party. He's an ass, I always said in answer to her queries. He's a pompous ass, I said when she pressed.

But flippancy doesn't really cut it in life. At some stage, you have to share with those you love the complete contents of your heart. I had to explain to Gita about Anji's death. If I started that story, though, I would end up in a purgatory of cross-examination and psychoanalysis. Gita knew me as a person who had a certain power and stability. She didn't know the uncertain boy who had started the process that led to Anji's destruction.

And where did that process begin, anyway? I began to puzzle over this question.

One morning, as I was sitting in my office, gazing out the big plate-glass windows at the Croissee, I realised that the space I now occupied had once been the mas' camp that had so captured my imagination as a little boy. It was where I had wanted to be. Gita could never imagine the Croissee back then, I thought. She herself knew it as a corner dominated by the glossy plate-glass of the Saran buildings. She couldn't picture the little concrete houses that had once taken up this space, she who had been brought up in upper-class comfort in the leafy Santa Cruz Valley. I started jotting notes in the intervals between work, playing with words that could bring the whole past alive, trying to find the links between the words. It turned into a continuing exercise, one that drew me back whenever I had time. The pages started piling up. I thought, maybe, if I could get the whole thing down, I could give it to Gita and stave off her inevitable questions. But my memories grew more and more chaotic. Eventually I decided to try to construct a straight narrative.

And, while I was discovering that I was writing a whole, big book, Gita turned fifteen and began to seek answers from another. She found my old, tattered copy of the paperback that bore her name, the Juan Mascaro translation of the *Bhagavadgita*, and started puzzling over it. I saw her with it on the sofa in the living-room one day, her brow wrinkled as she turned the yellow pages.

I realised she couldn't possibly get a grasp of that book without some background, since it is, in fact, the climax of a vast epic called the *Mahabharata*, the longest poem in the world. So I sat next to her and began giving her a potted version of the ancient legend.

'Two sets of brothers – sons of brothers and hence cousins – had rival claims to rule a mighty kingdom,' I explained. 'But the oldest of one of the sets of brothers has a gambling problem, and ends up losing everything he has, even his wife, to his cousins . . .'

Gita stared at me, her eyes round, her hair seeming to stand to attention. 'Now that's a jackass!' she said. 'He sound like Cheryl's father.'

I was stymied by her instant judgement. Potted versions couldn't convey the full human drama of the original, but the *Mahabharata* is comprised of over a hundred thousand couplets, so what does one do?

'He was young . . .' I smiled entreatingly. 'Too much testosterone in his backside.' Gita's hair quivered as though it was full of electricity. I felt like one of those bumbling old pundits I had listened to when I was her age. 'I hope you don't come out a pundit!' Ma had said when I showed an interest in these books in my early twenties. She must have known what she was talking about. I had major pundit-genes in me: her own father had been a celebrated pundit, a learned man, and deep inside, she had wanted to be a pundit as well. But she had squelched that desire, focused on practical things, and compelled me to do the same.

Now that I was over fifty, though, my pundit-genes must have woken up. When I picked up the book lying next to my daughter to search for some way to introduce her to its beauty, its first line brought back the old, inner trembling it had always evoked.

'"On the field of Truth, on the battlefield of life, what came to pass, Sanjaya, when my sons and their warriors faced those of my brother Pandu?"'

I persisted in trying to get Gita to see the human dilemmas the ancient texts contained. 'Yudishthira wasn't bad,' I said. 'He just had a weakness. The cousins were the ones who were bad – total psychotic. They made a deal with him. He could have his wife back if he left the kingdom for a whole lot of years. Go into exile, he and his brothers.'

Gita wrinkled her nose.

'You see, a small mistake could cause you to live many other lives trying to make up for what you do.'

She pursed her lips. She wasn't going to agree or not agree. But Gita's weakness was information. She liked to know things. So she waited for me to continue with the legend.

'But even after Yudi and his brothers had honoured the gambling debt, stayed in exile for the requisite number of years and went through hell, the cousins ultimately reneged. They refused to recognise the other guys' claims to the kingdom. The only way to get it back was to fight. And that's where the *Bhagavadgita* begins, when they are about to launch the mother of all wars.'

I opened the book and started reading the lines of the text, giving notes as to the characters. '"Krishna, the Lord of the soul, blew his conch shell."' I emphasised the line; '"Arjuna, the winner of treasure, sounded forth his own."'

'I thought Krishna was God!'

'Yes . . . well, Krishna was a friend of this ruling family. He couldn't take sides in the dispute. So he offered them all a deal. One side could have all his weapons, all the thunderstorms and earthquake and misery God could make. The other side could just have him. So what you think the bad guys chose?'

She squinted at me. 'The weapons?'

'Of course. And Arjuna, the leader of their warriors, the supreme warrior, chose to have Krishna as his chariot driver. Just as his chariot driver. Nothing else.'

She was intrigued now.

'So the armies are lined up to do battle,' I pressed on, 'and Arjuna tells Krishna to drive his chariot to the front of the troops so he could do a final review. And when he gets there, what does he see? On the other side of the battlefield, ranged against them, is his entire family – his cousins with whom he played as a child, his teachers, his uncles.'

I turned to the book and read Arjuna's reaction aloud.

When I see all my kinsmen, Krishna, who have come here on this field of battle, life goes from my limbs and they sink, and my mouth is sear and dry; a trembling overcomes my body, and my hair shudders in horror. My great bow Gandiva falls from my hands and the skin of my flesh is burning. I am no longer able to stand, because my mind is whirling and wandering.

I glanced at her. She was studying the words intently. Gita actually loves poetry, always gets top marks in it at school.

'"Thus spoke Arjuna in the field of battle, and letting fall his bow and arrows he sank down in his chariot, his soul overcome by despair and grief."' I paused dramatically, before continuing. '""I will not fight, Krishna,' he said."'

My Gita, my own soul and my treasure, uttered a word. 'Wimp!'

I sighed and pointed to the text. 'As he says,' I argued, 'what's the use fighting for a kingdom if you are going to kill all the people you have loved? The people with whom you have shared your past? That's a terrible dilemma. See? "In the dark night of my soul I feel desolation."'

'But he didn't see them for years! So what if it's his cousins and his half-brother? He should pass them out.'

I was shocked at her insensitivity. 'Gita . . .' I said, 'you don't know what it is to have a brother.'

She stared at me and then raised her eyebrows. 'You know?' she asked mockingly and turned back to the text. When she looked up again, there was a gleam in her eyes. 'See what Krishna says?' Her index finger stabbed at the page. '"Whence this lifeless dejection, Arjuna, in this hour, the hour of trial,"' she read. '"Strong men know not despair, Arjuna, for this wins neither heaven nor earth."' Her eyebrows rose meaningfully. '"Fall not into degrading weakness, for this becomes not a man who is a man."' She started putting stresses on the words. '"Throw off this ignoble discouragement, and arise like a fire that burns all before it."'

She kept nodding over and over.

They felt like stabs at my heart, my daughter's nods that evening. I had come close to finishing the manuscript I was working on in my office, and had been looking forward to giving it to her. I had been imagining her relief at understanding why I had kept silent about Anji for so many years. Now I knew it wouldn't be enough.

Late that night, as I sat in the darkness of the wooden verandah in my old plantation house, listening to the chirp of crickets and breathing in the scent of the giant flowers in my valley, I realised there was only one thing to do. For Gita's sake, I would have to publish and be damned.

October 2004
Rome, Dominican Republic, Amsterdam